By the same author:

Lightwood

River Rogue

Devil's Elbow

I0822514

THIS
IS
ADAM

THIS
IS
ADAM

A novel by Brainard Cheney

MM John Welda BookHouse

2012

Published by permission 2012 by MM John Welda BookHouse
Eastman, Georgia

ISBN: 978-0-9839365-4-1 (Hardcover)
LCCN: 2012938325
The Lightwood History Collection: Book 4
First Edition

To the Memory of

ROBIN BESS

(Whose character and works inspired this story)

THIS
IS
ADAM

1.

BALANCING THE LAST and largest lightwood log on his shoulder long enough to lift the end above the level of the board fence, the good-sized Negro man, like a dancer in a stately quadrille, turned with it and pitched it from his wagon onto the woodpile in the back yard. Then, picking up his hat and a large fish from the wagon seat, he got over the fence himself. He moved across the yard toward the big chinaberry trees at the back porch of the house, with the same upright, deliberate dignity. Flourishing a blue bandanna handkerchief, he pushed his broad-brimmed black wool hat onto the back of his head and mopped his face, a glistening ginger color in the bright morning sun. He approached the empty porch above the back steps under the trees, as assuredly and almost as ceremoniously as an actor advancing to the front of the stage to take a bow. As he halted at the foot of the stairs, he brought a jack knife from his jumper pocket and, bending over, rapped smartly on a step with it. "Here's Adam," he called in a raised, toneless, measured voice, "Adam Atwell."

Almost as if they had been waiting in the wings, a slender, black-clad white woman and a boy, looking out around her shoulder, were poised for an instant in the doorway to nod to Adam. Then the red-haired boy, in a striped blouse and knickerbockers, brushed past his mother and hurried forward.

In one automatic gesture, Adam took off his hat and lifted aloft the fish. Strung from a palmetto thong, the sleek white shad, with closed mauve fins and quiet tail, manifested a sacrificial assent to the offering. "Hit's the last un, I reckon," Adam said.

The small boy took the fish, a look of eager responsibility on his pale freckled face, and retreated through the doorway, with a flash of bare legs.

"Have they started work over on the Ridge yet?" the woman said, advancing to the top of the steps. There she halted, to glance matter-of-factly down at the man in clean blue denim meeting her gaze from the yard, his hat clasped to his knee, unconsciously, his stance, as unrestrained and straight as that of a pine tree.

He lowered his chin to emphasize his deliberation, and a light came into his luminous brown eyes that softened the gravity of his face and suggested detached humor. With a preparatory jerk of his jaw, he broke into speech. "N-nome. I-I ain't seen no signs of farming over on the Ridge—by black nor white!" His lips, obscured by a scraggly mustache, worked convulsively for an instant, then he continued without stammering, "But there's still time." He resumed his attitude of grave calm.

Mrs. Hightower shook her lifted head, shrugging her shoulders so that the edge of the short, black cape she wore about them fluttered to reveal a flash of the white shirt-waist above her black skirt. It was a gesture of tried patience. The frown gathering on her slim face drew up her cheeks about her eyes to accent further a fine but rather long nose. She wished she had the Peavys out of there.

Looking up mildly, Adam spoke the lines of a familiar dialogue, his guttural bass rising to a key of protest and subsiding into depths again. He had seen Mr. Peavy over at McIntosh shops with a broke-down wagon, when he came by bringing his cow to the bull on Thursday. Mr. Peavy had been laid up some, had been laid up.

For a moment Mrs. Hightower glanced askance at the eerily moving shadow skeletons of the trees on the hard-swept yard with her long, serious, gray-blue eyes. Her silver-streaked brown hair was coiled on top of her head in a pompadour, baring a high, well-moulded forehead that gave her face composure, and her long fine features, in repose, presented an aspect of disciplined resignation. But now her lip trembled, and she turned quickly and moved toward an upright pipe to a faucet and, reaching over, cut down the stream of water flowing from it into a covered wooden milk box at the edge of the porch. She regarded the box for an instant with distaste, before she straightened up again to her calm. She said she ought never to have let the Peavys *come on* the place, but, sighing, she came back to stand again at the head of the stairs.

They were standing now as they had stood on most of the Saturday mornings since her husband, the late Colonel Marcellus Hightower, had died eighteen months before—exorcising a world across a flight of steps that separated them in manifest social accommodation and joined them in an inscrutable fate.

Adam gave a ritual remonstrance, his voice breaking forth so suddenly that he did not stutter: the black folks on the Ridge were no better! He swiped the straight graying hair on his head with a claw hand and spat tobacco juice beyond the edge of the steps expertly to regain his composure. He had seen the widow Watson on Thursday, *too*. Her boys, she had revealed, were down in the swamp, fishing! He had made her get in the wagon with him and they had gone to the swamp after the boys, they had gone after them. This morning, when he came by on his way to town, the boys *done had their big field half broke*. He smiled, and the smile lighted up his eyes and his high smooth forehead with such a sign of detached ironic intelligence as seemed to belie his features and manner of speech.

Mrs. Hightower shared it but wryly, resuming where she had left off, resuming, with lifted gaze, where she had resumed many times before. It did look like she would have known better—would have absorbed something over the years she had lived out here—better than to take them on the place—and, of all of them, anywhere, the Peavys!

Adam's smile faded but a wraith remained, as he spoke with tempered reassurance, propitiatory words. Mrs. Hightower, the old man would put in a crop, even if the boys didn't help him and he was late getting it in the ground—he would put in a crop. He turned aside, his glance lowering, and formally paused, reviewing the ground before him, to be full fair about it. It was not *too* late yet! A rhetorical note came into his voice as he went on. Look at Adam Atwell! He had got in his corn in the Sand field, but what about the swamp? Yessir, the river was still in the swamp and the Wyche field was under three foot of water. He looked at her for a moment almost as if he expected her to reply, then a soft amused smile wrinkled his face and he went on. *Ordinarily*, it didn't get dry enough to plow the swamp field till later than this. He had planted cotton there as late as June and made a crop! His face began to glow, and he lifted his arm and the hat, like the soaring wing of an eagle. Yessir, he had catfish gnaw his corn off the cobs in the old Wyche field and then replanted and made a crop. He smiled with an absorption oblivious of the point he had set out to prove. But then, to be sure, there was not another piece of ground in this end of the county like the Wyche field!

Mrs. Hightower had not been drawn into his admiration of the prodigious field, but looked off into the distance in perplexity. She was glad that it wasn't yet too late to plant, but she still did not know how she was going to get the Peavys at it.

Adam calmed down, lowering his soaring wing, and nodded thoughtfully. He had been studying about it coming to town. And again his attitude was invocatory. Couldn't they put a *sleight* to it, maybe? Mr. Peavy never had brought her that syrup from last fall that he was supposed to bring, had he? Why didn't she drive out there to get it—she could be coming on to the homeplace too, to draw off some scuppernong wine, and then she could be *plum* thunderstruck to find out that they hadn't broken their ground yet. Of course she wouldn't get any syrup, but that would put them to work.

The Peavys didn't make good syrup, anyhow, Mrs. Hightower murmured abstractedly and turned away. Then, lifting a remote face, she gazed off into space, in a way that gave her slim, black-caped-and-skirted figure, a sibylline appearance.

Adam's smile straightened and he glanced at her sidewise. She had that far-off look now two or three times!

Feeling the inquiry of his eyes, she glanced down abruptly, remembering something she had been about to forget. She got an envelope from her pocketbook and drew pince-nez glasses on a fine chain from under her cape and fixed them on her nose to give her countenance a formidable intellectual glitter.

Adam, as she read aloud, stared at her face as if afraid of missing a syllable, then dropped his head to ponder the ground. One hundred and seventy-eight trees: was that everything, everything the sawmiller reported? he asked. He seemed almost obstinate about it. Well, then, it ought to have been just a hundred more.

Mrs. Hightower's nostrils quivered and her bearing stiffened, as if in fright, as she balanced above the steps. Severely, she asked Adam if he were sure, absolutely sure. A saddened expression took over her face, as his response reached her.

His mouth stretching ruefully, he stuttered with a formal reluctance, like a man admitting error, "Y-yessum!" He was sure. He dropped his hat, picked it up, and thoughtfully laid it on the steps. Finding a chip, he brought out his knife. He turned the wood edge up and skimmed a thin shaving off before his deliberate blade. He would have to take it that Mr. Berry's hands just hadn't reported the stumpage over in the bay, he said. He looked up, meeting in her face a propriety that half concealed ironic amusement. He said, a twitch of his mustache dimly reflecting this, "Put a sleight to it, Mrs. Hightower. Send the check back to him and tell him you had rather have it all at one time!"

They nodded at each other ceremoniously.

They might have been a priestess and the petitioner for a profane commons, for all of their unconscious formality and devotion to the business in hand. Although, at that time, in south Georgia their ritual was not uncommon.

When Mrs. Hightower had laughed softly, her face momentarily looking young, and restored the tally sheet and the check to the envelope and the envelope to her pocketbook, she hovered over it for a moment, as if she had something more to bring forth. Finally, she drew herself up at the top of the steps, taking off her pince-nez and holding them out in her hand and clearing her throat. "It may not amount to anything, of course," she began, giving forth the words guardedly, but unable quite to check her quickened breathing. She glanced past Adam's sharpened face and repeated, "It may not amount to anything, but there's a big land buyer from Philadelphia in town, with his attorney and woodsmen, and he has sent me word through the bank that he is interested in buying my swamp."

"Swamp?" Adam exclaimed, in empty astonishment.

"Yes. Mr. Littleton at the bank says the man means business. His name is Lincoln and he represents big money. Big money." Her deliberation vanishing, Mrs. Hightower's words were now coming rapidly, in spite of herself, and round red spots showed at the cheekbones of her pale face. "I'm to meet him soon."

Suddenly buck-eyed and buck ague in his voice, Adam groaned, "S-swamp!"

Scarcely hearing him, allowing her glasses to zip up the gold chain and out of sight under her cape, she went on. "Yes, Mr. Littleton says the deal will run into *thousands* of dollars, thousands of dollars! that it should give us some capital to open up several farms and make the place profitable and, of course, I need the money, Goodness knows! My older daughter will be ready to go off to college before long and I don't know what all . . ." She checked herself with a wry smile and drew her hands together on her bosom, under the cape. "Of course, I'm just talking on: nobody has offered me anything at all yet and we don't know that they will—anything that we can accept." She paused to look at Adam, as if expecting his reply, yet immediately resuming, "But I thought you ought to know about it, in case you ran into any strange men out there, cruising the woods." Now she halted and tightened her lips and blinked at him inquiringly, resting her chin upon her clasped hands under the cape. But before he could speak, she added, "Cruising the woods—of course they will be looking you up, probably, to show them the land lines!"

Adam backed up a pace or two, clawing his hair, his jaw trembling uncontrollably. He got out: "Yed-yed-yes-sum! Yessum!" As he struggled to speak, his neck swelled and his ginger-colored face darkened with blood. "You ain't gettin' ready to sell the Wyche field, is you?" he asked, with a smile poised shakily between humor and fear.

"The Wyche field?" Mrs. Hightower swayed a moment in surprise and dropped her hands down to balance herself. "The Wyche field!" She hastened to reassure him. "Oh no, of course not, Adam. I don't intend to get rid of the Wyche field—they wouldn't want it anyhow: they're after timber." Her head bent a little forward, as if over a plate of fine promise, eyes glistening, cheeks convolving, she went on confidently. "And I'll reserve the clay deposits . . ."

"And the oil slick?" Adam put in.

"Yes," she said, "and the oil slick—all of the mining rights. We'll put a sleight to it," she concluded triumphantly.

At this point, the red-haired boy came back and stood beside her and she put her arm about his shoulders. Rubbing one bare leg against the other, he interrupted them. “Adam, that shad had the most roe in ‘im I ever saw—biggest *shad* I ever saw—sure a fine shad!”

She ran her fingers through the boy’s hair and gave him a proprietary inspection. “Oh, yes,” she said, turning back to Adam, “we surely do appreciate the white shad!”

The Negro was picking up his hat from the steps and he straightened up before he spoke. “H-he ‘uz the last un—the season’s *bin* gone. I had kept ‘im in a basket.” He turned away deliberately and moved toward his mule-team and wagon outside the gate.

2.

ADAM SMACKED THE RUMP of his gray mule with the rope reins, as his team pulled the wagon into the road between broad shoulders of carpet grass, to pass the long, gray, gabled house with its encircling trellised porches that he had just quit. He muttered: “Git in there, you contrary scamp, and pull!” But, as the gray tightened the trace chains beside his young red mule and they broke into a rattling trot over the silencing sand of the three-path thoroughfare, Adam sat back on his plank seat and enjoyed the sight of the finery of Riverton. The team took the dip, with Adam grabbing onto his hat, and bounced across the tracks of the railroad that bisected the village and turned into a broader grassless street along which, on the side opposite the shallow channel of steel rails, stood a flat-topped, two-story brick house, with grilled iron porches and a fountain in the yard. It was the town’s finest, and he always liked to drive by and look at it. A rich steamboat captain who owned three boats lived there and sometimes he was on the porch and spoke to Adam, who had known him on the river. It was said that he was a hard but fair man.

Beyond at the depot, on the railroad side, the bearded stationmaster, standing on the freight platform, called to him by name and Adam bowed and lifted his hat, and with the same motion thrust his hand into his overalls for his chewing tobacco. "When you comin' back to the bight fishin'?" he yelled, as the team moved past. The stationmaster shook his head and his beard and nose bobbed up and down, like the features of a puppet Punch, without carrying any sound to Adam.

At the hitching racks, behind the stores, a half-dozen country men, taking out their animals to water and feed them, saluted Adam. Three of them were white and three Negro. To the one group he touched his hat, to the other he raised a hand, with the same easy enjoyment, as he crossed the dung-strewn, hoof-pitted common at his sedately strolling gait.

He came out onto Riverton's Main Street, at the corner of a long row of brick stores fronted by a covered sidewalk. Turning away from them, he crossed the intersection toward the Riverton Bank, a corniced, cream-colored brick building (the town's only one), that sat back from the street. He entered its columned archway, stepping carefully over the tiny colored marble tiles to the recessed doors.

When he pushed inward one of the heavy portals with the beveled glass in them and the gold letters on the glass, he let it swing to behind him while he stood for a moment, as he always did, a little dazzled and trying to get his bearings. The magnificence of the marble slabs, the golden oak paneling and frosted glass behind which the banker and his money bags were caged, the fancy white-shaded electric lamps, the ridged and crinkled white ceiling—made of enameled sheet iron, Adam had been told—and the fine high tables where town people made out their drafts on the bank and, above all, the little barred windows with marble slabs for sills from behind one of which Banker Littleton usually sang out before he had got his eyesight re-aimed to where he could see through them—in short, the high and rarefied atmosphere of the bank always put him to a test.

But this morning he was able to steady himself, remove his hat and approach the front window, before Mr. Littleton spoke. Indeed, he stood at the window for some moments, unnoticed; during which he eyed the fat piles of leather ledgers, and, on the desks, open ones at which the two men in their vests, black false shirt-sleeves and white collars and ties were working; during which he picked out the human and tobacco smell of the men from the heady odor of money and banking; during which he scrutinized the bright steel frame, with its thick, studded, steel door, open on the dark doorway to the treasure vault, itself—and he felt himself, with his seven hundred dollars in that vault (or working for the bank somewhere just as safe) a part of this strong top world.

Finally, the big banker looked up from his desk. "Who's that?" he called, in his big hard voice, peering over his spectacles, then added, as recognition came, "Oh hello there, Adam! What do you want?" But, without waiting, he pushed his chair back and heaved himself up—a huge man of rubber—ring chins and balloon belly. But he advanced to the window, with sure-footed ease and, leaning on the counter, pushed his long nose close to the wicket. His voice having put off some of its ballast, he said: "You'd like to get a little cash?" more in statement than question, and picked up a pad of counter checks and, with light, graceful strokes of his pen, wrote on the line in the top right corner, "March 21," and after the figure nineteen in the next blank, the figure "10," in fine flourishing script, and on the *Pay to* blank-line he wrote the word, "Cash."

"How much?" he said: his voice had taken back on some of its stone.

Adam looked up sharply, with a flash of eye-whites. His mouth worked convulsively and, after a moment, he got out: "Yeh suh!" In the pause that followed, it could not have been said whether it was due to his impediment of speech, or his considering the banker's question, or the banker.

But the voice did not put him off. Adam remembered a time four years ago, when Banker Littleton had cashed a big cotton check for him and would not let him stay at the window to count his money. But he had taken it a little way down the hall and had knelt down on the floor and counted it, twice. Then he had got in line and come back up to the window and said to the banker, "I think you done made a mistake."

The big hard voice broke out: "We don't correct any mistakes after you leave the window!"

And he had come back, "All right then, that suits me fine—"

But the banker had pitched ballast fast and called him back in another tone of voice. Yeah he even thanked him: it had saved him twenty dollars!

Now Adam's eyes twinkled with a dim ambiguity. "Reckon yuh better let me have 'bout fifty dollars," he said.

The long nose seemed about to stick out between the wire palings and the sloping forehead wrinkled up under a stiff forelock of graying hair. The voice demanded brusquely, "What do you want with so much cash, here in March?"

Adam's two knuckled fingers resting on the window slab remained motionless. The smile on his face broadened good-humoredly. "W-well you kain't always tell by what a fellow sez. I mought be gwine to pitch a bender, go on a spree!"

After an instant, in which he stared into Adam's face, Mr. Littleton, gradually withdrew his nose, saying in a vindictive tone, "If you bought liquor with all that money, we'd have to spend another fifty to bury you!"

Adam chuckled and took his time, but he noted well that Mr. Littleton still looked at him questioningly. Finally he said, not without a hint of pride in his voice, "I pays cash for my furt'lizer."

Mr. Littleton erupted: "You don't use all that fertilizer, down there on those swamp fields you're tending?"

"Dat's right, Mr. Littleton!" Adam said, as if it were a pleasure to admit it. "But then I wanted to git me some hemp rope and cant hooks and have sompin' to pay a little loggin' wages with."

"Where you going to log?"

It was, as he had hoped, the inevitable question, the one for which he had waited. The Colonel had said one time: *Bankers want to talk to you like it's their money: just remember it's the money that talks and it ain't their money!* Adam straightened up from his bent over position at the window and said with casual assurance, "There's still good timber in that cut-over cypress in the Hightower swamp. I reckon the Colonel's widow'll let me cut it."

Mr. Littleton unloaded himself on the slab again, his face at the wicket. "I reckon she won't—not if I have any weight in advising her! She's got the chance of a lifetime to sell it, right away."

"She is!" Adam counterfeited surprise. "How's that?"

"There's a big buyer here from up North, represents big moneyed interests in Philadelphia. He says he wants to buy five thousand acres of swamp, if he can get it together without too much trouble. And, of course, we don't mind taking a little trouble to help him. It would be a big thing to get that much money in here now."

As he gazed through the bars at the banker, Adam's face sobered and his eyes widened, like a man seeing a storm flag hoisted. "Y-you think they really mean business? They really got the money and want the swamp?"

"They've got the money, all right—I know that. Buying land is the man's business." Mr. Littleton put his pen behind his ear and canted his head with a redistribution of his double chins to squint at Adam. "How come Mrs. Hightower didn't mention it to you, when you asked about cutting that cypress?"

Adam turned away from the window and stared abstractly across the bank lobby and fumblingly let go his grip on the marble slab. Finally he said, without looking back, "I-I ain't axt'er. . . .I hyur her sayin' sompin', but I didn't ketch on."

The banker followed Adam with a shrewd gaze, and, after a moment's speculation, stepped back into the interior, returning to the window with a filing case. He spun the accordion pockets with deft fingers and took out a slip of paper. "Adam," he said, looking down at it, "I believe the second note you gave Bright on that piece of land you're buying falls due the first of July: I have a notation on it here. If that's going to press you too hard, we'll pay it off for you and take over the mortgage?"

Adam turned back in surprise. He looked incredulously at the banker, his countenance kindling with an impulsive warmth for an instant before his loosened lips righted themselves in a wry smile. His regarding the solicitous massive face seemed to buck him up. He laughed out loud and, taking hold of the wicket, he looked down at the pad with the check on it that Mr. Littleton had not finished filling out. "You better let me make my mark and git my money and go," he said, in high humor. "That money of yourn too high priced for me!"

The banker ignored his amusement and, leaning toward him over the counter, continued in an objective manner to utter his professional verdict. "You've got enough here on time deposit to take care of the mortgage this summer, but you've got to have the cash to make your crop with, too."

"Y-yessuh?" Adam agreed ambiguously, but he could not keep back his satisfied smile. "Hit don't cost *so much* to make a crop on cash, Mr. Littleton!" Cavalierly, he reached through the bars and touched the end of the pen and picked up his money. Holding it in his left hand like a glove, he walked, at his strolling gait, to the door before he began to count it.

Beyond Riverton, when his team had clattered across the bridge spanning the little river that separated town and country, the question jumped at him from the silence of the sandy road: *Why did you have to be so big Ike about your money in the bank?* Now the banker's face, with the chopped-off-and-sewed-up look that came on it as he left the window, rose before him disturbingly. He squinted across the glare of a white sand bank in the afternoon sun to the greening black-jack oaks beyond.

A banker was always out to hook you for something if he could (especially if your skin was black) but you had to live with him. The money that he had in the bank—and it wasn't so much—might be gone by July, when his note came due—might be gone, in this uncertain world he lived in now! Yeah, so big! He didn't even count his fifty dollars cash til he got plumb out of the bank—it would have served him right if the banker has short-changed him!

As his mules leaned against their harness to climb the sand hill ahead of them, he considered their rumps: he didn't have the Colonel to speak for him now! Then, reflectively: the Colonel wouldn't have let it puff *him* up, like that! His favorite image of the Colonel trod the warm air above the sand hill: a big, erect man in a linen suit and a panama hat, bearing his gray calvaryman's beard and bold high-bridged nose titled up a little, and above his florid cheeks, the small blue eyes that looked into you so sharp and calm and took everything that happened so unshaken—the quietest, easiest voice so big a man ever had.

He had seen the Colonel mad, but he had never seen him puffed up—though he walked like he might be that way all the time. The Colonel would have thought about all sides of it. But then the banker wouldn't have tried such a trick on the Colonel!

As the wagon topped the hill, another hill, higher and crookedly seamed with still deeper sand ruts, rose beyond him. With the weight of the wagon now on the mules, they broke into a trot downhill and across the bottom and, beginning to mount the farther slope, they threw themselves stubbornly against the harness. About half-way up, Adam got down from his seat and walked beside his team, because of the load of guano he had on the wagon. He pushed his wool hat onto the back of his head, as sweat ran down on his forehead.

Well hadn't the Colonel been tricked after all? He was *dead!* That was *one* thing he hadn't figured on! In pain, Adam yanked the hat back down on his head. He plodded on beside the wagon to the top of the hill and, mounting the hub of a wheel, he climbed up again. But when he was on the seat his chest still ached with his frustration and sense of loss.

It had been to settle down and make money that he had come to the Hightower place, ten years ago, after his wife went off to stay the first time. But he had been ready to come a good while before that. He had done caught up on turpentining and rafting timber and sleeping with strange women. He had already found out, in turpentining, that a fellow feel big, but it still didn't make him rich. And an honest rafthand never got anything for all his trouble, except *frozen* feet and wet butt and sun stroke—even a rogue never got hold of anything that stayed with him. And he had come to see that it wasn't only his ma that made Malinda leave him. He had caught up on being the best man in the woods, on the water, and in the weeds. "It waun't nothing but 'gaitor-bellering and gopher money!"

The Colonel had already talked to him a couple of times about coming on the holding and opening up a new farm. But when the big house on the homeplace burned, and he offered to rent the homeplace to him, Adam had appreciated that he was giving him his chance. The Wyche field then was nothing but a crab-apple thicket, but the Colonel had given him three years in which to bring it back. He had told Adam that the old swamp field would put the power to the cotton roots, but that had not prepared Adam for what came to pass; it had not prepared him for the yearly snow-storm of cotton bolls that rose up out of that yellow river mud!

"Stay with me, Adam, and I'll make us all rich!" was the way the Colonel had put it, pulling at his beard and giving him that sharp clear look that got inside you.

That had been four years ago, late of an afternoon, as he spoke from his buggy to Adam standing against the wheel. And during the twelve months following there had been a stream of men who had come out to the Hightower property. There had been clay men, brought there by the Paley boy, now grown to be a man, and he, Adam, had led them through the swamp. They had dug a hundred holes, it seemed, to test out where the kaolin and terra cotta deposits lay. Then there had been the crew of railroad surveyors, and old man Christian DeBow, one of the Colonel's partners, with them—they ran lines clean from the Riverton Corporation to the Oconee River bank.

The next year the Colonel himself moved, lock, stock and barrel, from where he'd been practicing law, to Riverton. Then he and Mr. DeBow and another man—a little squeaky-voiced fellow who the Colonel once said was going to put up the money to open his clay works—took to coming out together and he, Adam, had heard and overheard talk of big things. Big things! The railroad crew began to cut out the right-of-way—a railroad to run, they said, all the way from Anniston, Alabama, to the city of Savannah.

It was during this time that the Colonel had said to him that he would make him, Adam, a foreman in his clay works. It would have paid him *seventy-five* dollars a month *cash!* With Jake and Reuben, his oldest boys, big enough to tend to the farming, under his watch, they would be able to keep the Wyche field turning out as much cotton as ever. It looked like what the Colonel had promised was just about to happen. It looked like they were going to get rich.

Whatever the ups and downs, things had always gone finally the way *he* figured it out: the price of cotton, timber, and corn, the weather, the crops. Before, he had never failed to do what he said he would do. Never! Way back, on that rough day, when the judge had sent Adam to *the Mines,* the Colonel had said: “Go along and be a good boy, Adam, and I’ll get you out after awhile.” And he had kept his word then. . .

Adam left his team in the lane, before the barn, for the boys to take out the mules and unload the guano, and passed through a paling gate toward his four-room, weathered-gray house that squatted behind its boxwood-bordered porch on the hand-swept, gray surface of the yard, like a duck asleep on a pond. When he had reached the great water oak with the pump under it, a little way beyond the gate, he encountered his mother, with an empty bucket in her hand, approaching from the stand of wash tubs at the edge of the clearing.

Though old and thin and no bigger than a child, she walked with upright bearing, the same sedately strolling gait with which Adam walked. She halted when she saw him and stood regarding him from deep eye-sockets, with a dignity that was increased, not diminished, by her dull leathery skin and the gray, plaited pigtails splayed over her head. After a pause, she said with a sharp certainty of voice, “Whu’ a-matter, son?”

He had halted too, and returned her gaze. Now he frowned, and beginning to move again, said, “Nothin’, ma, nothin’. . . .Heah, le’ me have that bucket and I’ll fill it for yuh!”

After he had pumped it full, she moved off with it toward the tubs, but continued to regard him over her shoulder from time to time.

Adam filled the gourd dipper with cold water and, taking off his hat, squatted down at the roots of the big oak to drink it. When he lowered the empty gourd from his mouth, his gaze was arrested by a torrid, cloud-spattered, blaze of sunset, sending its orange rays through the scuppernong arbors and across the yard toward him. He stared with an uneasy stomach. . .

Such a curious sunset had been lighting up the side porch, just beyond where he stood inside the Colonel's sickroom that last time he saw him alive.

"I may not make it, Adam," he had said, when they were finally alone together in the long room.

It was August and so hot that they had all the sashes up in the bay window and the doors to the back and side porches open to make a draft. And he (Adam) was fanning hard with is hat, as he shook his head in response, but sweat filled his eyes, anyhow.

"Oh, there's no use to deceive ourselves," the Colonel told him, from the mound of pillows that propped up his head, his face white with beard, except for the bluish washes of cheek on either side of his gaunt nose and the glint from his pale eyelids. "Every man has to die. Man proposes and God disposes."

His voice was low, but it carried.

"Still it couldn't come at a worse time. . . Always before I've been able to stay with a thing 'til I could make it work or save the investment, or get out from under. But *this* time is different.

"McClosky was the third man I had interested in putting up money to develop the clay works—he lost a hundred thousand dollars on his olive groves—today he's just about broke. Yet I might have found another backer if it hadn't been for the railroad reverse. . .You can't get new railroad projects started every day. . ." He paused to catch his breath.

When he recommenced, his voice was more edged with anxiety. "Paley came up on my blind side, I guess—every man has a blind spot. I was completely deceived in him. He was a smart, hard-working boy, and I thought he had character. I spent a couple of thousand dollars on his education, I guess—sent him to Pennsylvania to study ceramics, helped his family while he was in school. . . ."

(Adam had thought that he might have told him different about Paley, any time had he asked him.)

"But he really fixed us! Mr. DeBow and I together could have raised twenty-five thousand dollars on our timber. And that would have been enough on which to shoe-string it—if Paley hadn't betrayed us to the Filcher faction among the railroad backers.

"It is a little hard now to see why—it sunk him along with us. He won't be able to go it alone—he certainly won't have the confidence of the men to whom he betrayed us." The Colonel's cheeks twitched, and for a moment, he tried to raise his head. "I-I-it's hard. . . ." He let his head ease back on the pillows, and after a pause, went on. "But I must harbor no hate against Oswald. . . I don't. I guess he has his blind spot, too: over-ambition. It made him blind to gratitude, to loyalty, to honor, and finally to good judgment and his own interest.

"My wife would lay it to his family background. She says that I ought never to have believed that I could make a gentleman out of a poor white—but I don't know . . . .I'm not convinced of that and after all his folks were not all white trash—his old mother was a good woman.

"But anyway Paley has alienated himself from us. Mr. DeBow, of course, knows it, but this fact is not generally known. I have told my wife. And I tell you now, Adam, for a reason.

"I know that, at sixty, I could not count on many more years of activity, my boy is still a child, and I had expected to lean on Oswald...I tell you for a reason, Adam. My wife—poor Lucy! I've never discussed business matters with her—in our whole married life. She doesn't even know how to make out a check. I'm troubled, Adam, troubled. She is utterly unprepared to manage the property I'm leaving. All sorts of people will try to take advantage of her. She doesn't even know anything about managing a farm. I always wanted to do everything for her, and now it seems that I have only robbed her of the experience that would have equipped her to take care of herself and our children!" He shut his eyes tight, and turned a little on one side and lay there silent for awhile. Then he resumed:

"Now I've got to leave her future, their future, in God's hands—where, God have mercy on us, it has always been, of course. But I can do mighty little about it; however, the Almighty expects us to do our part always—all that we are humanly capable of, within the bounds of honesty and decency. And I must make what practical plans for her future that I can. . . It's so little, so little!"

He managed to raise his head off the pillow. "But, Adam, I hope I can depend on you with the farming and timbering on the homeplace. I am counting on you to advise her the best you know how and look after the place, regardless of who comes on it. I know it won't be easy, because of your color and your station. There will be a lot of barbed wire and picked padlocks in this—it will put you to the test many times. . . . There are others, it should be said, more properly placed to take this responsibility, but I confess to you that I don't have confidence in them. I've tested you, Adam: you take responsibility—and you know as much about the homeplace as anybody. . . .It's my last request."

Adam had come near the bed to hear better by that time and was bending over to him. But the promise had been easy. What else could he do? He couldn't fail the Colonel and he had never had any notion of failing him. It was what the Colonel had said at the last, after he lay back on his pillows.

"There are things that count more than money, Adam. There are things that are worse than not having enough to wear and to eat—and I've known want. . .when you come to die. . .I know now that where I made my mistake was in not taking *it* into my calculations."

Then he had turned away on his pillow, pressing his head into it until his nose was bent, and three days later he was dead. . .

"Whu' a-matter, son?"

His mother appeared at the edge of his vision, still fixed on the dying fire in the west. Not turning his head, he replied, in the same low voice, "She goin' ter sell the swamp."

"Wyche field, too?"

There was a sudden chill on the air, coming from where his mother stood like a dark foreboding shadow. Adam shuddered and repeated, "Wyche field, too." But as the words came off his tongue, the yellow mud plot of cleared river swamp seemed to him a tenuous, a chancy, a slight assurance to the future. *Calculations!* What was it that the Colonel had been talking about?

3.

LUCY HIGHTOWER, her Sunday dress protected by a blue checked apron, swung the swing in which she sat on her front porch. Its short, sharp oscillations seemed to increase in tension and then relax, like the jumping of an irresolute diver on a springboard. But she was aware of no impulse to leap out into the dusk gathering over her lawn. She would not have conceived of any leap as taking her out of her responsibilities. Her pale reserved face was set in emotion compounded of aggravated annoyance and restrained alarm. A little distance away, dimly outlined by a white dress, Elinor, her elder daughter, faced the trellis of wisteria vines, in a motionless armchair. Their silence grew more ominous as they waited.

Finally, two small, dim, hurrying figures paused in the distance beyond the fence at the far corner of the lawn. There was a half-audible sound of boys' voices on the air for an instant. Then one of the dark blots beyond the pickets moved rapidly down the street and the other climbed over the fence at the corner and began trotting across the lawn, in the general direction of the front porch entrance.

At the sanded walk to the steps, the floating form deflected its course obliquely away from the house toward a gate in the fence between the front lawn and the back yard.

Mrs. Hightower's peremptory call cut through the silence. "Come here, Marcellus!"

The dark blob of knickerbockers between pale extremities came to an abrupt halt, as if winged in the air, and stood still. Then out of the shadows a boy's treble voice, trying to sound natural, cried: "Is that you, Mamma? I didn't see you!"

Mrs. Hightower came to her feet. At that moment, as if by prearrangement, the big electric arc lamp, swung between the poles over the street corner, glimmered and burst into a flood of light that uncovered the anxious face of her eleven-year-old son blinking and squinting at the foot of the steps.

Her voice lowered but grew more peremptory. "What do you mean, coming home to milk at this time of night? . . . And there *is* no milk! You did not separate the cow and calf this morning!" Her mouth stretched ruefully and she paused for an instant to give her disclosure effect, then went on with sharp inflection. "And where have you been, that has kept you into the night, like this?"

The boy shrank visibly before the inquisition. Rubbing one bare leg against the other automatically, he tried to give assurance to his voice. "Oh, Mamma, I think I separated them—I put the cow in the big field."

"And the calf with her! The gate is wide open!"

He dropped his hand and after a pause mumbled, "Somebody must have . . ." his voice trailing off.

"No," Mrs. Hightower said relentlessly, "it is just as it was when you propped it open last night. . . .In your trifling, good-for-nothing way, you just didn't go back down there after breakfast to put the calf in the chicken-yard!"

“I’ll go right now!” he cried and he jerked the foot he was rubbing against his calf down to move at a jump.

But she halted him. “No you won’t—not in your good Sunday clothes! You come in the house and put on your overalls!”

He came up the steps warily and sped around her to keep out of her reach and, hurrying through the front door, started down the dark hall.

She made no movement toward him from where she stood at the head of the steps, but she now called out, “Don’t you dare run from me!”

And he came to a halt, yanking his cap off his head.

She continued, as she approached him: “Here it is, after six o’clock at night! Where have you been?”

Elinor had disappeared into the house unnoticed and now brought a lighted oil lamp into the hallway below them and placed it on the hall table beside the unabridged dictionary. The boy gave her a suspicious glance, before he turned back to his mother, assuming an elaborate air of surprise. “Where have I been?” he echoed, incredulously. “We just walked down to the Big River bridge! Me and Walter! And went across to look for flags in Brickyard bottom!”

Her stiffened face showing no effect at this rhetoric, she pursued: “Who else was along?”

Her son tried to add incomprehension to his incredulity, “Who else? What do you mean, Mamma?”

“In the crowd?” she said, impatiently.

He twirled his cap on his finger with measured deliberation. “Oh there was Robbie and Mack and Ray and Paul Douglas and a couple of others. . .”

Her voice made the hard consonants accusatory: “And Cale Kiger!”

Marcellus winced and looked sharply around at Elinor, disappearing through the curtains to the rear hall. Struggling to keep a quaver out of his voice, he echoed, "Cale Kiger?"

Mrs. Hightower detected the telltale flush rising to the freckled, roughened, thin skin of his pale broad face, and this confirmation tightened her lips. "Yes," she said, revealing his complicity in a stricken tone, "and you went off into the woods with him, too—where there was a bunch of big boys and men—*gambling!*"

His small, deepset eyes tightened and the flesh at his cheekbones blanched. He moved his stiffened lips once without sound before he got out feebly, "They were just playing setback!"

"How do *you* know?" she said, insinuating further guilt. "Didn't you see money on the ground in the circle? And a bottle of whisky?" These details were Mrs. Hightower's own deduction, but they rang true. The little girl in the group of girls who had been following along behind the boys had only told Elinor that she got close enough to see those men sitting around in a ring. But Mrs. Hightower had heard before of these dissolute Sunday gatherings.

As she pressed toward him now, he backed away, dropping his cap. "I didn't know what they were doing, Mamma, 'til I got there," he said, in a crumbly voice.

She lifted a hand toward the door to his room on the hall. "Now you go in there and put on your overalls and go down to the lot and get that calf out of there and lock him up in the chickenyard—securely, *securely*: do you hear me?. . .And then come back to my room: I want to see you."

Mrs. Hightower moved down the hall to the door to the kitchen on her left and stuck her head into it. After a pause, she said in a husky, wrungout voice to her nine-year-old daughter, Lucinda Morrow, who was turning down the oil stove flame under the teapot, "Don't put the toast in the oven yet, Row." And, without awaiting an answer, she wheeled about and crossed the hall to her bedroom, closing the door behind her firmly and thumb-bolting it.

In the sanctuary of her room, Lucy Hightower bent toward the shaded student's lamp on the green baize-covered reading table beyond her bed, anxiously fingering an open Bible. Her sensitive brows were knit, her jaw loosened, her full bottom lip trembling, as she read the concluding lines of the Nineteenth Psalm, repeating in a whisper with her eyes closed, the last verse: "Let the words of my mouth and the meditations of my heart be acceptable in Thy sight, O Lord, my Strength and my Redeemer!" Then she turned to the Ten Commandments, marked the place, and closed the book.

She dropped to her knees at the side of her bed, where she prayed silently for a time, twice wracked by shuddering and once giving way to a sob. After which she rose, dried her eyes, and walked firmly to the door. Opening it upon her son, outside in the hall, leaning dejectedly against the clothes chest, she took him by the hand, not ungently, and led him in. They came to a stand beside the reading table and Mrs. Hightower, with a slight unconscious shrug, picked up the Bible and opened it, reading the marked passage.

Marse's face was drawn and pale and his freckles stood out on it, as he stared at her. He seemed appalled at the fate overshadowing him. His eyes cautiously searched the table, the bureau top, the bed, the mantelpiece. *Honor thy Father and thy Mother, Thou shalt not—*

Mrs. Hightower closed the Bible resolutely, looked down at her son with a severe, sad countenance and began, "Marcellus, I can't understand how you, in the way you've been brought up, could deliberately go off with such a boy as that Cale Kiger! Into the woods where reckless, godless men were at their debauchery!" She laid the book on the table. "You couldn't help but know that it was wrong, that they were evil men, that you had no business there!"

As she paused on the inflection, Marse swallowed the lump in his throat and said, "Mamma, I—I didn't know—"

She frowned and responded incredulously, "How could you stand there? How could you be with men of that sort?" She pressed upon him. "Why didn't you run away when you saw what it was?"

As his small vague eyes blinked automatically, confusion mixed with the apprehension on his face. "I—I don't know, Mamma!"

Straightening up, she shook her head and glanced aside.

"I cannot understand you! I don't know what has gotten into you! I suppose the devil got into you, but"—she turned dark, dilated, accusing eyes upon him—"you don't care about anybody, or anything, but yourself. Your household duties, nothing makes any difference to you. Instead of taking responsibility, here you are, the only dependence your widowed mother has—instead of growing up like your father, who worked hard and took care of his mother and father, the whole family, and even sent his younger brothers and sisters off to college, where he hadn't been able to go himself—yes, you, you walk off from here, leaving the cow and the calf together—so you won't have to milk—or just simply because you haven't got the wit to remember—or care!"

The boy looked up at her, tight-eyed and bemused and made no response.

She was just catching her breath and swept on at a higher pitch to her climax. "And you take up with gamblers and drunkards! You might have got shot and killed, even! And what would happen to you if you followed such a course in life is far worse! But you are not going to perdition because I have failed to do my duty, if I can help it, Marcellus! With God willing, I'm not going to fail you!" Her high chalk face now growing tinged at the cheekbones, she cried, "Go into that room and wait there!" She pointed beyond the washstand to the open door to his room, with the moving finger of Fate.

The boy's mouth began to work and he broke out imploringly, "Oh, Mamma, don't whip me—it won't happen again!"

"Go!" she decreed, still pointing.

As he quit the room reluctantly, she stepped to her bureau and took out of the top drawer a bottle of hart-shorn, sniffed it and put the bottle in her apron pocket, then she hurried out of the room to her wardrobe in the hall and after a moment, returned with a bone-handled ladies' riding whip. She moved swiftly and grimly to her duty.

When she collared him, in the dim small room, he began to blubber and, as she raised the whip to strike, he fell to the floor and slid his bare legs under the bed. "Get up, Marcellus!" she commanded and, irritation giving her a sudden access of strength, she yanked him from under it. "You begin crying and I haven't struck you with a blow!" And she whaled away on his shoulders. "But I'll give you something to cry for!" Her breath held, her face drawn up bitterly, she brought the whip down again and again.

"Oh, Mamma, oh Mamma, I don't know why you do this to me!" he yelled and his voice rose agonizingly, "Oh, I do-on-n't!"

The sound of it penetrated her like pain, stirring her anguish, her disgust, her fear. *Why, why did she?* Her stomach sank sickeningly, and her loins began to quake. It was as if she were striking into her own vitals and the whip wavered and paused. "Oh, God, give me strength!" She groaned and brought the whip down, down on his back again. And again she had to drag him out from under the bed.

When the lash struck his bare legs, he bellowed so loudly, so inordinately, and scrambled so frantically to get back under the bed, that her anger rose again and she found the strength to lay on the riding whip thoroughly and without faltering at the excess of his outcries, until she was out of breath. Holding the whip at last, panting, her brow wet with perspiration and two red spots flaring on her drawn cheeks, she leaned over him and said, between gasps, "Marcellus, I hope this teaches you a lesson!. . . I hope you know that I did it only for your own good?"

He did not respond, but lay heaving and sobbing on the floor, and she turned away and quit the room, shutting the door behind her.

As she came through the screened inset for bathing, athwart the passage from the boy's room into the main part of the long room that served as family sittingroom as well as her bedroom, she tossed her worn stubby whip, with its jaunty bone handle in the shape of a horse's foreleg and hoof, onto the bed, with some of the old imperiousness of her riding days—though this was a reflex act not in her consciousness. She moved, still breathing heavily. Here weariness descended on her like a pass, and she turned back and strode unsteadily to the mantelpiece where she fingered among its numerous oddments for her heart pills. Getting the round pasteboard box open and fumbling with the tiny strychnine pellet, she wondered if the boy was worth it all. A moment later, as she sank on the bed, she tried to raise the voice of duty to discountenance her doubt, but allowed herself to relax numbly on the pillow without answering.

Lying there, stretched out on her back, her hands folded on her breast and on her face the pallor of death, she looked like the corpse she felt herself about to become. But thought stirred uneasily, the voice of doubt pursued her. Would Marcellus ever grow up? Could she make a man of him? Half a feeling, hardly a thought, was her sense of repugnance in knowing that he had all of her weaknesses, and—the breath of a frown touched her brows—he was stupid on top of it! It was not merely in size and looks that he was unlike his father!

She stirred on the bed and thrust clenched hands down by her sides. How could she know this wasn't only her own mean irritability? To think such a thing! His father had not been depressed by his—his backwardness—maybe not really backwardness, but lack of ambition, laziness, triflingness and wool-gathering wits! When she had almost thrown the book at the boy's head over his slowness with his reading, Mr. Hightower had said with a smile, "We Hightowers take our time!" And when the boys at school had taunted and even hazed Marcellus and he didn't fight back, his father had not been the least bit disturbed about it. "We Hightowers are slow to wrath," he had said. "However, if there has to be a fight, we don't run away!" But Mr. Hightower was so absurd! He insisted that the boy's hair, that now looked like bristles on his head, would begin to curl when he was sixteen—said his had been the same way.

But then, she thought, feeling out with her hand for some cover to put over her, her husband at sixteen, before he was seventeen—so his cousin Rufe said—was leading a company of other boys his own age and younger, through the smell of gun powder and fright at the Battle of Atlanta—Joe Brown's Boys, armed only with pikes, because the Confederates had run out of guns. It was enough to curl his hair! And to have made a man of him, too—since he had come through it alive.

Lucy Hightower opened her eyes and stared up at the gray painted ceiling, high above her. She had not known this about Mr. Hightower when she met him that first summer at Indian Springs, but there was that in his bearing that let her know he might have led a company, she reflected. She was a city girl then, fresh from Charleston, and this Georgia Colonel—she still sniffed a little at the ostentatious title that the rural, less educated people here conferred on a lawyer—should have been too loud, too crude, and too old for her taste, with his powder-gray politician's hat, his already turning hair, and middle-aged paunch. But once she had met him, once he had spoken to her in that quiet, intense, musical voice of his, she never noticed these things again.

She shifted in the bed, turning onto her left side. To be sure, before they got married, she had made him dispose of the hat and afterward, after she had his diet in her charge, she made him dispose of his paunch, too. Yet she was still a little shocked at herself—even twenty years later—marrying a country lawyer and coming out to the Georgia backwoods! It had shocked her father and mother and Charleston friends at the time, but she, she reflected, had been too ignorant then of what the backwoods was like to know what she was about.

She found the handkerchief at the belt of her apron and blew her nose gently. They had not lived long at the Hightower plantation, however—though it came near being too long—and he had always *done things;* they had done things together, in Lancaster and later in the much bigger town of Leegrant. And small-town life for the wife of a leading lawyer was bearable. And then Riverton! But it all had ended in Riverton—yes, Riverton was the jumping off place!

The Morrows were never a first family of Charleston, but her father had been highly respected in the medical profession and even more so in the Methodist Church which he had served as treasurer for twenty years, and their cramped circumstances had always afforded them three servants, adequate wardrobes for her older sister and herself, and summers at the beach and watering places. And they moved in literate, well-mannered, highly respectable circles. After all Edward Louthan, who had been her early sweetheart and to whom she had been engaged, was now principal of Charleston's remarkable Boys High School. If she had married him, at least she would not now be a moneyless widow stranded in the rawest, roughest, most degenerate, most immoral small town she had ever encountered! Coarse Yankees, sawmill people, gamblers, drunkards, men living openly with disreputable women!

She sat up wearily, but her head swam so that she put her hand to her brow and leaned over on her knees. What a surrounding for her boy to grow up in! How could she keep him away from such people? She forbade him going with the Kiger boy, but half the boys in his class at school were not much better! And the case was scarcely happier for her two girls. Lines of anxiety creased her face and she straightened up. "What will my boy grow up to be, if we stay here?" she murmured fearfully. . . . Wasn't it time? She answered it herself.

Surely it was time for her, for them, at last, to quit this country and go back? Memory of the pungent smell of fresh warm baker's bread came to her, and the more pervasive, barely sensible smell of the harbor, and through her bedroom window, the sight of Walker, the butler, on the stoop, polishing the brass railing in the morning sunshine.

Oh, if she could only afford to go back to Charleston, at least for her children's education! If only the sale of the river swamp would bring her enough money. Eight thousand dollars seemed like a substantial sum, but was it enough for all four of them to stay four or five years in Charleston? Besides, Mr. Littleton had warned her not to live off her capital, but use it to open up more farms.

She rose resolutely and strode over to the washstand and poured a little cold water from the pitcher into the basin to bathe her eyes. An uneasy thought arrested her hand as she set down the pitcher. At their meeting in the back room at the bank the other day, when she had said that she must reserve her mining rights to the swamp for Marse's future and wanted to exempt the Wyche field from the sale, nobody had seemed to treat her exceptions seriously. Frowning, she told herself that she didn't like this at all. And, as she put the wash cloth into the water, she resolved to have it out with them, with all of them, for even Mr. Littleton did not seem sufficiently impressed . . . . Think: five years in Charleston would put Marse through high school!

A soft knock came on her hall door and she said, "Yes, Elinor?" and went on to bathe her eyes with the cloth.

A muffled voice said, "Mamma, we have some hot toast and tea for you."

"Thank you—just a minute!" Mrs. Hightower emptied the basin, moved to the door and, taking off the thumbbolt, opened it.

Elinor stood with a steaming pot of tea and cups and saucers on a waiter and behind her stood her small sister with a tray of buttered toast and a jar of preserves. "Come on in!" said Mrs. Hightower, smiling mildly as they moved in to the table with the green baize on it and began setting three places for supper.

Approaching them, she added, "You'd better put on another plate for Marse—he ought to eat something—you know we've got to go to church tonight." She sighed, shutting her eyes, thinking: Riverton does keep us on our guard! And Marse loves the singing.

The younger sister, in the act of placing the linen napkins around, shook her bobbed, tow-haired head, without looking up, and said, "I think he's in the diningroom now, Mamma."

Mrs. Hightower's mouth tightened automatically, then relaxed in a smile of relief.

4.

"THAT'S A MESS OF CARP you got there!" said the familiar voice. Adam, in the bow of the bateau at the edge of the wilderness-bound river, looked up from the fish he had just strung to inspect the low bluff above him. On it stood the tall, ramshackle, black-hatted figure of Hinshaw Slappy, his nearest white neighbor.

"Hit's a good mess," Adam agreed, running the wooden needle through the gills and out of the mouth of the foot-long fish to let it slide down the string to the gasping pile. "But then I hadn't fished my baskets in two, three days." He shifted his gaze again to Slappy, seeking to find out why he had come. The long, loose-lipped, pallid face seemed prepensely empty. Adam detected the .22 calibre rifle that Slappy held against his off side, half-concealed by the loose leg of his faded overalls—detected it, not so much by sight of it, as by Hinshaw's familiar posture and his own knowledge that Hinshaw rarely went to the woods without it. "H-how kin you tell a *he* squirrel from a *she* squirrel in these high trees this time of year?" Adam said with loaded casualness. At this season the females were carrying their young, and responsible hunters didn't take a chance.

After a poker-faced pause, Hinshaw Slappy said, "I hain't tried to."

Adam could not discover the weight or bulge of game in jumper or pants pockets and nodded in a confirmatory manner, but what brought Slappy to the bluff? After a moment he ejaculated, "Y-you fished your baskets this mornin', didn't you?"

Slappy's face relaxing, the bags under his pop eyes loosened, and his mouth sagged to return the ravaged look that it usually wore. With an odd mixture of a rogue's taciturnity and an undertaker's unction, he began to talk in a drawl that seemed long and lachrymose even in South Georgia. "Somethin' bin after my chickens, Adam—hit looked like a mink—I come off to the woods a-trailin' him." He lifted his rifle to view, making the belated gesture of disclosure with a vague air of apology. He lowered it. "I was just a-thinkin'—walkin' along, Adam, about that swamp line we run out back there in 1903, before old man Sumner died."

Adam lifted his gaze from the fish in his hand deliberately, glancing at Slappy before he let it settle on the broad expanse of the river to his left that moved past in tense stillness, its muddy waters purpled by the sinking sun. Slappy's land lines again? That one undersized lot of land of Slappy's had, with its various owners, been the cause of more trouble than all the other land bordering the Hightower place put together! "Yeah?" he said.

Slappy's pale eyes had bulged ambiguously as he stared at the noncommittal negro; now he reluctantly smiled and said, "You 'uz there, waun't you, Adam?"

Adam put his fish on the string. "I did the chopping and blazing for Mr. Sumner."

"I was a-looking' round down there at the bottom of our lot and found the old line this mornin'—walked right to it." Slappy carefully disengaged his glance and, using the muzzle of his rifle as a pointer, began to demonstrate on the ground before him the position of the imaginary line—"a runnin' east and west. Then I stepped it off. Hit passes just a hundred and ninety-six steps below our hog killin' grounds."

'Y-you mean the old pit that's always bin there?" Adam said. Not looking up, Slappy nodded his head, and Adam stared at him for a long moment speculatively, then snorted. "You ain't found no east-west line, no hundred and ninety-six steps below that old pit, Mr. Slappy. That line runs right by the pit."

Slappy looked away, his brow knitting, while Adam spoke. He met his gaze with pious earnestness now. "Yes, I did, Adam. I found the old chops and blazes, overgrown!"

Adam shrugged, then stood up carefully in the boat. "That must be the old wrong line by which your paw-in-law cut the Colonel's timber, til Mr. Sumner got us straightened out on the right line. It must be the line Old Bull Brownin' made up way back yonder!"

"Naw," Slappy said, "there's a jog in the deestrict line beyond us and hit carries through on our bottom line, carries through to Rison Creek—cuts all them lots on the River short." He added vindictively, "Even old man Sumner admitted to that!"

Adam listened attentively. Now he spoke to his twelve-year-old son in the stern of the bateau, as if he might be consulting him about the disputed line, but he said, "Steady it, Bo!" He stepped out of the boat to the bank, with a quick shift of his weight, then turned and put a foot on the prow to hold it for the oversized, lumbering boy, in knee-length, cut-down overalls, saying the while, "They're short, all right, but the River do that." He faced Slappy with a remonstrative smile and his jaw worked convulsively before he jerked out, "Whut you tryin' to tell me, man! That jog in the deestrict line is on the top side of your place—I've seen the plat. Don't you remember when Mr. Sumner showed us all the plat? And don't you know I wouldn't forgit it?"

Slappy waited till Adam had climbed the bank, then he resumed in an argumentative, whining drawl, "I couldn't be that much off, Adam! And then I found the old marks. I knocked a knot off of a big old sycamore tree and found a blaze with a date burnt into it—I could just barely make it out—'1857'!"

"Burnt into it!" Adam repeated, in surprise, now handing the long string of fish he had borne up the bluff to his son, to give close attention to the white man whose purpose he did not yet understand. As they began to move away from the river, he said, "That must be the corner old Bull Browning made up when he and the Colonel's pappy, Mr. Zach Hightower, *fit* over the line that time the Colonel told about. Didn't you hear him tell it?"

Slappy paused, bridling suspiciously as if he would scarcely have admitted to his own name; then he resumed motion, cautiously picking his way along the faint wilderness trace without speaking.

After a speculative glance at him, Adam gazed off, off into the trackless gray swamp as if it were tapestries of history, and pursued his story. "The Colonel told us about it that day Mr. Sumner had the plat there at the Hightower place showing it to us. The Colonel said he was there when they fit and separated 'em. It happen a few years after the War when he was just grown.

"He said his paw was a tall, keen-built feller, dark like a Frenchman and like to joke. Browning was a big fleshy feller, weighed over two hundred pounds, and talked loud. He liked to bully folks and he claimed that the jog in the deestrict line was on the lower side of Lot 133, just like you bin sayin—the county surveyor and them along with him had run the lower line sure-cuttin' trees in the way and only off-settin' where he had to, choppin' and a-blazin'—slap across the Hightower holdin' from the far deestrict line and hit come through right past that hog killin' pit, like I said. The county surveyor then was a man named McArthur. He told old man Brownin', No, the corner waun't where he had put his blazes, but further up, that he just had 'im a shallow lot. The Colonel said Bull Brownin' wanted to argue about it.

"They stood there where the surveyor said the corner was and Bull kept walkin' back toward the wrong corner he had sot up, looking at all them fine trees he was going to lose and he said, "Hightower, you brought this man by your wine house before you all started, damn you! He's tryin' to take my best timber away from me!'

"Old Zach laugh and say, 'Bull, the pasture always looks greener to you across the fence—what you mean is that he is tryin' to take *my* best timber away from you!'

"And Bull beller, 'I won't take that off'n nobody!'

"Then, the fit. . . ."

The two men fell into single file to walk a footlog over a slough that mired the road, and the boy, who was lagging behind, now bearing the string of fish on his back, hurried to catch up with them. They all crossed silently, in the towering silence of the swamp.

Finally Slappy spoke, a note of protest turning his drawl into a whine, "Who would have burnt that date into a corner blaze? Who, except the man who bought it from the old original Mr. Hightower back there? It must have been done when they run out that inside line for the first time."

Adam, now in the lead, did not pause or respond until he reached a point where the road began to ascend higher ground. Here a dim trail branched off to his left to crook its way out of sight around a rusty, abandoned steamboat boiler, half-sunk in the mud and overgrown with vines. He turned back to confront Slappy, for a moment gazing about him at the low swamp that surrounded them with endless spaced trees whose big gray boles were made identical by the pale mark of high water and made a misty maze by straggling tails of Spanish moss on the sunless saplings that grew between them. He glanced down beside him.

“Heah the old steamboat boiler,” he said, a note of triumph in his voice. “The line we bin talkin’ about a-comin’ ‘cross the Hightower place, runs by just above us, yonder”—he indicated the spot by a nod—“and hit ain’t more’n a mile from here to your corner. I still know where every chop and blaze is Mr. Sumner had me put there—I kin walk the line out with you?” Adam waited til Slappy came abreast of him and repeated, “I kin walk it out wit you, right now?”

But the lanky white man did not alter his loose swinging gait, as he moved past Adam, up the main road. “Ain’t got time now,” he muttered over his shoulder.

Adam fell in behind him, and they continued to walk in silence for several minutes, until they climbed a hill to emerge from the upper swamp into open piney woods and, a little further along, came to the gate to the lane that bisected a large field and, in the distance, passed Adam’s house. Slappy halted at the gate for Adam to open it. And, as he undid the latch, Adam turned back to confront him:

“How come you so worked up over that line *now?* I ain’t heard you mention it befo’ since Mr. Sumner got it all straightened out, seven year ago!” Slappy moved as if to go through the gate, but Adam did not get out of his way. “What’s this all about?” Adam said.

Slappy grew still. Leaning back against the wire fence, he relaxed, pushing his wool hat onto the back of his head with his gun muzzle and then allowing the rifle to slide to the ground, its butt beside his foot. His face took on an odd look of uncertainty that seemed to mingle amusement and pain, but his voice was matter-of-fact. “That land buyer, Adam, ain’t the least bit interested in the widow’s clay deposits, nor that oil slick—nor the Wyche field, for that matter. But she says she’s going to hold ’em out on the deal and he won’t stand for that. He’s buyin’ to sell and he don’t want his titles all cumbered up. He won’t buy! He don’t have to—he’ll back out!”

Adam, blinking, frowned; then glancing up at his boy who was standing a little apart, listening, he opened the gate to him saying,

"Go on now, Bo! Take them fish on up to the house!" Then, he turned back to Slappy. "Whut makes you think he won't buy?"

"He's done said so—said it to me and to Peter Bright, in the presence of Banker Littleton!"

Adam closed the gate thoughtfully and latched it and leaned against the gatepost before he spoke. "So you calculate to put 'em *above* the line to the land he's buyin'—the deposits, the oil slick and the Wyche field? But hell, Hinshaw, there never was any line like that comin' back through the Colonel's swamp—never bin claimed there wuz—wrong or not! And the blazes and chops on the *true* line can still be found!"

Slappy shook his head and came upright from the fence, leaving his gun behind. Without shortening his drawl, his voice took on a surprising drive. "Sho'. That won't make no difference, Adam, no difference, 'cause that upper line of the swamp land this Philadelphia feller wants to buy *fee simple* ain't ever goin' to be run out. That's 'cause he wants to lease the adjoinin' lots, too, for the slash pine in the upper swamp and bays—wants twenty-five year leases—neither, me nor you'll be here, likely, when that time comes! And he don't give a damn 'bout no land line for the sake of the land—what he's after is timber!" Adam, who had been holding Slappy's gaze, now lowered his face meditatively, and Slappy began automatically to advance on him, his voice rising, "What he's after is timber, I say, and he'll have that, *fee simple* and *lease!* And hit won't make no difference to him which."

Slappy, pausing, shifted to a sidling approach and his voice lowered and became cajoling, "And you know, Adam, while the clay deposits seem important to the widow now, 'cause she heard it from the Colonel, the things that made 'em worth somethin' ain't there any more. I mean the Colonel himself and that railroad—it's for sho' now goin' through way below us on the other side of the lower river." His face clouding, Adam had turned away as Slappy drew near him. Now

Slappy stood close, talking into his ear with conviction. "If she ever tried to do anything about that clay, which I doubt that she will, she'll quick find out it ain't worth a dime. Hit sho' ain't worth ruinin' the sale over! And as for that oil slick—hell, you know there ain't no oil in this here country!"

Adam turned his back to Slappy resolutely, opening the gate. "I don't know nothin'!" he said.

Slappy pursued him, still at his ear, like a hound that has treed his quarry. "Listen, Adam, he's goin' to give us little land holders six dollars an acre, *fee simple*, and five dollars for our slash pine—cash! Cash on the barrel head, Adam, think of that!"

Adam moved through the gateway hastily, shaking his head. "I got-a git on up toward the house," he said.

Slappy started to follow him through, then ran back to pick up his rifle, saying the while, in a raised voice that shook with honest unction, "But we kain't sell without her, Adam! He's not interested in us little chinquapin holders unless the widow'll sell her thousand acres, *fee simple*, and six hundred acres, *lease*. She's the main deal, we're just the fill-outs!" He put his hand on Adam's shoulder, like an act of love. "Hit could mean better'n six hundred dollars for me—six hundred dollars cold cash! That's more money than I've ever before bin able to git together at one time in my whole life!"

Adam moved toward his house, against the straight rows of the fields on either side of him, as if he were ploughing up the ground with his feet. And Slappy pursued him—it was almost as if Adam were the plow behind a team of relentless invisible mules and Hinshaw were an unsure plowboy, trying to keep up with it; but the whining voice held them hard upon the furrow. "Adam, if'n you lose the Wyche field your bonanza's busted—I don't have to tell you that! Your good times'll be over. And you're a-throwin' hit away too—for nothin', nothin'. That damned Philadelphia Yankee don't know nothin' bout cotton land—don't know how scarce hit is around here—and don't give a good Continental damn!"

When they reached the second gate, the gate by the barn, Slappy was before Adam and blocked their progress by holding onto the latch. "Listen to me, Adam, this thing means the most to me and you, both of us, both of us! And we got the clue to it!"

His back to the gate rails to catch his breath, Adam drew out his handkerchief and mopped a face drawn as if in pain, his wide, dancing eyes evading Slappy's look. At last he breathed out heavily, "Hinshaw, we kain't git away with nothin' like that—you'll just git us in trouble!"

Slappy's ravaged face had an ugly twist on it and his voice shook. "Look Adam, where's old man Mort Sumner now? Dead! And the Colonel's dead, too. Everbody's dead who knew anything about the *wrong* line, or the *right* line twixt the low swamp lots and the hill lots—everybody, 'ceptin' *me* and *you*—me and you, Adam!"

Cold sweat stood out on Adam's now gray face, but he finally met Slappy's gaze. He looked like a man who had swallowed poison, but he spoke collectedly. "They ain't as dead as you think, Mr. Slappy—they ain't as dead as you think!"

Slappy's tightened features slumped, sagging into a look of raddled frustration. He released the gate latch and reached into his jumper pocket for his chewing tobacco.

On the following Friday, Adam pushed open the beveled glass door of Riverton's dim house of finance and, before it could close behind him, Banker Littleton's voice bellowed out: "What's this I hear about you getting the widow Hightower mixed up on her land lines?"

Adam, blinking fast, scanned the lobby to see that there was no one else to answer but himself. He got out without too much stuttering: "I—I don't know whut you hear, Mr. Littleton, but the Widow ain't asked me 'bout no lines, since this big land deal come up—I reckon that's whut you talkin' about?—and I ain't told her 'bout none."

The banker's long nose and gray forelock picketed the wicket. "Why is it then that she keeps saying she's got to reserve the rights to her clay deposits? Ain't they on the lease lots?" But before Adam could begin, even if he had been eager to answer, Mr. Littleton added, "Look, the land buyer's lawyer, Colonel Slater, is over at Colonel Duke's office now—this thing is causing trouble—they want to talk to you and see if we can't straighten it out." He pointed a finger through the window. "Go on over there! And tell 'em I'll be along after awhile, if I can get away."

Adam turned back toward the door with reluctance. Peter Bright had sent him word to meet him at the bank. Had sent him word by Hinshaw Slappy. The word was that old man Peter was going to have to have his money from Adam in July—payment on the rest of his mortgage loan, since it looked like the land deal wasn't going through. Adam had got the significance of it, all right, would have understood the threat in it, even if old man Peter hadn't used Slappy to bring it to him. He had figured that Hinshaw would tote his land-line tale to take the Widow's clay deposits out of the deal around to their neighbors; he had even figured that most of them would want to believe it enough to swallow such a flying-frog story. But he hadn't expected banker Littleton to go for it! He still had six hundred dollars in the bank, even though he had his crop to make yet. He had counted on help from Littleton. Adam paused for a moment, as he held open the glassed, gold-lettered, weighty portal, to glance back at the wicket, but the banker had not relaxed his forward pitch. Adam shrugged and released the door.

He approached the squat, white, frame building up the side street from the bank with misgiving. The banker's words disturbed him deeply. Mr. Littleton ought to know better than to believe Hinshaw

Slappy! Could it be that he would let the others do in the Widow on her clay deposits just to get the deal through? Who was Mr. Littleton *for* in this thing, anyhow? Picking his way across the low porch that fronted it, Adam stood before a glassed door with words painted on it in black. Who was this *they* that wanted to talk to him? Wasn't it enough that he had to sacrifice his own interest in the Wyche field and to make an enemy out of a white man and neighbor to keep his word to the Colonel—without this? *They*, whoever they were, would all be white men in on the deal and anxious to believe Slappy's story too! Adam's eyes narrowed. He supposed the black marks on the door said, COLONEL DUKE. He had never been in the office of the Yankee lawyer, who mostly represented the big sawmill in Riverton, and he had never even laid eyes on the land buyer's lawyer, who would doubtless be a quick-talking Yankee, too. How did lawyers get in on such a thing as this?

Uncertain whether he should knock, loath to enter at all, he knocked twice and waited for the second sharp call to *Come in!* before he opened the door. The same voice called again, "In here!" And he found his way across the dark, empty front room and through an open door into a back room.

His eyes widened and his hat slipped out of his hand. His misgivings had not prepared him for what confronted him. The room blazed with blinding light from an electric lamp suspended from the ceiling at the center of it and beyond the ball of brightness, posted against an unpainted, tongue-and-groove wall, their faces almost like it in color and stiffness, were seated a row of white men that ran all the way around the room. Adam bent down to pick up his hat. He took his time in straightening up to get hold of himself.

The same voice he had heard before, said briskly, "Get you a chair out of the waiting room!"

As he came upright, Adam made out to his left the Yankee lawyer, Colonel Duke, in a swivel chair, backed up against a roller top desk.

He was young and smooth looking. His fine store clothes had a special cut to them, and he wore a vest with a little gold chain across the front of it. He said again in a flat cheery voice, "Get you a chair!"

Adam backed automatically toward the doorway he had just entered. With a single spasmodic jerk of his jaw, he got out, "Dat's all right, I kin stand up." But fenced in and his eyes dazzled, like this, he couldn't tell who any of these white men were. It was like facing a law-jury, a jury that had already made up its mind and all put one face on it!

"Adam, I guess you know why we sent for you?" The bright brown eyes in Duke's tinted face seemed to Adam to leer at him in a mercenary way. "My clients here believe that Mrs. Hightower may have got her erroneous misconception from you. Mr. Bright remembers your telling him—"

A bugle-like voice sprang at Adam from across the room. "Swamp field's above the river lots, ain't it, Adam?"

The smile on Duke's face hardened as he sat up in his chair to single out the questioner.

Adam's eyes walling, he turned toward the sound. He leaned to one side to peer around the glare of the incandescent light, getting out in words that shook with eagerness as well as with stuttering, "Ain't that you, Mr. Peter? Mr. Peter Bright?" Now he made out the white head, the lean face and thin nose and gray loosely twisted mustache, giving the mouth the seeming of a smile, that identified old Peter Bright for him. "Whut'd you say, Mr. Peter?"

But the other white men around the room shuffled their feet and shifted in their chairs, staring at Bright censoriously, and he became stiff as a waxwork and looked away.

"I will do the talking, Adam."

It was Duke again, but Adam did not yet turn to him. Retreating until his hams touched the door open against the wall adjacent to the roller-top desk, he found moral as well as physical backing in the support. He made another appeal to the circle of his white neighbors. "I know some of you white gentlemens, but they's some more here I don't believe I knows?"

"That's right, Adam."

Adam saw out of the corner of his eye that Duke had turned his chair toward him and was smiling up at him with an intense, smooth, cold smile. The faces in front of him gave back no recognition.

Duke went on. "And to start with, let me introduce you to Colonel Slater here to my right. He has something to say."

The long, starchy man in gray serge and glittering pince-nez moved in his chair, as if to get up, lifting a hand, but when he saw that Adam did not budge from the door, he resumed his position, saying merely, "Martin Slater—not 'Colonel Slater'! I'm Mr. Lincoln's lawyer." Taking an envelope from his breast pocket, he continued, "I have a letter here from Mr. Lincoln, who is now in Brunswick, and he is disturbed over the exemptions that Mrs. Hightower and Mr. Latrobe, I believe it is, down at Bell's Ferry—he has asked to exempt a river field since he heard about Mrs. Hightower's wanting to do so—Mr. Lincoln is disturbed over these proposals. And he writes me that he is on the point of abandoning the project altogether and, instead, buying a tract on Catherine Island where he won't be bothered with reservations." Amid a nervous shuffling of feet, the man refolded the letter with long-fingered, bloodless hands and returned it to his pocket, without ever having looked at it. Then, with a brief excuse to Duke, he nodded and left the room.

Duke, who saw him to the door, took his stance between the white men and the negro, half-facing each, and addressed his questions to Adam as if he might have been a defendant on trial. "Present here is Dr. Parkerson, who, as you know, is one of Riverton's most prominent druggists. Dr. Parkerson remembers that in conversation with you and Hinshaw Slappy one day more than a year ago, you told them that the field you tend, known as the Wyche field, was in the upper swamp."

Adam shifted first left, then right, peering around the lawyer and the light, to locate a pale, wide-faced man, in his shirt-sleeves, wearing a white collar and bow tie. "Kin you sort of refresh me on where we wuz when we had this conversation, Dr. Parkerson?" he asked, his air of honest perplexity in sharp contrast to Duke's hortatory manner.

The man addressed, whose curly hair drooped over his forehead, and purplish lids drooped over his eyes, and black mustache over his mouth, did not look up. "This is the first chance I've had to sell that cut-over swamp Pa left me," he murmured, "and it may the be last!"

"That has nothing to do with the case!" Duke said sharply, taken by surprise and too slow on the uptake to cut Parkerson off. He went on. "But we have others here, well known to you, who are even better informed about the lay of the land on the Hightower place. There's Mr. Milt Murdock and his brother, Mr. Lou, over there. But to get to the heart of this thing, coming with the Brights here, is Mr. John Hightower, the late Colonel Hightower's own brother, as you know, the only one remaining alive." Duke moved nearer Adam to intercept the roving eye. "He recalls an old false land line set up by a man now dead that he believes may have confused you. He remembers that his father had a fight with this man about it, and it took the county surveyor to straighten it out."

Adam turned toward the lawyer and was on the point of asking him why, instead of all of this fuss, they didn't call the county surveyor again, when he heard the nasal, mumbly, yet unmistakably Hightower voice of the Colonel's youngest brother. "Old man named Browning—where Slappy lives now—"

Adam's mouth tightened. The timbre of John Hightower's voice set up a trembling in his entrails and his leg quivered. He looked off above their heads and out of the rear window. It hurt him that that voice could be raised against—against whom? Yes, against the Colonel and his widow! That was what it came to. This was sorry business! Adam was cold and shaky but he felt his ribs swell and he spoke out to Duke. "T-tell Mr. Jawn I'd heard about that. But I hadn't figgered it to holp us none!" Then he turned to the group, a wry smile limbering the scared look on his face, and thrust out his hands. "My Gawd, y'all don't think I wants to quit tendin' the Wyche field, *do* ye?"

A blowsy, empty laugh swept the room. Someone cried, "It wouldn't make sense if you did!" There was more laughter at this, Adam joining in, and someone else said, "Where's Hinshaw Slappy, anyhow?" Adam had been wondering about Slappy.

At this instant the telephone on the wall beside Duke's desk rang to interrupt them. In a moment, Duke who had moved to answer it, turned back from the mouthpiece and said to the gathering. "It's Mr. Littleton—he doesn't see how he can get down here—he wants to know how it's *going*?"

A dark, bony-faced man with a lean red nose spoke out in a raised voice, modulated by an inner merriment, "Tell him it's not *going* (he imitated Duke's voice elaborately) a'tall: it's *gwine* and it seems to me hit's *gwine fine*." His bright raccoon eyes caught Adam's gaze and he smiled artlessly. "How about it, Adam?"

Adam felt embarrassed. Milt Murdock was an honest, kindhearted man. But what could he do? He looked helplessly about the circle: the white men's faces all wore a quizzical, expectant air. His insides slipped his grip and his head began to float. He gave them a wrenching, ambiguous grin. "S-sort-a looks like I'm outcounted!"

Duke spoke for them. "Well, what do you say then, Adam?"

Adam's wry grin widened, but his voice, when it came, was as soft and bland and uncertain as custard, "Look's like ya'll done *decided* 'bout de line—"

Accepting this as assent, Duke turned back to the telephone and said, "Say there—I believe we may have just got an agreement." When he turned to the room again, he reported, "Littleton says not to forget there's forty thousand dollars cash involved in this deal!" He walked back to his chair.

But the others in the room continued to stare questioningly at Adam.

In the pause, the door in the side wall opened and Hinshaw Slappy entered the room. Looking in Adam's direction but avoiding his eye, he called, "Hey there, Adam, I told them I thought you just got mixed up betwixt which wuz which line!" He turned toward the room with an exaggerated manner of speaking confidentially, "You know fellers, I saidst to myself awhilst we wuz a-talkin' about hit and a-arguin', I'll bet he's just got his lines mixed up, *whichun's which!. .*"

Adam stared at them, as if Slappy had swallowed fire before them, and would at any moment drop dead.

In the tightening silence that followed, Slappy clomped awkwardly across the room to a vacant chair without looking back; old Peter Bright reached in his hip pocket for his chewing tobacco evading Adam's gaze; and the lawyer, Duke, studied his fingernails.

Swaying, Adam shifted his stance to steady himself. He saw on their faces that they all knew that Slappy was lying. And, wincing, he saw more: he saw that, though ashamed of it, they meant for *him* to pretend to believe Slappy, too! Then his shifting gaze came to a halt. What he saw through the rear window made his back prickle and his eyeballs burn: the hook-nosed profile of Oswald Paley, as he disappeared around the corner of the building. He had been in the other room with Slappy! Paley was in on this thing! Sweat ran down Adam's face and he got out his handkerchief. Paley's being around made the thing look rotten as well as rough!

Somebody said, "We all got to be together on this!"

Duke leaned toward Adam, holding out his hand. "This understanding is going to be better for everybody," he said, and his smile seemed almost genuine.

Adam looked at the proffered hand, feeling the wall of pressure bearing down on him.

"I-I ho-hope so!" he stammered, wondering what he meant.

There was a laugh and someone said, "Shore as shoutin!" And the white men began to shove back their chairs and get up.

But Adam did not take Duke's hand. Instead he abruptly lowered his own hands to his sides and stood there trembling, his ginger-colored face, gray and pinched with fear, his eye-whites shoaling up. Bracing against the door, he said, in an intense smooth monotone: "Why don't y'all git the county surveyor to prove that line, white fo'ks?"

Duke came out of his chair as if he had been touched by a hot poker. "Why don't *you*?" he shot back, in more vigor than sense; then he added quickly, "The land belongs to Mrs. Hightower—my clients are not involved—it would be highly improper. . . ."

Adam saw the white men sit back down in their seats, saw their faces stiffen—around the circle, saw only the eyes of strangers. And in their eyes rose a familiar hostility—a community of hostility—a hostility that strangely he could not bear. He shrugged, feeling his backbone give way. He smiled submissively and moved away from the door, out into the room toward them. He said jokingly, though there was a quaver in his voice, "Maybe y'all *better had* let me look at them land lines ag'in!"

5.

THE LONG, LEAN, BLACK MAN, wearing a slick black serge suit and a celluloid collar without a tie, got out of Adam's buggy at the mail box. He and Adam had halted on the side of the deep-rutted sandy road that crooked its way out of a flat stretch of stunted oak and pine and palmetto. The man faced about and Adam handed an oblong, corrugated cardboard box over the wheels to him, saying, "Here yuh liquor, Kiger!"

He took it, steadying himself with a spread-legged swagger. The dull black pigmentation of his long face faded into large ash-white freckles on the front of his cheeks and on the bridge of his big, pointed, pock-marked nose, which, as he now lifted it, gave him a little the look of a shark, breaking through dark, foam-crested waters. This similarity was sharpened when he opened his wide, toothy mouth, flashing two gold front teeth. "Maybe a feller of color wid so much business wid de buckra oughter have another drink!" Kiger said, in a high-pitched voice, pulling a quart bottle out of the box.

A reddish tinge in his cheeks and his eyes glittering, Adam shook his head, then smiling said, "Shut yuh mouth, Kiger!"

Kiger was unaffected by this half-hearted rebuke, turning the bottle, three-quarters full, about in his hand, gazing at it. "Soloman's Supreme, aged in the Rock of Ages!" he said. "I'd be pleased to give yuh another one. How 'bout it?"

Sitting a little stiffly in his seat, still smiling, Adam took the bottle, swung it above his mouth for a swig and handed it back. Then he slapped the reins over his red mule's rump and that nervous animal jerked the buggy into the road and was gone, Adam waving goodbye over his shoulder.

The drink was Adam's fourth and that was more than he ordinarily took—except on special occasions. He slapped the lines over the mule's back again when she showed signs of slowing down. The special occasion, he told himself, was Kiger Steele's getting his monthly shipment of liquor under Georgia's prohibition law. But that, he knew bitterly, despite the warm surge of alcohol in his veins and the soothing blur on his brain, had *not* been the special occasion for him. He had felt completely washed out when he got away from the white men in lawyer Duke's office. He damn sure had needed a drink, and he was only too willing to help Kiger sample the new supply. He had been glad to give him the lift home. Kiger was at the hitching racks, across the street from Duke's office and had seen them when they all came out together.

His passenger was a brother in the Corinthian Lodge, and Adam was glad to have his company, along with his liquor, even though Kiger had tried to *pick* him about it over their drinks on the way out. Of course, he hadn't told him a damn thing. He wouldn't talk before a man of Kiger's kidney, or mouth!

As the mule trotted along over the firm road of the flatwoods, Adam, sitting lithely forward on the cushions, diverted himself by flicking leaves off the bushes along the way with his buggy whip. But after a time the road ran out of flat country upon sandhills that brought the animal to a dead walk. The sound of the buggy wheels in the sandy ruts was like ashes in his ears; the slow pace made him sluggish, and he put up the whip and slipped down in the seat to doze.

But he did not sleep. Quickly, the cat's clay of conscience pricked his brain. He hadn't answered Kiger's prying, sweet-tongued questions, but he had acted like a *bank-walker!* He had let Kiger and his liquor puff him up! The red-rayed sun was setting and there was now little warmth from it, but a cloud of dust hung over the sparsely covered hills and seemed to hold the heat upon them. Adam began to sweat profusely and felt a touch of nausea at the pit of his stomach. Nobody had less room to be puffed up than Adam Atwell, in these risky, April-fool days! At best the round at the lawyer's office was a dogfall for him. They *think* they have got me, he told himself—and I did come pretty near to knuckling under!—still they're not sure, and that makes a damned shaky situation out of it!

Dropping the reins over the dashboard, he came out of his overalls jumper. As he was unbuttoning his shirt collar, the question struck him, struck him with sudden aching clarity: *What do you mean, trying to buck all of those white men? Don't you know you're just a nigger?* He stared at the red mule's rump, as if addressing it. *Banker Littleton and the Colonel's brother John and Peter Bright! And, why, why, why? To do yourself out of the best piece of cotton land in the county! Have you gone slap dab crazy?* He pulled a bandanna handkerchief out of his hip pocket and mopped his face and, putting his feet up on the dashboard, he discontentedly lowered his head between his knees.

After a time he perceived that the rig had begun to go downhill and, pushing back in his seat, he pulled up the reins and the mule broke into a trot. Could he have kept the field? Hinshaw Slappy was the only other man who knew where the true line lay. He,

Adam, could fall in with Hinshaw's fraud about the line and get to farm the Wyche field for another ten years—maybe longer! And the boy, when he grew up, might never even look for the clay deposits! A lot could happen in ten years!

Passing a grove of oaks in front of a double-pen log house, Adam was seized with wonderment at how he had let himself get crossed up with those white men. He searched the clean sandy ground to discover his answer there. What *had* made him swell up and get so stiff-necked? An image of the white men, confronting him around the tongue-and-groove walls rose thinly before the trees. What was it, looking into the white men's faces, there, and them trying to ease him into a lie—what was it that had made him balk? It seemed now to him as if there had been some kind of pushing game between them—like, like they were trying to push their electric lamp onto him—and him, trying to push it back at them—by just thinking about it and wishing it hard, not saying anything out loud. He shrugged and mopped his face again with the red cloth. Somehow, in not taking their bait, he had held out against them—and if he'd swallowed it, there would have been a hook and line to it—they would *own* him now!

They were together against him from the start, but they didn't get mad till he charged about the county surveyor. Why the hell did he have to do that? Quick as a wink they all froze, froze into one look and he was no longer Adam Atwell to them, but just a nigger who had offended them, white men all together and they hated him!

The image before Adam grew achingly vivid. His insides were rising into his throat. He jerked the mule to a halt. They were now on top of another sandhill, and, pulling out of the road, he drove a little way among the scattering of blackjack oaks and sage brush in the dusk and, leaping from the buggy, began to retch. He vomited heavily. Finally he wiped his face and eyes and restored his handkerchief. Leading his mule out into the road again, he got back in the buggy.

He had seen *that* look on a crowd of white men's faces once before. And, only one time before: after the riot in Lancaster that sent him to the Mines, thirty years ago! The white men in the courtroom at Lancaster—and there weren't any niggers there, except the cowed little bunch of which he was one—had had that same look on their faces. The courtroom was packed full; however, deputies, walking up and down the aisles with clubs in their hands, kept everybody quiet. But they all had the same look on their faces. The white men who sat in the jury box had it, and, in front of the jury, the white men at the other table that the Colonel said were the prosecuting lawyers, even the judge behind the big desk looking down on them from his throne—all of them had it!

Every white man had had that look on his face, except the big, calm, young red-headed lawyer, who was Colonel Hightower, and the judge had appointed him to represent the niggers.

Adam had been in Georgia only six weeks when he got mixed up in the Lancaster riot. He was only nineteen years old then. He had run away from his old home in North Carolina, or as good as run away, not even letting ma know he was going! He told himself that he was leaving the old Atwell place, coming off down here to get to fresh turpentine woods. The truth was that he was trying to be on his own, and it was more to get away from his mother and old man Atwell, the white man he was named after, that he came. It didn't take him long to be sorry of it!

He had been boxing trees for Mr. Christian DeBow at Riverton for five weeks, when he went on the excursion to Lancaster—mostly for the ride, though they aimed to make the big brush-arbor meeting at Samson's Grove—he and two more turpentine hands—and one of them was that fool they called Trotlucky and old man Ezra, their uncle, who had come from up around that part of the country.

"My Gawd, whut a swarm of blackbirds!" old man Ezra said, when the train had stopped at Lancaster and he looked out the window—and he was black as any of them, himself! It was then about seven o'clock in the morning and excursions had been bringing them in all night. There must have been a couple of thousand of colored people there around the depot and on main street. They were everywhere: prancing up and down and jostling each other about, sitting on the station platform and on the stacks of cross-ties along the track, on the benches under the covered sidewalks to the stores, which lined the far side of each of the streets running alongside the railroad track that split the town open.

His memory of the fateful crowd came back to Adam so vividly now that he felt a strange sense of awe of it. He could hear again the buzz of that good-humored talk and laughter, as it had reached him that morning, before he got off the train. A lot of them had brought baskets of victuals or at least something in a sack for breakfast. They were eating and strewing baked sweet potato peelings and egg shells and watermelon rinds about the street. A lot of them were dressed up in fine long-tailed hand-me-down coats and second-hand silk dresses and even at that early hour were strutting up and down to show off their clothes. Everybody seemed as easy and amiable as folks could be.

Some of them were heading out toward the Grove, which was a mile beyond the town, but most of them were waiting for the drug stores to open, because that was where liquor was sold in Lancaster then. There were nine liquor-selling drug stores there that day, he had been told.

He and two other boys and their Uncle Ezra waited, too. They did not have any breakfast with them and they had not had much sleep the night before and old man Ezra said he needed a dram the worst sort.

At that time, he, Adam, didn't know the taste of liquor. The only thing he had ever had was a little scuppernong wine. But he was powerful curious to test it out. The other boys were older than he was and had been around such things more—especially Trotlucky Bostick—but, of course, he wouldn't let on that he was just breaking in on it.

The drug stores opened at nine o'clock. There was such a crowd, however, that Ezra didn't get his bottle till an hour later, and it was past eleven and the morning meeting had started when they finally got to the Grove. They had stopped three times along the way to have a drink and they had tried to find some breakfast somewhere, though without any luck. He, Adam, had managed to get down his drink all right each time they passed the bottle. He kept on smacking his lips as if he liked the stuff, but he couldn't keep his eyes from watering. By the time they got to the brush arbor he was already feeling the liquor too much, but he still had a hold on himself and could walk straight.

A long way off the beat of a bass drum reached his ears. The steady measured booming came out of a clump of woods that, off there beyond the rows of houses and open fields, looked to him like a dark green cloud on the horizon. The top pitch of singing voices and a faint riffle of tambourines came to him between the beats. He was just a smooth-faced boy then, and the strange sound of it made his eyes bug out at his companions—though it was Trotlucky who spoke up: "Man, listen at that thing!" Everybody he could see in the broad stream of bobbing heads and shoulders on ahead of them seemed to be moving faster and not talking, set on getting to the Grove. The sound grew inside him and made cold chills run up and down his back. The pop-skull from the inside and the drum skill from the outside had him half-scared to death by the time he got to the meeting.

He was shocked, too, by the size of the brush arbor. It spread out and out and on and on, between the scattering oak trees—that ran up through the sparkleberry and persimmon brush of the roof to make it look like a big burrow—the biggest in the world! And packed full of singing and shouting people.

Uncle Ezra said, "Boys, we better bust up and each man find him a hole!" And they scattered without so much as thinking of how they would get back together. Adam stumbled down an aisle on the far right-hand side, and found a perch on the end of one of the benches.

The music stopped just after he sat down and the people down the row from him nodded to him in a friendly way.

The ground sloped toward a hollow in front of them, where beyond the benches there was a low platform built out of new planks. In the middle of it, raised upon a throne and sitting behind a fine furniture-store pulpit, in a highback chair of the same sort, sat a big bright-skinned woman, in white robes. She looked like she might have been cut out of marble, she was so smooth and calm.

Next to him on the bench somebody leaned over and whispered in his ear, "That's Mother Mary Magdalene Call—Mother Mary, herself!" He turned to find the broad, brass-spectacles smiling face of a middle-aged dark woman.

He nodded and began to look around him, suddenly feeling the closeness of the place. It was August and sultry under that arbor and there must have been a million palmetto fans, making a breeze back and forth, all around the big semicircle of heads and shoulders and moving arms, but he couldn't feel it. Sweat popped out all over him and began to run down his face and his grip on his head began to slip. His stomach seemed to swell and quiver, then it turned a flip and he could taste the liquor in his throat again. A trembling nausea took him.

At this juncture the singing began again. Men dressed in white clothes stood up on the platform to lead it and in the middle in front of the pulpit sat the man beating the bass drum he had heard on his way and on either side of him were women, shaking tambourines, high and low, and dancing about as they shook them. The singing swelled and people, here, there, and yonder, down front began to shout.

Then somebody beyond Adam on the bench was making his way out to the aisle to shout, and when Adam tried to move his knees out of the way he slipped off the end and hit the ground. Heaving, but holding his liquor down, he got to his feet to find that the pulpit was pitching and rearing and the whole place was beginning to spin. He knew he had better get out from under the arbor as fast as he could, so he headed about and started back up the aisle. But now the aisle was weaving and twisting and he couldn't follow it and found himself mixed up against people's knees between the benches and his feet slipped out from under him and he went down.

They right kindly—he realized even as scared and sick as he was—helped him up and with somebody on either side of him, heaving and choking, he got out from under the arbor. And, after they were out in the light and the fresh air and walking around, he got enough of the water out of his eyes to see who it was. There was the old woman in the brass spectacles on one side and a skinny, shrivel-faced, man on the other. The old man shook his gray head and said, "Son, if she wants to come up, let 'er come—hit'll make yuh feel better!"

It was the first time and the liquor threw him hard. He had never known anything like it before. He was so weak when he got through vomiting, he could scarcely walk, and still drunk, too.

The old man had hung around for him to get straightened out, and when he saw that Adam still couldn't walk right, he led him back down the road to his house, which was only a quarter of a mile away.

Everything before Adam's eyes on that journey was painful and weaving and blurred and he could not tell much about it. The man, he remembered, took him to an old batten-and-board house behind a rail fence, and on the back porch the old man pumped water on his head, then led him into a shedroom with a big pile of shucks on the floor. Here Adam had collapsed on the whirling shuck pile, soon to be tossed into a black and dreamless sleep.

When Adam was awakened that evening, coming to foggily at first and choking and suspended in air, a baleful dim light somewhere behind him, he thought, maybe, he had gone to hell and was about to be thrown into the sulphur pit. Nothing had happened to him later that night, nor during the next three days for that matter, did anything to lighten or clear up that impression!

Soon he realized that a hard fist had hold of his shirt, was twisting the collar to choke him, while pulling him to his feet. In the blur of voices he distinguished the cold bitter tones of a white man saying, "Yes, yore belly full of red-eye, after you've ripped and roared around—gone dog mad and killed a white man, why you just lay down like the beast that you are and sleep it off!" Then as Adam tried to scramble to his feet, he shook him hard, twisting the collar till the button popped off, barking, "Git on yore feet, you yaller-skin son-of-a-bitch!"

Adam, in an open-mouthed, bug-eyed daze, stood before a tall white man in a flat-topped straw hat that shadowed his face except for his long jaw. The man jerked him around and he saw a second white man in the doorway of the shedroom, holding a lantern in his hand. But his incomprehension of his situation was so complete that he could not move. The first white man, now holding him by the belt, cracked him over the head with a club saying, "Maybe that'll wake you up—Goddamn you!"

It did help, Adam found. At least he knew now that his punishment was not a nightmare, but incredibly real. He was shoved out onto the back porch, where the man with the lantern set it down and pulled Adam's hands behind his back and tied them together with a length of rope, which he had cut from a coil of new plow line he carried with him. In the dim light, Adam now saw that the tall man with the club had a silver badge on his right gallus strap and a pistol in the holster at his belt. Guessing that he must be the *Law*, Adam tried to speak, but he found his throat so dry and aching, his jaws so locked together that only a whisper came out.

They did not even notice it. They hustled him down the steps and around the house and out of the front gate, where there were other white men, carrying shotguns, guarding a mule-team and wagon. He was quickly boosted over a rear wheel and made to lie down in the wagon bed, where he found another bound negro already lying.

The night's slow, broken, fearful ride, during which the wagon took on three more roped negroes, finally brought them to what he later learned to be the county jail—a square oak deal building, with barred windows in it. While the man with the lantern stood holding it above his head, they were all unloaded and led inside, where three other white men, like hell's pale angels, stood guard in a bare front room from which a dark hall ran down, he felt sure, to a rope, firewood, and a tree.

The man wearing the silver badge stopped before a table just inside the entrance and said, "All full up?"

Across the table from him, a man with a gold badge on his galluses, and a revolver laying on the table beside him said in a dead voice, “Stand ‘em over there with the rest!” nodding over his shoulder toward the far side of the room.

There were four more negroes, with their hands tied behind them, standing with their faces to the wall there. Adam and his fellow passengers were pushed along over to the wall beside them. Here they all stood, the nine of them with a white man in the middle of the room holding a gun on them—stood, leaned against the wall, or slumped down on the floor, for the rest of the night.

Numb beyond any pain, except a perishing thirst and still without a hint of why he was there except that seemingly a white man, somehow, somewhere, had been killed, and almost mindless in his confused uncertainty and fear of what might be in store for him, he was still limply kneeling, and leaning against the wall six hours later, when day broke and the jailer entered with a big tin pot of coffee. Adam remembered that night, would always remember it, as the nearest thing to hell he could suffer on this earth.

The jailor had a negro boy with him, carrying a new tin cup. The boy held out the cup for the jailor to fill with coffee, then he held it up to each prisoner’s mouth while he drank it, each in turn. When they got to him, Adam had mustered up enough voice and desperation to croak, “Could yuh gimme jus’ a little bit of water, please suh?”

The jailor’s bloated face stiffened, like he wasn’t going to do it, then he shrugged. “Damn if you don’t look like you need it, all right!” he said and motioned the negro helper toward a cedar water bucket on the table by the entrance. That water had felt like hot lead running down his throat, at first. . .

The mule halted and Adam roused himself to see, in the gathering dark, that they had arrived at the first gate to the Hightower holding. He got out of the buggy to open it. He had known after he gulped down that tin cup-full of water that he was going to live and that even if later they did hang him, nothing else could be as bad as the night he had just passed through, nothing could ever happen to him again as bad as that had been! He lifted the latch and pushed the gate inward. It was hard for him to recall now just how he did find out all about the riot, Adam reflected, leading the mule through the gateway.

He had heard one of the white men in the jail read out what was in the newspaper. There was some talk amongst the prisoners during the two days that followed though they didn't seem to know much about what happened—or wouldn't tell it. The long tall deputy who arrested him—fellow named Smithson—had talked to him about it some. Then the Colonel told him, too. Any way you learned it, it was a hard thing to believe. It seemed that his people went plum crazy mad that Sunday afternoon. Of course Redeye was responsible for a large part of it—the popskull that the white men in the drugstores sold them. But there was more to it than that. The devil got control of that bunch of niggers. Not those under the arbor worshiping. It was the ones outside, drinking and gambling.

One nigger lost his watch to another nigger, but when he got ahead again, he wanted to buy it back. When the man who won it wouldn't let him have it back he called the marshal, who arrested the one with the watch and started to take him to the jail. As they crossed a ditch on the way, this nigger tripped him and broke loose and ran. The marshal said later at the trial that he and his deputy fired up in the air to make the man stop running but there was so much confusion with all those black folks around that he didn't know just what happened. Anyhow the running man got killed by a shot from somewhere and all those drunk niggers thought it was the marshals that did it and started after them.

The marshals ran and got out of the way. But by that time the black people had lost what little sense they ever had. The devil was driving them like a drove of wild hogs. Mad because they'd lost the marshals and mixed up and lost, they came—a thousand or more of them, in a mob—a running into town, looking for their meat. They rounded onto the main street and came running up it.

Another excursion train had just come and gone, bringing on it a young white boy from Pineville, son of a big rich Yankee sawmiller there. There was, also, at the depot a bunch of colored people. When this white boy, walking up the street, saw this mob running toward him, he looked back at the depot and saw the crowd there—it was just curious to see what was up—running toward him from the other direction, and he got scared and broke and ran, ran between a couple of stores.

That wild drove of niggers went after him—not having any better sense than to think he was one of the marshals they'd been chasing. They ran him into a big house where white people lived and started to burn the house down, but the white people let some of them come inside to search for him (not knowing the boy was in there) and they found him and dragged him out and killed him.

He, of course, never knew that poor white boy, never did see him; but he had always felt a peculiar sort of sympathy for him. The white boy was nineteen, too, and just happened to come in on one of those excursions. And he didn't have a thing to do with all of that hell that a bunch of reckless white men and rioting black men made up there in Lancaster any more than Adam did. Poor boy! Not a thing! Those hell-headed niggers that day were yelling, "Kill white man, kill white man, but don't kill Yankee!" when they cut that Northern boy's throat. . . .

Adam found the second gate, the gate to his own place, open and Bo standing beside it. The boy jumped up on the back of the buggy and Adam drove on down the lane. . .

At the trial the Colonel had stood up in that unfriendly courtroom and had told the judge that if he had a little time he believed he could prove Adam's story that he was asleep on a shuck pile in a man's house during the whole riot and did not know a thing about it, but the judge wouldn't agree to it and the jury gave Adam a life sentence to the Mines, along with Trotlucky and the other sixteen on trial.

After the case was finished the Colonel had called him over from the benches where he was sitting with the other prisoners, to his table. That was the first time he ever got a good look at the Colonel. He was fuller faced then, with his sandy, curly hair parted on the right and combed back smooth off his forehead, and was wide and smooth, too. But he had those little, real blue eyes that were as clear as a baby's conscience.

He said to me standing there before him—even then he called me by name—he said: "Adam, they didn't treat you right! And I couldn't do anything about it, this time. An innocent white boy has been killed and feeling is running high. I can't get you a fair trial in Coventry County now. But this is not the last of it."

He didn't take no oath, he didn't make no promise, he didn't raise his hand, he didn't write no paper, he didn't even riffle 'em on the table, he just kept right on talking, putting one word after another, but I could see that he meant it. He said, "Adam, you go on up to the Mines and be a good boy and I'll get you out. . ."

"Whut yuh sayin', Paw?" Bo spoke up from behind him, interrupting his thoughts.

He had mumbled out loud! Adam shrugged and looked about him, peering through the dark. They were at the yard gate. He sniffed and cleared his throat. "I say, Git in the seat here and take the mule on to the barn! And make sure you give him twelve good ears of corn when you feed him!" Handing the reins to the boy, Adam got out of the buggy.

6.

NO FROWNING, but that hard scared look that will kill you, Adam decided, remembering the faces of the white people in the courtroom at Lancaster, as he eyed a green bay thicket by the road, the following morning.

He had beside him in the wagon the last load of lightwood of the season. He was on his way to Riverton to make his weekly report to Mrs. Hightower and to do his regular Saturday trading. Thoughts that had pursued him through the night were at him again, as his image of the old trial continued to haunt him. *The thing was that those white people had denied him a human skin. And that was what he had seen again on the white men's faces in lawyer Duke's office!*

Bringing the small rusty remnant of a tobacco plug out of his overalls pocket, he had brushed it off on his shirtsleeve and turned it about to find a place to bite off a chew. He would reckon it was because the Colonel did not look at him *that way* that he had believed him when he said he would get him out of the Mines. Adam took the chew and turned it over in his mouth. Of course, he was *done on his way to the Mines,* whether he believed the Colonel or not that morning!

He secured the tobacco in his jaw. There had been more reason for his belief in the Colonel than that, however. Although he had been a young man then and Mr. Atwell was already old and they didn't look alike, there was something about the Colonel that had reminded him of the gray-bearded old master of the plantation to which his mother had returned when Freedom came and where he had grown up. There was something alike in the Colonel and old Mr. Adam—Mr. Adam, who knew the white blood in him and though it wasn't any of his, had treated him almost like he was his own son. Adam couldn't put his finger on it, but there was something about what the Colonel said that day like what Mr. Atwell might have said. But there was more to it even than that, than just the man. It was somehow the thing itself—somehow. Adam wagged his head. . .

When he first saw Lost Mountain Prison, it had scared him.

He and the other prisoners from Lancaster rode there in a cow car on a narrow-gauge railroad, from the last town where there was a regular railroad. There were a couple of fellows in the prisoner bunch who never worried about *nothing, no time,* and one of them was that Trotlucky Bostick. He just didn't seem to care. And he and a big dark fellow called Luster were singing and joking and they got most of the crowd to singing with them on the way over there.

They had been traveling through the roughest, wildest mountain country he had ever seen, country without a sign of life in it, the whole afternoon. The sun had already dropped behind the peaks. Suddenly they rounded a woody slope and, there in a big hollow, filled with the gathering dark, on a low rise, sat a dead white city, a ghost settlement.

A hush fell on that crowd in the car, as they swarmed against the slatted side to look out. Adam, clamped to one of the slats, peering through a gap, grew weak behind his knees. Then that damn fool Trotlucky had come out with, "Gawd, hit look like a clabber cheese!"

They all quick found out it wasn't. But the whole stockade—a big three-story jail, an eating hall and a guardhouse with a high plank fence around them—was kept white-washed.

Nothing else was. The prisoners were all colored men and the guards looked just as black as the niggers did, when they came out of the coal mines at night. And the whole time he was there Adam never saw anything that looked like daylight, but those white-washed walls. There was a little while of daylight on Sundays of course. The guards rattled the chains on the doors to the big long rooms they slept in at four o'clock in the morning and they were loaded in the cars and on their way underground by five-thirty, and it was evening dark when they came back up.

It was a rough, hard place. The eating was rough: cornbread, sowbelly and beans—mostly beans and the corn meal was sometimes moldy. The work was rough: there were twelve hours of it every day, except Sunday, and four men got killed in the mines while he was there. Rougher still were the men: there were a few mean white men among the guards, who liked to use the rawhide; but meaner than the guards were the prisoners—some of them, and they could get at you more. Some of them had got so low down they had lost their nature. It was one of these trying to bugger him that had almost got him in trouble.

But the thing that was hardest to bear, the thing that you couldn't forget, that followed you around like your shadow, that were in you like a pox, that tempted you most and ran some men crazy, were those bars in the windows, the chains on the doors, the day-after-day gun in your back, and those white-washed walls that cut you off from the rest of the world.

There was a lot of talk among the newcomers about breaking jail. It went on every night behind the chained doors in the sleeping halls. They didn't hardly talk about anything else. And nobody stopped them. The old-timers didn't join in. There were old-timers there who almost seemed to like it. At any rate they wouldn't get stirred up about making a break, about how easy it would be to get out of the old rotten plank windows and over the plank fence. The warden didn't even keep a pack of bloodhounds. But the old-timers, when the talk came up, just shook their heads and walked away. A little, one-eyed, bald-headed trusty on Adam's hall told him once, "You kin git out, but yuh kain't git nowheres else!"

The bunch of them out of the Lancaster riot took the lead in all the planning and plotting to break jail. They all claimed to have got a raw deal in the court. None of them would admit to having anything to do with killing the white boy, though one of them admitted to Trotlucky that he had gone in the house to search for him. And Trotlucky had told Adam once that he had been near enough in the crowd to see the boy when they drug him out. But none of them denied being drunk and mixed up in the ruckus, except himself, Adam. Yet they had all got the same sentence. To him this continued to be a reason for hope.

Except for Trotlucky, he didn't know any of the men sent up from Lancaster and he didn't talk with them much. He went ahead and did what the white bosses told him to do just like they were paying him good wages for it and *come* night he got in his bunk and went to sleep. It seemed to him like the best way to get along and he still held on to what the Colonel had told him in the courtroom.

The bunch talked every night after the lights were blown out and the trusties were asleep. They sent Trotlucky to him to get him to join in. Squatting there by his bunk in the dark of a night, trying to get him to go with him to the privy where the others were gathered, arguing with him in his up-and-down sandy whisper that crazy big-mouthed nigger began to break into Adam's sleep. Why did he believe the Colonel would get him out? Adam dodged answering that question, because when he tried to put his answer into words they sounded silly.

Trotlucky came to his bunk four times. Finally he told Adam that it was his last chance to get in on the thing. If he changed his mind later, they wouldn't talk to him. Adam had been there almost two months then and he had not got word of any sort from anybody in the outside world and with Trotlucky disturbing him every other night with all sorts of persuasions and contentions, he had got to dreaming about his mother's being sick, about her having to leave the Atwell plantation, and all sorts of things. But more than any of it, the white-washed walls got him. Trotlucky kept saying, "In another week we'll be long gone from this here boneyard!" It made Adam's blood leap to be gone with them and his heart ache at the thought of being left behind. On the last time that Trotlucky came to his bed, Adam went back to the privy with him to talk to the bunch.

A light was kept burning in the long narrow closet, bare of everything except white wash and a wall bench that ran the length of it. There were already five others there, sitting on the privy holes. He and Trotlucky pulled down their drawers and covered two more.

Trotlucky always looked like a scared goat, about to go stiff. He had wall eyes and even a little whiskers on his chin. He now rolled his eyes around the watching group, allowing them to come painfully to rest on Adam and said, "The onliest way a nigger kin git justice where *we* come from is to *take* it!" He lifted and shifted his head about, looking at the others, as if he might be about to jump off his perch and run the next minute, then came back to Adam. "Take it, and be long gone for somewhere else!"

Adam grinned wryly and shrugged but said nothing.

"No white man don't give a damn 'bout no nigger 'cept to work him!" He looked up and down the line for confirmation, then added, "The quicker you knows that, the better off you'll be, boy!" He glared at Adam for a long moment in stiff silence, then went on in a different voice. "There ain't no guard on the northeast corner of the far wall after two o'clock in the morning. We got two hacksaw blades. We kin cut that chain on the bunkhouse door in thirty minutes. There's a trusty on the inside of the outside door who we kin handle. The guard, he go to the guardhouse to eat at one-thirty and leave it without nobody on the outside til he come back."

Sitting there, hearing him detail the plot, Adam still tried to argue with himself, but the voice he usually listened to got further and further away from him and sounded more and more like a green boy's voice. The Colonel, if he had ever thought again on what he had told Adam, had surely forgot it by this time. And Adam could feel himself moving through each operation as Trotlucky described it and finally climbing the high white-washed fence and gaining cover and freedom in the woods.

He had just got over the fence with those fellows, in his mind, listening to Trotlucky talk, when a voice, not his own, said to him, Why do they want to take *you:* you're a lot younger than they are and didn't want to go in the beginning and might lag behind in the woods and make trouble for them. Why are they so anxious to take you along? Somehow Adam recognized the voice as the Colonel's voice and it was a sharp question. He froze back on his seat and spoke it out, “Trotlucky, I just wonder why you all want so bad to take me along?”

Trotlucky jumped up like he might have been waiting for that question. He sort of pranced when he walked, anyhow—like his feet were tender. And he jumped up off the hole with his drawers hanging down and his black backside shining in the light and pranced around in a circle. “For luck,” he said, “for luck! I knows luck when I sees it. Ole Luster over there thinks you be lucky for us, too.”

Adam laughed, but somehow it had a quieting effect on him and after he got back to bed and to sleep that night, he had a very quiet dream, in which the white boy killed in the riot came to him and stood by his bed, and he knew him though he had never seen him before—he was very pale and had a big purple scar on his throat and did not speak, but he shook his head in warning. And on top of the dream, Adam woke up in the morning with the words of the little one-eyed trusty on his mind: “You can git out, but you can’t git nowheres else.”

The hints were plain and he took the warning.

Trotlucky and the other sixteen of them broke jail three nights later. They got out of the lock-up and over the wall and into the woods all right. The warden and the guards did not kick up much of a stir about it. According to the one-eyed trusty the search party used a bob-tailed train with searchlights on it to run up and down the railroad to see that they weren’t following the track and they telegraphed to the sheriffs in various towns around the outskirts of the mountains to pick up the runaways if they happened to get there. But that was all. Everything went along like it had before. The warden didn’t get any stricter and the guards didn’t talk or act any tougher.

They had broke out on a Monday night and it was the next Sunday morning that the first batch—five of them—dragged back to the stockade. They gave up to the guards on the main gate, like they were glad to see them. The warden marched them into the eating hall—it happened to be right at dinner time—in the front door and clear around the hall where everybody could get a chance to see them and then on out the door to the kitchen, not letting them stop for a bite to eat or even a drink of water.

They were scary to look at. They were the worst beat up and run-down animals Adam had ever seen pass for human. Their clothes were torn off of them, they had scratches, cuts, and knots on them, they could barely drag along and they were so famished that their big swollen tongues hung out of their mouths. He, Adam, had been where he could look through the door into the kitchen and he saw the guard finally water them. Most of them just stuck their faces in the dipper and slobbered. But one got hold of the dipper and the guards had to knock him down to get it back.

Three days later four more of them dragged in, looking even worse used up than the first batch. Six of them gave themselves up at the town of Alum Well, to get a drink of water. Nothing was heard from Trotlucky and Luster for several weeks, but finally some hunters found their bodies at the bottom of a ravine, not far from Lost Mountain. A month after the runaways got back, those that did, they were given forty lashes apiece, with a cat-o-nine-tails.

Adam was feeling grateful to the Colonel for his good advice, even if he never did get out of the place, never did get out of it. But just two days after the warden had had the runaways whipped, he got a call to the warden's office. There was a transportation officer there with a court order to get him another trial. The man took him to a place called Gray, to the Jones County Courthouse. When the man brought him into the courtroom, they found there the Colonel and Mr. Christian DeBow and his mother and the old woman and her husband he had met with under the brush arbor—it was the same old man who had led him to the house, where he, Adam, was sleeping off his liquor when the patrol got him. The Colonel, also, had a paper from Mr. Adam Atwell, to give him a good name. And it didn't take a full hour with all of these things and the Colonel taking his part, for that second judge and jury to turn him loose—clean free!

But when Adam stood at the foot of the Hightower back steps, under the shade of the chinaberry trees, the image that colored his consciousness was not of his delivery in the Jones County Courthouse, but that of the hostile faces of the white men in lawyer Duke's office yesterday. It gave him a pervasive anxiety that showed in the solemn dullness of a glassy eye and a monotonous voice, as he reported on the high water still in the swamp field, about the planting going on at his place and the farms of the two other tenants.

At the top of the steps, Mrs. Hightower, in her black skirt and white shirtwaist, listened, the attractive shifting of her reserved gaze giving the only sign that she observed anything unusual in his manner. She asked few questions and when he had finished she nodded and, glancing away distractedly, moved to the milk box and adjusted the stream of water flowing from the faucet. She looked up abruptly, saying, "Adam, did Mr. Hightower ever speak to you of Oswald—Mr. Oswald Paley?"

Adam stiffened, then leaned over deliberately and picked his wool hat up off the steps before he responded. "W-well, yed-yed-yessum," he said, his stammer hammering out the repeated syllable like a steam drill. He still looked at the hat. "Just how do you mean?"

Mrs. Hightower was conscious of the constraint on Adam and seemed to consider the issue of his reserve, walking back to the steps before she spoke, but she went on firmly, "I mean the sort of man he turned out to be, after all Mr. Hightower had done for him."

Adam nodded, finally meeting her gaze. "The Colonel spoke to that, too, spoke to it the last time I saw him alive."

Her grave eyes lifted to the distance. "I just don't know, Adam!" she exclaimed in perplexity and halted. After a moment she went on with more composure, "Mr. Littleton has been representing to me all along how difficult it was going to be for me to get the land buyer to let me reserve the clay deposits and the Wyche field. Especially the field. He said, as he understood it, the field lay in the middle of a lot and keeping it would involve roads of *ingress* and *egress,* not only across *that* land lot, but two or three other lots Mr. Lincoln is buying. When I held out for these things, Mr. Lincoln talked about calling the deal off, although he already had five thousand acres under option. He even went so far as to go off to the Coast to look at other timber lands."

Lowering her eyes to Adam, she made, with a certain reserve, a wry face. "Now, almost overnight, it all seems to be changed!" She shook her head in doubt, continuing, "Mr. Littleton tells me that there has been a mix-up all along about where—that is on which of the five lots they want to buy and the three they want to lease—as to where the clay deposits lie and where the field. Mr. Littleton says that Oswald Paley has come forward—though I don't know how he got into it!—with the blueprint of a minerological survey made five years ago, showing the clay deposits in the upper swamp; that is, on Lots 132, 131, and 130, not on the lots we had been thinking they were on!" She frowned with impatience. "It's this confusing business of land lines again! They always appear so geometric and simple on the map and, actually, they seem to give the greatest trouble, not only in running them out, but in running them down afterward. So much trouble to find them, so much uncertainty about where they are! Mr. Littleton asked me if I didn't have the original of the blue print among Mr. Hightower's things. But you know"—her gaze now closely examined Adam's face—"I can't find any such map!"

Adam winced with a proper concern and then lowered his gaze with a proper thoughtfulness, shaking his head, but nothing in his manner implied any suspicion of Mr. Littleton or Mr. Paley. "That so?" he said.

Still eyeing Adam, her full lower lip quivering for an instant, to be quickly drawn tight, Mrs. Hightower said abruptly, "Yes, it is!" After a moment, her gaze shifted to the distance in speculation. As she continued her thought at length, a slight hesitation came on her pale blue-veined face. It became almost a surface embarrassment as she spoke. "Mr. Littleton keeps saying—anyhow, he feels that we are mistaken, mistaken in our judgment of Oswald Paley. I am speaking of Mr. Hightower and me. Mr. Littleton says that Mr. Hightower had some misinformation, but I can't go into all of that here, of course—I—Adam"—she broke off and walked over to the milk box, standing there at a loss for a moment, before she turned back ruefully smiling on Adam. "It would be fine if this Paley blueprint *were* right, wouldn't it? All of our problems would be solved!"

During Mrs. Hightower's disjointed recitation the anxiety pervading Adam had come out plainly in his countenance: in the stiff down-setting of his mouth, the melancholy anguish in his liquid eye, and in perspiration. He shrugged, drawing forth his handkerchief. As he mopped his face, he asked in a non-committal voice. "Hit didn't show the field?"

He was dodging her! But now that the thing was boldly before them, she seemed to welcome his evasion of the point of her inquiry. Under stress of the moment, she responded with a warmth of feeling that she would not have allowed herself in a state of composure. "Let me say, I'm not going to let you down on the Wyche field, Adam! I'm *not!*"

He turned aside. Still swabbing the sweat on his face that grew, not less, but more, he spoke through the handkerchief with convulsive effort. "Yessum!"

"Were you with them when Mr. Hightower and Mr. Paley and the geologist and all made the survey of the clay deposits back there"—the inflection in her voice flattened out as she added parenthetically, "I think it *was* five years ago?"

Adam put away his handkerchief with resolution and turning back to her, straightened up. "Y-yesum. I was along. But I never did see the plat when they got through." His lips moved on, as if there were more he would say, but the sound had dried up on him. He shrugged and turned about again and took a few steps. Looking up to find her still waiting questioningly, he shrugged again and added with reluctance, "I think Mr. Paley borrowed that plat. Or more'n apt he just had a copy of it, but anyhow I think I seen him with one, way back 'bout the time of the survey. It might have been a blueprint I saw!"

Mrs. Hightower drew her feet together and her slim figure erect at the middle of the stairhead, and composure came upon her. She eyed him, toying with her pince-nez glasses, zipped up to a spring metal button at her left shoulder. "But you were with them on the survey," she repeated. "And after all, what difference does it make! Adam, you *know* where the clay deposits are, don't you?" She was asking, she obviously thought, a rhetorical question.

The mimetic smile that had begun to form on his face vanished and his eyes glazed over and the glistening ginger color of his cheeks took on a grayish tinge, as he stood there in stiffening silence. Finally he swallowed and lowered his head and, with one convulsive jerk of his jaw, said quietly, "Well, 'um, I thought I did."

She pulled out her glasses automatically, going on in an almost girlish tone of relief, "I *know* you know where the *Wyche field* is!"

"I kind-a thought I did," he mumbled grudgingly.

"Do now, Adam! You know where all of the land lines are. I know you were with the group when the lines were run out. Mr. Hightower told me before he died that you knew. You *know* where the land lines are!"

"Yessum," he said, but his phrase was not affirmative. He did not look up, and after a pause he went on. "I-I hear some talk going 'round 'bout an *old* line—going back behind the ones we run out—back to the olden times. *Mr. Jawn* spoke about hit. Mr. Jawn Hightower!" He halted, nodding, lifting vacant eyes above her head with an inflection of manner that would raise to issue the whole question of land lines, of whose moral responsibility for whose land lines and finally of his own status to speak on land lines at all, in the disputed circumstances.

Staring at him with open disbelief in the implications of this speech, she stood in shocked silence for a time, then exclaimed, but half-conscious of her words, "John, John, pshaw!"

He avoided her gaze, his face becoming a drawn gray mask, and his voice shaking as he continued his evasion. "N-not only Mr. Jawn, but Mr. Peter and Mr. David Bright and—and a lot more, in this thing!"

She frowned out of a sympathetic fear at his appearance then shook it off. "Pshaw!" she said again, "They don't know! I won't listen to them! Mr. Hightower said you know where every land line on the place is!"

"White mens!" he went on, in deadly quiet. "All together!" He finally met her gaze in a grim wry-faced appeal. 'You-you ought to have that line run out again by the county surveyor? Hit wouldn't cost *so* much."

"County surveyor! County surveyor?" She lifted her head, zipping up the pince-nez, with an air of dismissal. "Adam, we haven't any money for a county surveyor! It would cost fifty dollars, at the least. I'll take your word for where our land lines are!"

When he had turned away and moved off toward the gate, she heard—or for a moment she thought that she had heard, a groan.

7.

LUCY HIGHTOWER had seen the letter in the morning mail, but her thorough sense of discipline restrained her. She had gone on with Lena, her negro cook, to the chickenyard to pick out the pullets for Sunday dinner. She had come back by the vegetable garden to see that the hired negro gardener working there suckered the tomato vines. And she had set Lena to her special Saturday cleaning in the house, before she allowed herself to pick up the mail from the ledge of the walnut secretary in the bay-windowed alcove of her bedroom-sittingroom and, lowering the writing board, sit down to read it. She had already seen that the fat linen-paper envelope bore a Charleston postmark, had recognized, not without a quickening of blood, the handwriting of the superscription, and even vaguely apprehended that the letter might bear a peculiarly personal message, though this shadowy feeling she had repressed.

As she sat with her slender forearms resting on the green baize inlay of the board, inserting a brass letter opener under the sealed flap, a hint of pink came into her white pale cheeks and her rather harried countenance was enlivened with a look of expectation. She unfolded and flattened the pages of the letter on the desk and began reading the small, worm-crawl script, closely and interruptedly.

Wellington Arms, 31 Rutledge Avenue
Charleston, S.C.
May 1, 1910

Dear Lucy,

The "celestial city of our youth," this bright May first morning, has all of the color and salubrious breezes that that old euphemism would celebrate. I was about to add, all of the reminiscences, too. But they don't appear to me quite as reminiscences. Of course I live here—as we Charlestonians do, you know—as if the city were my shell. And I am scarcely conscious of it, but it is all here with me in the present tense. There has not been the discontinuity to establish a proper sense of reminiscence.

(Lucy Hightower's slim face limbered in a vague smile, offsetting the sharpness of her slightly knitted brow.)

I was walking on the Battery earlier this morning, and the water was never bluer than under the nine o'clock sun—you know that ethereal indigo hue that sun and distance and season can give the harbor? And as I sit here now, writing, I hear the singsong of a colored fishmonger in the street below, crying (as well as I can make it out) "Shark steaks! They need no gravy!"

(Her lips twisted in a quick automatic sign of her amusement, without altering the focus of her eyes.)

But the wisteria that you mentioned in your last letter was scarcely up to its usual luxuriousness this year and it has all just about gone by.

The description you give of Riverton shocks me. I can quite understand your being there with your husband, while he was developing his enterprises and the ways and means toward the establishment of a permanent home, even in that vicinity. But now that you are widowed and, as you say, utterly unequipped to carry out what he had scarcely well begun, it seems to me that every consideration would indicate your withdrawing to a more tenable position—more tenable for both you and your children, who certainly should not be allowed to grow up amid such backwoods illiteracy.

(Lucy caught her breath and glanced aside briefly before she read on.)

Since you cannot properly operate it, it would seem to me, sensible for you to sell your property there, or lease it, if you can get anything like fair terms.

(She sniffed, almost without sound, and automatically stroked her nose.)

And of course, there is only one place in the world for you to return to, Lucy: Charleston, your home.

(She paused to glance away, and her jaws tightened until the muscles moved in her cheeks. After a moment, she shook her head and resumed reading.)

I saw Lizzie M. (now W., of course) at church last Sunday and we were talking about your situation and she fully agrees with me (and Julia W., as I said in my last letter) that there is nothing left for you to do but to come back home to Charleston. She told me that she was going to write you to that effect within the next few days.

Lizzie has grown a little stouter, of course, but she is still the same old Lizzie of yore, who, for a lark, unconscionably led your father and the Texas bishop each to believe the other was deaf that time! She is just as full of fun and outrageousness and as big of heart and, believe me, she is just as devoted to you, as she ever was.

(Lucy's face limbered briefly, as if she were beginning a smile, but she only wet her lips and read on at a quickening glance.)

But the purpose and intent of all the foregoing, dear Lucy, is merely to set the stage for your sympathy and to stir within you, I hope, fond memories. For Lucy, there is one realm in which time does stand still, changes not at all.

The night you first kissed me, Wade Hampton marching by (when you were ten and I was eleven), till the next time, when I kissed you, on the evening you were graduated from Meminger (in the side garden of the Morrow home), till the more mutual occasion on the Murchison's moonlit front porch on Sullivan's Island, when you made me certain undated and as yet unfulfilled promises, is all one day, in the freehold of my heart. And that day is the unending NOW of my love for you, Lucy.

(She drew a quick, sharp breath and held it, as color began to fill her cheeks.)

Why do you think I have remained unmarried these twenty long years? I have always loved you, Lucy, and I always will.

If you will marry me now, . . .

(Lucy stared at the words, ceasing her reading, letting out her breath, while tears welled up in her eyes and blinded her. After a time she shook her head and reached for her handkerchief in the band of her apron, looking around self-consciously to see that no one else was in the room to observe her. She dried her eyes and began the sentence over again.)

If you will marry me now, I will provide a home for you and your children here, back where you belong—where all of you belong! True it must be a modest one, but in circumstances not unfamiliar to you once and now I could make you comfortable and secure.

And once you were back in Charleston you would find that you have not been away so long, my dear—not too *long at any rate.*

With affectionate devotion,
As ever,
Edward.

Lucy stared on at the name signed at the bottom of the page distractedly, her eyes beginning to dance. "I'll go! Edward, Heaven alive, I'll just go!" she whispered. All of them together. Go. Just get out of this Godforsaken town! She folded the letter, then opened it out again and reread the last page. Edward did love her! And he had a right to love her! Why shouldn't she marry him now? Now? It wasn't too late! She got up from her chair, feeling suddenly invigorated. But she must put the letter up for the present! Pushing it into a pigeon-hole, she lifted the writing board to close up the secretary and its litter of papers. Adam should be coming shortly to make his report and she better see how Lena was getting on with poisoning the bedsteads before he got here. She pushed the lid of the paper-stuffed desk shut and, taking a bunch of keys from her apron pocket, locked it, then turned on her heel briskly. Last Saturday, after Adam left she had been reduced to shedding tears, she had been so depressed and uneasy over her situation, and nowhere at all to turn! She smiled secretly. Well, if it got too much for her now she could just move out!

But, after Lucy Hightower had, in the middle bedroom off the hall, for a time watched Lena dip the long turkey feather into the bottle of poison and apply it to the joints and corners of the bedsteads, just to be sure that no unmentionable and unbearable insect life got into them, and had given Lena a few more specific and general instructions, she found herself around on the side porch, in the big rocking-chair, behind the trumpet vines, again thinking about the letter. She did not review Edward Louthan's words, or think about Edward Louthan. She did not, indeed, reflect on the letter at all. She just enjoyed the warm secure feeling she got from its being there, locked up in her desk, like a gold nugget to be kept in reserve against an emergency. And to be sure, to be given a fuller consideration later.

But now she did not feel inclined to cry when she thought of the dark and devious Land Deal, so deeply involving her and on which so much depended. She suspected that every man connected with it was trying to take advantage of her. Unless it was poor Adam, and he was scared, too—like herself! In her ignorance, she could not quite make out just how they intended to do her in, but there was something smelly about the behavior of every one of them. She recalled Peter

Bright's lank face at the meeting at the bank, when she had asked how they all happened to have heard her clay was in the upper swamp, and his mustache had actually taken on an ironic twist, as he looked past her at Littleton with a dead blue evasive eye. None of the others selling their land would be frank with her, either; none of them was really friendly with her. And when Mr. Littleton spoke up for them there was an oversoft core in his big bluff voice. She rocked the big chair and looked beyond the green screen of leaves away into the sky. This change of attitude of Mr. Littleton about her clay deposits, what did it mean? Could the land buyer be trying to dupe her about the clay deposits? Even Littleton, her supposed friend, seemed to be in on it, somehow! Or could this, this whatever it was, be something Oswald Paley was trying to pull off—could it be a Paley plot? Was Mr. Littleton taken in by Paley? Or was it all just the emotionality of an ignorant, frightened woman? She sighed and stopped rocking. Still she could not but believe there was something, something! And all of them were in on it—all of them, except Adam.

An *olden* land line! *Not only Mr. John, but Mr. Peter and Mr. David Bright.*

The words of her negro overseer came back to her and Lucy felt disturbed. She saw again Adam's troubled, wry face, as he stood at the steps, uttering the sounds, tocsins that betrayed even his inveterate reserve, "White mens. . . all together!"

She sat upright, her face gathering in an anxious frown. Adam seemed to be under real pressure! He had not wanted even to *intimate* anything against those white men. She turned a gravely inquiring face, her fine nostrils dilating, on the blankness of the shuttered doors at the end of the porch to her left. Of course it was characteristic of him never to say anything against white people, and she had not thought of it then, but could it be possible that *those white men had been trying to scare Adam, somehow?. . .*

Lucy had grasped the chair-arms and was on the point of coming up out of her seat, when she heard a sudden, small, penetrating sound. She halted abruptly, recognizing it as the whir of the wings of a hummingbird, and, easing back into the rocker, guardedly turned toward the deep screen of vines. Her glance found the bird. Within the dim cloister, he hovered, a small feathered missile of changeable green and gray to scarlet, poised between two dark blurs of wings before an open red trumpet flower. Unmindful of her gaze, driven by his whirring power, he gracefully thrust with his long, slender, black beak down into the blossom. Then out again he darted, moving backward with the same swift grace, to poise in air. And, cocking his small head toward her, his tiny black beads of sight met her tender eyes in the white, still face, in an instant of mysterious recognition. Abruptly, the humming of the wings changed and he was gone.

Lucy smiled and began to rock the big chair back and forth. *Wade Hampton marching by!* she repeated to herself absently, her previous anxiety now out of her mind. She might not have remembered the incident but for Edward's poem about it later. Yet she did recall the day. She was wearing her hair in curls down her back (having had it up in papers the night before) and a long-waisted black velvet dress. For it happened to be poor Russell's birthday: the day General Hampton paraded through Charleston streets in the campaign that made him Governor and finally ended the night patrol in the city, ended Reconstruction. Her gentle younger brother's birthday, and none of them suspected then that it would be his last! And it was Edward's birthday, too. That was how he happened to be at their house.

After their party was over, she and Russell were walking piece-the-way home with Edward, who lived just over on Market Street. They were loitering in the edge of the little park across the street from the Morrow house, trying to blow a tune with a willow leaf held between the thumbs, when a troop of horsemen clattered by, bearing torches, though it was not yet dark. It was only a short parade and seemed to be made up largely of negroes mounted on mules, but there, near the end of it, Wade Hampton rode on a milk white charger, sure enough, great-bearded, grand and gentle. He waved to her—or them, for the three of them stood on the sidewalk by themselves and just a few feet away from him, wringing their hands off, in their excitement.

And when the parade had passed on by, they turned to congratulate each other, and she suddenly swelled with the bigness of the moment and the nearness of heroism and threw her arms about her brother and kissed him. And when she turned to Edward he looked so forlorn, standing there and it was his birthday, too—that she flung her arms around his neck.

And they had all laughed and danced around in a circle and she would probably not have remembered it but for his verse later.

The Louthans were, like the Morrows, German, and Edward's father was a steward at Trinity Church, where her father was treasurer, and the families were old friends. She and Edward were more like brother and sister than sweethearts. Indeed, she even felt older than him, in some ways. Though not intellectually, to be sure! At school she worked hard and managed to keep within hailing distance of him, but she knew that she was no where near as bright as Edward. He was so quick and he remembered everything! It was a foregone conclusion that he was going to be valedictorian at Boys High and he finished almost two points ahead of the rest of his class. She had made salutatorian at her school, where the competition was not so keen, but by the hardest work and only with his help and inspiration.

Rocking her chair, Lucy fixed an absent gaze on the red trumpet flower recently invaded by the hummingbird. She could remember the second one, too; when, as Edward said, *he* had *first* kissed *her*. *Lucy, would you kiss me, if* I *were still eleven?* That was the refrain. She had received his verses that day, along with the silver wishbone broach that he gave her as a graduation present. The poem sounded a little like Wordsworth, his favorite poet.

"Two of us our birthday marked
"And one came straight from Heaven,
"Wade Hampton, passing, dropped a spark—
"Lucy, would you kiss me now, if I were still eleven?"

There were several more stanzas but she could not remember them now.

He had kissed her that night when he escorted her home from the graduation reception, kissed her at the bottom of the Morrow side garden by the big jessamine bush. He had been awkward, but so had she!

She could remember the houseparty on Sullivan's Island, too. That had been three years later, and he had just graduated from the College of Charleston. They had been pretty far gone on each other that summer—yet not *too* far gone, because she knew that he could not marry her. He had got his bachelor's degree, *magna cum laude,* and a fellowship and was planning to go on in the fall to get his master's degree. Yes, the kissing *had* been *more mutual* on the houseparty, but not without a sense of responsibility, at least on her part. He had talked about their going on and getting married, but she had known better, she had kept her promises strictly undated—his father and mother would never have forgiven her! Really it had not been her concern about them so much, however, as her own pride in Edward. It was obvious that he had a brilliant academic future ahead of him. If she had diverted him then, or held him back, she would never have forgiven herself.

And he had fulfilled his promise. Doctor of Philosophy from John Hopkins at twenty-four, an assistant professorship, full professorship and finally the chair of Latin and Greek at a university in the North—

even though it was Catholic—all before he was thirty-six! Over the years, the news of it had thrilled her! Of course his taking a place at Boys High was merely a way to get back to Charleston, though likely the principalship paid him more than the Catholic university had.

She had thought when she urged him to go on to get his master's degree that she was committed to waiting on him to finish his education. She had grown up on that idea, you might say. It hadn't occurred to her that her father's health might break down. Although, it was hard now for her to see why it didn't occur to her, for her poor father had been moving from his bed to his patient's beds for years! Her most characteristic memory of him was in lying down on the hall couch with his graceful thin hands on his chest holding onto a big silver watch to get five minutes sleep between calls—to be able to keep going!

"Heaven alive!" she said aloud and, giving the chair an abrupt rock forward, got to her feet. She couldn't have waited on Edward! Who could have? She moved toward the slatted doors at the end of the porch. At the doorway she paused and looked back. Marry him now? But he hadn't waited! Too much had happened to her in the last twenty years! And to him, too, probably. She opened the shutters and entered the house. To her: six children, for one thing. And the *deaths of three of them!. . .*

"Lawd-a-Mussy! Miz Hightower! Miz Hightower!" The raised, moaning voice of the quiet cook, Lena, floated down the hall. "Come heah quick! I'm scared Marse done hurt hisself in that autymobile!"

Lucy Hightower clutched at her throat, for an instant transfixed, then hurried across her room and ran up the long hallway. At the front door she met her saturnine flat-nosed cook whose usually black face was ashen. Wall-eyed, Lena pointed toward the railroad embankment in front of the house a hundred yards away. "I just seen 'im as he went over it!"

Lucy caught on. Both women then ran down the porch steps and over the lawn to the front fence.

Across the sand road, on the wide grass-grown shoulder of the railroad cut, stood a half-dazed boy who stared at them in white-faced fright and mumbled defensively, "He liked to run over me!"

Beyond the embankment, Lucy glimpsed the corner of the black canvass top of an automobile. She gripped the pickets to steady herself, then falteringly summoned her resolution and moved toward the front gate.

But even as she fumbled with the gate latch, up over the edge of the cut climbed Marse: small, and white-faced, his freckles standing out and his stiff red hair standing up on top of his head. He got to his feet and came gingerly across the green to the edge of the road and halted, looking very much like a fly that has just swallowed a frog. "I don't think it's hurt much, Mamma," he said ruefully, "it went over easy!"

Lucy swallowed, taking her hand down from her throat. She found speech still difficult, but wetting her lips, she summoned what firmness she could to ask, "Are *you* hurt, Marse?"

One of the legs of his overalls was gaping at the knee. He discovered it with astonishment and felt of the knee. "No, Ma'am, Mamma, I ain't hurt a bit!" He added, with a hint of professional familiarity in his voice, "I was just creeping along in *low gear.*"

Tightening her hold on the pickets she gripped in each hand, Lucy stood speechless for a few moments while color came back into her face. Finally, she said with resolution, even sharpness, "Marcellus, I can scarcely believe my eyes and ears!"

He hung his head and with automatic swiftness rubbed a bare foot up and down the denim-covered calf of his other leg. "We were just going to run it a little along the green here!"

Lucy leaned on her support and, frowning, managed a tone of indignation. "The idea! The i-de-a!" She shifted her glance briefly toward the visible part of the overturned car. "Do you know whose automobile you have torn up?" She turned her head to include the other boy, "Jerome, do you know?"

The boy backed away, shrugging. "I just cranked it! Marse said he knew how to run it."

Lucy Hightower allowed her face to show only a grave concern, but resentment began to stir inside her. She *suspected* this Cranford boy, who, living next door, was always coming over without invitation. His father was the town's leading doctor, but there was gossip about his mother, an obviously underbred woman, whose behavior supported such talk. And all of the Cranford children, girls and boys, and there were seven of them, were *wild.* She frowned. She was sure Marse would never have thought of taking over somebody else's property in such fashion, if Jerome Cranford hadn't suggested it! She spoke with a hint of severity. "I asked if you knew whose automobile it is, or was, before it was wrecked?"

Jerome loosened himself assertively, thrusting his hands in the pockets of his navy blue knickerbockers, and even trying a grin, though it didn't come off. "Old Halley McGrew's," he blurted out, half as if she ought to have known and yet in pride of the revelation, too. "He left it out here last night, with a flat tire."

"Mr. Halley McGrew!" Mrs. Hightower said firmly.

"Yessum," Jerome agreed and now managed a quick grin, "He's just twenty-three!' He turned away and kicked at the grass with a shod foot. "And he ought to not have left it out here on the road with a key in the switch!"

"On the road?" She began, but broke off. It had not been *on the road,* as she only too well appreciated: it had been left in front of *her* house, because Halley McGrew did not dream that *her* son would molest it! The very thought embarrassed her. "And how old are *you,* Jerome?" She said, with an ambiguous tonelessness.

The Cranford boy glanced back at her suspiciously, saying "Hunh?" Then, he reacted to the high reserve on her face and he jerked his hands out of his pockets, adding confusedly, "Yessum, I mean! I-I'm twelve—be twelve next month."

Mrs. Hightower nodded. She thought as much: a year older than Marcellus and fully a head taller! And handsome, with his well-shaped head and good features, but already the look of a rowdy about him. And how could she keep Marcellus away from him? On what basis? They were all even members of the same church! She said with a slight tone of irony, "In any event, Jerome, I think that you had better run along home and tell your mother about this." Dismissing him, she glanced toward her son. "Come along with me, Marcellus!" she said distractedly, deflected by the sudden thought of Edward Louthan's letter in the pigeonhole in her secretary. She turned back toward the house. What better reason could she have for accepting Edward's offer than to get Marse out of this place and to get him a *father!* She looked back at the stubby boy, who still remained standing at the edge of the road, staring at her from his small, deep-set eyes, the large round nostrils of his flat nose spreading apprehensively. She thought with astonishment, was it *Marse,* Marse who stood between her and Edward?

8.

THE SOUND OF THE AX seemed too deep into the swamp, when Adam heard it from the back field. It was a long way off, of course, and the wind might be toward the River to take it that way. But then, on the other hand, he knew that Hinshaw Slappy didn't have any hardwood timber left to cut. The woodsman must be on Hightower land!

Adam was chopping cotton, and he took a chew of tobacco, shouldered the hoe, and climbed over the fence on the side toward Slappy's and moved into the bay along the dividing line. He hadn't gone two hundred yards into the swamp before he could tell for sure. He thought, By damn, that itchy-fingered scamp just couldn't wait a minute! But, of course, it wouldn't be Hinshaw, himself, throwing that big chip. Hinshaw didn't believe in sweating over an ax handle, and Adam was close enough now to tell that it wasn't Slappy's lick, anyhow.

Adam circled a wide crab-apple thicket to his right and moved up behind a low-bush holly. He looked out around his cover to see a lean, long-armed, black man, swinging his blade into a high ash tree.

The man was wearing, not overalls, but a ragged white shirt and black britches. Adam stared for a moment and then with a shrug, moved out from behind the holly, his hoe over his shoulder, sauntering toward the action at his deliberate upright gait.

"That's a p-powerful heavy ax you swinging there Brother Steele!" he called out good-humoredly. He advanced a step or two, as the axman delivered his blow and halted to look around. "When I heard that loud lick up the branch I didn't expect to find y-you aholt of the hickory!"

To a casual listener Adam's voice would have sounded entirely amiable; but, judging from his reaction, Kiger Steele detected more in it—though to be sure, there could be additional reasons for his self-consciousness. After his first startled glance over his shoulder, he became studiedly deliberate in drawing his ax from the tree. And when he turned toward Adam, there was something vindictive in the care with which he rested the ax head on the ground with the blade up-tilted. Looking up from his tool, he said in his high-pitched voice—that seemed louder than was necessary—"You wouldn't expect Kiger Steele to muffle his licks none?"

Adam must have taken a couple of strides before he replied and his voice, in contrast, sounded sonorous. "I just didn't know you for a w-woods sawyer."

The arrested axman's momentum and pitch seemed to carry him on. "Kiger Steele's a man of many ways and turns—you liable to run into him wherever a solid dollar kin be made!"

Adam swung the hoe down from his shoulder and folded his hands on top of the handle. "Hit's bin said that no sweat's dishonest and I'm always glad to see ye." He smiled in what seemed to be pure reminiscent pleasure. "Hit's bin a long time since we took that d-drink together out'n your jug, in my buggy. And you wouldn't think I enjoyed it the way I did, and me not returnin'it in no way. It's bin on my mind, but it look like I couldn't come up with ye no wheres befo'."

Pausing, he unfolded his hands and hoed down a straggling fern or two in front of him. "I'd hoped to give you a mess of catfish, or carp, or maybe some scuppernong wine afore now." He looked up sharply out of the corner of his eye, as his hoe came to rest.

Kiger Steele's mouth worked a couple of times without saying anything and he studied the blade of his ax. He turned the blade down and spoke noncommittally. "I bin movin' about."

"T-timbering?"

"Some." Kiger began to seem more relaxed.

Adam shook his head and canted it suavely to one side, thrusting out his hoe handle. As if it were an Elizabethan courtier's staff. "I just hadn't figured you for no woods sawyer—and you here, cuttin' this ash by yourself!" He looked away and continued as if speaking a stage aside. "Mostly woods sawyers have a podner and use a c-crosscut saw these days." He surveyed the tall tree the axman was working on. "But then with ash timber as fine as this, I reckon you don't want-a share none of the profit!" Abruptly he looked Kiger in the eye. "By the way, Brother Steele, how you cuttin' this ash?"

Adam's formal *Brother Steele* was a reminder of their mutual moral obligation in the Corinthian Lodge, and it may have been responsible now for Kiger's drawing forth his sweat rag to mop his face, before he undertook to reply. But when he had mopped he still did not speak, but shook his head indecisively, restored the rag to his belt and, turning back to the tree, swung his ax into the cut. This, by the second lick, seemed to work up his resolution and his dander and he yelled over his shoulder, "I don't reckon that's any of your business, Atwell!"

Adam took two steps nearer and continued, as if he had received an entirely amiable response, his voice only raised a little to be heard above the cutting, "Do you buy yo' own stumpage, or work for the other feller?"

Kiger tossed his head, halting, his ax in the tree, and again turning to Adam. His voice was challenging. "I works in various ways!" He added defiantly, "Ye ain't got no timber ye want to sell me, is you?"

Adam shook his head. "I ain't got any timber for sale, myself, but if it aint' too c-curious in me, who you buyin' this ash ye're cuttin' here, *from?"* He eyed Kiger steadily, his mouth drawn as dry as pine dross.

Kiger went on, hitting another sharp lick as he spoke, "I ain't said I bought it!"

"How's that?" Adam called out and Kiger halted and looked around to repeat his insolence. "O-o-oh!" Adam soughed, lifting his face. And his jaw loosened and he took a swipe at his mustache. "I see—cuttin' on s-shares! Who'd ye deal with?"

Kiger barked, "I ain't said I'uz cuttin' on shares!"

Adam cleared his throat. His voice when he spoke was still good-humored, but it had a carrying quality and he spoke without stuttering. "Kiger, as I said, I ain't askin' you out of curiosity." He paused, trying to catch Kiger's eye, "I don't want to see you git in no trouble!"

Swinging his ax to his shoulder, Kiger turned toward Adam, as if he were about to move on him. His face was twisted, his voice was high and hostile. "I ain't called on you to look out for me! Who you think you gonna bully 'round here, Atwell? I got this stumpage from Hinshaw Slappy, it's his timber and I'd like to see you stop me from cuttin' it!"

Adam moved toward Kiger as if Kiger did not have an ax on his shoulder—or anywhere else, speaking, as he moved, in the same even tone as before. "I ain't goin' to stop you from nothin', Kiger. But the Court kin sho' stop you from collectin' a cent for your labor. And I'm here to tell you that it *will!* And I intend to take part in seein' that hit do!" Adam squirted a stream of amber twenty degrees to the right of Kiger's left foot. "More'n that: it may cost you a court fine."

Kiger raised the pitch of his noisy defiance, but he backed slowly away from Adam. "Atwell, you can't bluff Kiger Steele!"

Adam halted, a grin spreading his mustache upward. "T-that's a curious thing, Kiger—a curious thing. I ain't any mo' bluffin' you than a rattlesnake's whistle." He halted, as if to reflect and again chopped at a fern with his hoe. "Maybe you don't know hit, but I look after the Hightower holdin' for the Widow Hightower. And maybe you don't know hit, but you kin prove it by the man you are cuttin' this timber for—there's a d'spute over a land line that lies on beyond you up there and accordin' to what I know about it, you are below the Hightower line, a-cuttin' the Hightower timber. Likely Mr. Slappy told you sumpin' different, but that's not going to take care of you in court." He looked at Kiger kindly. "Hit don't make no difference who's right and who's wrong, with these white people—who wins and who loses—you de nigger and you gointer lose, Kiger—if'n you git mixed up in it!"

Kiger was impressed. He relaxed his grip on his ax, allowing it to turn, blade down over his shoulder, but he was not yet prepared to surrender. He backed toward the tree to get more distance. "Look here, Adam, I'm in the clear. I bought this stumpage on what Mr. Slappy said, for fair. I'm in the clear!"

Adam, eyeing him sharply for the first time, spoke short to him. "Kiger, maybe you don't think you're a black man, hunh? Put up yo' ax and come on!" He snapped the hoe up on his shoulder irritably. "We're goin' up to see Hinshaw Slappy. I'll git it out of his mouth that you on d'sputed ground—I'll do better'n that, if he fools 'round about it!" He moved in close.

Kiger shook Adam off, turning his back, to face the tree again, sliding his ax off his shoulder to the ground. "I ain't goin' nowhere with you, Adam! I ain't goin' nowhere!"

Pausing, Adam laughed. His face and voice softened and he said gutturally, "I didn't mean to be short with you, Kiger!" he moved nearer Kiger, still smiling, catching his eye. Adam's twinkle, as they stood thus, firmed to an amiable insistence, then held the other man's defensive gaze with demand, his strong eyes burning luminously. As Kiger's glance faltered, Adam powerfully commanded him. "Come on!" he said, taking Kiger by the arm. . .

But they had scarcely reached Slappy's hog-killing grounds on the way to his house, when the sparkleberry bushes on the far side began to shake and Hinshaw himself came pushing his way through them and out into the clearing, holding his .22 rifle by the pistol grip.

"Hey there, Mr. Slappy!" Adam called out cheerfully, "you done saved us a walk!" He led the way into the clearing from the opposite side, without saying anything more, but observing the lank, loose-faced white man alertly.

"How's that?' Hinshaw said, his features tightening, as his gaze fixed on them. He eyed first one and then the other. "What you colored boys up to, anyhow?" he said, lowering the muzzle of his gun.

Adam halted, smiling. *Hinshaw Slappy was already prepared to write Kriger off his books!* As he watched Kiger pass him to get nearer the white man, Adam wished *he* could be as confident as Slappy was that Kiger had deserted him. He said pleasantly and almost as if he were jesting, "I thought maybe you'd come to meet us, I thought maybe you'd *sent* Kiger down beyond the Mort Sumner line to cut that ash timber?"

Kiger looked quickly at Slappy, lifting his big sharp depigmentized nose. He opened his mouth as if to speak, his gold teeth flashing, then he seemed to break in the middle almost as if he had received a blow, his long frame swaying limberly and he shifted his stance to take a look at Adam. "Atwell, here, talkin' about some sort of line," he said.

Adam continued as if Kiger hadn't spoken, eyeing Slappy. "Because he didn't have no saw podner and it took so long, I got down there afore he got a tree down. Howsomever, we going to have to take out that un he 'uz hackin' on. Hit'll make us hoe and ax handles enough for the next five year."

Kiger looked from one to the other suspiciously. "I reckon y'all kin stop me if you git together, like this, but I aims to git paid for my time! I aims to git paid!"

"You don't happen to be sayin' that to me, do ye Kiger?" Adam said quizzically.

Kiger, who had kept glancing about, at this point allowed his gaze to settle on Slappy.

Adam was constrained to join him in this. "Did you send 'im down there, Mr. Slappy?"

Hinshaw's mouth worked a couple of times, loosening his lips, then he lifted a sharpened glance to meet Adam's. He said glumly, "Send him whur?"

"Down below the Mort Sumner line!"

Hinshaw shifted his stance and lowered his gaze and pushed over a large toadstool near his foot with the barrel of his rifle. He grunted.

Kiger spoke up again. "Somebody's goin' to have to *pay me!*"

"Down below the Mort Sumner line!" Adam repeated.

Slappy's face sagged into its dull ravaged look for a moment, then twisted tight with a desperate anger. "Look-a-here," he said sharply, his voice quivering as he went on, "I don't know whur you found 'im"—indicating Kiger with a nod—"and I ain't admittin' to nothin'—no ash trees, no Mort Sumner line, no nothin'." He glared at Adam. "But whut difference would it make to you if'n I did send him down in the swamp?"

Adam raked his foot back and squirted a long stream of ambeer at the bushes left of Slappy, then he chuckled, shaking his head. "Sho' not enough to make you mad about it, Mr. Slappy!" He had spoken with feeling, but he appeared remarkably controlled, looking about him interestedly and, after a moment, taking a step to chop down a stray weed in the clearing with his hoe. He turned again to Slappy.

"The onliest thing is, I'm gointer have to report 'bout this to Miz Hightower." He spat and shouldered the hoe, observing mildly as he turned away, "Hit do look like you goin' to make us have to call in the county surveyor to run out that swamp line ag'in!" He turned his back, without waiting for a reply and made his way again through the sparkleberry bushes. Before he had passed out of earshot, however, he could hear Slappy say, "Hell, Kiger, let's git on up to the house!"

Mrs. Hightower leaned over the mailbox on the back porch, inspecting the small red-cheeked yellow crab-apples that filled a two-bushel split-oak basket. She filled her lungs with the sharp odor of them. "They're really fine this year!" she murmured to the basket.

Adam, in the yard, looking at the hard little apples from the opposite side, said, "They's better than usual and there's plenty of 'em. Ma and the chillum picked a lot of 'em and wanted to send you some."

Straightening up, Mrs. Hightower said, "They sent so many! I hope they have some left for themselves?"

Adam glanced up with a brief twinkle in his eye. "More'n they got sugar for, I reckon," he said.

"Anyhow, Adam, I am very glad to get them and thank your mother and the children for me, please. Those Old-Crumley field crab-apples make the best jelly of any I know about. The girls and I will have a jelly-making!" She started to move away, but turned back for an instant and, selecting one ruddy apple from the heap, carried it to her nostrils, then slipped it into the plaid pocket of her gray cotton dress. "There is something I think I ought to tell you about, Adam," she said thoughtfully, as she, with the hand hidden in her pocket, wrapped the round fruit in her handkerchief.

"You know so much about so many sides of it. And you know the source of the claim as well as any of us now living. I'd like to know your opinion."

Adam had been moving as she moved along the porch and now they stood, respectively at the top and the bottom of the steps, at their appointed stations of which they were unconscious, to resume a morality play of which they believed themselves unaware. As she met Adam's grave countenance, she added, in qualification, "It seems pretty incidental, I know, but it disturbs me. Mr. Littleton brought me this, this report, himself and in all seriousness. . . .Oswald Paley"—her voice lowered unconsciously at the mention of his name—"has been to him with *this* tale. He says that the original mineralogical plat made of the clay deposits—the surveying which you attended, you know—the supposed original plat, which we haven't been able to find anywhere (nowhere in Mr. Hightower's papers and you had never seen such a plat as Paley had turned up with a blueprint of) and which we only learn about through Oswald Paley, who now says it is at a Macon blueprint office! Paley says he believes it's there. He says Mr. Hightower sent it there not long before he died." Mrs. Hightower tightened her lips and, putting her hand in the pocket of her dress, walked back and forth across the landing, while Adam digested her news.

Adam retrieved his broad-brimmed straw hat from the top of the milkbox where he had laid it, to fan himself with, for the morning was sultry and the chinaberry trees, with their deep shade, were as much a trap for the heat as a protection against the morning sun. "H-hit's one of those things that might, or might not-er happened—who kin say for certain," he said temperately. He fanned, turning his cheeks judiciously to the breeze. "Just thinkin' about it, I don't know that we need to know sho-nuff, whether the Colonel did that or not."

Mrs. Hightower looked at him quizzically, shrewdly, but she was not sure of his point and asked, "How's that, Adam?"

Adam's straw hat moved back and forth with dramatic deliberation before he resumed. "In the twenty-odd years I knowed him, I sca'sely ever heard the Colonel *condemn* a man—not to say, wholesome condemn him as no good. But the last thing he ever said to me about Oswald Paley—and the Colonel was then lookin' the *end* square in the face—was the deepest damnation I ever heard him make of any man." Adam halted his fan abruptly. "Miz Hightower, that's enough for me!"

Mrs. Hightower nodded. "Yes I know. Oswald Paley is a treacherous man."

Adam resumed. "And Miz Hightower, hit ain't my part to condemn no white man that ain't done nothin' to me and I don't believe I ever have befo'. But I'm gointer say about this particular man that all I've seen of 'im supports the Colonel's words."

"Yes, a treacherous man," she repeated, her face still questioning.

The hat, held between his hands, Adam rested on his chest decisively. "We may not know whether the Colonel sent a mineral plat to a Macon blueprint man or not, but we do know that any contention, that Paley makes 'bout it, is to our harm on the Hightower place!"

Mrs. Hightower shrugged and nodded. As she stared on at Adam, the gaze from her long, serious, gray-blue eyes going through him and growing abstracted, a frightened look came on her face. "Yes," she said finally, "yes. If we only knew what he was up to!" She walked thoughtfully over to the basket of crab-apples, saying, "Well, thank your mother and the children for picking them!" She took a few in her hand and abruptly dropped them, as she remembered what she had intended to do about them, exclaiming, "And—oh, here! Let me give you this!" She hurried through the back hall into her bedroom and returned after a moment with silver in her hand. "Give this to your mother for her church circle" she said, counting out eighty cents into his hand. "And tell her I do appreciate the crab apples!" She turned away toward the hall door again, adding disconnectedly, "I wish I could impress Mr. Littleton with what we know about Oswald Paley!"

Adam raised his voice. "Miz Hightower!"

She turned back in surprise. “Yes, Adam?”

He smiled apologetically. “As you sort-a e-expose, there's a lot-a crooks and turns to this here Land Deal. And it looks like I'm gointer have to ask you to pass some word out among the folks in it, for me, if you don't mind, please ‘um!”

Mrs. Hightower came back to the head of the steps and looked down at him with sharp attention.

Adam stood before her in upright ease of posture, at that incalculable but exact distance away from the steps that gave his uplifted face command, rather than appeal, but a command unasserted and potential and covered with a distant twinkle in his eyes and a slightly ironic compression about his mouth—an action that was automatic and an appearance that was unconscious with him. “Sort-a pass the word ‘round that you're ‘bout to get the county surveyor to run out the line between the low and upper swamp lots, please M'am!”

Mrs. Hightower's eyes widened in surprise. She said frowning, “But, Adam, we don't want to do that! We can't afford it!”

Adam's smile grew more pronounced. “I-I didn't say, Do hit. J-just pass out the word that you aim to.”

The tightened lines at the corners of Mrs. Hightower's eyes and mouth began to relax, as she stood speculatively eyeing Adam's countenance. She shrugged. “Do, Adam! What's this all about?”

He lowered his eyes, as if the lids were curtains and lifted them again as he began to speak steadily, without stammering. “Yestidy afternoon I ran across a feller on a Hundred-and-forty-two, close to Slappy's bottom line, a-cuttin' your ash timber. He hadn't even got the first tree down when I flushed ‘im. He ‘uz a colored man and I reckon you don't know ‘im. I had my suspicion from the outset as to how come ‘im there.” As his smile threatened to broaden, Adam glanced away swiftly to restore his gravity. “This colored feller—though I bin knowin' him a long time—waun't a bit quick to git on confidential terms with me. Which made hit pretty sure he already knowed he didn't have no business there. Howsomever, I persuaded him to go with me to talk hit over with Mr. Slappy."

Mrs. Hightower began shaking her head and smiling. "Enough said," she broke in. "What did that pious-faced snake in the grass, Hinshaw Slappy, say?" she asked, in tart amusement.

"He didn't say much," Adam said and added laconically, after a pause, "and then he took that back. What he said mostly was that he waun't goin' to admit to nothin'!"

Mrs. Hightower sniffed and began to pat her foot in annoyance. "That sounds like him, all right!"

Adam now spoke blandly, as if what he was prescribing were a specific with which both were familiar. "I told 'im we might have to git the county surveyor to run out that bottom line twixt you and him!"

She began to frown. "What *is* this about the county surveyor? And who was the colored man cutting the timber, anyhow?"

Adam looked down at the steps carefully and gravely. Then he looked up again with the same care and gravity, a dim apologetic smile in his eyes. "Miz Hightower, I don't think you knows that colored feller," he said, his voice raised in disparagement of her interest, "and if you'll just trust me and put out that word, like I axe you to, I'd be much obliged."

Her slim face cleared and she smiled reluctantly, with appreciation for his reservations. "All right, Adam—all right, if you say so. . . ." She nodded, placing a steadying hand on the post near the water spigot. She started to move away from the steps, and turned back. "But whom am I to put out this word to—which one?"

Adam lifted a stiff face and his mouth worked convulsively before he could get out the words. "I don't think hit matter too much, Miz Hightower, which one. You'll be seein' the banker Littleton, likely. You kin just leave it with him. The next time you see 'im."

Lucy Hightower's eyes widened. Then she laughed out loud.

When she had recovered from her amusement, she looked down to see that Adam had left and was already half way across the yard. She started to call him back, then she halted, resting her hand again on the post, and stood watching him as he moved through the gate. She smiled reflectively, repeating to herself, "I sca'sely ever heard the Colonel condemn a man." She nodded her head. Yes, Marcellus didn't *have to*. Yes. And neither did Adam! Suddenly she felt defended against all of the deceit and trickery and connivance of the twenty-odd weak, avaricious, fearful men who appeared to have joined together against her, merely because she had property and was a woman too inexperienced to protect it. She watched Adam mount the hub of a wheel and get into the seat of his wagon and give his guttural command to his mules, "Git in there, Gray! Don't let Red tote all the load!" Yes, thank God, there was one *man* in the lot!

9.

ON MONDAY AFTERNOON, on her return from McDowell's general store, where she had gone to settle with Halley McGrew for the damage to his automobile, Lucy Hightower approached her yard by the side entrance the better to survey the activity of her children. On the way home she had come to a high decision, but recognized that she must for the time lower the focus of her thoughts to her daily duty. From the sidewalk she could see the game of scrub going on a hundred yards away in the dead-end street that made a neighborhood commons between her place and the one next door. She paused long enough to pick out the stubby figure of her son, knickerbockers hanging down his bare legs, catching the ball behind the batter, and to detect the sound of her younger daughter's high-pitched voice among the fielders at the far end of the playground. She had been made aware of her eldest child's dutifulness already by the sounds from the piano in the parlor. Elinor was practicing her piece for the commencement recital. Reassured, Mrs. Hightower passed through the gate quickly, crossed the narrow side lawn, climbed the steps beside the trumpet vine and entered her bedroom by the window-door at the end of the porch.

In the back hall she intercepted Elinor. "You sounded pretty good from the street," she said, adding routinely, "Did you practice a full hour?"

Framed in the portieres that marked off the rear from the front hall, Elinor paused, raising the leather music roll she held in her hand in a vaguely defensive gesture. "As a matter of fact I went five minutes over time, Mamma," she said, a little self-righteously, a glint in her gray-green eyes, "I was so absorbed!"

In the dimness of the hallway, Mrs. Hightower gave her daughter a sharpened second glance. A strong gaze, a prominent nose and slight sallowness, coupled with an ingenuity for mischief only in recent years brought to taw, of which Mrs. Hightower was conscious, gave Elinor, for her, an aura of mystery. "So absorbed?" she repeated ambiguously.

Elinor relaxed her stance and, turning back to the table just behind her, laid the music roll on it. She grinned. "That, and I got mixed up on the clock, too!"

Mrs. Hightower tossed her head, eyeing her daughter's mouth still widened by her smiling, "Well, get Marse and Lucinda into the house and start supper. Lucinda will help you. Tell Marse to get to work on his arithmetic—in *his* room; I'm going to be in mine." She smiled, turning away. "And push in your teeth!" (This was a reference to Elinor's eye teeth that had denticles behind them and had to be constantly "pushed in" against their spoiling her mouth.) "Aw, Mamma!" Mrs. Hightower heard, in protest, as she swept on toward her bedroom-sittingroom and her exciting purpose.

Seeing a disordered pile of school books on the reading table in her room, she scooped them up in her arms and took them out into the back hall where she unloaded them on the linen press. "Tell Marse his books are on the big chest!" she called out to Elinor, now on the back porch in the act of summoning her younger brother and sister. "And I mustn't be disturbed," she added, as she reentered her room. She thumbbolted the door behind her.

Edward, she told herself without any conscious relevance, had to have a great deal of experience with boys to have been principal of the High School as long as he had. Though, of course, he was not really old! She took off her hat swiftly and put it on a shelf in the closet, moving on to the secretary in the bay window. When she saw him at her mother's funeral in Charleston three years ago he didn't look very much changed—a little thinner and there were lines in his face that made his nose more prominent and there was a thin spot on the crown of his head. But he was still handsome. And he was attentive still and had about him his appealing air of innocence.

She began a search of the stuffed pigeonholes in the desk for a letter Edward had written her after her mother's death. She wanted to see what it was exactly that he had said about her appearance. Even mourning had not spoiled the quality of her *complexion?* Doubtless he had not actually referred to her complexion, but somehow he got over that impression. Of course, Mr. Hightower had been with her in Charleston and there wasn't much occasion for Edward to show her attention during that three-day visit. But he had nevertheless, been able to give her the feeling—now that she thought about it—that he still bore her a deep consideration. And that had not been *so* long ago! She *did* exist in the flesh for him! A little color had come into Lucy's face, now drawn about the eyes and mouth in an anxiety of eagerness as she picked among the confusion of papers.

After all, *she* had been responsible for Edward's not marrying her!

"I'm not going to take it!" he said then. "This has gone on too long already." His voice was raised in protest, but he spoke soberly. "I can get an instructor's job at the Citadel and we'll get married!"

They were sitting on the old green plush Sheraton sofa in the Morrow parlor on Wentworth street.

She had said, “Don’t be absurd! Only six such fellowhips are given out by John Hopkins, Peter Miller tells me. Why it’s like being picked to be bishop!”

Shaking his head, he frowned, staring at the brass shield that covered the fireplace. “No,” he said, “I’m not going to!”

She had taken hold of his hand then to cry, “Look at me, Edward!” His dark liquid eyes were widened in pain, and she, with as much of the oracular as she could give to her voice, went on, “You’ll be a doctor of philosophy some day. I know it!”

A frightened look came over his face, and she had thought then that it was merely the challenge of his future at Johns Hopkins that affected him.

Lifting a rusty hardback ledger out of her way, Lucy paused in her search for Edward’s old letter to consider.

She had been unfair to him!

But then, she was also unfair to herself. And she had kissed him on that occasion, too. A kiss of betrayal, it turned out to be! She did not think of it so at the time, to be sure, but she had known that, within reason, she was not going to get to wait three more years to marry Edward! Her father was then already planning to retire and move to an up-country farm. That had been an evening in May. Within a month she had met Marcellus Hightower!

A small heavy envelope fell like a plummet out of the ledger that she had taken up and lay before her on the green baize. She stared at it in mystification. The superscription spoke to her from the vigorous forward-slanting though fading script:

“Miss Lucy Morrow
Aiken Co. Aiken, South Carolina.”

The words carried a command.

She knew the letter, though she had not seen it in many years. He had written her only five times after she removed her family to Aiken, after they were engaged. They were his only love letters; she had kept them all. But this one alone had come through the years. She took the sheets out of the container and spread them out before her. It did not occur to Lucy that she could refuse to read his letter.

He had written her on his professional stationery. A box in the left-hand corner announced: "Special attention given to selling, buying, paying taxes, leasing and perfecting TITLES TO WILD LAND." On the right, in print: "M.B. Hightower Attorney at Law," then in his hand: "Adair, Ga., Dec. 3d, 1886."

Her eyes took in the familiar script as if it were a returning presence.

"My dear Lucy,"

"Your bright messenger of the 24th ult., was read on my return from Clarksville, the county seat of Clark County where we hold our Superior courts.

"I have about decided not to try to visit you this week, as I have to be in Coffee County next week and I could not more than reach you and return by that time. I will have more time after then and I will not have to hurry back so quick.

"You will not feel more disappointed than I do but I believe you feel too much interest in my affairs to have me neglect a matter of so much importance to me (or us). Nor does this make you a secondary consideration either, as you are sometimes half persuaded to believe."

There was Marcellus Hightower! Every word and syllable of it was him. Lucy shook her head. Looking over the unselfconscious script again, she became aware for the first time (though she could not say how many times she had read it) that there were no paragraph indentions, no punctuation in it. She had always supplied them unconsciously herself, so conscious was she of the rhythm and sound of that voice that had seemed sometimes to come to her through her chest rather than her ears. So conscious, of its commitment!

> *"Now, if your cheeks are rosy when I go to see you, you will pardon me if I insist on what you so often refused me? It was perhaps impudent to make such a request, but you know, my dear, how much I love you! It is you alone, Sweetheart, who can make me happy and I am lonely without you, forgetting all the rest."*

Well the test of it was not in the words!

> *"It is hard to foretell the future and we cannot tell how much sorrow may come or how soon, but if tonight I knew we would be congenial and happy, it is all of life I would wish. And I tremble when I think that either one of us should spend the rest of our lives unhappy?"*

Lucy lifted smarting eyes and looked away, her breathing grown labored. Our *lives!* The voice was coming to her through the chest now. . .

"Of course my humble prayer is that you will not be disappointed. We cannot escape the stern realities of life and you have seen enough of the country perhaps to guess whether or not you could afford to spend all the rest of your life on the banks of 'My own Oconee.' It is doubtful whether or not I could make a living for you in the city, is why I hint what might be your fate if you continue to trust me."

Oh yes, she was confident that she had seen enough of the rest of the country to *know*, the first time she read this letter! Then, she had known! Lucy pulled the handkerchief from the band of her apron and wiped her eyes. She sat up in her chair and took the last lines in a clump.

"When you write Miss Julia again tell her I appreciate the compliment and hope the Earthquake may never visit her home any more and 'May her joys be as deep as the ocean, and her sorrows as light as its foam.'

"I shall be happy to hear from you soon, dear,

Yours as ever,
M.B. Hightower"

Lucy got up abruptly, still dabbing with the crumpled linen cloth. It was now almost dark and she strode to the reading table and lighted a lamp. But, *why, why, why?* Shrugging she moved to the window-door to the side porch and drew in the blinds. Edward's voice echoed in her head: "But they are dead; those two are dead!

"Their spirits are in heaven!"

And isn't that the unalterable, the controlling fact of the whole situation, Lucy? She asked herself, still in Edward's tones. She strode to the table again and, picking up the lighted lamp, she bore it over to the secretary. *The Earthquake!* How odd! The Earthquake and Edward!

She did not, as a rule, believe in earthquakes, or fires, or storms, as providential. But she had thought that about the Charleston earthquake. The Morrows, she and her mother and father, had already, in mid-summer, moved to Aiken. And she had already become engaged (though it hadn't been publicly announced) to Marcellus Hightower and had written to Edward, breaking the news.

That really accounted for their being at the Hibernian Hall at the annual German that evening. He had an engagement for it with her from the year before, but she would not have filled it, would not have come down to Charleston for it, if he had not gone on so wildly. He telegraphed her that he was coming to Aiken to put a stop to her engagement and she had to wire him that he must not come, that she was on her way to Charleston to visit her eldest sister and would see him there.

She did not see him until he called to take her to the ball. He was going to give up the fellowship and not go to Johns Hopkins he vowed, and they were crossing the ballroom floor, when the first tremor came.

A fragmentary sense of its chaos smote Lucy now and she shuddered. It was as if the old high-ceilinged hall was having a hard glittering chill. But nobody was in doubt as to what it was for long; as incredible as it seemed. Even as they stood there transfixed by this realization, the floor heaved and the gas lights were broken. As they grasped for each other—she could always see Edward's face, empty, gaping, and bulging with strain—they were thrown asunder, into the enveloping darkness.

Lucy could hear, could feel, could tremble again to that invisible bone-loosening rattle that went on into a hideous, ear-splitting, paralyzing roar—it was as if the jaws of hell had opened and Apollyon's heavy artillery belched forth. The floor of the hall rocked up and down, like the deck of a ship in a storm.

Where was she? Who could say! She remembered sliding on her knees, rolling on the floor. In the formless dark. Then the room over them split wide open and part of it caved in, pilasters fell about them and on them. And suddenly, in the darkness a flame ran up one wall—one of the fallen gas jets had caught the draperies.

She could not say what happened in the melee. People were whimpering, crying, shouting, screaming, and praying. She probably did some of each, herself. She could not say. Nor could she say quite how she got out of the place. But, as she was pressed against the wall near the door by the panic-stricken people, all trying like herself to get out, and thinking that she was going to get crushed, trampled, another quake pitched the crowd in the opposite direction and suddenly she was moving at a drunken, rocking reel through the doorway to fresh air and the unsafe outside.

As she turned on the sidewalk, seizing the train of her ball dress in her hand for better walking, and began hurrying away from the building, she had, beyond her confusion and consuming fear for her own safety, some dim notion of seeking aid to get Edward out of the place. But the streets, if not as dark, were quite as appalling as the hall had been, with great gaps in the pavement, piles of debris and still falling stones. A fragment of a cornice grazed her shoulder and she shrank back, turning toward the street. She stumbled out into the middle of it, where after wandering about for a time, she perceived the dim outline of two men on their knees in the attitude of prayer. Gratefully she got down on her knees beside them.

While they were thus, a fire broke out in a building nearby. One of the men turned and, staring at her for a moment, exclaimed, "Little Lucy Morrow!" Then he got to his feet and helped her up, for the quake was beginning to subside, and she recognized the big bluff form of Dr. Middleton—her father's friend. He reached down into the darkness and came up with his medicine bag. He shook his big bare head with its heavy gray mane and blinked his pop eyes at her. "Ha, Miss Lucy, now we've got to do something about all of this!" he said. But he faced about uncertainly, surveying their surroundings and shook his head again. "The puzzle is how and where to begin!" Then he turned to his still kneeling companion and forcibly brought him to his feet. Lucy saw that the man was his colored driver. "We've called on the Lord for His help, Ephraim," Dr. Middleton said, "now He expects us to do our part. . .I have it," he went on, looking at her, "the little park over at Wentworth, beside your old house! It won't do to go to the Battery—there'll be more of these quakes coming and likely a tidal wave." He took Lucy by the arm. "I am sure that you'll make a nurse, a good nurse, Miss Lucy. I've heard your father say that you don't faint at the sight of blood and can take directions."

But she held back and, after a moment's confusion and questioning, she got it out. "It's Edward Louthan, my escort—in the Hibernian Hall!"

He sized her up. "Since when did ladies start rescuing their escorts!" He barked. Then his manner softening, he said, "He may have been knocked out. But we can't go into the hall now—it's split wide open. We couldn't find him in the dark, anyhow. And we're going to get another quake any minute here. Let's hurry!"

Lucy could not say how they made their way over the four blocks of rubble and darkness along Meeting Street to Wentworth, but they did—driven by the fear that another quake would hit them before they could reach the safety of the park. Somewhere along the way she tucked the hem of her dress under her basque for more freedom of motion. They made it just in time! Again the earth opened up to belch forth the awfulness of a nether region. And buildings wobbled and split open and fell. And people of all sorts shouted, screamed and prayed in agony. But the second quake did not bring the personal confusion for her that the first had. They were relatively safe now and they had a base from which to resist chaos. Moreover, the second quake was actually less violent, she felt sure.

At the park Dr. Middleton recruited two able-bodied white men to serve as stretcher bearers and a wooden window blind to use for a stretcher. The negro man built a fire and dug up an iron pot from somewhere and water to fill it. She had volunteered to find sheets to tear up for bandages and she did, after a time, across the street, in the disordered household of the man who had bought the Morrow house.

The third quake came before she got back to the park and she was thrown down in the street and suffered bruised hands and knees, but she didn't have time to think of her bruises then and the violence of the third quake was less even than that of the second.

When she got back to Dr. Middleton's emergency station, he had several patients stretched out on the grass and a second stretcher team going after more. He put her to work making bandages out of the sheets she had brought.

Throughout the night she urged one or the other of the stretcher teams to go through the ruins of Hibernian hall to look for Edward. They reported to her that they did go—and they brought back with them two injured men—but they found no trace of Edward. She wanted to go with one of the teams, herself, but Dr. Middleton wouldn't hear of it. Later she wished she'd gone anyhow! She did not know what had happened to him until the following afternoon. She had been relieved from duty to go home and sleep, exhausted, of course, and a sight to behold, in her ruined chiffon dress. But she went by his house and found him there, in bed, his head swathed in bandages.

It was terrible! A falling pilaster had knocked him down, cutting a great gash in his head and he had lain unconscious on the floor of the hall most of the night. Someone had found him about daybreak and had taken him to another emergency station.

He was pale and shaken and did not rise up off his pillow when Lucy knelt down by his bedside. She told him what had happened to her and of her night-long efforts to locate him. He winced sympathetically and apologized, but he seemed too ill and depressed to take much interest. The wholesale grocery store, in which Edward's father worked as chief clerk, had been wrecked. Edward was absorbed in the enveloping distress on every hand.

She sensed that their personal affair would be out of taste, if it was not, in fact, out of mind. He did not mention the argument they were having when the first convulsion came. He did not ask her again to break her engagement, he did not even ask her to come back to see him.

Perhaps the blow he had received did put her and her concerns out of his mind. At all events, five days later she returned to her home in Aiken, without having seen Edward again and without his ever having asked to see her. The falling pilaster, she decided, had struck more than his head!

10.

ANYHOW, SHE MARRIED Marcellus Hightower, *forgetting all the rest* and taking title to wild land on the banks of his Oconee.

And she had not finished writing the thank-you notes on all of their wedding presents before she discovered her awful mistake.

Not in the man. She did not doubt Marcellus then. She had never at any time during their marriage doubted him, though it was well that she could not see more than a step ahead on how they would *spend the rest of their lives!*

But she did not have the experience or imagination to envision the circumstances in which such a man, at forty, would be enmeshed. To begin with, she was not prepared for the backwoods.

She was wholly, provincially urban and had only romantic, ignorant notions of this country. Contrary to her expectation, her two years at Aiken had been no preparation for it, because the place her father had bought was only three miles from a fully civilized town, where, despite his poor health, he still engaged in the practice of medicine, and although he had directed the setting out of the vineyard, none of them actually knew or did anything about cultivating the grapes.

Perhaps, Mr. Hightower's looks and dress and manner had misled her, though, Heaven knows, no man could be less pretentious than he was, less self-conscious! Perhaps it was simply that she had expected no king to have so mean a country. On that first ride out from the railroad at Riverton, they had stopped en route at the baronial place of the Adairs. Mr. Adair was Mr. Hightower's biggest client then and he had come to Aiken for the wedding. The size and grandeur of the Adair place, ugly though it was, had been an unhappy preparation for a giddy bride, just come from Niagara Falls, when two miles further into the piney wilderness, she and her frock-coated lord came upon the Hightower house. There it stood, behind a rail fence, in a grassless yard: a double-pen-log—if pressed for a designation then, she wouldn't have known *not* to call it a—*cabin!*

Lucy refolded Marcellus Hightower's letter, still open on the writing board of the secretary, and put it back in its envelope. She should not make too much of the size of the place. There were nine rooms in it, upstairs and down, besides the dog-run. Nor even of its primitiveness. She came to appreciate the dog-run and even to find a sort of mellowness and grace about the balanced log pens, behind the shady front porch, under the high, gray-shingled ridge roof. It went well with the Spanish moss and the great oak and magnolia trees about it.

But the place was not really the point, it was the people. Backwoodsmen, whether to the manner born—that is, whether born on a River Road plantation or on a pine barrens patch (a distinction that was not at once apparent to her by their looks and speech)—were a peculiar breed. They were of a temper quite unknown to her. She never got over their drawling speech and their understatement. They always made her feel as if she was *gushing*. And she had never before in her life been made to feel so. More serious, she could not tell by his demeanor, when she had offended one of them. At first she thought they were hostile all of the time, all of them. But when she had hurt somebody's feelings he seemed no different!

But she would have gotten adjusted to that, too, to be sure, in a few months time. Eventually, she believed, she would, even for them, have ceased to be so offensively a *city girl*. After all, didn't she have the blood of Methodist circuit riders in her veins!

But it wasn't merely that she was a little airy and citified that the Hightowers held against her. It was that she had married *Big Bud!*

There were eight of Marcellus' brothers and sisters left. The oldest boy had been killed in the War, another brother had gone west, and their father and mother had been dead almost fifteen years. Three of the girls were married and only one of them lived in the vicinity. But two of the boys remained unmarried, and one of these was a roving hunter and fisherman, rarely ever under the parental roof or any roof, and the other and youngest was in law school at Georgia University. Yet she had blasted their hearthstone! She was an interloper and an upstart. And the worst of it was that she could not understand that she was.

When the elder Hightowers died and the inheritance was divided, Marcellus declined to accept any part of it. Such was his big-brotherly feeling for his family. Then he had bought the place from his brothers and sisters and ever since had been maintaining it, in as unchanged a way as possible, as the family home. Moreover, he had sent all of his brothers and sisters off to college, as often and as long as they would go. And from time to time he had done other things for them. There were substantial reasons why they didn't want the old order changed.

But she might even have tried to carry on this way of life, have joined in, if Caroline, Mr. Hightower's spinster older sister, who had been running the place since the death of their parents, had only made a few concessions.

Perhaps not, perhaps she could never have made herself over into a member of the Hightower household. At all events, their general differentness (if that phrase can describe the relation) finally took a specific form in contention over the servants. When the two sisters and the brother, the two cousins and an aunt, who had gathered for Big Bud's homecoming with his fancy bride (and even John, called *Fox,* the hunter, came by for a day or two), when they had all departed and Lucy was able to establish just who was who, she found out that the leaner, older and more ill-favored of the two women who haunted the kitchen and presided over the meal table was supposed to be the cook, a Mrs. Warrick. The other was Caroline.

She was able, too, to detect a whine in Mrs. Warrick's drawl and a tendency in her to eat with her fingers. (Caroline was brown and smooth and would not have been bad looking, but for the lipless, vindictive expression on her face.)

With the visitors gone and Mr. Hightower gone about his law practice (which took him away the greater part of the time) they became three lorn women gathered at common board. The kitchen and dining room, as was customary in that country, were housed apart and only connected with the main dwelling by a long porch, and she had had little to do with them at first, except to be escorted out to meals.

She was astonished to find the Hightowers, anyone in this country, in fact, with a white cook. And of course, she had never heard of a household where the cook ate with the family. It seemed to her that Mrs. Warrick did less waiting on the table and more eating with the family than Caroline did. But she wouldn't have said anything—indeed, she didn't say anything for a month—if Caroline had come even a little way toward her. With the others gone, Lucy found herself excluded at table, excluded by Caroline and the cook. Their conversations, with the barest of civilities, ignored her.

This was merely one aspect of a widespread exclusion. Mr. Hightower had given her a saddle horse as a wedding present. She loved to ride and finding so little possible company on the place, she rode a great deal. All too often, she rode the two miles over to the Adairs. Mrs. Adair, herself, was an outlander. But their whole place, and it was relatively new, was, so to speak, an importation—from library, with its ten thousand volumes encased from floor to ceiling around four walls, to the Italian marble baths. Mrs. Adair was a Godsend to her, but Mrs. Adair had a two-year-old son and was again in confinement. And, after all, Lucy could not live at the Adairs! And having no one to ride with her, Lucy had galloped along those dim sandy traces, through solitary miles of pine woods, alone, a young and generally-considered handsome married woman, whose husband was afar, all by herself. In Clark County this was a scandal and it was dangerous, too, as even a much less opinionated woman than Mrs. Warrick would know.

It had required great discipline of Lucy to sit at table with the cook and remain polite, especially during conversation with which she could scarcely keep a polite connection. Only her deep devotion to her husband and a strict sense of her Christian duty made this at all possible. But when Mrs. Warrick essayed the role of her monitor, it became out of the question.

Abandoning her awkward hints one day at dinner, Mrs. Warrick looked down her gray turtle's nose at Lucy and said, "I've heard of ridin' for bizness and I've heard of ridin' for pleasure—be it church or courtin'—but there's one of us 'round here's plain ridin' for a fall. And it's liable to be by a hack in some turpentine nigger's hand!"

Lucy gasped, but she was able to rise from the table and leave the room, without further reply.

That had ended Mrs. Warrick's services in their entirety. But her going did not improve Lucy's relations with Caroline. Nor did Lucy's temerity then, herself, to take over her own kitchen.

Through Mrs. Adair she got hold of a negro woman cook and a likely young negro man whom, it was deemed, she might train as a butler. Caroline, during those days, stood by silently, her lipless mouth like the seal of doom. She only spoke when she was spoken to and with the coldest civility. But Mr. Hightower, at home for a few days then, encouraged Lucy, even if his jesting seemed heavy. She established a new kitchen and a new cuisine, for she had found the food as difficult as anything else. It was working well, despite the silent disfavor of the sister and the sceptical humor of the brother.

Then, maybe she over-extended herself. When she brought down an old broadcloth frock coat of Mr. Hightower's one day to dress up her butler more properly, Caroline gasped and Marcellus broke into a laugh. For a moment there, they were country Hightowers, and she was Lucy Morrow of Charleston and she wanted to have no more to do with either of them!

Mr. Hightower finally defended his levity by saying, "If you give that negro that long-tailed suit it will be the last you'll see of him. I warn you!" (And here Caroline permitted herself something almost like a cackle.) "He'll go to preaching," he added.

And that is what he did! But it would only have been a broad joke at her expense, if she could have convinced herself that Caroline had not run him off and if Marcellus could only have seen the seriousness of the situation. She, a bride and a new mistress by *coup d'etat*, was being made ridiculous in her own house. To top it off, the cook left too!

Lucy, probably, was not quite serious herself, when she first broached the subject of their moving away to Mr. Hightower. But his amusement over it greatly annoyed her. Feeling herself made light of, she did take it up seriously then. She eventually told him, and with all the earnestness at her command, that so long as his older sister lived and other members of his family regarded the place as home, she wanted Caroline to keep it there for them. (Technically, the whole plantation was hers, Lucy's, for in a gesture of devotion at the time of their marriage—and sadly, in his desire to give two things most dear to him closer union—he had deeded the homeplace to her.) She, Lucy, wanted it to remain the Hightower homeplace, she said, but she and Caroline could not run it *together*.

He confronted her with, for him, an unanswerable question, *But where else would either of you go?*

Lucy went home. To be more exact, she went first to Charleston to visit Lizzie Murchison; and, on leaving her husband, she in no way intimated that she would not return. She did not even intimate such a thing to herself, though she packed up all of her trousseau and took her trunks with her. And, after two weeks in Charleston, she went on to see her mother and father in Aiken.

She was still there two months later, when Marcellus came for her. He didn't ask her whether she intended to come back with him, or not. He didn't in any way intimate that such a thing had crossed his mind. But he began, on the first evening he was there, by telling her that a giant land company and sawmill enterprise in the new town of Lancaster had put him on a large retainer and had given him so much business that he felt it important to their future to move to Lancaster.

There had been only one moment of revelation: when, after they had settled the question of making Lancaster their new home, she told him that she was going into her fourth month of pregnancy. He steadied himself with the back of a rocking-chair. He was a full-blooded man and wore no beard then, only a mustache, and his cheeks were smooth and a little florid, but as he stared down at her, where she lay back on the pillows of their bed—for they had gone to their room—his face got white and drawn and he was speechless for a full second, before he cried out in delight. . .

Mrs. Hightower heard a brief indeterminate noise beyond her hall door and, turning with lifted face after a pause, called, "What is it,

Marse?" And to the mumbled response, she said, "Yes, you can have it. And light the oil stove and put on the tea kettle!" Then she sighed and shook herself and, reaching into a box of white linen stationary drew out a sheaf of it and laid it on the board before her. But after writing the heading and date of her letter and the salutation, "Dear Edward," she ceased. She began to make cross hatches on a piece of scrap paper and shook her head. "Our lives!" she murmured. Our lives—then she had had her inning.

They had been married eight years, and could anyone have been happier! Lancaster was a small town, but there was considerable wealth in it and quite a few interesting people. The Coventry's big sawmills in the suburban village of Pineville had brought other Yankee capital to new Coventry County that bore their name and a new people to the newly-established resort hotel at Lancaster, the county site, to bask there, in southern sunshine and the salutary airs of pine forests, to entertain themselves and to look for profitable investments. There was opportunity, there was enterprise, and there was a cultivated community.

She could not have been happier anywhere this side of Charleston! They now owned a nice, new, comfortable house on the best street in town. Her mother and father—the vineyard venture at Aiken had not proven profitable and they had had no ties there since her marriage—had come on to live with them and were a great comfort to and company for her. Her father was practicing medicine, with an office at the house and no night calls and, at seventy, had more practice than he would well attend to. And even Mr. Hightower was not out of the circuit so much and was more at home during those days than ever before. He enjoyed the parents, too—especially her father. Of course everyone admired him, he was a good doctor. But Mr. Hightower never ceased to remark his enterprise, at seventy, and his agility. "Dr. Morrow can get up, turn around and sit back down, while

I'm (of course he was twice as big) getting up out of a chair!" he used to say.

But the center of the household then, the center of everybody's thought and devotion, was their two daughters, Patricia, six, with yellow curls to her waist and as fair as an angel; and Miranda, four, with black ringlets over her head and Irish blue eyes. (Although, since she was born on St. Patrick's Day, they had given the elder daughter the Irish recognition.)

Their first-born, a son whom they had named for her father—their first-born who had only lived two days and of whom she had had so little impression after his birth, because she herself was in precarious condition and was not told of his death until after he had been buried—their first-born had been *replaced.*

If Marcellus Hightower ever sorrowed for that son, he never allowed her to see it. He was utterly devoted to his two young daughters and in the instance of Miranda, that winsome child with mischievous eyes and deceptive dimples, it amounted to infatuation.

But everybody was taken with Miranda. Her invalid grandmother, in whose bedroom slippers she might hide a spool that would break a toe, could not be annoyed with her when the child ran out from behind the door to throw her little arms about her neck and say, "Miranda loves you, Grandma!" Nor did her sister's stiffly mannered playmate, Fanesta, feel hurt when Miranda would imitate her gestures and tone of voice, sharing the family's amused astonishment. For Miranda always ended her act with her arms about Fanesta. Her father she met at the front gate at dinnertime, with her mother's apron around her shoulders like a frock coat, her mother's handbag carried like a portmanteau, matching her father's ponderous stride with her plump little legs.

Lucy was sure that Marcellus would not have been able to eat his meal, if he had not found her there to cry, "Co't's A'jown!" as he opened the gate and she put her arms up to him. Sometimes this make-believe with her father went on throughout the meal and, to his unallayed amazement, she remembered from day to day the things he taught her. It was precocious in a four-year-old.

The child was brought to her father's office by its mother. They came in a spring wagon from the mill settlement in Pineville. He had a sore throat and had lost his breakfast. The symptoms might have signified any one of a dozen complaints. Since the little boy was running a temperature, her father gave him something to reduce the fever and instructed the mother to put him to bed. Since he had not recovered by the next day, her father called on the child on the day after. He found him broken out with a rash.

She, Lucy, had not known of the existence of the patient up to this point. Afterward, she did recall glimpsing the mule and spring wagon at the hitching post before their gate. But, before her father told her, he had called in the other three doctors in Lancaster and they all had agreed with his diagnosis. Together the doctors consulted the Ordinary at the Courthouse and had the little boy and his family quarantined.

Scarlet Fever.

The terror of those two words, even now, made them almost unpronounceable for Lucy.

In telling her about the case, her father took care to assure her that he had taken every precaution in examining the patient. His office had its own outside entrance at the side of the house, and the boy and his mother had not come into the other part of their dwelling.

Four days after the quarantine began, the little boy died, and three new cases were discovered in the Pineville school and one in the Academy at Lancaster, and the Academy there had been suspended too.

On the day the Pineville school closed down, her father had removed to the hotel to live, and he began sharing the office of another doctor, as a precautionary measure for her children. For he was the most experienced physician in town with the disease—and he was fearless and extremely conscientious. And, in spite of his years, he went night and day during the epidemic.

But it was the most virulent epidemic anybody had ever heard of. Children kept dying within two or three days from the time they were stricken. Parents, moved by mortal terror, burned smudge pots in their yards and in one case, the house burned, too. Some of them guarded their premises against the scourge with shotguns, others tried to run away from it. There was a story of a ten-year-old boy seized on the train and dying in the car seat. By the end of the second week eight children had died in Lancaster and Pineville, and there were thirty cases of the dread disease in the county.

The academy had been closed and Patricia had been home almost a week, when it came on her: the sore throat and the vomiting after breakfast. Lucy put the child to bed immediately and sent for her father. She committed Miranda to the care of her mother and Susan, the colored nurse, with strict instructions that they keep her downstairs. She took up her own post in Patricia's room. And she telegraphed Mr. Hightower.

He was away at court when the epidemic broke out. She had wired him about it then and that the children were all right. He had wanted to rush home at once, but since the Pineville school was closing down and a general quarantine was going into effect and her father was moving to the hotel that day, she had telegraphed him to stay beyond the confines of Lancaster, because the regulations might hold him there once he came.

He was in Dublin, a town not too far away, but almost inaccessible by railroad. A telegram from him, urging her to bring the children to him there, reached her two days before Patricia was stricken, but she had been unable to make up her mind that this was the thing she should do. She did not believe in trying to run away from a disease—

there was that much of her father in her! She could scarcely have left her invalid mother there alone in the house by herself, with only the servants, and her mother would not leave her husband. The trip would have been too much for her. There would have been a seven-hour lay-over in changing trains in one direction and a four-hour lay-over in the middle of the night in the other direction to get us to Dublin. She had not had a chance to ask her father's advice about it beforehand, but he pointed out to her afterwards that Patricia undoubtedly was already infected and might even have come down with the fever on the trip. None of this, of course, had been any consolation to her later; but what was done was done!

When he came in answer to her summons, Dr. Morrow did everything he knew how to do for Patricia. He said there wasn't too much he could do—it was simply up to God, until she had passed the crisis. But, after this point, the treatment she got would make a great deal of difference in the after-effects of the malady. He spent more time and effort on Miranda's isolation, standing guard over the food and water brought in to her, allowing no one to enter her room (it was really her grandparent's room) except the grandmother and the nurse.

It seemed there was so little that could be done, however, and even less time to do it in! On the morning following the night Mr. Hightower got there in the cars, Miranda went down with it, in spite of all they could do. At first Marcellus lost his head and wanted to take her to Macon to the hospital. She was so sick with vomiting and burning alive with fever and every minute calling on her papa to help her. That night she lost consciousness.

Two days later, she was dead.

She, Lucy, did not see Miranda alive after she was stricken. Indeed, she had not seen her younger daughter since she had taken up her duty in Patricia's room. But it was some consolation to her that Marcellus had been able to be there with his ewe lamb, whatever the agony of those last two days.

At the funeral, Lucy could scarcely recognize him. His face was a bluish gray; he had lost ten pounds and had aged ten years. Circumstances allowed for only the bare essentials in the last rites for Miranda and not quite all of them. There was no preacher available and Lucy's father had had to say the burial ritual and there was no music. Still, she believed that Dr. Morrow was as near God as any of Lancaster's men of the cloth.

Marcellus had been bludgeoned and he was dazed, but he did not break. After Miranda's death, he was there beside Lucy every minute—in the long watches at Patricia's bedside, at the meal table, in their room—with his deep voice (the very vibrations of which were a support to her) and the clear steady light in his eyes. It was these that sustained her through the rest of the nightmare that held them in its thrall: while Patricia began to recover, during the period of her peeling (desquamation, the doctors call it) and convalescence, even then her condition still remained uncertain; and in the lightning-stroke aftermath.

The final blow was almost as staggering as that of the scourge itself. After Patricia was out of bed, they fumigated the house, under Dr. Morrow's direction. Parker, the stable boy, who was helping them, somehow let the carpet in the back hall catch fire and the house burned through the floor and got under the house. The men—Marcellus, her father, and the boy—crawling under the building with buckets of water, were able to get it out, but in the process her father got drenched. He developed a cough before the end of the day that with his weak bronchials and in his run-down condition went into pneumonia in twenty-four hours. He who had done so much for others, who had lost only four patients out of the forty he had treated in the epidemic, was powerless to help himself. In forty-eight hours he was dead. . .

Lucy lifted her face and drew in a long shuddering breath and shut tight her eyes. She sat in this position for some moments, holding onto the writing board, then she opened them and they came to rest on the small, thick envelope that had plummeted out of the ledger into her afternoon's great intentions, to carry her off on this intractable train of thought. She shrugged and put the letter back into the stiff-backed book.

If her father had lived, if things had been different, she could not say what Mr. Hightower's reaction to their tragedy might have been. He never got over Miranda's death. He was never the same again. But he never faltered. At no time over the years had he ever questioned her father's course of action in the epidemic. At no time, had he ever brought up with her the fact that the fever's first case came to her father's office, in their house. He never mentioned the circumstance of her parents living with them. He never, even once, suggested that his telegram to her to bring the children to him might in any way have altered their fate. And he never once, over all the years, allowed her to condemn herself in his presence, in any way for any of these things.

He had always hushed her with the invariable comment: "Everybody did the best they knew how. Things were taken out of our hands. Don't question the ways of the Almighty!"

Never, yes, never! For even when the invisible thief took its final exaction of them—when, six years later, after they had moved to another place (to Leegrant) into a new world, where they had built a new life and God had sent them three other children—when, on a cloudless, quiet, calm Sabbath morning, without their having had any premonition or the slightest preparation, they found Patricia dead in her bed (little Elinor, who had slept the night with her, came crying to their door, "Mamma, I can't wake Big Sister up!), when this last and incalculable blow had fallen on them and, she, Lucy, had sunk under it into melancholia; it was Marcellus' words—those same words—in his quiet voice, under his steady eyes, that had reached into the morbid and destroying shadows to her and brought her back.

Everybody did the best they knew how. Don't question the ways of the Almighty!

11.

THE ODOR OF WHISKEY assailed her keen nostrils, and Mrs. Hightower, without shifting her position at the steps before Adam, drew up into a posture of more reserve. She was astonished and a little disturbed. Except on Thanksgiving and at Christmas-time, he never came to the house with drink in him. But she took the letter.

Adam, a foot on the bottom step, was extending it toward her, though he seemed to look off beyond her shoulder. His eyes were puffy; a swelling throat darkened his face with blood; a peculiar cloudiness covered his ginger-colored skin.

He said: "H-hope you don't mind to read it to me, please'm? My boy Jake sez its postmarked Milledgeville. That's whur my wife Malinda is in the asylum. I ain't never done this befo', but hit didn't seem right to let them chillun read after theah po' sick ma. Didn't want to take it to Mr. Slappy, or Mr. Peter Bright. Hope you don't mind? You know I ain't never axed you nothin' like this befo'." The convulsed jaw had opened and the words had flown out of his mouth like a flushed covey of quail.

“Well of course not, Adam!” Mrs. Hightower said, her eyebrows lifting in surprise. Then, as if the words had hit her eardrums in an unintelligible clump and were only now unfolding their meaning, she blinked and looked down at him abruptly and audibly released her breath. He had drunk only to nerve himself to seek her help! “I’ll be glad to read it to you, Adam,” she said and, turning it over in her hand, took a hair pin out of her hair and slit it open.

Adam had withdrawn his foot from the steps to take an upright stance, his face uplifted to listen, but he had not yet mastered his embarrassment in making the request and his jaw worked convulsively again and he got out, “Y-you knows I sho’ wouldn’t a-dun it, if I could read it myself.”

Mrs. Hightower looked at him sympathetically, as she took the letter out of the envelope, and the restraint about her mouth softened to release a quiver in her lower lip. “I appreciate the mark of your confidence, Adam,” she said quietly. Unfolding the sheets, she added, “And you can rest assured I will never mention it to anyone at all.” She drew forth her glasses from the spring button at her shoulder.

Adam scrutinized her face, as she glanced diffidently down the page of lined tablet paper. Then he looked abruptly away, his mouth beginning to work again. “Hit’s a hard thing! We wouldn’t-a put ‘er there, ‘cept she tried to kill me and ma, both—gone clean out’n her head. It wuz the Court put ‘er there.”

Mrs. Hightower examined the large childlike but regular script a moment longer to get the hang of it, then lifted her gaze without altering her attitude. “I had heard she was at Milledgeville. I know how very distressing it must have been for you all to have to put her there!” She looked back at the letter and a firmness came on her face as her eyes focused on the writing. “I will begin reading,” she said and cleared her throat.

"Dear Adam,

"I am all right now. My mind's been clear for a long time and I stay in good shape. I'm clean cured, for sure, but the superintendent keeps on keeping me in here, because they get paid so much a head for us—"

Mrs. Hightower's voice slowed for an instant and hesitated, but she resumed without commenting:

"and they don't want anybody to get out I know for a fact."

Mrs. Hightower lifted an eye to conjecture on the reasonableness of this, but the sight of Adam's face halted her. It was swelling and he blinked reddened eyes. Her hands began shaking and her throat got tight. This unprecedented show of emotion in him upset her. She felt weak in the knees and turned away and took a step or two to regain her composure. She cleared her throat sharply and took off her glasses deliberately. "Now Adam, don't get too disturbed," she said, in a low voice. "I don't think we can take everything at face value here. Remember she may still be sick." She cleared her throat again and put on her glasses to read.

"And they don't give you nothing"—("anything, that is," she corrected the script tardily)—"to eat but mouldy cornbread and watery bean soup and black strap that ain't fit for a dog to eat."

Mrs. Hightower paused, reacting to this grim intelligence with compressed lips and sharpened brows, but she did not hazard another look at Adam. Taking a deep breath, she read on in a forced monotone.

> *"They work me hard, too, and I don't get anything for it but abuse. I have to work in the fields and I'm past the time for it. I got a deep cough that don't ever leave me and I ain't fit for field work."*

A suppressed sound, like the grunt a man gives when he's been hit in the midriff, halted Mrs. Hightower and she heard the shuffling of Adam's feet. She lifted her glance waveringly to see that he had turned his back to her to hide his disturbed feelings. She read on, her monotone grown crusty now, shaking a little.

> *"Please get your white folks to get me out of here! I know the Colonel could do it."*

Her voice caught on the last words and she had to stop completely. It seemed as if this family confidence for which Adam had had to blunt himself with whisky was going to prove too much for both of them! She removed her glasses and took a turn across the landing and back before she tried to go on. She finished under a strain that made her voice harsh.

> *"The doctor says I tried to kill you again was why I am back in here. It was in a spell if I did. And I ain't had a spell for a long, long time now. I am well. Please get me out! Your loving wife, Malinda"*

Mrs. Hightower lowered the letter as if she had finished with it and moved over to the milk box, giving her attention to adjusting the flow of water from the spigot. She seemed absorbed in reflection on the letter's painful appeal, but after a moment she glanced at the sheets of paper in her hand and said, "There's a postscript. Shall I read that, too?"

Adam was using his blue handkerchief and did not turnaround. His voice came to her as if from the bottom of a well, in a hard stammer. "Y-essum," he said. "Read it all!"

From beyond the water pipe, she covered her eyes again with the glitter of her pince-nez and resumed with the letter, now more collectedly.

> *"I won't mind your ma being there any more. It wasn't your ma so much as the way I saw you looking at Babe one day that made me sick the last time. But I don't care any more. I'm done past my time of caring. You can keep—"*

Mrs. Hightower halted abruptly, then after a pause, in a voice raised in protest, yet faltering, she said, "Adam, I don't think I'd better go on with this. Obviously her mind is not right. There's no sense in making you suffer needlessly. . . ."

There was a silence, then Adam said in a hoarse, harsh voice. "Read it!" He turned about to confront her. His face was stiff and a bloodless gray, but it now wore the grim quiet of a man who has prepared himself for the doctor's knife. "I got to hear it, Miz Hightower, please'm. She my wife, sick or no. If you can stand to read it, I got to hear it!"

Reluctantly Mrs. Hightower straightened up again and lifted the letter to read, as if it were an instrument of torture. She sighed.

> *". . .Babe."*

She completed the sentence she had broken off, without going back to reread it. She sighed again

"Just don't let me stay in this jail full of crazy people any longer, please, Adam, please."

"Another postscript," Mrs. Hightower said, going on.

"If your ma would take that hex off of me, I would have already done been out of here. Please, please, get the Colonel to. . ."

"That's all of it, Adam," Mrs. Hightower said, dropping the hand with the letter in it to her side. She turned away and, shaking her head slowly, she walked back and forth across the porch, gazing at the floor boards thoughtfully. She found Adam's situation baffling. His show of emotion—Adam whom she had never seen give way before at all!—distressed her deeply. And he seemed to take his wife's illness all upon himself, in moral blame! Insanity was always disturbing to contemplate, whatever your relation to the victim. But she would doubt that Adam had any responsibility; indeed, she thought it very likely that he did not have any part in her mental sickness. The chances were that it was the effect of the dread social disease that was so prevalent among *them*. Though her father had once told her that suffering of the brain was a rare thing among negroes!

"Course it kain't be the Colonel; but you reckon they ain't some way we kin git her out?" Adam's voice bore the hollow, wrung-out calm that follows hard suffering.

Mrs. Hightower came back to the head of the steps reluctantly, not knowing how to begin. She said in mild protest, "But, Adam, she may not be well, at all! What makes you think that she is well?"

Lifting his head, Adam blinked only once. His voice had not lost its calm, but was now assured. "Hit's the fust letter she ever writ me from there. Least ways, the fust one I ever got from her. She at herself in that letter, all right!" He laid a foot on the bottom step and looked down at the rough, worn cowhide encasing it, as if to reassure himself of its familiarity. "Don't you think she sounded all right?"

Mrs. Hightower observed the shoe, too. "I don't know her, have never seen her. Of course it would be hard for me to tell." She paused and looked up at him and said crisply, "Do *you* believe that your mother has her hexed, as she says?"

Adam shrugged, taking his foot off the step. He smiled feebly. "No'm. But *she* may believe that." He looked off into the distance. "They's somethin' curious between 'em. They never did get along. Yet they never quarreled nuther. Ma ain't the quarreling kind."

"But that may have been the *result,* not the *cause,* of your wife's condition."

Adam straightened up, shaking his head. After a pause he said, "She had some hard times with us back there in the beginning."

Mrs. Hightower's mouth compressed and her brows gathered and she turned away to cover the difficulty she felt. She saw that he meant "times" that were somehow the responsibility of himself and his mother. How could she get at the business of telling him better? "My father, Adam, was a doctor, and a good one. He practiced in Charleston." She faced him again. "He once told me that insanity was a disease, like—like smallpox. Sometimes it was inherited, he said, but most of the time it came about as an after-effect of a physical disease. Like smallpox," she repeated.

She paused, her mouth tightening and her hand automatically drawing forth her glasses on their chain, as if she were going to put them on. She felt reasonably sure that Adam understood the disease to which she thus obliquely referred and which propriety forbade her to mention. From her reasserted distance, pince-nez before her pedagogically, she resumed in a tone of patient deliberation. "Now think. Did your wife ever have any physical disease back yonder? Any organic trouble, like with her kidneys or heart? Or any rheumatism that the doctor said was incurable?"

Adam shook his head. "She never had no doctor for nothing', ceptin' this last boy of our'n. She never were sick."

Frowning, Mrs. Hightower let go the glasses and stared off into the leafy cloister of the chinaberry trees. . . .Of course Adam's report on it proved nothing! She said firmly, "Adam, I would doubt very seriously that anything you or your mother ever said or did to your wife had the least thing to do with her mental sickness, despite your not remembering her having the disease. The fact is, she might have had it without its ever having any noticeable ill effects on her, until her mind was affected. She might well have become infected with the disease before you ever knew her. The fact that she tried to kill you and your mother doesn't prove anything, except that she was insane."

The only visible reaction her words brought to Adam's face, now natural looking except for its hollow-eyed, tear-stained appearance, was a steady blinking of his eyes. After a pause, he spoke with detachment. "Ma said I treated Malinda mighty mean back there right after we 'uz married." He turned aside and strode along by the steps. "I've thought on it, too, and I reckon now that I did. Though I didn't think about it that-a-way then. Because I never give Malinda a short word at no time. But I was raftin' timber durin' them years and I was gone on the river most of the time. Howsomever, it waun't just that!" He paused and stroking his jaw, studied the ground, obviously under constraint as to how to speak with propriety about his behavior to Mrs. Hightower. "W-when I-I was away from her, which was most of the time, I didn't act like no husband, I know now. And I reckon she knew it then, or suspicioned it." A wry, mirthless smile rose dimly to his eyes. "I reckon I'd a knowed hit then, too, if'n I'd stopped to think about it. But the ole River give a feller a rough loose life back in them days."

Mrs. Hightower responded with a like smile, gingerly. She felt at sea. But she recalled something her husband had once told her of Adam's wife and she felt curious about it. "Adam, Mr. Hightower, once told me that your wife, Malinda, was a widow with a child when she married you. And that she was five years older than you?"

"Y-yessum," he said. "Dat chile was Babe. You've seen 'er." His face-clouded with an ambiguous constraint and he looked away. "Malinda was always a jealous woman. Right from the start. It seemed to eat on 'er!"

Mrs. Hightower pursued her point obliviously. "But it puzzles me to know why you, Adam, should have married a widow with a child, a widow five years older than yourself."

Adam raised his eyebrows, astonished at the question. But not because the answer was obvious or came easy to him. He seemed embarrassed and uncertain. After a pause, he shrugged to muster a show of detachment, of humor. 'W-well, for one thing, she wuz a school teacher. I reckon I aimed for her to teach me how to read and write." Hitching up a shoulder and thrusting a hand into his hip pocket, he pulled out his tobacco plug and bit off a chew, all in one automatic motion. "But somehow we never did come to it." He turned the tobacco over in his jaw. "And then, her bein' a widow . . . .maybe!. . .My ma, you'd say, was a widow." He chewed vigorously for a moment and dropped a mouthful of ambeer carefully beside his foot. "C-course, I don't know! Who knows 'bout a thing like that? I didn't, to say, think about it one way or tother. I just thought I wanted to marry her."

He continued to chew on the tobacco, obviously unconscious that he did so (he rarely took a chew of tobacco in her presence), caught up in his own thoughts. He did not stutter as he talked on. "I was full of myself then—full of doing, not thinking. I took more rafts down to Darien one year back there than any other man on the Oconee. I didn't see what was coming up. Until I come home to Long Pond one day after I'd been gone for 'bout three weeks—hung up in the Narrows, not far above the Nightingale plantation with the chillun—her'n and our'n. She'd gone back to her folks over in Coffee County."

Gazing at her now lean and middle-aged overseer, talking on in his dignified composure, Mrs. Hightower began to see, with some astonishment, the reckless young river rover of twenty years before—the champion axman, raftsman, shot, who accepted the favors of women (their color made them more, not the less, women) along the river bank, doubtless on the Nightingale plantation and in Darien—a visiting hero. Yes, that would harass an older wife at home alone—black or white!

"It was then I sent for ma, to come live with us and keep her company. I began to think about getting' off the River, too. But I didn't do it for another five years.

"Ma's being there, I come to find out, only made it worse. Malinda suspicioned ma doing ever sort of thing to her, or tryin' to. And of always taking my part. And I had to be showed the hard way that I was wrong, and not treating Malinda right. Two years before we come on the Hightower place she went out'n her head the fust time and tried to kill ma over a wash pot with a stick of stove wood. All on account of me, she said. She tried to kill me, too, and two or three more, before we got her committed."

Could such a situation drive a woman actually insane? Mrs. Hightower went on with her thoughts, as she listened, obscurely disturbed by the sound of his voice. What did his mother do? What was old auntie's dark part in this—this unwitting domestic tragedy? Could she, Lucy, dare believe his story?

"Then, just before I moved on the place, I went to Milledgeville to see her and she seemed alright. The Colonel *holped* me git her out."

Would Mr. Hightower have done this if she had had softening of the brain? Would the hospital have let her go?

"Ma stayed over on the other side of the River and lived with my brother Deadman, when we first come to the Hightower holding. She stay there. She didn't cross the River 'til our last child, DeBow, was born a year later and Malinda had so much trouble. Ma come on to nurse her then.

"Hit was about four years a'ter that she went off ag'in—trying to kill ma and me both with an ax she had hid under the bed, accusing me about Babe, who waun't more'n twelve or fourteen then. Accusing ma of hexing her with conjure pills and breathin' down her back when she was asleep. . .Malinda!"

As he halted, Mrs. Hightower's long gray-blue eyes were rounded in hypnotic staring. She was in the woman's skin. She felt familiar fear-filled shadows enveloping her. *She*, Lucy, had not suffered syphilis. It has been Life—and *death*. It had been the action of others, when she succumbed to melancholia! As the pause lengthened, she started and shook herself and abruptly turned away. She said in a sharp voice, "I don't believe it!"

After a silence Adam's surprised, mystified words reached her. "But she in there, aint' she?"

Mrs. Hightower faced him, "Yes, but I don't believe that you and your mother put her there."

Adam's face suddenly suffused with blood and his eyes watered. With a heaving catch of his breath, he turned away, unable to utter a sound. He began to walk up and down and finally to speak. "But she in there, Miz Hightower. Behind those windows with iron bars in 'em and those walls! She bein' mistreated! She nigh starvin' and sick!"

Mrs. Hightower drew herself up firmly on the landing and spoke sharply. "Now stop that, Adam, and listen to me! Your wife is *sick*—still mentally sick, I believe. If she were not, why would they keep her there? There are hundreds of other mentally sick people being crowded back into county poor houses because there's not room for them at Milledgeville. There's great demand for space there. They wouldn't keep her if she weren't sick!"

"Behind them walls!" he ejaculated, still walking.

She grew brusque. "Now stop it, Adam! This is not like you!"

Adam brought out his handkerchief and wiped his eyes, his body jerking a couple of times with heaving, then he turned toward her. He stood for a time very still, upright and stiff-faced, blinking his eyes. He said finally, quietly and very carefully, without stuttering, "Miz Hightower, you may be right and more'n apt you are. But things don't always happen like they oughter, in this world. 'Specially for colored folks."

Lucy's countenance clouded for a moment, as if in pain, and her body relaxed. After a pause, she said gently, "I know, Adam, I know." She looked away. "Besides, neither of us could ever sleep again at night with that letter on our minds and our not doing anything about it." She lifted the sheets of tablet paper which she still held in her hand and looked at them once more briefly and folded them and, taking the envelope out of her pocket, restored them to their encasement. "Arthur Adair is our state senator and he'll be running for re-election soon," she said matter-of-factly. "I'll write to him today."

12.

THE THING THAT PROVIDENCE made Lucy Hightower a witness to must, in any event, have driven her to do what she did; though the incidents of that Friday afternoon piled up to convince her that it would only have happened in Riverton. She had no premonition of the approaching crisis, or of the day or the hour, as she sat, in petticoat and corset cover, before the marble-top bureau, in the privacy of her bedroom, fixing her hair. It was a first Friday and she was dressing to attend, at three o'clock, a meeting of the Methodist missionary society of which she was secretary and treasurer, and she gazed into her looking glass alertly.

There was in her gaze, to be sure, a hint of a deep distraction that may have contributed to her feeling about Riverton. Her thoughts by duty and habit were given to a review of the state of dues payment in the missionary society. But behind this conscious downstage activity of her mind there loomed an affective backdrop of a mingled emotional texture. It heightened for her the drama of everything she was doing and brought her occupations to issues as means toward the end of resolving her dilemma. Almost three weeks had passed since she had received Edward Louthan's proposal of marriage, and she was still torn between the desire and reasoning that would take her and her children back to Charleston and a fear of what this might do for her son, Marcellus, and his future commitment to the Hightower holding, to his father's dream.

When she had finished her hair, she glanced behind her at the nickel-plated clock on the mantelpiece. Turning back, she hurriedly opened the top drawer to the bureau and drew out a chamois skin to dab her face with chalk dust. In new vim she lifted the white lawn shirtwaist from the back of a chair and put it on, fastening the high net collar, supported by two bone stays around her neck, whose thinness she was self-conscious about. From the clothes closet across the room she brought a white gabardine skirt with mother-of-pearl buttons down one side, stepped into it and, with practiced economy, drew it about her hips, fastened and straightened it. She took a leghorn hat from a closet shelf and, circling by the mirror, pinned it on top of her pompadoured hair in two tries.

A minute later, she emerged from her front door, an airy lavender scarf about her shoulders, a pair of white silk gloves in her hands and the missionary society account and minutes books under her arm. She drew on the gloves between the steps and the front gate and, facing left on the sidewalk beyond it, she began to move at a firm, decorous step along the thoroughfare split by the railroad tracks.

The distance to Mrs. McLester's house, where the Methodist ladies would gather, was no more than a quarter of a mile and the direst hazard along the irregular, grass-bordered, sandy path to it—since the sun was descending a flawless amethyst sky—would seem to be getting dust on her white shoes. Mrs. Hightower, nevertheless, proceeding with modest aloofness, was aware of other perils on the streets of Riverton.

She did not glance toward the Cranford house as she passed, because, like her own, it sat sufficiently far back from the street for the passer-by not to be expected to recognize anyone sitting on the porch. Moreover, on one occasion, she had unguardedly allowed her eyc to take in the porch and Mrs. Cranford, in wrapper and boudoir cap, from the bench swing, had called out to her in a strident voice. Her own voice was too weak to make itself heard! And really the distance was too great for an exchange of greetings! But beyond Cranfords, Mrs. Hightower, moved by sympathy to less caution, gazed at the bare, gray, boxlike dwelling that sat in the middle of an unkempt yard. She did not expect to greet the woman who lived there, though the front porch was in speaking distance. The poor, ill-dressed mother of affliction in the gray house never spoke or never even appeared in view if she could help it. Mrs. Hightower's glance had been impulsive and uncalculated.

Yet, out of an experienced wariness, she assured herself thereby that the woman's idiot son, who sometimes stood at the fence and yelled obscenities at passers-by, was not in sight. Even so she quickened her pace a little. She wondered again, as she had often before, about poor little Victor. The long-headed, well-built child would be actually handsome but for the confused tortured look on his face. He did not look like an idiot. She suspected that something could be done for him if he were anywhere except Riverton!

She was not past the yard. But she slowed her gait only to hear a moment later, from the railroad tracks to her right, a shrill whistle and a shouted word, which, though she had never heard it before, she sensed was obscene.

From the corner of her eye she saw, standing amid the tracks with his back toward her, a man in overalls and a workman's cap. Before she could resist the impulse, her glance had already gone beyond in the direction he faced and she saw on the street across the tracks a young mulatto woman, moving away—saw, below straight unfaltering back, her hips suddenly wiggle in an assenting response. She heard the man laugh.

Mrs. Hightower shrugged and shook her head, and fixed her gaze steadfastly on the distant clump of chinaberry trees in the street ahead of her that marked her destination. She shook her head again. Surely, there were negro prostitutes and licentious workmen in other places, she told herself, but only in Riverton would a person know (and she did) the brakeman, whom she recognized even with his back turned and who had children in the public school. And only in Riverton would one be acquainted with the prostitute, whom she knew even at a distance to be the chambermaid—and a good one—at the Riverton hotel!

Mrs. Hightower was prepared for the ordeal of *passing* the hotel. The spread-out, rambling, two-story, frame building, painted gray with white trimming, faced, from across the railroad tracks, the town's main street. A bannistered porch extended the length of its front, only a few feet from the way she must come. Here drummers, loafers, and gossipy old men sat with their feet propped up on the railing, smoking and chewing tobacco and spitting across the grass plot onto the sidewalk, and making their half-audible remarks, chorused by chuckles or guffaws, about the women who happened to walk by. The porch was now lined with them, but Mrs. Hightower, with the missionary society books under her arm, passed at her prudent gait, giving no evidence that she knew she was being remarked on, or even observed. And she overheard no word, nor chuckle.

She had got quite beyond the hotel and along the picket fence that framed the McLester lawn, when the unseemly side of Riverton emerged again. Seeing men whom she knew, on the walk before the gate in unusual attitudes, she was puzzled. They were bending over with hands on knees, kneeling down on the ground and squatting on their haunches. As she drew nearer the wide stretch of hard ground under the shade of the chinaberry trees, she discovered to her astonishment that they were playing marbles.

. . .Marbles! Mrs. Hightower stopped and stared.

She saw a big-bellied fellow rise from his squat with surprising agility: Mr. Johnson, the butcher! And there was Wallace Bender, the turpentine 'stiller and the town's wealthiest bachelor—baldheaded and bay-windowed—getting up and down like a bandy-legged baby. Though he was using a gold-headed cane to help. Then she determined that the oversized hulk on the ground, squirming about to get a prop on his elbow, was the sawmill superintendent's six-foot-three-inch son, engaged to be married—trying to thump a marble at a hole half the size of his hand. And beyond him, the town's *mayor*, on all fours, was drawing an X (as she had seen Marse and his playmates do) before the hole to hex the shot.

Again Mrs. Hightower shook her head. Only in Riverton could grown men so far forget themselves.

But at this point a florid, jowlish, baggy-eyed young man, whose face seemed creased by lines from laughter, bounced up from a squatting position and, taking a step in her direction, bowed with easy informality. "Hello, Mrs. Hightower!" He smiled on the scene at his feet good-humoredly and went on in a deliberate, soft, yet carrying voice. "Don't mind us, Ma'am! Come right on by!"

She nodded and sidled toward the gate, lowering her gaze, as if she would ignore the whole thing.

The man's china-blue eyes were bloodshot and the flush on his face was obviously alcoholic, but his manner was unperturbed. He spoke in amiable deprecation. "Looks like the boys wouldn't've picked this spot for their marble game this afternoon! They are going to *scandalize* mommer!" He implied that the matter was something over which he had no control. Then he met her gaze, his eyes suddenly filling with a twinkle as if with tears and he chuckled softly.

Mrs. Hightower shook her head again. This was Mrs. McLester's oldest son: in his middle thirties. The town's hardest drinker and chief idler. "Do! Robin!" She managed a wry smile. "You all are not *playing marbles?*"

He shrugged and moved to open the gate, while some of the others rose to bow, or merely nodded at her from the ground. He said, with a jesting air of confession, "Well it's the only thing mommer would let us play, over here under her chinaberry trees!"

Mrs. Hightower's gaze withheld approval as she passed on through the gateway, but she turned back to respond to his nonsense. "And I suppose you picked this afternoon for your game, just to please her, too?"

He lifted his chin with gravity. "Mrs. Hightower, it's a critical moment! You might not believe it, but we are playing for the world championship! We're the challengers." A twinkle glimmered in his eyes, as he nodded at Bender. "And we are now four holes ahead of those bullies!"

There was general laughter, but Mrs. Hightower did not join in. She was about to turn away, when Robin spoke again.

"Mrs. Hightower?"

"Yes, Robin?"

"You missionary ladies needn't spend your efforts on China this time. You can begin the work of salvation right here at your gate. This Bender bunch ain't going to have anything left to save when the game's over but their souls!" He laughed.

And Mrs. Hightower smiled in complicity, but her face sobered as she spoke. "I'm afraid you all are *hardened cases.*"

The men all laughed boisterously at this.

As Lucy Hightower moved down the white sand path with its border of castellated brick, she glimpsed in the tail of her eye proof of her suspicion: two of the men had eased away from the group and were slipping into a small building at the far corner of the yard. Ostensibly it was a butcher shop, but as everybody in town knew except, she supposed, Robin McLester's mother, it was a private bar for him and his cronies. It was just as she suspected: the marble game was only an excuse and a blind for their hanging around that butcher shop to drink!

Her glance swung to her left, off beyond the vine-covered summer house that obscured the farther view, where the hotel abutted the lawn. Here steps and a hall door in the gable end gave entrance—entrance that, she had been told, they used, under cover of darkness, for an intercourse even more immoral.

She fixed her gaze on the tall, magnolia-shaded dwelling in front of her. Beyond the front door, with its big frosted glass, set amid little dark blue and red and orange panes, giving forth its dim, rich, discreet glimmer, were gathered *their* wives and mothers—to bring Christianity to the Chinese! Here it was, assembled on one stage: *Riverton!* She gripped the missionary society books tightly against her side. Could the Hightower holding require *this* of Marse? And why should her girls have to grow up here? Could there be *any* reason sufficient to keep them here? Why did she hesitate?

When she had returned from the missionary society meeting an hour and a half later, Mrs. Hightower found it necessary to go to the barn in search of an egg for the charlotte russe. None of her children was at hand. She and Lena—before Lena left—had made the dessert for supper and put it in the milk box to chill, but they had not whipped the cream to put on top of it and she now found that the cream wouldn't whip; she needed the white of an egg.

Mrs. Hightower changed her almost-new white shoes for old black ones for the trip. She would have changed all of her clothes on her arrival at home but for the fact that she expected visitors in after supper. Mr. Littleton was going to bring Mr. Lincoln and his attorney, Mr. Slater, around for a preliminary talk before what they hoped might be the closing of the big land deal on the morrow. To the old shoes she now added a straw hat of Marse's to protect her pompadour against cobwebs. And, tightening the strings to the gingham apron she had put on earlier, she set forth.

As she reached the chicken yard, Mrs. Hightower was startled by a flash of lightning and looked up to find, to her astonishment, prodigious piles of dark, lowering clouds. Her surprise bore some realization that events might be making up about her of which she, in her absorption with the ills and contingencies of the moment, was unaware—indeed, that these events might be beginning to transpire. For she perceived the encircling gloom. But how could she have anticipated where the Light would lead her? A sense of the sky's portentousness hastened her step across the chicken yard and hastily she opened the barnlot gate. At a distance, amid the bog of mud and manure about the cow brake by the back fence, she saw the empty milk bucket on the milking block, as on an altar, gleaming immaculately in the ghostly light. So that was why Marse hadn't answered her call! But she saw merely the familiar bucket and turned away in her hurry, thinking only that it was early for him to be milking, and moved toward the first stable on the near side of the tall unpainted barn. She opened the door and looked in the hen nest under the feed trough, but it was empty. She made a similar search of two other stalls, as she moved toward the far end of the building.

Beyond the barn, she met the force of the storm and, glancing up, was frightened by the tossing tree. The outspreading boughs of the giant oak at the outside entrance of the barnlot churned tortuously and she—in her alarm, pausing for an instant to stare—saw Sook, the cow, beyond the paling gate of the tall framed gateway. She wondered where Marse could have got to, but another lightning flash, followed immediately by jarring thunder, spurred her on toward the stalls on the breezeway. Yet even as she moved she noticed that Rosa, the heifer, had not come up with the cow. She decided that Marse must have gone to look for her.

Mrs. Hightower was standing a little way inside the breezeway, facing the slatted front of the middle stable, when the next lightning bolt struck. The barn, the dim interior of the stall, blazed with that sudden, appalling fullness of light that illumines lightning strikes, nightmares, and apparitions and that, in the fraction of a second, etched on the retinas of her eyes this three-fold vision of Marse at Rosa's head, holding onto her horns and looking backward with gaze possessed at the remote, high, livid, agonized face of Jerome Cranford—and in the remaining fragment of that same second the same lightning bolt knocked her to the ground and in an earthquake of sound that jarred enough loose hay through the hole in the loft above her to bury her in it. . . .

Mrs. Hightower never quite knew how she got back to the house, but she was set with rain and so out of breath from running when she entered her room that she thought she was going to collapse on the floor in spite of herself before she could get a heart pill out of the box on her mantelpiece and swallow it and fall on her bed. For ten minutes she lay there on the white counterpane, staring at the ceiling, her eyes wide and her face bloodless, as if she were in a trance. Then abruptly she rose up and walked to the telephone in the back hall. She rang the Riverton hotel and got Mr. Lincoln, the land buyer, on the line. "This is Mrs. Hightower, Mr. Lincoln," she said stiffly. "Mr. Lincoln, this may sound extraordinary to you and I will apologize beforehand for presuming on your courtesy, but can you come to my house at once, alone, for a private talk with me, now, before the meeting tonight? I assure you my reasons *are* extraordinary!" After a short pause, she said, "Thank you, Mr. Lincoln! I believe the rain is already beginning to hold up."

13.

ADAM ARRIVED at the back steps in a state of morose anxiety. His wife Malinda might or might not still be crazy, but he suffered to think of her being behind stone walls and iron bars. And with the suffering had come resentment. It was when he wasn't directly thinking about it that resentment most rode him—resentment, it would seem, at the whole world around him. On top of him, would more aptly describe his feeling about it. At some unguarded moments he even felt his situation like that grim childhood time of slavery that he knew through his mother. And he was moved almost to open anger at white jails for colored people.

But, as he waited for Mrs. Hightower to come out on the porch, he sobered his feelings with the practical consideration that not very much *could* have been accomplished in Malinda's behalf in a week's time. His wait was long and he began to move about under the chinaberry trees, fanning himself with his black hat.

When Mrs. Hightower finally hurried through the back door and out onto the landing, he saw at a glance that something serious had happened to her. As he took in her pale, tightened face—brows gathered, her full lower lip flatly set and her abstracted gaze politely trying to focus on him—momentarily, he felt betrayed. At this hour, her crimped and netted pompadour against her loose house dress made him think she must be dressing for a trip. And an urgent one, since she was holding her gold watch out in her hand. His eyes widened in concern. With only a slight reluctance left in him, he moved toward the foot of the stairway above which she stood. His jaw convulsed and he jerked out in an anxious guttural voice, "You had bad news, Mrs. Hightower?"

"Oh Adam, we're so upset! I've just had word that my sister in Summerville has had a stroke!" Mrs. Hightower's gaze finally gave him recognition.

Adam shook his head, his face wincing sympathetically. "That's sho' bad!" he said.

Mrs. Hightower looked at her watch. "Yes. We got a telegram only about two hours ago. It happened last night." Her voice was raised, carrying in it a note of harassment. "She's my only sister. I'm trying to get off on the one-thirty train."

Adam continued to shake his head and repeat his words of commiseration.

Suddenly, before him, Mrs. Hightower lost control, her features twisting in pain and beads of perspiration popping out on her brow. "And it comes on top of everything else!" she said, in a tone of desperation. "Your trouble, Adam! And the plague-take-it old Land Deal! And. . .and Marse! And I—I don't know what all. It just couldn't be worse!"

But even as he sympathized Adam's face set and he backed away a little. It was too much! He was suddenly conscious of her odor, the thin, sickly-sweet odor of white people. It set off or rose out of some deep inner conflict that seemed to be going on inside him through his senses. He couldn't catch hold of it with his mind, but it was there. Then Adam brought himself to a halt. He straightened upright, his mouth tightening in an act of will that disregarded the smell and the inimical appearance of her face. He wiped his mustache with the back of his hand, took out his tobacco plug and bit off a chew. Thinking back over the past, he recalled that he had not been conscious of the white man's odor for a long time. . .a long time. He recalled, too, that way back when he was a boy in North Carolina and lived for a while in the Atwell house to build fires and run errands, he had come to be conscious of the *negro* odor of the field hands, in their shanties. He carefully turned the chew over in his jaw and spoke sedately. "T-t-this the sister, live in South Ca'lina?"

"Yes. She's still unconscious, the night letter said, but they think she will live." This turn of thought (and his deliberation) seemed to give Mrs. Hightower more self-control. The tone of her voice was grateful. She went on speaking of her sister, lowering the hand with the watch. "She is ten years older than I am, but there are only the two of us. I have no other immediate family, on my side, except her and her three children."

Adam nodded and resolutely picked up his hat from the top of the milk box, where he had laid it. "W-well, you ain't got no time for me and my troubles here this morning. You better git packed to git on that train. You don't wanta git left. Just tell me whut you want me to do while you're gone." He paused with the hat held to his bosom. "Whut's going to happen 'bout the Land Deal?"

"Oh, the Land Deal, Adam!" Mrs. Hightower's upsetting excitement seemed to come back, making the hand with the watch rise up shakily. "The Land Deal's called off! That is, it's postponed. We're not going to try to do anything about it today."

Adam lowered the hat to his knee, in a surprise that turned to puzzlement. He finally asked, "You mean, nothing 'til you git back, don't ye?"

"Well—" Mrs. Hightower's lips pursed, as her loosened jaw hesitated, faltered. She stared at Adam. Then her gaze lifted above his head and she swallowed, the hard lump going down her throat visibly and bringing a heave to her bosom. "Well," she said again, blinking as she paused. "Well, yes and no! There will be nothing done, all right—'til I get back—if then!" Faint pink streaks began to show in her face, just below the cheekbones and her eyes glittered and, in shifting her stance, she somehow appeared to be trying to keep her balance above uncertain footing. "I am thinking—that is, we. . . Something has come up. . . ."

Her effort broke down with these words and she stood in silence for a few moments, finally focusing her gaze again on Adam. This time her long, serious eyes were assured. "I would like to tell you something confidentially, Adam," she said in forced quiet.

His gaze and the barest nod of his head gave assent.

She went on, still collecting herself. "It is in strict confidence, for what I am about to tell you is now known only to Mr. Lincoln, his lawyer, and myself." She took a preparatory breath. "For my own purposes, yesterday afternoon before last night's meeting to get ready to consummate the deal today—before the meeting to which Mr. Littleton was a party, I talked to Mr. Lincoln by himself and told him about our Okefenokee swamp land. . .You remember about it, don't you, Adam? You've heard me refer to the fabulous twenty-five thousand acre holding in the Okefenokee swamp that Mr. Hightower bought what he believed were the best existing titles to, haven't you?"

Adam nodded. "I—I remember the Colonel going down there to, he said, *'splore* it. Tole me he'd a-took me with 'im, could he a-got me word in time." Adam's eyes twinkled reflectively. "That's whur he crawled up on a log to sleep at night because they waun't no dry land, and found a twelve-foot 'gator up there to 'spute it with 'im!"

"Yes," Mrs. Hightower agreed, with a smile that vanished quickly as she resumed her confidence. "I told Mr. Lincoln about the big stand of cypress on it, that there were big sawmills operating around the outer edges of the swamp and that Mr. Hightower had always believed that our cypress would become very valuable as soon as these sawmills began to exhaust the timber around the edges and moved deeper into the swamp. He had believed it enough, and believed in those titles enough, to pay fifteen thousand dollars for them—and you know there wasn't a better land lawyer in south Georgia."

Mrs. Hightower seemed to take so much interest in these details that Adam began to wonder if she were trying to postpone telling him something else about the deal. "Y-yessum," he said, "hit ought to be worth somethin'."

She went on. "Well, Mr. Lincoln's lawyer made a preliminary examination of our chain of title and was impressed, and Mr. Lincoln said he might be very much interested in that timber and. . .and—" Mrs. Hightower paused and looked about her, as if she had unexpectedly come to the end of her way and was searching for another foothold to leap to. "And he wanted to have it cruised right away and it was he who suggested that we take no action in the other deal until he could consider the Okefenokee property and possibly make me. . . make me"—Mrs. Hightower halted again to look about her—"I suppose you would say an overall offer."

Adam nodded. "Y-yessum, I see," he said, though he didn't see entirely. "And do that have some effect on the clay deposits and the Wyche field?"

Mrs. Hightower, her gaze roving, nodded energetically but mechanically, in what seemed to be an effort to gain time to reflect. She broke forth with the sudden impulse of decision. "Oh, yes, Adam—the Wyche field and the clay. I thought it had been decided that they are on lease lots!" She smiled. "Anyhow, they may drop out as an issue altogether. Just out of it."

"That's fine!" Adam said, without much conviction. There were still red splotches over Mrs. Hightower's cheekbones, as she ceased speaking and still some sort of agitation in her eyes.

She could not quit talking. "Oh yes, and I got around to saying something about our having to have that swamp land line proven by the county surveyor to Mr. Littleton. He didn't say anything, but wasn't pleased."

Adam nodded again, with restraint. "That's fine," he said, turning away. "Well 'um, wuz that all?" He raised his hat toward his head. Then he saw her eyes and abruptly lowered the hat again. They were wide and strained and seemed suddenly frantic. "Wuz they sumpin' else, Mrs. Hightower?" he said with concern. He stared at her in apprehensive wonderment. . . .Then he exclaimed on dim impulse, "Oh yes!" He turned back. "Marse say somethin' 'bout coming out to the Oconee fishin', with Mr. Robert Bruce's youngest brother, when school out."

His words were telepathic. Mrs. Hightower responded in an eagerness that released her eyes from their bafflement to glisten brightly, and loosed her mouth in a tender smile. "Yes," she said, "he and his little friend, Walter Bruce, were planning to come out Monday, I think. . ." Now she paused and looked distractedly at the watch again. Her other hand lifting as if she were intent on the message she sought in its face, she talked on to herself. "Monday. And I don't see . . .I don't see why they shouldn't go on out there. A neighbor, Mrs. Walton, is coming over to stay here in my absence, but the girls could get along without him. . . . Why not out there? It might be better. . ." She came to herself, glancing down at him again now. "That is, of course, Adam, if you can put up with them, if you're not too busy?"

"I sho' ain't too busy," Adam said abruptly. "My corn's been plowed and I still kain't git into the swamp. The Wyche field's still under two foot of water." Again he took his hat between his hands to put it on and moved along beside the milk box in the direction of the gate, but, turning his head, he saw that Mrs. Hightower, gaze afar, watch still in hand, and balancing uncertainly, was not yet willing to quit the porch. He decided to take the time to speak of his own concerns. "M-miz Hightower, anything happen about Malinda yet?"

"Oh yes, Adam! I was coming to that." She lowered her hand. "I wrote Arthur Adair, as I said I would. And I've just gotten a reply. It came this morning, too! I meant to bring it out here with me, but everything was in such a state of confusion. . . ."

Adam interrupted. "That's all right You kin tell me whut he said, kain't ye?"

"Yes, Adam. It's this way." Mrs. Hightower paused for an instant to collect herself to set off on this new train of thought. "He has written a letter to the superintendent of the asylum. I know what Malinda said about him in her letter, but Senator Adair says that under Georgia law there's no way to get her out without the superintendent's consent. He doesn't take any stock in what Malinda says about that. He says that the superintendent will be only too glad to turn her loose, if she's well enough to come out."

Adam glanced at the ground to drop a mouthful of ambeer near his foot. What Mrs. Hightower was saying did not come as news to him. All of it was what he had expected from a public man and a white man. And the *facts* were probably with Senator Adair, the official facts. But he, Adam, was not convinced—not convinced even though he would not dispute these facts. Adam's eyes clouded over, his gaze moved off to the distance. . . .As he looked back, the stammering tic seized both of his cheeks before he even moved his lips to speak, "I—I'd be willin' to try her, out of there!" he finally got out.

Mrs. Hightower nodded sympathetically. "Yes, I know how you feel, Adam. Let me tell you that I impressed it on Arthur that we wanted to get her out. And he said this: he said he would go up there personally, if we wanted him to. He said he would talk to Malinda and the superintendent both!" Mrs. Hightower nodded her head and her voice asked for a sign of his approval. "Now that's something, isn't it, Adam? That's something."

"Ye-yessum, yessum!" Adam responded with more noise than feeling. Suddenly he was oppressed with a dim sense of his having made a deep mistake to bring Mrs. Hightower into his domestic trouble.

She was turning away, back to the hall door, when he saw her shoulders give a convulsive heave and heard her catch her breath. "Marse!" she moaned, with a quivering elongation of the word. And abruptly she was facing him again with pain twisting her face. She spoke out of irrepressible need. "I *don't* know, Adam!. . . I'm so worried about him!. . . I hate to leave here now!" It was a painful, impulsive confession. She strode slowly across the porch, towards the far landing post, gazing at the floor boards. "At the same time I—I feel so unequal to his situation. . .He—he so much needs a father right now—just at his age, eleven years old, going on twelve. I—I don't *know!. . .*"

She had lapsed into silence, still moving slowly over the boards and Adam continued to study her face. He looked away reflectively, then after a moment, he shrugged. His voice limbered and he spoke in a reassuring, gruff, half-amused tone, without stuttering.

"Mrs. Hightower, you wouldn't know, of course, but boys Marse's age—and I kin tell you, color don't make no difference 'tween 'em at 'leven and twelve—I tell yuh, a boy at dat age, he ain't quite a beast and he ain't quite a man. . .Don't take it too serious if'n he acts scandalous! Against Nature, even!"

Their eyes met and were jointed in an intimate recognition. There was no absence of the usual reserve in the glance they exchanged. There was not sexual consciousness in it. Yet there was confidentiality on Adam's part and tender appreciation in Lucy Hightower's moist gaze. In a common human communion, they confronted elemental human experience.

She nodded. "Yes?" she said.

Adam went on. “They can do things, make you wonder what it is you done brought into this world!” He shook his head, with a brief grim smile on his face.

And she responded wryly, saying again, “Yes?”

He resumed. “But if'n they don’t go crazy or kill somebody, if'n they git a chance to come along like they oughter, along with right thinkin’ people, they’ll grow out of that kind of thing.”

Mrs. Hightower stared, first shaking her head slowly, then slowly nodding it—nodding her understanding. “Yes,” she said. “Adam, I believe you—believe you know!. . .”

Abruptly she lowered her gaze and resumed her slow stride back and forth. She walked the length of the milk box and, on her return, half-pausing at the spigot, cut down the stream of water. Then she resumed her position on the landing, at the middle of the steps and drew herself up collectedly. Her eyes were wide and dark and glistening with excitement, and she breathed audibly and her lip trembled when she went to speak. But there was a calm on her face. “Adam, why couldn’t I leave Marse out there on the homeplace with you, ‘til I get back?” Adam ducked and glanced away. Her voice pursued him with inflection. “It will be no more than a week. The little Bruce boy will be with him. They can camp in your yard at night.”

Adam shrugged. “Sho’!” he responded, not looking at her. . . . “They can sleep in the old wine house—hit’ll keep ‘em dry.”

She lowered her gaze, too, and said distantly, “And if you think anything should be said, maybe you could talk to him, Adam?”

“Sho’!” Adam said again and nodded stiffly, without lifting his glance. . .He moved off toward the gate, still holding his hat in his hand, still staring at the ground with a troubled, uneasy gaze. Suddenly the white smell was at him again, anathema in his nostrils.

14.

THEY WERE FISHING in Murdock's millpond, a wide, creek-fed oval of clear water that grew reddish brown in its depths. Adam stood in the sun on the earthen dam, near the spillway, with a short line on his pole, trying to snag a pike. His two white charges were with Bo, in the shade of the sweetgum trees that rimmed the sides of the pond. Marse and Walter Bruce sat in comfort on the slant, root-clutched bank with their poles stuck in the ground at their feet, watching the corks on their fishing lines, floating on the placid surface. Beyond the spillway, on the far side, at the foot of a big tupelo tree that overspread the water, sat Adam's mother.

She wore an apron of blue checked calico and, of the same material, a shovel bonnet, out of which came smoke from a clay pipe. Her knotty black hands worked with the mixture of corn meal mush and lint cotton in her lap, making balls of it to put on her hook. She was fishing for carp. Between Bo and Marse stood a bucket of minnows and between Marse and "Little Walter," as Mrs. Hightower called him—he was as big as Marse but three years younger—sat a can of wiggle-tails and a perforated box filled with grasshoppers, crickets, and catalpa worms. And on a tree root over the water alertly squatted Bo's pet coon. The boys were fishing for anything that would bite.

Adam kept the scene in the corner of his eye. In the corner of his consciousness trouble clouds kept him company. But above him was a cloudless June sky and about him, the bursting summer. Cattails, with their sharp, green, sword-like leaves thrust at his feet along the edge of the dam. And mixed with their velvety brown clubs were white blooms of arrowhead and the blue of day-flowers. The big bed of Cherokee roses against the millhouse behind him sent him a smell of fresh sweetness. His senses were filled with the immediate pleasure of being.

Bo yelled out. There was a burst of scuffling on the right bank and Marse, teetering on the brink of the pond, brought up his bending pole with such commitment that, bursting from the water, the small sailing fish on the end of his line went up into the trees and stuck there. In the hubbub that followed, both Marse and Bo tried to disentangle the line. Then Marse threw off his hat and grappled the trunk of the big gum that held his fish.

"Hold on a minute!" Adam called. He had already laid his pole down on the dam and he hurried along the water's edge to the boys. "We might have to fish for you, and you f-fall out'n that tree!"

Marse continued his scrambling embrace of the tree and moved upward laboriously, but his efforts did not bring him near the bottom limbs. By the time Adam reached him, he was winded and sliding back down.

"Gi' me the pole, Bo!" Adam said, taking it out of his son's hands. He swung the end of it out in the direction whence it had come and examined the tangle of line around the tip of the pole, saying "H-hit pays to take yo' time. G-go easy 'bout it." Gradually he shortened the line until the pole was tight against the tangle, then he used the pole to lift and draw the line from the leafy branches.

Just as he brought down the line, the fish fell free. There was a shout and a scuffle. The three boys slammed into each other, grabbing for the fish.

But the coon, quicker, went in under them. The coon came off with the catch. Back on his tree root he washed his paws and lifted it finically to his mouth. The black bars in his ruff beyond his muzzle looked like an exaggerated smile as he eyed them. Bo tried to console Marse about it. "T'waunt nuthin' but a little ole stump-knocker!" he said.

When Adam got back to his pole, he found Hinshaw Slappy coming across the footbridge from the millhouse. "Are they bitin' any this mornin', Adam?" he called out, in his sad-sounding drawl.

Adam wondered whether Milt Murdock had sent Slappy word he was here. He saw that Hinshaw carried the .22 rifle at his side. "M-mighty little," Adam replied, with a train caller's tonelessness.

Abreast of him now, Slappy smiled dimly, in painful affability. "Ain't this a long way from the Hightower place for you to be fishin'?"

Adam took his remark to be more than casual, detecting an undertone of agitation in Slappy's voice. He picked up his pole. "A-anywhere's a long way for me to go a'fishin'," he said. "But we come out here because of the high water in the swamp." He stood, removing water moss from the bunched fish hooks on the end of his line. "They're not b-bitin' here," he said finally. "I bin tryin' to snag a pike."

Slappy swung the small rifle across his shoulder and looked with vague anxiety out across the pond. His loose features tightened. "Who those white boys ye got with ye?"

"That's young M-marcellus Hightower and Mr. Robert Bruce's littlest brother." Adam lowered his hook into the water, managing to keep the glum, lank figure in view.

His pale pop eyes blinked and his long jaw dropped. "Is that so?" Slappy said. He took a dry tobacco *cud* out of his mouth, as if he were relieving himself of an impediment and cast it aside. "I believe I'll just go down there and speak to Marse a minute. . . ." A moment later, beyond the end of his lowered pole, Adam saw Marse get up, gingerly stepping over his fishing tackle to shake hands with Slappy. And he could hear Hinshaw's pious raised-in-meeting tone of voice. Yet there was harassment in it! Slappy was asking Marse about his aunt's stroke—the one in South Carolina—and when his ma would be back. He hung around, as if he were going to ask him more. Marse's back was turned to Adam, but he could tell by his stance and the stiffness of his neck that he wasn't being very confidential. Hinshaw finally left without even going through the usual rigamarole about his friendship for the Colonel and how much Marse looked like him.

As he approached Adam on the dam, returning, he called out, on a note of vague hostility, "Old woman, how come you to git so far away from home?"

Adam glanced over his shoulder in surprise to see his mother coming toward them on the footbridge across the spillway. The small, upright figure advanced sedately, the boney face lifted in dark solemnity. She did not seem to hear the remark.

Slappy spoke again brusquely, when she was near them. "You gittin' deaf?. . .I said, you a long way from home."

She blinked barely discernible eyes in black caves and cupped a hand to her right ear. "Hunh?" she said.

Passing a hand over his mouth, Adam looked away.

Slappy shouted in irritation, "So, you're gittin' deaf?"

She responded tranquilly. "Carp ain't bitin'. Too much water here, too." She sat down at their feet, in the sun, and threw her hook into the pond.

He stared at her back with bulging eyes. "I didn't know she'd got so deaf!" he muttered; then, staring on, his face grew empty. Abruptly he looked up at Adam his features twisting as if in pain, and beckoned with his head. "Come here a minute, Adam!" he said, moving away toward the footbridge. On the bridge, lowering gray eyelids in a blank face, Slappy abruptly raised a staring interrogative gaze to let Adam have it. "I reckon you know that the Land Deal is blowed up?"

Adam blinked and stiffened. "Blowed up?" He examined Slappy's countenance closely. "N-no. I didn't know hit!"

"Didn't?" Hinshaw exclaimed. After a pause, he went on in an incredulous voice, "I 'lowed you knowed all about hit. Seein' as how you talked to the widow after the word came to us. Whut did ye talk about?"

Adam eyed him steadily for a time. "H-hit don't never pay to jump to no conclusions, Mr. Slappy," he said.

"What did y'all talk about when you went by there last Saturday mornin', then," Hinshaw persisted in a tone of sarcasm. "That's all the rest of us could talk about!"

Adam stood away from the railing, balancing evenly on his feet. "We talked about it some. She told me hit wuz put off 'til she got back." He looked away thoughtfully. "Whut're y'all so r-roused up about? She couldn't put her mind on no land deal, with her onliest sister on her death bed, there in South Ca'lina!"

"Naw! Naw, that won't do!" Hinshaw said in a voice of ridicule. "Banker Littleton done tole us different. Banker say hit wuz already done as good as put off in that secret meetin' the night befo'." He stared at Adam in open suspicion. "She didn't tell you 'bout that?"

"No," Adam said, but he paused to glance down at the swirling water slipping away from its brown depths under the bridge to fall into frothy whiteness beyond. Hinshaw's intelligence did come as a surprise to him: the widow hadn't taken Mr. Littleton into her confidence at all, sure enough! He hadn't realized that she meant quite this. He spoke quietly. "How did banker Littleton tell it?"

"Why tell you?" Hinshaw threw up his head in open indictment. "You know all about it!"

"I don't even know nothin' of the sort, Mr. Slappy," Adam said, in firm patience. "The widow just said it was put off. S-she believes for sho' hit's goin' through, when she gits back here. Mr. Littleton must know somethin' she don't know?"

"No. Banker Littleton said hit look like there might-a bin sometin' going on between her and the Yankees, *he* didn't know about. He said it looked like it, if'n he hadn't a-knowed better!"

Adam eyed Hinshaw intently. "Whut did Mr. Littleton say c-caused the deal to blow up at the night meetin'? W-whut caused it?"

Hinshaw winced and looked away. "I reckon you know that, too," he said after a moment. "You sho' ought to! Hit wuz because of her wantin' to have the surveyor run out that land line, you got her started on!"

Adam spoke impulsively. "Hit couldn't've bin!"

"Yes, hit wuz! Banker Littleton say they were sittin' there in her parlor—Lincoln and his lawyer, Banker and the widow. They were sort of fumblin' around, the lawyer talking' in them legal terms, gittin' ready to git down to brass tacks. When suddenly she come out with hit."

"Come out with whut?"

"Yes. She come out with hit, seemin' to say hit to *him,* Banker said."

Adam gazed into the depths of the pond. "To him! S-sez whut to him? I don't get it!"

"And the Lincoln lawyer sez, 'Well, Mrs. Hightower, that's your own business. If you want to have the county surveyor run out that line on your own responsibility that's all right by my client. But I want you to know that we will not share in the expense of it." Hinshaw raised his voice "Yes, they sho' waun't goin't to pay no part of hit!"

Adam turned back, keen-eyed, to press him further. "And what happened next?"

Hinshaw's face flushed a brownish-yellow and his voice shook. "Well, you damn well know! Don't you?"

Adam shook his head positively, patiently, persistently. "N-no. No, I don't, Mr. Slappy. I don't know."

"This lawyer said then that Mrs. Hightower had better go ahead and git the line run out before they tried to close the deal. That's whut he said!" Hinshaw's face took on an ugly twist. "And I want you to know, you're the cause of this whole thing, Adam!"

Adam's face stiffened. He frowned and the eyes he now lowered to the water wore a troubled look. But finally he shook his head with the detachment of a justice unbeguiled and turned back to Slappy. His mouth was grim, but he said evenly, softly. "Hit's my job to look out for the Widow's property. . .If'n the deal fall through, Hinshaw, you ain't got nobody to bl-blame but yo'self!"

That night it hailed for an hour. The roar of it waked Adam. He built up his fire, put on his clothes and ran through the outlandish storm across the yard to the old wine house. On the backside, where the door was off, the hail was beating in bad. Marse and the little Bruce boy had abandoned their blankets and buried themselves in a pile of cotton seed at the far end of the room.

Adam took them to his house.

Babe and his mother were in by the fire when they got there. He could see that his ma had made up the big double bed with clean sheets and turned the covers back. The women remained awhile to talk about the storm. His mother had seen it snow six inches deep in June once. Then they went back into the room on the other side of the chimney.

The boys sat on, around the hearth, Marse next to Adam and his chum beyond him, looking at the fire and listening to the hail hit the tin roof. The lightwood blaze illuminated the whole room, giving a golden tint to the old newspapers with which the walls and ceilings were papered and silvering his mother's sand figures on the floor, polishing the varnished beds and the bureau and making luminous the waxen flowers under glass on the taboret. From an easel between the beds, the glow was reflected by the glass in the large, white-framed, photographic enlargement of Malinda and Adam, at the time of their marriage.

Marse, who was more familiar with his surroundings, only took a sidelong glance now and then at the room's strange litter. But Walter, his jaunty nose uplifted, gazed about him in unselfconscious curiosity. The two small boys, in the duck-legged chairs, below the high dim mantelpiece, their bright hair, freckled faces and blue eyes transfigured by the firelight, constituted a curiously burdensome angelic visitation for Adam. He had never before given roof for the night to a Hightower. It was an honor. But he had not bargained for so much when he took on for a week Marse's guardianship. Adam frowned. For it was, also, an intrusion.

Marse cut his eyes, a little uncomfortably, at the white sheets of the turned down cover on the bed behind him. And Adam, seeing it, got to his feet. He took his pipe off the mantel and turned back to look down at the boys, his mouth limbering. "That ole wine house got pretty cold, hey?"

Marse nodded.

Gathering loose tobacco from an old cigar box, he began to fill his pipe. "C-cotton seed make cold cover?"

"I like it better here," Marse said.

"Does that phonograph play?" Walter asked, pointing at a varnished mahogany box with a large morning-glory horn about it, in the far corner of the room. He turned solemn, still chubby cheeks toward Adam.

"H-hit ain't made music in many a year," Adam said, bending down to get a blazing splinter.

Relaxed by the fire, Marse leaned back in his chair. As he gazed into the flames, his nostrils spread meditatively. "I didn't know Babe was married, Adam," he said at length. "Where's her husband?"

Automatically Adam caught his breath and pulled hard on his pipe. His face became the mask of a deaf man and he sat down.

Marse looked over at him uncertainly and said, "I just hadn't seen 'im anywhere?" Walter was interested, too.

Adam tossed his head and took out his pipe. He turned a gruff face to them. But his liquid eyes shimmered in an ambiguous smile. "He around," he said.

Marse's small deep-set eyes fixed Adam with a naked interrogative stare, then turned quickly away. His thin skin, transparently white under his freckles, began to color faintly in embarrassment. "Oh!" he said under his breath.

Walter leaned forward, lifting his nose. "Look, look!" he said, "Adam is pulling our leg. I'll bet Babe hasn't got any husband!"

Marse thrust out a hand to stop him, but he ignored it. He comically pursed his lips and puffed his cheeks, and said to taunt, "I'll bet Adam couldn't get her a husband!"

Adam stared into the blaze grimly for a moment, then turned a wry face to the boys. (Walter now sensed that his humor was misplaced and his puffed cheeks grew red.)

"Sometimes girls does have babies, without husbands," he began matter-of-factly. "S-specially with colored folks."

He pulled on his pipe, turning back to the fire. "Maybe Babe *ain't* got no husband she kin lay c-claim to. . . .Maybe I ain't took time to git her fixed up right." He glanced back at them distantly, speculatively. "Maybe I ain't h-had time—or mind for it. . . .But it ain't the worst thing kin happen to a"—he gave ambiguous emphasis to the words —'she critter'!"

He turned and addressed his remarks to Marse. "Maybe I bin too busy worryin' 'bout my livestock, here and whut's gone to Riverton, too." He said with loaded emphasis, pausing to add in a way that asked for an answer, "not enough time to look after 'em."

Marse's gaze shifted to the fire prepensely, self-consciously. But before he could speak or give clear evidence that he apprehended Adam's meaning, Walter had filled in the breach. "What's been after your livestock?" he said with interest.

Adam waited for Marse to look up at him, then he fixed him with a dim, grim, glint of a smile. "Little boys have been after my livestock," he said. "They bin abusin' my heifers!"

"You don't' say!" Walter returned unsuspiciously. "What they do to them?"

" 'Bused 'em!" Adam repeated with a communicative glance. "Got where nobody kin hardly git nigh 'em for the kind of business people supposed to have with livestock."

Marse grinned hard, taking it for a rough joke, yet his face reddened guiltily. He said, "Aw, go on!"

But Walter had more curiosity. "What did you do to those boys?" he asked unselfconsciously.

"Had 'em arrested," Adam said ominously.

Looking away, Marse blurted out, "Aw hell!"

"I didn't know you could have anybody arrested for that?" said Walter.

Adam waited until Marse looked up. He said solemnly, "It's ag'in the law of God and man."

Fright rose in Marse's eyes and they shifted quickly back to the hearth, as his broad face swelled in redness.

Adam did not look at him, but after a pause he murmured on in a mellow, detached voice. "Yeah, some boys may think a cow you milk, hit don't make much difference. . .just a cow-lot trick to take the pressure off yo' pecker. . . .You'd better-a grab an ax handle or plow handles and work hit off!. . .They's mens in the penitentiary serving ten years on the rock pile for that. And they ain't black nuther!"

Marse gave him a brief, appalled glance.

When the boys, in their shirt-waits and drawers, in Adam's double bed, were sound asleep, his old mother flickered noiselessly into the room and onto a low stool beside him. Marse had been shy about sleeping in Adam's bed, at first. He had insisted that he and Walter could just roll up in their blankets—which they had brought along, wrapping themselves in them to run through the storm—and lie before the fire. They didn't want to rob Adam of his bed, he said politely. Adam had assured him that he didn't ordinarily sleep in the double bed, anyhow, but in the other single bed that was also in the room. If they didn't mind sharing the room with him, he would keep the single bed and let them have the big bed. By that time Marse, obviously, had adjusted himself to the idea. Both boys were asleep within three minutes after they slid between the sheets.

For a long time Adam and his mother sat in silence, each staring at the crumbling lightwood and oak reflectively. Finally she spat into the coals and murmured in low gutturals. "Hit needn't to-a-happen to ye, and you had any respectability about you!"

Adam glanced toward his mother, eyeing her for a moment, then spoke gruffly. "I waun't just talkin'. I'd promised his ma I'd say somethin' to 'im, if'n I got a chance."

She shook a head of gray splayed pigtails. "Hit wuz a mean chance, and you a'makin' hit!"

Adam knocked out his pipe on a brick on the hearth. There was a note of impatience in his voice when he spoke. "Look, Ma, I know whut's on you' mind. You want to git at me to marry Babe. But I'm already married by law. I kain't marry Babe!"

The old woman snorted. "*Married!*" She took up a short, burned broom-handle poker and jabbed at the gray crust and red coals. "Out'n her head and in the 'sylum six year. And bin there befo'! Whut sort of wife that?" She turned on her stool to look up at him. "And whut sort of married is you? Hit ain't no real marriage!"

Adam shrugged and straightened up, glancing downward in her direction, in assumed astonishment. His face was wooden, except for the tenderness in his eyes. "How you know so much about marryin', Lectra?" he said, calling his mother by the strange name her mistress had baptized her with, back in slavery times. "You never did try hit none!"

She drew up on her dignity, like an aged sable pigeon, a hand on the poker, before her, as on a staff. But she deigned not to defend herself by word.

Adam shrugged and bent over on his knees. "All right, ma!" he sighed, in laconic apology. He gazed into the red pit of coals beneath the back log. He was not laughing at his mother's early misfortune—to be taken by her white master. He wasn't making small of the old story. How, back there in North Carolina, old Mr. Adam's daughter, Minerva, married a big planter with Lectra as her maid and part of her dowry. How inside of three years that hard man—drinking to fight and abusing everybody dependent on him—made Lectra his open concubine. How Lectra behaved so that when freedom came and she could quit her shame, she went back to the old Atwell plantation and Mr. Adam took them in. . ."B-but just the same, you never did try hit," Adam, at length, repeated.

She shrugged and turned away. Poking at the charred log ends and coals, she spoke to the fire. "Didn't do so bad, without marryin'," she said, "Got you and Deadman, didn't I?"

Suddenly shuddering, Adam said to himself, *You sure hell did!* And he glared at his mother's silhouette before him, hovering over the coals, as small as a child and as black and gray as the burnt back log in the chimney. Yet Adam had to reckon with the fact that he owed a debt to Sinclair Cauldwell, his outrageous father, whom he never saw to know or remember and who would never have admitted that he was his son. . .He sighed. And Lectra had *given* his father something, too—else he wouldn't have kept her as long as he did! He raised up and glanced back at the mops of yellow and red hair on the pillows of his double bed and laughed. It was a short, crusty, baffled chuckle. He wiped a tear out of his eye with the back of his hand and leaned forward again. "I hopin' to bring Malinda back home, well and cured, befo' too long," he said.

His mother sat up, startled. "Bring Malinda back?" she echoed.

"I got Mr. Arthur Adair workin' on it."

There was a silence, while they sat motionless. After a time she lifted a gaunt, distant face, turning her head, as if to catch a sound, the tight pigtails quivering like antennae. Then Adam detected a soft padding of feet on the porch outside their room. He stiffened, too. They both turned toward the door. After a moment Adam heard a muffled knock. It was repeated, harder. Then Adam decided that it came low down, only a couple of feet from the floor. He shrugged and chuckled. "H-hit the coon! Hit Bo's pet coon, done seen the fire through the cracks and want to git in!"

She shook her head slowly. Then looked at Adam and shook it again. He started to get up and she raised a hand to stay him. "Don't let hit in," she said, "hit's too close now!"

Adam stared hard at the face, now mask-like to him and felt the hair stiffen on the back of his neck. "Whut too close, Ma?" he said, "whut too close?"

She picked up the poker and gave her attention to the smouldering back log again, not replying.

He asked once more.

Finally she said, "Son, you needn't worry no mo' 'bout Malinda. She ain't goin' to git well. . . .She comin' here, all right, but 'twon't do us no good—nor harm!"

Adam jerked up from his chair angrily. "Ma, don't gi'me dat kind-a talk! Don't gi'me that!" He moved toward the door. "Here, I'm goin' to let the coon in by the fire to prove you wrong!"

She turned and, in the glow from the hearth, showed the glint of her eyes in their sockets, as she stared at him, but she did not move to arrest him. "I wouldn't," she said in quiet warning, "they won't be no coon there. . . ." She tensed to her listening, then spoke again. "Hit wuz close, close!" she said, "but hit went on by."

"Whut you mean, ma?" Adam asked, irresolutely halting, turning back from the door. "Whut you mean?"

She spoke over her shoulder, facing the fireplace, in a different voice now, a singsong. "Land lines and timber. . .boat in the River. . ."

15.

THE NEXT MORNING Adam put his red mule to the buggy. He was off to Peter Bright's place the first thing after breakfast. He hoped to catch the old man at home, before he started for the field to relieve his son, David, with the plowing, as he sometimes did. It was a long three miles over to Bright's.

Land lines and timber! He had enough on his mind already, without any of the trouble his mother predicted for him for the night before. She had, however, sometimes a way of putting it like she wanted it to be. He hoped this time it was her *druthers* and not the future that wagged her tongue. He couldn't make out what she meant about the lines and the River. But she had been near enough to overhear (pretending she was deaf) some of Slappy's talk with him. She may have thrown in the Land Deal just to give it a twist. If he did bring Malinda home, she would probably go back across the River to Deadman's. Yet she never really had a good word for Babe, either. She was a curious woman!

Adam got down to open his gate and he led his mule through it. He had left Bo with Marse and the little Bruce boy to entertain them.

And he had put Jake in charge, to look after them 'til he could get back. He told Jake not to let them get out of sight.

Adam latched the gate with impatience to be gone. Slappy's news was bad, any way you looked at it! He had better move fast. There were two good reasons for starting with Peter Bright.

Adam found the old man squatting down in the breezeway of his barn mending harness. He rose as Adam approached. The mild, fair, lean face seemed to smile as usual in the adornment of its handlebar mustache. But Adam was sharply aware of the constraint about the thin nostrils. He said, with more formality than he had once been accustomed to use, "I-I hope y'all are all well this mornin', Mr. Peter?"

"All well, thank ye!" Peter said in a crusty voice. In a posture not unlike a question mark, he continued to confront Adam with inquiry on his face.

Adam was disturbed by this coolness and decided to announce the warrant for his visit at once. "That's fine!" he said, going on, without pausing. "You know that note of mine is comin' due the first of July and you sont me word a while back you wanted to see me 'bout it."

Peter blinked and for a moment lowered his gaze reflectively before he could speak. "We didn't git to it that other time. I thought we might talk about it now?" Peter's face was unresponsive, but he continued. "You remember when we made it, you wuz w-willin' to let hit run til the first of the year. But I said I could give ye half of it in July?"

Peter turned away to hang the bridle on the wall. He said over his shoulder in a tepid tone of voice, "We'll talk about it." He began to move away. "Come along to the well. I want a drink of water!"

Adam followed him through the barnlot gate reluctantly. He had wanted to talk about the note *first*. He surveyed the gray, hard-swept backyard before the covered well dubiously. How was he going to reassure old man Peter about the Land Deal, anyhow?

There was water drawn in a cedar bucket, but Peter chose to draw a fresh supply. As the chain ran through his fingers, lowering the bucket down the well, he said, with a slight life in the pitch of his voice, "I hear the widow Hightower's boy is out stayin' at yo' place?"

Adam glanced down the dark barrel of the well to the distant dollar of water. So Slappy had been before him! He shrugged. He studied Bright's pensive downcast profile for an instant, then said circumspectly. "Mr. Marse and Mr. Robert Bruce's little brother, Walter, are out campin' in that old wine house. Doin' some fishin'. . . .I took 'em over to Murdock millpond yest'idy. But there wuz too much water."

Peter rested the dripping bucket on the shelf, saying in deference to manners, "Have a drink, Adam?" but going on, without pausing for a negative response, to take a dipperful himself. "We've got too much of everything in this country," he said, taking up Adam's remark with a will that denoted purpose, "except money!"

Adam acknowledged his wit with a wag of his head.

Peter drank and lowered the dipper, again offering Adam a drink, then he went on. "Yeah! Take corn. I got half of last year's crop in the barn right now and if I wanted to git shut of it, I couldn't give it away. And cotton. I done give that away, of course, to git out of debt to the bank. I don't know why we are plantin' ag'in this year?" He shook his head in token of his puzzlement. "Just for the fun of watchin' it grow, I reckon!"

Adam laughed politely. Seeing the drift, he pulled out a new slab of chewing tobacco and his pocket knife and extended them toward him. "Mr. Peter, you s-sound like a man as needs him a good c-chew of 'bacca," he said heartily to turn the edge of his homily. "Here's a fresh plug of Brown Mule. Cut ye a mouthful!"

For a fraction of a second Peter's blue eyes gleamed, then his face, almost imperceptibly, stiffened and his thin nostrils curved. "Don't believe I care for any just now," he said.

Adam, to carry off the rebuff with a show of manners, said, "Well, if you don't mind, I believe I'll take one?" He cut himself a chew.

"Same way with land—too much of it!" Peter's bugle-tone resumed. "And then when it looked like we're going to git the chance to sell off a little of it for real money that you can bite true metal and ring on the counter, why somebody goes and gits notionate." Peter plopped down, in demonstration of his disgust, on the bench between two of the posts of the well shed.

Setting his teeth in his chew, Adam decided to get the Land Deal out in the open. "Mr. Slappy tells me that banker Littleton thinks the Land Deal is done blown up."

Peter went on as if he did not hear him. "Notionate! First it's *except* this and *except* that. Then when it comes about that there don't need to be any exceptions, why somebody else gits 'er all upset over land lines! In five thousand acres of timber, what difference does it make where one land line runs, more or less?"

Adam repeated, "Mr. Slappy says the banker believes the Deal's off."

Peter looked up sharply. "I heard ye. Slappy *told* me too, *So* did Littleton!"

Adam went on in patient persistence. "If'n hit is, I don't b-believe Mrs. Hightower knows about it."

Peter wiped his mustaches with the back of his hand and staring straight ahead of him at about the level of Adam's overalls' bib pocket, said, "She ain't never knowed what was good for her in this thing!" He thrust out his hand abruptly. "Sit down, Adam. It's cooler under this shed."

Adam took a seat at right angles to him. He said, after the manner of casual inquiry but in a tone that loaded it with meaning, "M-mr. Peter, ain't yo' wife some kin to the Hightowers?"

Peter replied, with an air of judicious admission, "Georgie and Marcellus were third cousins."

Adam's mouth limbered in humor and he spat out into the yard. "Ye still kin, ain't ye?"

Peter swiped at his mustache again. "We ain't no kin to the widow! She don't hardly know we're livin'." He brought a small sandy piece of chewing tobacco out of the bib of his overalls. "She ain't never bin out here to see Georgie—not during the whole time she was married to Marcellus."

Adam said, in an apologetically-lowered-depth of voice, "She's always lived away from here mostly." He had taken a wrong track there!

Peter lifted the tobacco plug to inspect it and bit off a chew with a jerk of his head. "Oh, we've managed to git along without it," he said ironically. "All we interested in is the Land Deal going through."

Adam nodded.

Peter masticated his tobacco for a time then went on. "You keep gittin' her excited about those blamed land lines and it won't go through, howsomever. That Yankee buyer don't give a damn about her clay or the swamp field, either, but he don't intend to have his titles messed up. And, with all of the wild land in south Georgia that's beggin' to be bought, he sho' hell don't have to!"

Adam had been studying his face as he spoke and at the end of it he shrugged and got up from his seat. He walked back and forth before the well shed, gazing at the ground. Finally he came back and sat down on the bench beside Bright, but facing the other way. He spoke with a brief preliminary jerk of his jaw, without stuttering, and with deep assurance in his voice. "She ain't goin' to have that line run out,

Mr. Peter, I can guarantee you that—just between us not to go no further."

Peter moved the pin-point pupils of his incredulous eyes over Adam's face. After a time he said, still unconvinced, but impressed, "Well what's holdin' up the Deal, then? Why did she want to put it off, *indefinitely*—Littleton says, 'indefinitely'."

Adam spoke again with the same assurance under the scrutiny of Bright's gaze, "The widow told me for sho' that the Deal waun't off."

"Then what is she and them Yankees up to? Actin' so mysterious."

Adam let out his breath and turned the chew of tobacco over in his mouth, like a juggler who is balancing a ball on his nose, but he did not shift his gaze. "She ain't told me nothin', not a thing, mind you! But you know the Colonel owned a lot of timber land—a lot of land away from here."

Peter jerked up his head. "Oh the hell you say! I'd never thought of that!" He came to his feet. "She may just sell Lincoln some of that Okefenokee Swamp land and let this whole thing drop!"

Staring, Adam's eyes widened until their whites shone, then he winced and shut them on the scene of his misadventure and shook his head. He came to his feet. Old man Peter was moving away toward the barn and he caught up with him. "M-mr. Peter, you ought not to jump to no conclusions, like that," Adam pleaded. "I don't know a blame thing. Besides it would take a long time—crusin' the timber and clearin' the land titles—to work up a deal on the Okefenokee swamp. And she like the rest of us. She need money now."

Peter paused and looked back, taking a swipe at his mustache. "I reckon that's so," he agreed. "But I wonder why I hadn't thought of that Okefenokee tract before!" He turned back, opening the gate to his barnlot. He went inside and fastened the gate behind him. He started toward the barn, then looked back over his shoulder, calling out apologetically. "Oh yes, Adam. When the Deal fell through, I had to sell that paper of yours to the bank—you know, like I sent you word I might have to? Littleton's got it."

Adam's breath caught in his gullet and made him gag.

On the following afternoon, in the back room of the bank, he stood in front of the director's table, facing Mr. Littleton who sat behind it in a wide arm chair. Adam stood firmly, with his hat in his hand, in noncommittal gravity. He had waited a day to come to the bank to be able to think the thing over and pry around it. The Colonel had believed that such time was well spent. He wanted old man Peter to have time to get there with his story ahead of him, too. "M-mr. Littleton," he said evenly, "Mr. Peter Bright tells me he done sold my mortgage note to the bank."

The big banker nodded stolidly, his double chins like a bellows.

Adam kept his voice steady. "We had an understanding that I was to pay five hundred in July and git it renewed til the first of the year."

Littleton erupted in a mixture of a belch and a snort and, turning his head, dropped a mouthful of tobacco juice in the brass spittoon by his chair. Then his voice rolled out under the weight of his great belly. "What's this yarn you're spreading about Mrs. Hightower dropping the River deal to sell Lincoln her Okefenokee land?"

Adam was rocked on his feet, his cheeks tightening against the bone and his eyes beginning to burn. He had been afraid this was the way it would come out, ever since he got to town and overheard Paley, back of the stores.

"Well?" barked the banker.

Adam limbered his stance. His words came crustily. "I-I heard that too!" he said smiling wryly. "Here in town!"

Littleton blinked, aimed his long nose at him. "What do you mean, you *heard* it?"

Adam's face was still darkly flushed, but he had regained control of himself, his jaw loosening a little and his eyes bland.

"Yessuh! This mornin'. S-standing behind the Ocmulgee River Tradin' C'operation!"

Littleton frowned. "Well, what about it?" he said peremptorily.

"T-there to my left was a-standin' Mr. Milt Murdock, Mr. Hinshaw Slappy, and Mr. Oswald Paley, with his back to me."

His frown deepening, Littleton interrupted, "I said—"

Adam raised his voice. "Well, just a minute! Mr. Paley was sayin', 'She tryin' to work up a deal with 'em on her Okefenokee land. Hit'll leave us—' But just then Mr. Slappy, he seed me and hushed him up."

The banker had waited, pitched forward impatiently, with his mouth half open and his question ready. "What did you tell such a tale for?"

"What Mr. Paley is tellin' for me, I feel pretty bad 'bout it."

Adam gave him an indulgent smile of admission. "H-hit waun't much I said. But when I come to town and h-hear..." His voice sharpened. . . ."In fact, knowin' how Mrs. Hightower feels about Mr. Paley, I feels bad, sho' nuff! I feel like I could kick myself s-slap across the county, knowin' how she regard Mr. Paley!"

"Well you know," Littleton fairly bellowed, "Mrs. Hightower didn't tell you she had up a trade with Mr. Lincoln on her Okefenokee land!"

Adam thought he detected a subterranean note of question in his voice. He smiled wryly. "M-mr. Paley, he don't seem to think so! Whut interest Mr. Paley got in spreadin' that story, you reckon?"

Littleton spat again, frowning, and began tapping on the table with a celluloid ruler, in a show of annoyance. "Well, did you start it?"

In an otherwise grave face Adam's eyes shimmered with amusement. "H-hit would almost seem like I did, Mr. Littleton—to hear 'em tell it!"

"Well?" The banker's mouth now set in a labored display of patience.

“I asked myself that same question.”

Littleton broke in irritably. “This is nothing to get funny about!”

Adam came erect. After a pause, he said quietly. “I couldn’t hardly be more serious, Mr. Littleton, than I am right now”—his voice vibrated with earnestness—“not, if’n I wuz goin’ to be sont to the Mines tomorrow!” The banker seemed mollified. He went on. “I wuz only supposin’ to Mr. Peter, as a might-be-may-be, in strict confidence. He wuz the one jump to the conclusion that she might be workin’ up a substitute trade. That never crossed my mind!” He paused prepensely and caught the banker’s eye. “Did he say anything to ye ‘bout my tellin’ ‘im she waun’t goin’ to git no surveyor?”

Littleton bridled. “Hell, you’re the one who, all the time, has been getting her worked up over those blamed lines!” He leaned forward, his nose censorious. “She had told me that she *was* going to get a surveyor!”

Adam wagged his head, then his face smoothed and rippled in a bland smile that turned sly and then a little awkward, as if he were about to make a confession. “I ask her to do that—a while back.” He laid his hand on the table and leaned forward. “H-hit just happenstance that she got around to sayin’ it the same night!”

The banker rumbled meditatively, looking somewhat appeased. He leaned over and dropped a mouthful of ambeer into the spittoon. “Oh, so you put her up to that as a bluff, hey?”

“That’s right!” Adam said, still smiling and holding to the edge of the table.

Littleton turned his tobacco over in his jaw ruminatively. “Hum,” he murmured. . . . “The same night—” He suddenly frowned and glared at Adam. “What the hell you mean? The same night!” Adam winced and came upright. Still glaring at him, Littleton exploded, “Did she tell you—!” He broke off in a splutter, without finishing his sentence. He had swallowed some of his ambeer, in his outburst and it sent him into a fit of coughing.

But Adam had seen it in his face and he winced again and shook his head with foreboding. He had seen jealously flare up in the banker! Jealousy of the widow's confidence in him!

Littleton's spasm of coughing continued and he got up and went inside the banking room to the water cooler.

Adam stood by the table for a while, drumming on it with his fingers, listening to the banker cough. Finally, shaking his head, he quietly turned around and walked out of the bank.

16.

THE TRAIN, smelling of cinders and coal smoke, its air brakes whistling, moved ponderously into the Charleston station. Lucy Hightower sat poised on her Pullman car seat. Her shoulders were resolutely erect, though she felt very queasy. To add to her general discomfort, she had just realized that she had already given the porter her quarter when he brushed her off. Now she would have nothing to hand him at the step, where she always did this, when she got down.

She dismissed the thought with a frown. Trifles, vanities, and vexations seemed to have usurped her mind, when she should be immersed in distress over her sister, who might never speak or move again and who even now might have passed away! The Pullman itself was an extravagance now for a widow in her reduced circumstances, though she had never made the trip except by Pullman. But after waiting in Jesup for eleven exhausting hours, she felt she couldn't withstand the night ahead of her in the day coach and she had already finished rereading the volume of Dickens she brought with her. Though she had slept but little during the night she knew she looked more presentable.

This reflection caused Lucy's pulse to quicken. She shook her head. Compressing her lips and shutting her eyes, she said, under her breath but fervently, "Oh, God, forgive my vanity and help me hold myself together!" It would be disgraceful of her if she allowed an incidental thing to overshadow the purpose of her journey. If circumstances should permit, it would be justifiable to her to see him, of course. It was a matter of serious consequence that she and Edward try to get re-acquainted with each other, to see—she pinched the end of her finger with the other hand—to see whether this was not just a sentimental notion that would evaporate before the realities.

Yet the yellow telegram she had received aboard the train at Savannah, and now was stored in her pocketbook, remained close to her consciousness. It had given her a feeling of security that she had not had in a long time. It had said merely that he and her niece, Jessica, would be at the train to meet her. Lucy pulled her watch by its black cord out of her belt. She was already four hours late! Her hand shook as she restored the small gold timepiece. She felt disgusted with herself at this evidence of her suspense. But had she not been more than twenty-four hours on the road? She had a right to feel shaky. She could not be far from exhaustion. And beneath her tension, she was so weary!

She looked toward the window and saw reflected in the streaked, tarnished pane, her pale face. But leaning to look in the strip of mirror between the windows, she discovered a touch of pink at her cheekbone and felt a flutter of gratitude to the Almighty for giving her more than she deserved. It must be the excitement. Abruptly, she straightened up, sighing severely.

But at that moment the train came to a final stop and the conductor announced, "All out for Charleston!" With the short veil on her black hat pulled down and her pocketbook clutched between her gloved hands, she moved in the loose queue along the aisle, through the vestibule and onto the steps. She first glimpsed them, a man in a white suit and a woman in a light colored dress gazing up at the doorway, without identifying them. Then recognition came.

Just beyond the footstool, she swept her small niece up in her arms, murmuring "Oh, Jessica, Jessica, Jessica!" And they clung to each other desperately for a tense moment. Then she released her to ask, "How is she, Jessica?" There were tears in their eyes.

Jessica, her face flushed, embarrassed as always by any demonstration of feeling, said with lowered gaze, "I think she is *really* better, Aunt Lucy!"

Lucy considered *herself* undemonstrative. And it was a natural, deeply-felt greeting, yet she could not have denied that, all the while, somewhere in the obscurity of her mind, she was conscious of Edward. Somehow, she was aware of his standing there, a little way behind them, his panama hat in his hand, in polite reticence, yet his liquid brown eyes on them in a graceful sympathy. And this awareness was charged with suspense and a fluttering apprehension for the approaching moment.

Then, there he was, coming toward her, saying, "Lucy! Lucy!" And before she realized it he had kissed her gently on the cheek, then stepped back still holding both her hands.

She scarcely knew what she had expected, but she had been too astonished at this to present a cheek for him. And she was too caught up in the moment to observe Jessica's reaction. As she began to right herself, with Jessica on one side and Edward on the other, hurrying her along the cinder platform and through the waiting room and across the cobblestones to a hack, beside which stood a bowing colored driver—as she began to right herself, she felt the grace and youth of the old city descending upon her and offered up another prayer.

Edward lifted her and Jessica into the back seat and climbed into the front. While they waited for the driver to pick up her suitcase, Edward informed her that the next train to Summerville would not leave for another hour and forty-five minutes, and asked if she and Jessica would not come over to his flat on Rutledge Avenue to rest and have some tea? He was leaning solicitously over the back of his seat, and his deep, almost casual voice held the proper note of concern for her distress.

Lucy smiled wryly. "Do, Edward!" she exclaimed, out of shock. "And that would be across town!" She wet her lips to add lamely, "I can't let you be so extravagant!"

Shaking his head, he assured her that it would take no more than ten or twelve minutes. She must be very tired. There was only the extravagance of his pleasure in taking her. . . .And he promised, "I'll put you on the next train that goes to Summerville, without fail."

Lucy would never have considered such a visit beforehand, but confronted with Edward's warm invitation and getting no help from Jessica it did not now seem so callous toward her gravely ill sister, only ten miles away.

And at that point Jessica added, "Yes, Aunt Lucy, we couldn't get there a minute sooner if we sat in the station. And I know you are worn out and need the rest." She made a droll purse of her lips and smiled sweetly. "I think I would like a cup of tea, too!"

It was already sunset when Lucy finally reached her sister's sick room, in the rambling, porch-surrounded house in Summerville. The hour, the veranda, and an overspreading oak tree, she knew, all contributed their shadows to the scene. Yet Lucy looked shocked by her elder sister's appearance. This unfamiliar pallid visage against the pillow would have seemed the death mask of an old woman, but for the occasional twitching of a corner of her mouth. The iron-gray hair, the closed, deep-set eyes, in the gaunt face, seemed otherwise lifeless.

She was alone with her for Jessica had gone on to the kitchen to see about supper. Sister Prudence was ten years older than Lucy and temperamentally different, and they had never been close. But they had always borne each other a genuine respect and a peculiar sisterly affection. This, in a way, came of the family anxiety over Prudence's mysterious powers.

The now mask-like face, less than two years ago—there, with her in Riverton, at the time of Mr. Hightower's death—had been so alive, so lined with living, with its concern and care, to be sure, but irrevocably committed to life.

That was it, that was it, perhaps! Lucy thought of the afternoon at about this hour, soon after the funeral. Prudence and she were sitting on the side porch behind the trumpet vine, she vaguely talking.

Prudence interrupted her abruptly, asking, "Lucy, who is that coming in the yard?"

They were facing the side lawn that had a gate to the street. And Lucy stared in astonishment, saying, "Why, Prudence, I don't see anybody!"

"Coming up the path? A little girl in white?" she went on.

Lucy's heart had lunged, in alarm at this, for she was familiar with her sister's visions. And at that very moment six-year-old Lucinda was in bed with a fever.

Prudence had grasped Lucy's forearm, saying, "Don't! Don't be disturbed, Lucy!. . .It isn't here, it's back home!" Then she had shaken her head, adding, "I'm so sorry I mentioned it, but I just didn't realize. . . So sorry!"

The child of an intimate friend and neighbor here, in Summerville, had died at the hour of the appearance, to be sure, but the thing was that Prudence had not known it was a phantom! She was always embarrassed by her apparitions. It was that she could not distinguish between objective actuality and her visions, so enthralled by life was she. It was her unselfconscious commitment missing from her face, Lucy decided, that she found so shocking now.

She had a sudden guilty sense of having come too late upon the scene. She thought of their almost frivolous talk over their tea at Edward's flat with a twinge of conscience. . . .Conscience, before the sister of her bosom. . .and a vision of their father, in the family library, coming up off his knees after morning prayers, raising his voice in song, "A charge to keep I have, a God to glorify—" Lucy sighed.

On the bed, her sister stirred, turning her face toward her. Her lips moved, she mumbled, opening her eyes—*She had called Lucy's name!*

"Oh, Prudy! Prudy!" Lucy cried and dropped to her knees by the head of the bed.

Supper that evening was a subdued meal, but not without pleasure for her. Her nephews were at table. Debonair Jack, now grave, was home for the summer from college and Julian, the courtly, who for two years now had been practicing medicine in Charleston, was down to attend his mother, and incidentally, to greet her, Lucy, having been unable to meet the train. She was very fond of both of them. And Julian gave them the encouraging report that his mother was showing unexpected improvement for this stage of recovery.

Lucy, recognized as the most capable nurse in the family, took over at the bedside. She quit the sick room at 11:30 that evening, because of her travel weariness. But the next morning, she was again at her sister's side, where she remained throughout most of the week's daylight hours.

On the second day, late in the afternoon, Edward came by for a cup of tea. He had said, in the hour at his flat, with his good sense of propriety, "I know, Lucy, that you have only one concern now. But I will be visiting in Summerville and when you are adjusted to the situation there, I do hope you will let me see you?"

Jessica insisted on having them served on the porch, while she, Jessica, took over in the sick room. They didn't try to talk much, yet their *tete a tete* was not heavy for their silence. In the gathering twilight they watched, on a large bush by the steps, the milk-white four-o'clocks open, like eyes—like the eyes of an awakening but sympathetic Argus.

By Thursday, Julian was sure that the paralysis was going to be limited to one side of his mother's face and she had recovered some use of one leg and one hand. That afternoon Edward took Lucy for a buggy ride, as far as the tea farm, and urged her to stay on for another week, which she, of course, had no intention of doing! (She learned, after these twenty years and now irrelevant, that he suffered a concussion of the brain, from the blow he got on the night of the earthquake from which he did not recover for more than a month!) On the same day, Lucy received her first letters from Riverton—from Mrs. Dalton, who was staying with her children, and from her elder daughter, Elinor.

She had been procrastinating but decided the next morning that she must arrange for her return, not later than Sunday. Before she could bring the matter up that afternoon at tea, however, Edward and Jessica and finally Jack were all urging, even demanding that she stay another week. Thus far, there had been no sentiment between Edward and herself. He had been simply her life-long friend, deeply sympathetic with her in distress. They had talked about her sister's illness, about their own youth together, about his past academic career, and the married life behind her. He had not broached the subject of their future and there was a formal restraint in their manner. She was not, and she sensed that he was not, yet ready to bring their affair to final issue.

Now that her sister had improved so much and while she was in the neighborhood, it would be unforgiveable of her, he urged, not to take the time to see her old Charleston friends. But there was a great deal more plainly on his face, as he said these things. And he had, when she accompanied him to the steps on his leaving, said, almost desperately, his urbanity vanishing and his face flushing even into the thinning hair above his forehead, “We’ve got to give ourselves a chance, Lucy! A chance!”

When Lucy went to the beach on Sullivan’s Island, on Thursday afternoon, she wore a bathing dress! She had scarcely had one on since she had been married. Lizzie, Lizzie Murchison Worley, her girlhood friend, whom she was visiting, had dared her to wear it. Though Lizzie was always strangely persuasive with her, this alone, of course, would not have accounted for her doing it. The fact that Lizzie, with her generous proportions, did not hesitate to don such scanty attire, herself, had its effect. But what was more important was that when Lucy tried on the suit—a black one trimmed in gold braid with ample bloomers that Lizzie had outgrown—she saw in the mirror that she still had a figure—a figure, not too bad even beside Eunice’s (that of Lizzie’s oldest daughter, whose bathing slippers she was wearing, too), Yet even this could not have accounted for her doing such a thing.

As Lucy stood against the sand dunes, in the afternoon sun before the in-coming tide, still wearing a beach robe—the Worleys (Lizzie, Wentworth, and their four children) already at their beach games, and Edward in the surf—she had a sudden stage fright. What, in the name of conscience and high heaven! had come over her? Edward and Lizzie had carried her in such a whirl! Lizzie began it yesterday with a luncheon, two of her Morrow cousins and three of their old Meminger classmates at her house in Charleston. Then she and Edward had toured the town: the old museum (where he showed her some of the handiwork of her Morrow silversmith ancestors), visits to the old Circular Congregational Church, where a Methodist preacher-uncle of hers had filled the pulpit in supererogation and out of a scarcity of preachers just after the Civil War, and to old Trinity and Bethel Methodist churches, to the old Morrow house on Wentworth and into the side garden, of course! Then they watched the Citadel cadets parading on the green, and strolled on the Battery, and on to a fine seafood restaurant, and finally to a piano concert at the old Academy of Music. A Cook's tour, but with its peculiar necromancy—its way through the Looking Glass! And now, the beach party.

She looked up to see Edward running up the beach toward her and she stiffened against his approach. As he kept on coming, growing larger, she noticed fleetingly that his legs were thinner than she remembered. Then his sun-tanned dripping face came giant-like upon her, as he shouted: "A regular spring tide running, Lucy! A high rider! Come on! Man the boards!"

She gasped and her eyes were suddenly wide and an indigo blue, a girl's eyes. She threw the beach robe off her shoulders, letting it fall from the bathing dress. And, she stepped through the looking glass again. "Man the boards!" she cried and ran down the strand behind him. . . .

After supper at the Worley's cottage that evening, she agreed to go with Edward down to the beach again to see the moon rise over the water. It was first dark when they arrived. The moon was not as yet in evidence, and the dim strand was deserted. The breeze was still balmy and smelled of salt-spines and seaweed and distance. Edward took Lucy's hand and began to sing in a low baritone, "Just a song at twilight, when the lights are low." Lucy joined in. . . .

But as she sang, she was distracted by vague misgivings. In the gray darkness, she began to feel middle-aged again, in reaction from her brief burst of youth of the afternoon, when she had forgotten herself in the surf. And Edward was middle-aged, too!

They were now walking along the water's edge. And the dim slate surface of the sea had for her the look of the illustrations in her grandmother's volume of *Pilgrim's Progress*. Maybe, in a way, Edward *wasn't* middle-aged? He was still holding onto an expectation of youth's culminating experience, maybe!. . . And was she up to it? It was a grand and glowing thing for a woman to know that a man has loved her, has been devoted to her for twenty years! A man that she had loved—*does* love, Lucy corrected herself, frowning in the dark.

Edward said, "I don't hear you singing!"

She squeezed his hand. "All right. Something a little gayer in the dark, please!" And, after a moment, she added, "What about, 'Row, Row, Row'?" His hand was soft and strong. Suddenly, there was the wavering light of a distant boat, invisible in the darkness, to give point to their singing. She joined in with a will.

As they sang, seeing a hint of the moon's approach in faint light beyond the round horizon, she felt suspense and a glowing came on inside her. *But haven't I had love?* (She was aware somehow of Marcellus' compact, white, blue-veined hand.) *Haven't I loved already?* she asked, staring urgently at the skyline's prophesy. *Could there be something else?* Her faith was weak.

They walked along in silence a little way, resting from the exertions of their last song, both held by the dim, moving, immensity of the sea. He said, "Lucy, your fingers are cold!"

And after a pause, she summoned the bravado to reply, "A cold hand's said to be a good sign, isn't it?"

For answer, he laughed and broke into song again, a very old sentimental one of their childhood and she joined in with him. The edge of the moon was now above the water! They were far down a bare strand, far from the beach cottages. But this didn't seem important, as, singing, they moved toward the moon.

Suddenly, it was all before them—a shining mirror of the sea, as round and immaculate as love itself. It caught the song in their throats, burnishing the ocean with a stairway of silver from the horizon directly, it seemed, to the sand spit on which they stood.

She said, in a discordant voice, "This is too much!"

He put a hand over her mouth gently. And an arm around her waist. "It's time to forget everything else, Lucy!"

And, incredibly, as they stood there, staring into each other's faces, in that light, she began to forget. . .forget. Yet before all mind left her, she stiffened against her floating on and said hoarsely, "But we can't take this along with us, Edward!"

He shook her by the shoulders. "But we have, Lucy, we have!" he said, adding fiercely, "for thirty years we have!"

This emptied her mind of any further resistance to his faith.

The next morning, in Charleston, in the somber railroad waiting room, Lucy got her feet on the ground again. "I couldn't remember this last night," she said to Edward, beside her, smiling a little wryly as she sat erect, at the end of the dark rows of seats. "I—well, Edward, I don't want to lay the blame on you. But I had a desperate sense of needing to remember when I couldn't!"

"I'll accept the blame!" Edward said. His jaw loosened and his lips pursed and he made a vague incipient gesture, as if he were going to take her in his arms.

Lucy shook her head, as if against dizziness. "Please don't, Edward!" she said in a low granular voice. She touched his fingers in her gloved hand to soften the severity of her manner. "Now, let me see, where I was. . ." She focused on the clear sharp doorway. "Oh, merciful saints, yes! Here. I let you run on on the ferryboat, this morning, coming over from the Island, because—well, because, I hadn't quite steeled myself to it then. And maybe, because I wanted you a little longer by myself, alone—pretending that!" She drew in her breath and considered for a moment. "A woman," she said, a little sententiously, "is like a secret. Once it has been shared and its contents committed to others, whatever happens, it can never come to you the same secret again, solely your own, unattached."

Eyeing her from a clear, expectant face, Edward smiled lightly. "Your children?" He shrugged this off. "Well, of course! I have considered your children, all along, Lucy! Don't be absurd. From the very first. I wrote you so."

She shook her head again. "Ah, yes, Edward! But you have never had children—not of your own. You don't know, you *can't,* what the involvement is! You simply don't know what you are talking about!"

He said, with detached assurance, glancing over her shoulder, "Remember I am the principal of a high school. And I'm not entirely without imagination."

She caught the frown gathering at her brows, pretending to search for something in her pocketbook, until he had finished. "Oh, I know, I know, Edward!" she said, giving him her attention again. "If you weren't the most intelligent man I know, did not know me so well, weren't—if there were any less love between us, I wouldn't for a moment—"

He interrupted positively, "Listen, Lucy! It's been done before! And with a high degree of success!"

With her off hand she readjusted the position of the scuffed, tan leather bag on the floor beside her, beyond the end of the bench. "I wonder. And besides, *you!* Edward, how can I pretend to love you as much as I do and do *this* to you!" She lifted a hand to forestall his interruption. "No, no! I'm not being sentimental! You can't know what you are about to get yourself into! Can't!"

Edward gripped the arms of his seat, frowning. "Lucy, I'm used to children! You haven't forgotten there were seven in my family, four of them younger than I am."

Meeting his annoyed, open gaze, Lucy stared for a moment with her eyes widening, then abruptly pulled down her veil against their burning, to hide the tears. "If you didn't *love* me as much as you do, it would be a lot simpler," she concluded.

A sympathetic gloom overspread his sensitive face. He lowered his gaze and said grimly, "It isn't *love,* if it can't endure!"

She sighed. "But, Edward, you can't just marry *me*. You've got to marry my three children, as well! You've got to love them, too, to make any sort of a job of it—another man's children!" She put her hands on the arched metal arms and came to her feet, and he rose with her. "And the chances are," she continued, "at my age that we won't have any children of our own!"

He took her hand, and brought it under his arm and led her through swinging doors and onto the deserted platform beside the tracks. They walked a little way. Then suddenly he swung her into his grasp, crushing her against him, and kissed her with a paralyzing fierceness.

When she had righted herself on her feet, they walked on in silence. She leaned on his arm heavily, unable to do more than breathe for a time. Her feelings were a confusion, but when they finally settled down into some order, she could not find anything further to say. When they turned about to walk back, she raised her voice plaintively, with a feeble try at facetiousness. "One reason I'm marrying you, Edward, I might let you know, is to get Marse a father. I want to resign the job!"

She added, more ominously than she meant, "It won't be easy!"

17.

ON MONDAY AFTERNOON, Lucy opened the door and led the way into her own parlor, followed by Elinor and Lucinda Morrow. She moved across the room to raise the shade a little against the room's too dim sanctity. She allowed the cream-colored blind to roll up far enough to conceal partly its elaborate, embossed, silver and gold design of flowers. The girls had followed her in curiously, gingerly, and a little reluctantly. They stood, Elinor with an arm about Row's shoulders, on the angora goatskin rug at the entrance.

"Close the door and come over here!" Lucy said self-consciously, halting before the sofa. She had taken off her apron, as she came up the hall, and under it she held Edward's photograph. She had been back from Charleston for two days, and she had not been able to say a word to her children about Edward. It was almost as if it were a clandestine affair! She had to tell somebody!

The day before she had almost told Marse, then didn't. He had picked up out of her suitcase the envelope with the photographs of her nephews and niece and the one of Edward, crying out, "Is this something else for me, Mamma?" She allowed him to look at them and when he came to Edward's likeness, she had said, "You have heard me speak of Mr. Edward Louthan?"

"What kin is he, Mamma?" he asked.

She felt for a moment tongue-tied and said, when she did gain speech, perhaps with more feeling than she intended, "He's a very fine man. I've known him since we were children together in Charleston."

He had given her a surprised, curious look. And, with a little "Oh!" laid the photograph down and went on to something else. It did not seem to be the right moment! So Lucy had decided to begin with her daughters, in the privacy of the parlor.

"Sit down by *me!*" she said, in invitation, to Elinor, laying a cushion against the trim walnut arm of the sofa. Row took a stool at her feet. She cleared her throat and took Row's hand. Trying to speak in a noncommittal voice, she said, "How would you all like to live in Charleston?"

It sounded more mysterious than she intended. There was a pause, while both girls gazed at her uncertainly. She smiled to reassure them. And Row's little, lean freckled face crinkled into a nervous laugh. "In Charleston?" she exclaimed, emphasizing the first syllable comically. Jerking her hand loose, she cried challengingly. "Can I take Jessie Tucker with me?"

Lucy caught herself frowning and forced a tight-lipped smile. She shook her head patiently. "No, Row! This is not make-believe. This is real. Really and truly."

"Mamma!" Elinor put a hand on her knee. She spoke, conscious of the full maturity of her thirteen years. "You've talked about our going to school there. Is that what you mean?"

"Yes, and more," Lucy answered, looking toward her, still astonished at the difficulty she was having. "We might go there to live!"

Elinor lifted her nose to think. "It sounds grand," she said, more in wonder than enthusiasm. . . ."Will it depend on the Land Deal?"

This comment took Lucy by surprise and she lifted her eyebrows, considering it before she replied. "In a way, yes," she said. "But not altogether. There is something else." As she gazed away her eyes darkened with a look of mystery. "Something that deeply concerns Mamma and means a lot to her. Something that," she paused to choose her words, "that she hopes you all will want to join with her in"—she hesitated again—"well, in sharing." She went on more hurriedly, feeling somehow threatened by their mystified faces. "This would mean a big change for us all. But Mamma would not then be so alone in the world. She would have somebody to help her look after you all, somebody to protect her against land sharks and shysters. Like—like those lawyers, who rooked me out of your father's title records. . ." Beside her, the gray-green eyes, with their pupils as shining and slit-like as a cat's, before her the wide, questioning, almost blank blue ones, began to be unnerving. She said with a summary lift of voice, "And we would *all* have a protector!" She paused and began trying to extricate the picture from its wrappings.

"Yes, mamma," they both said.

Taking a deep breath, she unveiled the cabinet-size photograph, holding it up between her hands, the apron falling to the floor. "You all have heard me speak of Mr. Edward Louthan, my old friend?"

They looked at it judiciously.

"We have seen that before, Mamma," Row said, pointing at it. "What are you going to do with it?" Suddenly her face took on a glib, childish cunning and she cocked her head. "Are you going to marry him, Mamma?"

Elinor sat up, glaring at Row indignantly, crying, "Why, Row!"

Lucy lifted Elinor's hand from her knee and held it between hers. "Elinor, Elinor!" she remonstrated gently. "Row happens to be *right!*" She turned to Elinor, smiling. But behind her smile, the pupils of her eyes were big and staring with anxiety. "That is just what I do want to talk to you about. And I do so much hope you all will approve." Her voice growing more intense, she went on. "Edward is such a grand person! Such a fine man! So brilliant! Such a wonderful school principal. And has been devoted to Mamma for so many, many years. We were sweethearts a long time ago before you were born."

Row's upturned face had been growing graver and graver, as she listened. A frightened embarrassment caught her like a blow. "But what will Papa say?" she asked, with bated breath—knowing that God had taken her father away and he would not return, but that he looked down on them from Heaven.

For an instant Lucy's face seemed sympathetically to reflect Row's agitation, then she lifted her chin, her mouth sobering, and straightened her shoulder a little. "I'm glad you asked that, Row!" she said with too much insistence. "I think you all should know that your father very much wanted me to marry again when he died." This was the interpretation she was placing on Marcellus' having said, talking about property matters in his last troubled hours, "Lucy, I do hope you will find somebody to teach you to take care of these things better than I have." Yet she was sincere.

Row squirmed about on her stool, lifting clownishly a lock of her tow hair on top of her head. She had done so famously with her questions, she was inspired to go on, tilting her face again to ask, "Does he have lots of money, Mamma?"

Lucy accepted her inquisition graciously. "He does much better," she said, with a glowing firmness. "He has brains. And he is a very fine person along with it. And his position is an important one and pays him well. But we won't be penniless ourselves, Row!" she went on with assurance, "if Mamma sells the Oconee swamp. And maybe the Okefenokee swamp, too!"

Row nodded excitedly. But Elinor, Lucy observed, had remained distant throughout this with little to indicate her approval. She turned to her now, going on, if a little histrionically with a conviction that gave her persuasive grace. "Your mother's life, Elinor, had been shipwrecked by your father's death. She was left alone in the world with three small children and no experience in looking after things. Then the boy whom, a long time ago, she had grown up with in Charleston, who had professed his love for her in those early youthful days, before it was time to get married—this boy comes forward, now a man older than your mother. She had not thought of him since she met your father. But, he reveals to her that he has remained in love with her *all of these years. . .*" Lucy paused to catch her breath and to allow this testament to romance to take effect.

Elinor's already-shining eyes widened and a golden glow came over her usually sallow face. "How wonderful for you, Mamma! I never heard of anything so wonderful!" She turned to include Row. "Wonderful for all of us!"

Row clapped her hands. "Oh, Mamma, can I tell Marse?"

Lucy's face paled and, automatically, she clasped the photograph to her. . . "No. No, you may not!" she said crisply.

On the next afternoon, at the back steps, Mrs. Hightower was still the returned traveler, in her new white shirt-waist and skirt and shoes, handing Adam, who, with a foot planted midway, reached to receive them, the things she had brought back from Charleston. "Here's horehound candy for Babe and the boys," she said, "and a picture of Charleston harbor for your mother to hang on the wall and some tobacco for you—something special called perique that they smoke down on the coast. I thought you might like to try it."

Adam pushed himself back into a standing position with the paper bag in his hands, saying, "Ooee! S-so many things! That's mighty nice, mighty nice, mighty nice!"

She straightened up, smiling on him, a little color in her cheeks. "I guess you thought I wasn't coming back, at all?"

"Well'um, no'im." He looked down into the bag. "H-hit was a right good stay, though! Howed you leave yo' sister in South Calina?"

The glow remaining on her face, Mrs. Hightower replied, "She was much improved. And she recovered so rapidly after I got there that I really stayed on the second week almost as much to see some of my old friends and get about a little as to nurse her!" She added as an afterthought and a little as if it were a threat, "I liked not to have come back, you know?"

Adam, who had seemed a little preoccupied as she talked on, broke into a smile. "Sho, glad you got a nice trip out'n it, too!" Looking into the bag in his hand, he fished out the package of tobacco and smelled of it.

She eyed him, with a glint in her eyes, her brows twitching. "But I'm serious about it, Adam!" She paused while he finished sniffing the perique. "I'm thinking about pulling up stakes and leaving this country."

Adam smiled affably. "I knows how you feel! Charleston a fine city, I hear."

Mrs. Hightower bridled at this, half annoyed, but broke into a smile again. "No, really, Adam!" She paused to sober before going on. "While I'm at it, I think I'll just sell out, lock, stock, and barrel, and move back to Charleston!"

Adam's eyes twinkled and his lips loosened. He said indulgently, "S-sho wouldn't blame you!" He shook his head. "Hit's a mean ole land, to live *with* it. And the folks you have to deal with, such sorry folks! And all the trouble we havin' over this land deal on top of it. Hit's a rough world 'round this here place!"

Mrs. Hightower's mouth was firm. If he wanted to doubt her intention, she would give him the details. "When Mr. Lincoln comes back with his offer on the Okefenokee property," she said precisely, "I intend to get him to make me an overall price, including the homeplace and all. That should give us enough to live on in Charleston."

Adam nodded in ready agreement. "'Nuff to live on anywheres!" he said.

"I mean it, Adam!" she added, in irritation.

Adam laughed gleefully. "Couldn't blame you! Couldn't blame you! Just sell and git shut of it," he cried gustily. Sobering a little, he recalled, "Of course there's still trouble in the Land Deal, looks like." He shook his head. "Trouble. Then I reckon h-hit's the same ole world over there, at last, that we got here, ain't it?"

Mrs. Hightower's eyes were widening in astonishment and her brows, working nervously. Couldn't he understand? Could Adam be deliberately putting her off? "Well, you'll see!" she said grimly. "I'm just waiting on Mr. Lincoln's report. I'm going to sell out!"

Adam's laugh was wry. "Well'um, that's fine," he said, with no more belief in her threat than before, but in the sobering tone of one who wants to restrain an excited person. "H-hit looks like right now they goin' to sell *me* out!"

Mrs. Hightower gazed at him for a moment to see if he could be more serious. "Sell you out? What do you mean? Who?"

Adam's preoccupation had returned. After a pause, he nodded. "You know that little piece of ground I bought from the Brights? . . .The b-bank's 'bout to foreclose on it."

"The bank! What on earth have they got to do with it?"

Adam hesitated to consider and sighing, as if he saw no alternative, said glumly, "M-mr. Peter sold 'em my mortgage. Said he had to have his money, because of the land deal blowin' up—some of 'em claimin', since the Yankees left that hit's blowed up."

Mrs. Hightower drew in her lips, smiling slightly, in incomprehension. "Well, we know better than that, Adam!"

Nodding, Adam said ruefully, "Yessum. Look like I done knowed too much."

"How's that?"

"Well I should've kept my mouth shut when I didn't!" He shook his head. "And then goin' on to violate yo' confidence, too!"

"My confidence?"

"Brights and some more of 'em here think I knows more 'bout the Land Deal than I do." He went on, close-lipped, to detail his futile morning's effort to convince old man Peter otherwise, concluding, "But he jump too far—he said 'So she goin' to sell 'em that timber down there in the Okefenokee and just drop our deal, hanh?' And there waun't no way I could make him believe any different. . . .He told me then, that he done sold the mortgage to the bank."

Her shock over Adam's story left Mrs. Hightower staring. "Why Adam, you had the money to pay off half of that note, I thought?"

"Yessum. But he say he have to have it all."

She still stared. "But, if you pay half the bank will certainly renew it."

Adam lowered his gaze. "Mr. Littleton say, Nothin' on paper 'bout renewin'—say, Bank has to have full payment on the first."

Red flared in her cheeks. "What is this, Adam? I don't understand what's going on here? How does the land deal get into *your* business?"

"C-curious, ain't it?" Adam agreed wryly, guardedly. "But Mr. Lincoln went back up No'th and they think he's gone for good." He added, glancing at her dimly in passing, "Mr. Littleton, he don't know any different, nuther." He pulled meditatively at his mouth, chewing the ends of his mustache for a moment then said diffidently, "All of 'em thinks I had a hand in it."

Mrs. Hightower's eyes blazed. "Why, Adam, this is blackmail! Or something of the sort! Why!" She strode jerkily across the entrance and back again. "Why, they are not going to do such a thing to you! I certainly won't let the bank do us this way! I'll see Mr. Littleton today—I'll call him *now* before the bank closes." She added, in scorching irony, "Why, why, this *is* a fine come-off!"

Adam's face drew up ruefully. "I—I hates to git you into it, but look like—"

"Into it? Why, what about what I've got you into!" She crossed her arms on her chest with a sudden determination. "I'll borrow the five hundred for you, if I have to. But Mr. Lincoln is due back here now. We ought to be able to bring the deal to a head in a few days."

Adam wagged his head thankfully. "Sho' glad to hear that!"

But Mrs. Hightower's eyes were still hot with indignation. "I am really amazed at Mr. Littleton—and he is supposed to be my friend and adviser! And Peter Bright, too! It's low down of him!" She started her striding again. "All of them, all of them. Out to do you in, because you are colored and me in, because I'm a woman and a widow. . . . It's outrageous!" She turned back to the steps and, under the impulse of her indignation, to her original purpose. "Adam, I'm going to get out of this place. I'm going to get out and I mean it! I'm going to sell out everything I've got and go. I won't live here among them!"

Adam shrugged. "Hit do try you!" he agreed grimly. "I sho' couldn't blame you—couldn't blame you a bit!" He lifted a drawn face that worked convulsively. "Hit's m-more'n a widow like you ought to have to put up with! Hit sho' is! And I feels real bad 'bout bringing hit on you. But look like the bank was goin' to sell me out and take my land, after I done got hit more'n half paid for."

Mrs. Hightower's face was sympathetic. "Why the idea, Adam! It's I that got you into this! The idea!" She drew herself up. "But just the same, I'm not going to put up with it!"

"That's right!" Adam agreed fervently, "that's right—you oughter not put up with it!" He pondered the steps, picking up the bag of presents he had laid on them. "But it won't be *so long* now, Mrs. Hightower." He went on with an air of revelation. "Not so long. Marse, he beginning to grow up."

Mrs. Hightower batted her eyes and said, "Oh" in a low, startled voice.

"Yessum. Me and Marse got pretty well acquainted while you wuz gone." Adam nodded his head measuredly. "He growin' up and he growin' up *all right.*" By the tone of the last two words he conveyed what she wanted to know.

Mrs. Hightower paused, to stare out into the yard, then said finally, "I'm relieved to hear you say that, Adam."

"Yessum. . . He probably not goin' to be as big a man as his pa," Adam continued, conscious of the importance of his responsibilities. "But he goin' to be *like* 'im. Goin' to be like 'im where hit counts." He put a finger to his forehead. "He thinks like the Colonel. And whut he tell you, hits like that—you kin depend on it."

Mrs. Hightower swallowed, her lips loosening, her face gathering in warmth. "I hope you know that nothing could please me more than to hear you say this, Adam!"

Adam raised his voice in attributive astonishment. "H-hit would surprise ye, how much of his pa is in him!"

Mrs. Hightower came nearer the steps.

"Maybe you ain't never heard it, but they say that when the Colonel was a young feller right after the War." Adam set down the paper bag again. "And a dollar was hard to come by for anything. He took to raftin' timber. And he made a name for himself as a rafthand. They said he was great to ride a log—in assemblin' the raft.

"I seen 'im once take a pike pole in his hand and do it just for the fun, down at Bell's ferry."

Adam's voice shifted to the present time. "The Brights bin raftin' some pine timber at Hightower's old ferry, runnin' the logs out'n the swamp—water's still up in the sloughs. And me and Marse happen by there, while they wuz runnin' logs out'n slack water down to the boom.

"Marse, he watched 'em close a good while. Then he say, 'Kain't I try my hand at that?'

"Mr. Dave say, 'Sho!' And he give 'im a pike pole and show him how to handle it to balance on the log. And we stand by with a boat to pull 'im out if'n he slip off.

"But, Marse, he brought his log right on the boom.

"Old man Peter say he rode hit just like his pa use to!"

Mrs. Hightower, grown tense, broke her stance. "Do, Adam!" she said gently. "How could he tell?"

Adam shrugged. He said firmly, soothingly, "H-hit's not goin' to be so mighty long 'fore he'll be able to take over here. Hit'll surprise you one of these days." He picked up the paper bag and tucked it under his arm, adding softly, "He'll git done, at last, whut his pa waun't give the time to do!" He put on his hat and moved off toward the gate.

Mrs. Hightower continued to stand at the steps, staring out into the yard.

18.

"HOW YOU LIKE Hinshaw's new boat?" Kiger Steele asked from the stern of the shallow, narrow, green punt.

Adam, sitting at the opposite end of it, ten feet away, lifted his head casually to inspect the boat and the man in the stern. "Hit's all right!" he said politely. There had been a glint of a gold tooth when Kiger spoke, but his face, with its white freckles and shark's nose, was now bland and secretive. Adam gazed at the willow piles beyond him with a slight frown of impatience, and wondered what Kiger could be up to?

"All *right?*" Kiger echoed, raising his fishing pole to look at the bait on the hook and cast it farther out toward the current of the muddy Oconee. "Hit's better than that, ain't it?"

"I don't like these here shallow punts to fish in," Adam said, "you kain't move around in 'em good." Obviously they weren't here just to try out Slappy's skiff!

Kiger looked up from his floating cork and said heartily, "Sho' saves sweat at the paddle!"

Adam detected a lack of genuineness in his voice. Kiger had sent him word that he had something to tell him, something that he needed to know and that he would come out and go fishing with him. It wasn't the way he would have picked to spend the Fourth of July. And now Kiger was taking his time about getting around to his business! Adam spoke without looking up from his cork. "Bound Hinshaw Slappy would git 'im the easiest-paddlin' boat!"

"Look man, he went to a lot of trouble and expense over this thing!" Kiger said, in protest. "He got old man Green Fork, over in Riverton, to make it! Out of yellow poplar! It's made right! Just draws three inches of water!" His enthusiasm seemed forced to Adam.

Adam had planned to take his boys and Marse and his pal, Walter Bruce, seining, with a fish fry on the bank today. But he had had to call it off for this! He wouldn't be taking up his time with Kiger, if things hadn't come to such a strained, curious pass. The Yankees had never shown up and the Land Deal was still hanging fire. The widow had written to Philadelphia, but she heard nothing from them. The Wyche field had finally got dry enough to plow and he had been planting it to corn and velvet beans—too late for cotton now—and hadn't been off his place for a good while. But he knew by what he heard that everybody around him was upset. He knew, too, that they suspected that he had a hand in the mysterious delay. In the commissary at Adair, he had overheard Mr. Bright (knowing that old man Peter had raised his voice as he passed for just that purpose) saying to Mr. Milt Murdock, "She's a city woman and don't know nothin'—got 'im where he's so biggity, white people can't have dealin's with him!"

Adam glanced over his shoulder at the bow of the punt. "I could tell it wuz one of old man Fork's jobs by that chain and anchor he always puts on a boat."

"You got to chain it to keep it from runnin' out from under you!" Kiger bragged. "Old man Green named it, *The Green Ghost*. You kin see it there on the side of the bow, painted on it!" Kiger raised his paddle to point to the black lettering.

Adam resisted the suggestion of Kiger's gesture with a shrug, grimacing. "Just look's like an extry long c-coffin box to me!" he grumbled in irritation at this prolonged talk about the boat, about everything, except what they were supposed to go fishing for. He had had enough of it! He fixed him with a keen gaze. "Look here, Kiger, whut is it you want to tell me that I needs to know? Let's git on with it!"

"I'll git to it. I'll git to it, Brother Atwell," Kiger said, with jocular formality and a flash of his teeth. He lifted his nose. "But hit looks like yo' fish too well fed here around the Hightower landing. We bin here close to an hour and ain't had a nibble." He raised his pole and began to wind the line around it. "Pull in the anchor and let's paddle over to that old dead river you told me about."

When they had got to the mouth of the old course and moored the boat among the funnel-shaped trunks of the trees and the long tails of Spanish moss, Adam turned around on his seat toward the stern, ostensibly to get fresh bait for his hook, but said, "Well, Brother Steele, as you wuz goin' to say?"

Kiger had found it a hard pull across the river and he sat on, with his legs stretched out before him, grinning and shaking his head, as he panted. "Kain't say yet!" he soughed. "Devil's Elbow like to got me!"

Adam saw that his shirt was wringing wet—a white, store-bought shirt that looked new (the pasteboard collar button that came with it was still in the collar band). He wondered why Kiger always dressed up like he was in town. He shook his head, responding to Kiger's show of good humor. "Lookin' at that Sunday shirt you done sweated down, I wonder if'n you don't aim to preach to me?"

"No suh, no suh," Kiger began, still breathing hard, but lifting his nose to resume his public manner. "Kiger Steele aims first to *thank* you. He aims to thank you for givin' him good advice—good advice that he wants to let you know he *profited* by." He nodded his head in a pulpit gesture of reiteration. "Thank ye, and he appreciates it and that's one reason he's here now to try to return the favor."

Adam could not resist saying crisply, though with a twinkle in his eye, "Well hit must be a big 'un, for all this w-warmin' up you're doin'!"

Kiger picked up his pole but he only used it to gesticulate with, resembling, for the moment, an attenuated fiddler crab. His manner was hortative. "I'm more indebted to you than you knows, Brother Adam. And I want first to make you acquainted with the how-comes and where-withs of my indebtedness." He unwound his line, pausing in his harangue to put a catalpa worm on his hook and spit on it. "Ole thick-skull Kiger like the tomcat. Yeah, he like that cat, the monkey make pull his chinquapins out'n the fire."

Abruptly, he pulled in a bream out of the water and took it off the hook, but without interrupting himself. "Kiger is still a-singeing his paws on chinquapins. But it's a po' game that's all for the gander and none for the goose. And he done learn a thing or two. One is that monkeys likes to chatter. He learn how to listen. He learn how to lay around where he kin listen. That's how come he know 'bout whut he goin' to tell you 'bout. Hit's important to you."

Adam, pulling up his line to find his hook bare, said, "I better git you to spit on *my* bait!"

Kiger went on. "I know you don't think highly of those *monkeys* I bin doing business with. You ain't got no use for 'em at all. But I hopes you won't let it warp yo' judgment none. I don't aim to try to change yo' mind about them. I don't think I kin do that. But don't let hard feelin's make you soft-headed, Brother Atwell!"

Adam said, with dry detachment, "You means Palcy, too?"

Kiger nodded, watching Adam's face tighten. Then with an abrupt change in his manner, he said, soft and easy, as if he were breaking eggs into a skillet of salt water to poach, "I knows why the Yankees ain't come back down here to close the Land Deal."

Adam's hand jerked slightly, but his face remained impassive. Eyeing Kiger, he said laconically, "I hears a new reason-why ever day."

Kiger sat up to deliver his next words, as if a poker pot lay between them. "I've seen it in a letter from Philadelphia, signed with the name 'Archibald Lincoln,' in green pen-and-ink!"

Adam's nostrils tightened and he lowered his gaze. "Go ahead!" he said.

"Mr. Paley and Mr. Lincoln have swapped letters back and forth during the past month—that why they ain't closed the Deal!"

Adam's face darkened with blood and the whites of his eyes shoaled up when he raised them. After staring fixedly at Kiger for a long moment he lowered his gaze again. He said finally, "I don't believe hit!"

Kiger caught the end of the pole between his legs to release his hands. He pointed to one palm with the index finger of the other hand, as if he were lining out the words in a letter. "Mr. Lincoln write 'We understand yo' proposition, but we are afraid our arrangements'—yessuh, arrangements wuz the word"—Kiger's voice was sharply expository—"'our arrangements with Mrs. H!'—he didn't spell it out—'our arrangements with Mrs. H. have gone too far.'"

Kiger withdrew his finger for a moment to look at Adam. He went on. "Then he say this, 'We have agreed to exempt her mineral rights'—that means clay—'and she has agreed to withdraw her exemption for the Wyche field.'" Kiger lowered his long hands like a preacher dropping dirt into an open grave. "That wuz it, Brother Atwell—did I, or didn't I see a letter?"

Adam said gruffly, doggedly, "Where's the letter? I ain't seen no letter yit!" He tried, without conviction to make his voice derisive. "Yeah you done forgot to bring 'em with you, hey?"

"No, Brother Atwell. Not-a-tall, a-tall!" Kiger studied his cork briefly, then turned confidently toward Adam and said quietly, "You has always represented to me, Brother Adam, like you don't care so much 'bout the written word, that you never did learn how to handle it."

Adam shrugged sharply, his eyes smoldering on the distance. "I kin tell green ink!"

Kiger looked beyond him slyly, lifting his voice. "Mr. Paley wanted me to bring some of them letters. I wuz the one said I didn't think you'd appreciate it, if'n I did."

Adam managed to keep his swollen face expressionless. "Go on!" he said, making a muffled, wheezing sound.

Kiger suddenly grappled with his pole and brought it up, but the fish had got off the hook. He took out time to bait it again, saying in his high voice, "Well, who's pullin' whose chinquapins out'n the fire now, Brother Atwell?"

Adam said gruffly, with a glint in his eye, "S-so they sont you here?"

Kiger resumed without responding to this. "Mr. Paley answered that letter and yestidy he got back the letter he wuz lookin' for. Yes-suh, the one to the dot and to the tee!" Kiger let his baited hook swing out over the water and lowered his pole. "You kin guess whut that wuz, Brother Adam, kain't you? There wuz just eight words on the page of paper, below the *Dear-Suh* line. It said, 'If you kin work it, it's a deal.'" Kiger looked out at his bobbing cork and tightened his line, repeating the letter's message. Then he went on, "I reckon you kin guess whut Mr. Paley's proposition wuz, kain't you Adam? Mr. Paley propositioned Mr. Lincoln that he would undertake to see to it that the widow thought her clay deposits were on land lease, not the land bought fee simple, so that she wouldn't ask to exempt 'em. And after the deal was all over Mr. Paley would then buy the clay from Lincoln by the ton, as he dug it up. That's it.

"He tell me and Hinshaw—Mr. Paley do, that that the best clay in the State of Georgia, there in the Hightower swamp, and he knows the widow never would sell him a lump of hit, not and she could help it, anyway! He say he kin dig it and haul it to the river bank and barge it down to the railroad crossing. He aim to put up his clay works there." Kiger brought another bream from the water. "But Mr. Paley make a *condition* to his undertaking to keep the widow in the dark"—Kiger paused with the fish in his hand to find Adam's gaze. "And, yessuh, that's why I'm here, Brother Atwell. Because that condition wuz that Mr. Lincoln give *you* a ten year lease to the Wyche field and the right to renew!" Adam looked away, but Kiger's voice pursued him, saying, "That whut those words, 'It's a deal' means in Mr. Lincoln's letter. . . ."

Adam's throat was dry and his head ached. Avoiding Kiger's gaze, he got down on his knees, astride his seat, and washed his face in the river with both hands. He scooped up a handful of the water and swallowed it to wet his throat. Then he reached into a side pocket of his overalls and got out his tobacco and his knife and cut himself a chew. This he masticated, as he restored his plug and Barlow and resumed his seat, getting the saliva back into his throat. The astringent balm of nicotine cleared his head. Then he spat, with premeditation, into the river. "Kiger, I forgot to offer hit to you. Will you have a chew?" he said apologetically. "H-hit's Brown Mule."

Kiger, who had been gazing at him speculatively, frowned, and shook his head.

Deliberately, Adam pulled up his fishing line with its bare hook—the bait, he knew, had long been gone—and began to wind the line about the pole. He finished the job, sticking his hook in the cork, before he spoke. "Let's go home, Kiger!" he said, in a rough, off-hand voice, his face set. "You tolled me a long way off to bring me such monkey business!"

Kiger's long face seemed to contract, his lips sticking out, but he didn't say anything. Sullenly he wound up his own line, glancing at Adam out of the tail of his eye. Finally he spoke, in a low-voiced protest. "Now look a-here, Adam, you sho' ain't goin' to be that kind of a fool! A ten-year lease on the Wyche field!. . .And the other way you goin' to lose it, lose it for sho'!"

Adam looked at Kiger steadily, then contempt came on his face, and finally a grim smile. "I reckin that wuz Hinshaw Slappy wanted to git me that lease on the Wyche field, hey?" he said. He gave a short, harsh laugh and stood up in the boat. "Here," he said, "gi'me that paddle and le'me git where you are! I'll take us back across. I knows how to keep out of that Devil's Elbow current."

Adam kept his face set and his tone rough til he finally got rid of Kiger—though he thought he was going to have to knock him down to do it. When he was gone, however, Adam didn't know whether he was madder, or scareder! Kiger had come with him all the way to his yard and stood there at the pump, under the big oak and argued. He even went so far as to threaten Adam, in a way. "Look here, Adam," he said, "all these white men are against you. You done made 'em mad. They're worked up 'bout this Land Deal. They think hit ain't goin' through. You kain't tell whut Paley and Slappy might tell 'em 'bout you, if'n you don't play ball!"

"Kiger," he had said, at last, pointing down the lane, "that the shortest way back to Slappy's place. You got my word. Git goin'!"

But when Kiger was out of sight and his ma spoke up behind him, he jumped like he was shot.

"He a-totin' trouble, son?" she said.

Adam shrugged. "Look like h-hit's on my trail!" he said. He turned away, leaving her standing there, and walked off through the gate and down the lane, his eyes walling around as if, indeed, trouble were following him. It did not seem to him a thing his mother could speak to and he did not know where to turn. He walked all the way to the Wyche field. But he could not think of anybody he could talk to. He could not take it to the widow. Not til he could decide whether there was any truth in anything Kiger had told him. He did not really believe Kiger. But he couldn't make up his mind as to what actually had happened with the Yankees. He wouldn't talk to the widow til he had some idea how to handle it.

Adam leaned on the rail fence and gazed at the rich, dark-brown earth, stretching in straight rows across the field. He would still make a corn corp. And likely it would be his last one! Shaking his head, he looked to the right and left about the level expanse anxiously. He spoke aloud, as if he might be addressing the field. "Well, you kain't never treat with the devil!" He beat with his fist on the top rail. But who could he treat with? Who could he even talk to? His staring face tightened in horizontal lines til his jaw broke loose with a convulsive jerk. "W-who?"

The view grew misty and a current rose up through him, as if from the ground. A current from the old field itself—their experience together—of hunger and fulfillment, of high water and waiting, of sweat and strain and anxiousness, but at last the warming sight of a snowstorm of open cotton bolls. Till now. He turned his back on the field and wiped his eyes with his hand.

The Colonel had told him if he brought the field back, he could keep *on* tending it. But the Colonel wasn't here. His word didn't count any more. . . .If he could only *talk* to the Colonel!

Adam started back along the dim three-path road out of the swamp. Maybe he was going a little strong on it, about the Colonel's word. It still counted with the widow. Hadn't she always been straight with him, Adam? He slowed his pace thoughtfully. But wouldn't she like to sell out everything and get out? She might have agreed to something about the field, not really knowing. His step quickened again. She wanted to sell out. Didn't he see that in her face now? Adam halted a moment, in stillness, to watch, at a distance, a wild turkey hen cross the road, followed by a half-grown brood. No, he decided, no! She only *thought* she wanted to quit. He counted seven of the young turkeys. . . .The widow sometimes *prayed* over her troubles. His anxious feet were hurrying him on again, in the gathering dusk. It couldn't hurt, he told himself, slowing, it couldn't hurt! Again he halted. And he muttered aloud, a wry twist coming over his uplifted face, "Old Marster, Adam need help!"

That night Adam was tormented in his sleep. He dreamed that he was drifting timber down the Altamaha on high water. It came night, and he couldn't find a place to tie on the mainland, so he tied up his raft to an island in the river. After he had made camp, it came to him that this was Hannah's Island and supposed to be haunted by the ghost of a whore that a company of soldiers did to death during the War. And it seemed that he had no more than realized it when the ghost appeared to him out of the cane brake, naked, the color of a scraped pig, with smoke pouring out of her belly. And she ran toward him, crying, "The lighthouse! The lighthouse!"

Adam laid his frying pan down and tried to run and found that he couldn't run!

It was then that his mother woke him up, beating on his shoulder. She told him that he had been yelling out loud.

But he was heavy with sleep and in no time he was back, back on the Island, in the same dream again.

Adam could not see the ghost woman, but he could hear her crying out for help in the dark island jungle. And he thought that a strange fearful hardihood took him, scrambling along the water's edge, toward the voice. Finally he came upon the tall black shadow of a lighthouse and there stood the ghost woman, at the base of it, in a baleful glow, staring off into the canebrake.

He followed her gaze, and saw that there the soldiers were, creeping up through the vine-tangled brake toward her—only they were pale and jack-o-lantern-looking, like she was. And it seemed suddenly that he had his Winchester rifle in his hands and he started shooting at the soldiers. But he found that the bullets went through them, without any effect. And they kept coming. And he was cold with sweat.

Suddenly Hannah was beside him, whispering in his ear. "Find the lighthouse lever," she said. "That'll stop them."

Then it seemed that he clambered over uncertain footing to the lighthouse and fumbled around the wall, to see what he could feel out with his hands. On the back side of it, he came upon his mother, without feeling any surprise, and he called out, asking her where the lever was. He could somehow see in the dark that she was reading from a big black book, reading out loud from back to front. And she never paused. But as he stood, listening to her babble, not understanding her, he picked up the words, "On the other side, by the big gum stump." And he ran back around the tower, found the lever and pulled it back.

There was a great glimmering and whirling of shadows high above them, and the island began to spin. And suddenly he was seeing, not jack-o-lantern soldiers, but black men, in a great drove, running toward him up a street that he recognized to be Lancaster—and it seemed that he knew what he had never seemed to know, that these were the niggers who rioted there thirty years ago, and they were after him!. . . .But then the dream changed and he was staring into a big empty hollow, from which rose up a dead white city—Lost Mountain Prison!

Then the spinning slowed to a halt and the lighthouse was there before him again, with a strong light pouring forth from the top of it, in all directions. Yet it did not reach the island, but blazed out into space far above the tree tops. And the place seemed deserted. But in a moment he heard a woman's voice. It seemed familiar to him, though he couldn't recognize it. She was crying, "It's because I'm a widow!"

And he clambered around the foot of the lighthouse again and found Mrs. Hightower on the other side—only it didn't seem like her, for she was pale and transparent, too. She was pointing out into the brush and he could see jack-o-lantern men, but this time they weren't soldiers, but the landowners in on the Deal. "Light!" she said, "If we could turn the light on them! If we could find the other lever!"

Then he dreamed he began a new search of the base of the lighthouse. He went back to the big gum stump, but there were no levers there at all now. He scrabbled about in the half-light, thinking maybe he had got the wrong tree, but he could find no tree with a lever behind it. Then he heard Mrs. Hightower's voice, crying, "I'm going to sell out lock stock and barrel!" And, it seemed, he looked up, and there she was, climbing up the outside brick wall of the lighthouse. And he was scared. And, it seemed that he looked across the water to the mainland and saw eyes shining from a tree. On a second look, he recognized the eyes to be those of Bo's little pet coon. And the coon spoke to him.

The coon said: "The right lever to the lighthouse is over here on this side of the river, in the dark."

And he said, "But how kin I git over there?"

And the coon said: "There is a green boat hid under the bow oar of your raft. Get in that boat and paddle over here. But beware of the boat! It belongs to the men on the island."

And it seemed that he got in the boat and paddled it, without any trouble across the cut to the mainland, until he stood up to get out of it and all of a sudden it bucked up, like a Texas pony, and pitched him in the river.

But it seemed that by the time he came back up, the coon had him by the wool, pulling him out of the water. Then the coon took him by the hand and led him along a crooked path, slippery with mud, and overswung by vines. But they dodged this way and that way and got by everything and, at last, they were standing before a big iron lever, like the brake lever on a locomotive.

The coon pointed to it and he, Adam, took hold and heaved it forward. And, over in the lighthouse, the light swung downward and flooded the whole island. And from where he was Adam could see the Land-dealers pop, like soap bubbles, as the rays hit them—and Banker Littleton, the biggest of them all, popped like a paper bag.

Then the coon said to Adam, "Come on home!"

And he was grateful to the coon and went along with him, the coon leading him by the hand through the swamp. And as they made their way toward home, the coon gnawed tenderly at his hand, on the part between the forefinger and the thumb. And he knew that this was a friendly rebuke to him, it seemed. So he asked the coon why for.

And the coon said: "Trouble with you, Adam, is you went to the island without a boat. If you don't have a boat to get back to the mainland, we can't help you. You tried to desert us!"

And somehow, Adam knew that the coon was speaking for the whole creation of dumb creatures.

19.

LUCY HIGHTOWER looked up from the writing board of her secretary in surprise. She saw, through the window entrance, Marse, on the porch, coming toward her. A smile smoothed out the lines in her face and she lifted her voice. "What are *you* doing here, at such an hour, on a hot afternoon like this?"

Reflecting her good humor with only the barest glimmer of it, Marse said noncommittally, "I didn't go swimming this afternoon."

This astonished her even more, but simultaneously it occurred to her that Marse could take the letter she had written to Mr. Lincoln down to the post office, and her voice swept on to the second stimulus still bearing some of the tone of the first. "Didn't go, well that's good!" she said, "I want you to mail this letter for me." Her wry lips straightened. "You remember how to register a letter, don't you?" She picked it up. "It's important." Then she glanced at the page of paper before her on which she had written only the salutation, "Dear Edward." She had started it first and it had given rise to the second letter. And she had been staring at it in frowning frustration again, when Marse appeared. She sighed and turned it over as he drew nearer. As he extended his hand for the envelope she was holding, however, she suddenly lifted it out of his reach and stood up, another impulse now evident on her bland countenance.

"On second thought, there's no rush about it," she said, glancing at the clock, "the post office will be open for another hour." She faced the veranda again. "I see a breath of air, stirring the leaves of the rose vine. Let's go sit in the front swing!"

Marse, his nostrils spreading, bridled a little and seemed about to resist, then he nodded abruptly and faced about.

They walked alongside and around to the front of the house, her hand lightly placed on his nearer shoulder, in her usual restrained affection. Lucy, however, did not take the occasion to be usual. She had been back home nearly a month and she had never been able to tell Marse that she intended to marry Edward. She could have told him, of course! But she had never been able to establish the sympathy, to feel close enough to him to lead up to it properly. It was amazing: he had put forth a new personality under the strain of their nameless tension. She had decided to shift her ground.

"I have been thinking," she began, when they were in the swing and she looked back into the green gloom of the ivy-shaded corridor through which they had come. "I have been thinking, Marse, that we should really go ahead and move back to Charleston now. . . ." A cloud covered the sunset and brought twilight upon his silence. "I mean, of course, when the land deal is finally closed!" She turned toward him, a breeze lifting a strand of hair at her temple that had escaped her pompadour. His face was both questioning and non-committal, but at least it was not sullen, she decided. Examining, at the quartering angle, the soft seamless surface of it—made barer by blind, almost invisible eyebrows—she was suddenly struck with the look of his father in him. Strange. It was neither his forehead, nor his nose. She had always thought he had none of his father's physical features. What was it? Perhaps it was the numb expression. You could not tell what was going on inside a Hightower! She used to call it the ancient Greek in her husband.

She lifted her nose lightly to command his attention. "You see, if we wait til you are ready for high school, why, you won't be able to get in Boys High in Charleston from this school!"

Marse looked away abruptly, wrinkles of resistance gathering under his freckles at his cheekbone and his mouth, but after staring out into the yard awhile, he responded submissively, "Yessum."

Mrs. Hightower went on, meaning to dwell on the topic, "And, of course, there's Elinor. It would do a lot for her to have a couple of years at Meminger, my old school, before she goes to college."

"Yessum," Marse said again.

She was not sure why, but she felt surprised at his meekness. For one thing, he usually protested any mention of school during vacation-time. She pressed on the floor with the ball of her foot and the swing moved, with a squeaking of its chains. The motion made her aware of his clean and still-fresh blouse. And she saw that he was wearing a pair of his good knickerbockers, too. Oh for Goodness sake! She reached out automatically and took hold of the chain, in a balancing gesture. He had been to the afternoon revival services! How could she have forgotten about the revival?

Mrs. Hightower gave more official endorsement to these summer evangelical purges of Riverton's spiritual life than she really felt. She was a Methodist, but it was not her idea of religion. Of course, *God works in mysterious ways*. And it seemed that Riverton had to take its religion, like everything else, raw, sensationally, and fitfully. The Hightowers, of course, *had* to attend a Methodist revival, but she did not encourage her children to be active. She had been astonished at Marse's manifestation of interest this season. And, she must confess, a little disturbed. He was not a demonstrative person and really pretty serious-minded for a boy. She wanted him to experience Christian conversion, certainly—if he hadn't already. But at a revival! That would not be like a Hightower!

She placed her other arm on the back of the swing, behind his head. "Boys High in Charleston," she said, "has always been known for its high standards. And Mr. Edward has kept scholarship above athletics there." A glance from the corner of her eye disclosed no visible reaction in Marse to the mention of Edward's name. "Not that they don't have fine athletic teams, too. Edward, himself, used to be a good oarsman. And really expert at tennis!"

Doubling up a leg, the heel of his bare foot resting on the edge of the seat, Marse wrapped his arms about his knee. "What is an oarsman, Mamma?" he said diffidently.

Mrs. Hightower's face brightened. "An oarsman?" She looked about her helplessly, then tightened her mouth and began. "Well, we don't have rowing here on these rivers. We use paddles. But on the coast they have row boats and rowing races, with oars—you've seen oars! An oarsman mans one of the oars in such a race."

He nodded his head positively, but she wasn't at all sure she had made him understand. The revival meeting was probably responsible for some of Marse's recent strange behavior! She supposed he was, what the preachers call, under conviction. She gave him an uncomfortable glance. As his mother and a practicing Christian, she should be able to give him comfort and help. But he had given her no opening. Lucy frowned into space and swallowed. Do! An eleven-year-old boy! And her own son! She ought to be ashamed of herself. But he was certainly Hightower, not Riverton, in the way his conscience affected him. He took it dumbly and alone. She would not actually have known what was happening, if their neighbor, Mr. Wilson, the blacksmith, had not tried privately to return to her the dollar Marse gave him for watermelons he had stolen out of his patch. Mr. Wilson said that, of course, the boy was welcome to them and, anyhow, all six of them would not be worth more than half that sum.

She turned toward Marse. "It's a great sport on the coast. They have regattas. Edward rowed for the College of Charleston."

Again he did not react to the name! She could feel, on the seat beside her, the automatic shifts and muscle tensions of his body that registered his interest. But he looked at her guardedly. "Did you ever row a boat?"

"Heavens, no!" She laughed. Then, her eyes brightening, she said quickly, "I was in the cheering section—cheering for the College and for Edward."

He looked away, with his jaw clamped in an obvious effort at self-control, but he did not take fright, or get the dumb swelling, and she was inspired to go on. "I often went boating with Edward, back there when we were young, but I never rowed the boat."

He nodded, still gazing into space and, after a pause, said, "That must have been nice."

The encouragement was not great, but she would try to make the most of it. "I rode a sea turtle once!" she said dramatically.

His small, deep-set eyes turned on her like a shotgun. "You mean, out to sea?"

"Well, we were on the beach of an island."

"How did you get on?"

"You mean the island?"

"No. The turtle?" His jaw loosening, he threatened to smile.

"Oh!" It had not been deliberate, but this seemed to relax them a little, so she went on. "I was on a moonlight picnic, and we were turtle-egg hunting. And we found, coming over the top of a sand dune, oh, a half-a-dozen, I would guess it was, big barnacled, sea turtles, lying there on the sand, some distance away from the water.

Marse's face was gleaming, a burnished galaxy of freckles. "What'd you do?"

"We raced down the slope and leaped upon their backs!"

He grinned and hugged his knee. "Did you ride 'em into the ocean?"

"Almost. I stayed on top, with the help of"—he saw it coming and turned abruptly away—"my escort," she said, after a pause, in obvious substitution. . . .

They swung in silence.

Then Marse, his face still averted, wagged his head several times excitedly. Nursing his knee, he began urgently to jiggle the swing. He said, in a lifted voice, "Do you know what a pick-up raft is, Mamma?"

He seemed immensely remote. Mrs. Hightower was mystified, but she knew she had lost ground. "A pick-up what?"

"Do you know what a pick-up raft is?"

"Well, no."

"Did you ever hear the story about Mr. Pete Parkerson and the pick-up raft and Adam?"

Mrs. Hightower's brows sharpened in an unconscious frown, but she did not see how she could recover the initiative. She smiled ambiguously on her son and said, "No, Marse, tell me about it!"

Marse laid a cheek against his knee and gave himself over to the telling, with abandon. Once, starting with only seven logs—barely enough to hold them up—and a boat, Mr. Pete and Adam went down the river picking up timber (by river law "free logs") to make out their raft, all the way to Doctortown, where they were going to sell it. As Marse retailed the adventure of each log picked up, Mrs. Hightower found herself becoming involved and wondered at the seeming awe that he gave this raffish life. On one occasion, Mr. Pete—which he pronounced *Mistpete:* one word, as Adam did—had pretended some logs (seven of them) were his, having, of course, never seen them before, with the adverse claimants at the other end of them, with a rifle in their boat, and had bluffed them down. Eventually, Adam and Mr. Pete reached Doctortown with the largest pick-up raft ever to be *scaled* there.

Lucy Hightower, as she listened in forebearance, began to sense—in a world she knew to be muddy, smelly, raw, always too cold or too hot, mosquito-bitten, sallow-faced, shifty-eyed, tight-lipped and loud-mouthed—to sense, almost below awareness and quite without sympathy, that, in his telling, it had a grace of its own. Less rudimentary and repressed were the fears in her that this gave rise to.

"Then, after their getting there with the biggest pick-up raft in history," Marse added, in epilogue, "and getting a lot of money for it, Mr. Pete gambled the whole thing away, Adam said. Adam's part, too, in a poker game, in a goodtime house. And Adam, between trips up the railroad embankment to see how late the train would be, telling him, every time he came back to him for more money (he had made Adam the money man) that he was going to lose it all, if he didn't quit. And he lost every penny. And then, after losing all they had, forged a check on his cousin here in Riverton, Dock Parkerson. And had to run away to Texas." Marse shook his head with resignation, but with a reminiscent glow on his face.

The tale had given Mrs. Hightower, not a glow, but a chill. How could she temporize over their situation in this place? Marse's chief counselor and confessor, an illiterate, crude, barbarous negro! Even though he was honest and an extraordinary man. How could she?

"But you know," Marse said, still absorbed, "Mr. Pete liked Adam. And Adam liked Mr. Pete. Said he was accommodating with everybody, and open-handed and, if you were his friend, he would go to the bridge with you. He wrote Adam from Texas, sending him back his part in the raft and telling him that he would send him the money for his fare out there, if he would come to Texas!"

Mrs. Hightower's dry smile showed that her forebearance had worn thin.

"And you know what Adam did?" said Marse, his fervor unabated by this. "He took the money and went to Dock Parkerson and paid off that bad check and the court costs. Then he got a letter written to Mr.

Pete, telling him to come on back here, it would be alright now, that he'd better come, he had overworked his luck too long; he had better come back and marry and settle down. Adam told him that the law of averages operated in Texas just like it did in Georgia. And he was playing a losing game. But Mr. Pete wouldn't come back. The next year, playing poker with some Texas gamblers, he got killed."

Mrs. Hightower felt tired by her son's enthusiasm and the tale. A river rogue and gambler, his hero! She wondered how he was fitting this into the admonitions of the revival. She tried to give her voice a tone of soft irony, as she said, "And do you find Mr. Pete's example inspiring?"

"Oh, he was game, but he didn't know when to quit," Marse said matter-of-factly. He tilted back on the seat, his head resting on her forearm momentarily. "But Adam sure can tell a tale!. . . He can even make his stuttering count." Marse looked out into the dusk with a start. "Gee!" he jumped to his feet. "I'd better run on to the post office right now, to get that letter registered!"

"Oh, you don't need to go yet!" Mrs. Hightower urged, clutching at the chain. "The parlor clock just struck the third quarter."

He leaped down the steps at a bound. "But I've got to get back in time to eat supper and get to church early," he cried over his shoulder, as he ran across the lawn toward the fence corner.

Gripping the iron links harshly, Mrs. Hightower put the other hand to her tightening throat. He's *not* going to grow up in this insufferable place! She told herself fiercely, she told herself in the knowledge that the letter he bore to the post office proposed to the Yankee buyer a bargain price of their total land holdings.

There was a rhythmic sweep of palmetto fans. They moved to the swell of voices raised in song:

"Would you be free from your burden of sin?

There's pow'r in the Blood, pow'r in the Blood!"

The sense of this sound and motion was disquieting to Lucy Hightower, seated between her two daughters, near the center of the main auditorium of the crowded church. Her feeling did not come of the meaning the familiar words held for her. Nor even, in itself, from the emotion of the revival-goers, which had been building up for ten days and which she knew would be extravagantly demonstrative during the evening. This, also, was too long familiar to upset her. Yet she felt a strange jeopardy in the spiritual seething about her.

Her vulnerability lay beyond her and, she feared, beyond her control. It lay in the person of her son, seated, not with the family as usual, but on the far side, in the men's section of pews. There had been several songs. The evangelist had read his Scripture. The service was warming up. As well as she could tell from the corner of her eye at this distance, Marse was taking it with his characteristic reserve. But Lucy was apprehensive.

At the railing to the pulpit, the preacher thrust up an arm. "Wail, O ye oaks of Bashan!" he intoned, from his Scriptural reading. He moved into his sermon, speaking in a rapid, sonorous voice that had the compactness of his own thick body and smooth, dark, muscular face. The preacher warned again, as he did in every sermon that there was no half-way stop to salvation. Lucy was sure Marse had been impressed by this point, from something he had said, And, certainly, it was true!

The preacher was telling a story. The happenings in it were familiar to her through Marse's account. It was of the drowning of Jack Boswell, a riverboat pilot, in the Ocmulgee at Indian Point, earlier in the summer. . . At the end, the preacher said, "Boswell put all his faith in his own strength!"

Lucy, looking toward the faraway pew, thought that Marse's face seemed paler, though she could not be sure. It was a crisis in his life, she was certain. She could not say—she halted her fan—she would not dare say, of what magnitude. It should be of the greatest, and he was as serious as a boy could be at eleven. If only the circumstances were different—but she could not choose the circumstances!

At the railing the preacher's smile seemed sinister. "Ah, the river!" he murmured, "Smooth and pleasing its surface. But who can guess the treacherous current below it?"

But Marse had not sought her aid—he had, it seemed, deliberately avoided the subject with her. She feared that somehow, in a way he was not even conscious of, he had been estranged from her, already. Already? What did she mean?

The preacher shouted: "Jack Boswell had never met a force so powerful before!"

Lucy underwent a sinking in the pit of her stomach. Or could it be some indefinable guilt of her own? Some irresponsibility? Disloyalty?

The darkness at the open windows flickered with lightning. The preacher stood at the chancel rail, braced with his feet apart. He raised his arms abruptly, lifting himself up on his toes, and came down with a powerful thrust. "That river is sin!" He moved off along the railing, waving his arms, shouting hoarsely.

A moment later the choir eagerly led the way into, "What a Friend We Have in Jesus." And the aisles began to fill with people coming down to the railing to shake hands with the preachers—*those who wanted to live a better life.* As the crowd thinned out, Lucy glanced in Marse's direction, with strangely mingled feelings. She found him immobile in his seat and, in spite of herself, she could not deny that it allayed some of the apprehension in her.

But the evening's evangelical work went on. There were other descents to the railing by the assorted revival goers to other propositions. And still Marse remained in his seat. The evening was nearing its climax and conclusion. There were but few left in the house who had not been down on some proposition, or other. And as the choir broke into "Tell Mother I'll Be There," the preacher raised his voice above the singing to say, "All those who want to give their hearts to God, come down and kneel at the chancel rail!"

The time for those under conviction to seek salvation was at hand. It was the final and unconditional call, the high point of the soul-saving appeal.

The response was slower and more scattering. The preacher kept the choir going through the third and on into the fourth verse. Then Lucy heard the scuffing, padding sound of bare feet on the boards—it seemed exaggeratedly loud, a whisper magnified by a megaphone. She had to look across the wide arc of pews to be sure; though she knew she knew it already, yet she must establish it by her senses, too. There, on the far aisle, was the small, shy figure of Marcellus, moving uncertainly toward the pulpit, his body pitched a little forward by the slanting floor.

She caught her breath, laying down her fan. Hadn't she expected it? But she experienced a sense of shock at the actuality, nevertheless. She stared until he finally knelt at the railing and the pastor of the church put an arm around his shoulders. Then, she closed her own eyes and said, "Oh God, have mercy on me! Have mercy on me and send me grace to do what I ought to do *now!*"

Should she go down to pray with him? Anxiety drew Lucy's face into a knot. She had never been down to the railing to pray with or for anyone. She had never approved—but that was beside the point! Now the teacher of the young men's Sunday school class was on the other side of Marse. There would be nowhere for her to kneel—or get near him. These men were experienced and much better qualified than she was, she told herself. They were trained workers.

"Lay your sins at the feet of Jesus. . .He alone can bear them." It was the professionally modulated voice of the evangelist, moving about the kneelers, Lucy thought, like a doctor at a first aid station.

But Marse seemed to be finding it hard to do this. The time stretched out. Lucy had pulled her fan to pieces and twisted her handkerchief into a rag and had snatched Row back into her seat and straightened out her dress innumerable times, and still he was there beneath the arms of the coachers. Finally he was the only one left and still he did not lift his head. Lucy could bear this torture no longer! She put a firm hand on Row's knee, murmuring under her breath, "Stay here!" and the other on the back of the pew in front of her and got to her feet. "God help me!" she said silently and moved toward the aisle.

But, as she gained the open aisle and turned toward the pulpit, she saw that Marse was up and on his feet. The men stood up with him, their hands on his shoulders, reassuring themselves of his state. He nodded in response to their solicitations, but did not look at them, or speak. He seemed scarcely to notice them. He turned to the aisle on which she stood and started up to it. He did not utter a sound, though his lips were parted. His face was pale, but it shone from an inner light. He moved as a sleep-walker moves, up the aisle toward her, staring fixedly—she thought, at first, at her.

She moved a little way down the aisle to meet him, as people about stood watching. She saw, as he drew nearer that he was staring, not at her, but at the doorway behind her. He came abreast of her and kept moving. He strode past, as if Lucy were not there, to the open door.

She turned in time to see him, on the porch beyond the entrance, outlined by lightning. The thunder was deafening. Everybody knew that the church had been hit.

20.

"MARRIAGE IS FOR THE LIVING, not the dead," Mrs. Hightower said.

"Yessum," Adam answered noncommittally, his stuttering taut. "Hit hard to say some time whut hit's for!"

"That is the wrong attitude, Adam!"

She stood with him at the back steps, all in white—shirtwaist and skirt and shoes—though it was only eleven o'clock in the morning. She could scarcely say why now. The sunless day was sultry, the air seemed as warm and thick as soup, and faint beads of perspiration covered her upper lip. She was dressed to go with Marse to the church in the early afternoon to meet their pastor, for though Marse had been baptized as a baby, he had never been confirmed, Mr. Hightower insisting that this await Marse's mature decision. And now seemed to be the time. She decided that her getting dressed so early must have been due to heat derangement. Already she felt the back of her shirtwaist unpleasantly damp between the shoulder blades. Yet it could have been complicated by a cross purpose that came to her in the middle of the night. She had been dreaming fantastically of the time in their early marriage when Mr. Hightower came to Aiken to fetch her back to Georgia, as if it were going on then, and she had awakened with a desperate determination not to be trapped.

She was speaking now, not of her own marriage ostensibly, but of Adam's. She added, "You have gone already way beyond your marriage responsibilities."

He glanced up at her, then lowered his gaze to the dimness of the hallway behind her. "H-hit hard to say where a man's responsibilities ends in marriage," he said, shaking his head.

Her eyes widened and darkened in bafflement and her mouth twisted impulsively, as if for retort, but she turned without speaking and walked away. Taking up the white pocketbook which lay on the tool chest against the wall, she extracted her handkerchief and dabbed her mouth and brow. She faced him again and said positively, "I believe very little in divorce. But the law recognizes insanity. And in a case like yours it is the same as death!" Arthur Adair had brought back the report from the asylum that Adam's wife, Malinda, was now confined to a padded cell and, though it was problematic how long she might live, she would never be out again.

Adam, his voice from the depths of his chest, spoke with dry and solemn succinctness. "Hit l-like death, but hit ain't!"

Mrs. Hightower turned around and stared at him, saying flatly, "Yes, I know. It's worse than death!" Then she lifted her head in what seemed a gesture of defiance. "But you can't let it drag you in after it—into a cell!" She came back toward the steps. "I think you ought to go ahead and remarry, Adam."

He mopped his face and the back of his neck, moving alongside the entrance, in meditation. What was it? he asked himself. The heat? Everybody got a little flighty this kind of weather. Or was she agreeing with his ma and getting after him obliquely for not marrying Babe? "H-hit's bin a corn crop, not marryin' on my mind!" he said finally, with a trace of a wry smile.

"Ah, this weather!" she exclaimed, dabbing her face again.

"And the Land Deal!" He turned about, grimacing, still mopping his face. "Whut you reckon's happened to them Yankees?"

For only the fraction of a second, Mrs. Hightower's serious eyes brightened with something that looked like glee, then she drew in a quivering breath and sighed, "The plague-take-it, old Land Deal!"

By common impulse, they both glanced at each other diffidently. Each would allow the other the initiative in beginning. Each shook his head with an air of reluctance and misgiving.

Finally Adam, in a change of manner, said, "Marse anywhere 'round?"

"Marse?" Mrs. Hightower blinked at the steps. "I'm afraid he's not!" Then, her face softening, she added, "He's gone to take the girls swimming. The girls go to the swimminghole in the mornings now. And he went along with Mr. Henry Bruce and little Walter to make another man to help pull them out, if need be."

Mrs. Hightower had got a little involved in her explanation and Adam, nodding, said repeatedly, "'S-sall right! 'Sall right! I just wanted to tell 'him how sorry I am we didn't' git to go seining on the Fourth of July." He smiled indulgently. "And to tell 'im, too, that the River's right and I got a trotline I want 'im to help me run, one night soon."

Mrs. Hightower's face reflected Adam's expression and she said, in the conventional way, "I know he'll be delighted to go fishing out there!" Though, after she had said it, she had an uneasy moment of wondering, since the evening before, what Marse might want to do.

Adam turned away casually and said, a detectable wariness in his stance and in his voice, "Y-you know I went fishin' on the Fourth with that crazy nigger, Kiger Steele?"

"Oh, yes!" she daubed her brow with her handkerchief. "Kiger Steele." She had not got the report straight and had forgot, too. "What was that about?"

He continued, without altering his attitude or tone of voice. "H-he had a long tale to tell. I-I don't know whut to make of it. He puts out to me that Mr. Hinshaw Slappy and Mr. Oswald Paley, in touch with the Yankees; that this feller, Paley, has writ to Mr. Lincoln; that they havin' truck with 'em!" He glanced up at her briefly, without shifting. "I don't know whut the truth is," he said, tensing a little, as if he were listening to the sound of his own voice, "I sho' don't! Mr. Paley, he might have writ 'em a letter with some sort of scheme up his sleeve. I wouldn't put nothin' past *him*. B-but I kain't think of anything much, any proposition of his'n, Mr. Lincoln apt to be taken in by."

Mrs. Hightower's eyes had widened as Adam talked on and she lifted a hand and felt for her glasses at her left shoulder. "Paley!" she murmured, her breath quickening. Jerkily she zipped the glasses up and down on their chain. "Do you think Mr. Lincoln would listen to such a man?"

"W-wouldn't seem so, but you kain't never tell, kain't never tell." He turned himself about carefully, as if balancing on a plank.

There was open alarm on her pale face. "My Heavens, Adam! What could Paley propose to Mr. Lincoln?"

"I don'—I don't know, Mrs. Hightower," he said balefully, glancing up at her. His eyes showed a pain, of which he was not conscious. "But that man sho' would like to git his hands on your clay!"

"But," she broke out, "Lincoln has always seemed less interested in the clay than, than"—she faltered, lifting her gaze above his head. "Than other things."

"Y-yessum," Adam said, his eyes following her, now in conscious, questioning pain. "How's that?"

She frowned, meeting his gaze, hers still remote. "Well, until it came out that the field might be on a lease lot Mr. Lincoln would hardly talk about exempting it," she said ruefully.

"Yessum!" There was tense pressure in Adam's stuttering and he shifted heavily. "Did you 'gree to anything, any time?"

"Well, let's see—it seems so long ago that we talked about it!"

"Yed—yessum!" His stammering was a steam drill.

"He said if he exempted the Wyche field, he would have to exempt three other fields, that somebody could lease the field from me and put up a sawmill down there and cut his timber, without any way to catch them, or stop them. . .Why, Adam?"

"He did?"

She lifted her eyebrows, continuing vaguely, "Yes. He talked about another way of handling it, handling it another way. But then you all said the field was on a lease lot. And it wouldn't make any difference! I don't know. . . ."

Adam's pain made him grimace and he turned away. *She must have,* he said to himself, not finishing, not needing to finish the thought. After all she was just a woman and didn't know about things. Lincoln could trick her. Maybe she agreed to it, not meaning to! He began mopping and walking back and forth again. What did that crazy dream he had last week mean, anyhow? His mother had been cryptic when he told her about it. "I done told you, once," she said, "you'll recognize it when you come to it!" She probably just couldn't figure it out. What connection could Mrs. Hightower have with Hannah or Hannah's Island? That lighthouse business? What are they going to turn on about this land deal? And how could he, Adam, have a part in it? He shrugged and glanced over his shoulder. Did she say something? In his preoccupation, he had forgotten her for a moment. "I don't know'm!" he said, in a lifted, sing-song voice, just in case she had. It reminded him of Kiger's voice and he recalled his own words of advice to Kiger about a nigger getting in the middle in a white-folks contention! "Don't know whut to make of this thing. I sho' don't!" Now Adam did not have to be guarded or listen to his voice any more. His conscience was clear. She wasn't talking, he would not talk, either. "I kain't tell what's up. I don't doubt that Paley writ a letter. But maybe they just fishin' for whut they kin ketch!"

She looked at him, puzzled. "But what is Kiger after, Adam?"

"Yessum." Adam's teeth chattered.

"What did Kiger tell you?"

"Well-'um, h-hit didn't make too much sense." He consulted the distance of the street beyond the fence evasively. "You know they all think I got some connection with the Yankees a-puttin' off the deal . . . .Maybe Kiger just playin' me along with his talk to see if'n I won't tell *him* something. I don't know'm!" He returned to his preoccupied pacing.

Heaving a sigh and wiping her mouth of perspiration, Mrs. Hightower revived her spirits with a shake of her shoulders. "Well, anyhow," she said briskly, "we ought to hear something soon from Mr. Lincoln." She looked at Adam until he turned his head. "I have written Mr. Lincoln a registered letter. He will have to sign a card to accept it. At least we'll know that he gets it. And surely he *will* answer it."

Adam cleared his throat. "Whut'd you tell 'im this time? If ye don't mind a-sayin'."

Mrs. Hightower began frowning, but turned it into a smile. "Oh, I told him, I told him, he had better come on down here and close out the deal, before we all backed out," she said, passing it off as a jest. She regarded Adam's watchful gaze self-consciously. "Mainly, I tried to get him down here!" She shut her eyes tight then, for a long moment, and opened them wide, facing Adam resolutely. "I told him, Adam," she said, with great firmness, staring, staring hard at the quiet, informed, unshaken, ginger-colored face of *familiar reality*. But the words wouldn't come and she shifted her gaze, laughing nervously. And then, in a different tone of voice, with—they both fully realized—different meaning, she continued, "I told him I would sell him *everything* at a bargain price, if he'd come on right now and close it out!" Her shoulders slumped and she shrugged. Her words were only a joke! "I'm getting so worn out with this thing!" she added plaintively.

"Ain't we all!" Adam laughed, in the same rueful way. "It's done gone on too long! Too long! Gittin' me scared the thing kain't be brought off. It's got to where I'm havin' bad dreams 'bout it!"

But Lucy would not, could not leave the subject of her effort. Her face sobered, sharpened again. "Adam?" she said distraughtly, her lips drawing tight, her eyes staring darkly, "Adam?. . ."

But he did not hear her. It was, as if the same compelling spirit possessed him, too, as he stood, rooted to the foot of the steps, staring into the depths of the open hall, with bright vacant eyes. *Lincoln's letter. The widow's deal. Make Kiger produce it, if they have it.* That would settle it, one way or the other! Settle it! His face flushed darkly.

A third time she said, "Adam," but it scarcely sounded like her voice, and plainly her attention was with her averted gaze, staring, staring back up the aisle toward a boy and a dark doorway, hearing a familiar voice say: *Everybody did the best they knew how; don't question the ways of the Almighty!*

"Yessum?" he answered hollowly.

And the voice that was scarcely her voice went on, without willing it, saying, "Marse joined the church last night!"

Finally moving out of his tracks, Adam said, "Y-yesum, whut'd you say?"

And, looking down at him, her eyebrows lifted, daubing perspiration at her temples, she responded. "I was saying—Oh yes, I was saying, what will we do, Adam?" And after a moment's silence, she added, "Maybe we'd better pray over it."

But Adam shrugged and turned away.

21.

ADAM NOSED the narrow green punt out into the current. Here, with an overhead sun on the river's flat surface, the light cut out the picture sharply. And, in front of him, though six feet away, Adam could detect movement at the throat muscles from the back of Kiger Steele's lean neck. Was Kiger uneasy?

Adam dug the heavy paddle into the yellow water, pushing the boat against the current, toward a far swamp-lined bend in the course. Maybe Kiger knew enough about those letters to make him uneasy!

He, Adam, had negotiated this *fishing* trip, through a Corinthian lodge meeting. Kiger was cold to his idea at first. It took two weeks to work it out. They were on their way to the swamp up above Burnt Island, where Paley and Slappy were cutting timber. There Kiger would meet Paley and pick up the letters, while he stayed with the boat. Then they would angle back across the river to land below the Island and go out to the Bright's place. Adam had agreed that he would take Peter Bright's word for what the letters said. And Adam had given Kiger the grip on his telling the widow nothing about it.

He switched the paddle to his left hand. But Adam didn't have confidence in old man Peter any more. And Adam had made further arrangements. He had primed Marse to meet him out at his cousin Bright's that afternoon, as if by accident. He had laid the ground carefully, though he had not told him all of the reason why. If Marse was there and he demanded that they let Marse see what was in the letters, it would be hard for them to deny him. And, if the letters did show that Mrs. Hightower had wobbled over holding on to the Wyche field and it came to it, then he might get Marse to help him uphold his mother's hands. Adam pushed the end of the cord-bound fishing poles out from under his foot. The truth was he did not believe that Mr. Lincoln wrote them anything in a letter saying he would deal with them. A Yankee would be too sharp for a thing like that! And he doubted now that there was anything about a side deal with the widow, either. Why would he tell *them!* Still Adam had to know. He gazed intently through the clear noonday at the steadily enlarging wall of gray-mantled cavernous trees at the river bend. He had to know!

Kiger picked up a tin bucket by the handle and held it up, turning half around on the seat limberly, his dark profile convolved in a gold-toothed grin. He said, "Night crawlers. We might do a little fishin', sho' nuff. After we git our other business wrapped up."

Adam nodded. But he got the way that Kiger kept looking him over, while he talked. . . .Kiger *was* uneasy! Why? Adam released the end of the paddle to take a swipe at his wide straw hat, pulling the brim down lower over his eyes, against the glare. This was a chancy piece of business for everybody! But it *had* to be done. His shoulder muscles knotted as he held the blade behind the boat for an instant at the end of his stroke, to keep straight. His gaze searched the water front along the low-lying shore, pried into the caves of dimness among the gray-boled trees. He could feel a firmness of muscle on the top side of his stomach that registered his own excitement.

The mistrust and meanness around this land deal had got so thick anything could happen.

He lowered his glance to the boat. All right, suppose Paley and Slappy didn't have any such letters as Kiger had lined out to Adam! What then? He had certainly foreseen this possibility. Would they try any rough stuff on him, up here in the swamp? No. Too many. Too mixed. Paley was sure to have some sort of letters out of Lincoln. It would be easier and foxier to them to try to bluff it on the letters with old man Peter's help.

Adam changed over his paddle, deliberately tipping the surface to skeet up water as he went to sink the blade in the river again. Some of the spray reached Kiger and his long back collapsed in a nervous shudder. "Sorry!" Adam sang out foggily. "This heavy paddle of your'n!" He made the stroke good, pulling the paddle through. Yeah, Kiger was *anxious*. . . .Adam measured his strokes. And the fishing poles! How did they come into it? A cover up? Alibi? He saw the black lettering beyond Kiger on the side of the shallow boat. Yeah, the *Green Ghost*. It would be easy for the Ghost to shake a fellow off of his back!. . . But what good would that do? He could outswim Kiger and Slappy and Paley, all put together. And they knew it.

They rounded the bend. A few moments later, there was a slight muscular rhythm through Kiger's body and he turned back to Adam again, this time from the other side, pointing into the distance. "You kin pass the island through the cut and save 'bout a half-mile of paddlin'!" he called out, eyeing Adam once more.

Adam nodded, still more puzzled. They were a good half mile from the cut and it would take him a quarter of an hour against this current to get there. But Kiger couldn't wait fifteen seconds to tell him—and take another look! Steadily Adam climbed the river, with his measured strokes. He searched far and near, reviewing every incident, from the first fishing trip to the up-coming moment, yet he could not account for the secret anxiety in Kiger. This tightened his own nerves.

When he and Kiger had landed at the steamboat wood racks on Persimmon Bluff and Kiger had gone off into the swamp toward the distant sound of axes, Adam's nervousness increased. He left the boat and got under the bluff, squatting in the cavity that high water had cut into its base. Hinshaw Slappy was a good shot with that twenty-two rifle, from behind a tree! He didn't have much nerve, but it was hard to say what a fellow would do when he thought he could get away with it. Looking about him, Adam picked up a few sticks of wood that had fallen in loading the steamboats and laid them beside him. They would have to come in here to get him. And he would put up what resistance he could.

When Kiger returned, Adam came out from under his cover warily, moving away from the boat and coming up on top of the bluff behind a tree that gave him a protected view of the whole surroundings. But he saw no living thing, save the lank, swinging figure of Kiger and a couple of swamp hogs. He joined Kiger on the bluff and walked a step ahead of him back to the boat. He got in, moving to the bow and facing the shore, when he sat down. "You want to pull'er awhile, Brother Kiger?" he said, keeping the trees around the edge of the clearing in his eye. And so he sat, as Kiger paddled out into the current, turning downstream and angling for the other bank to take the cut on the far side of the island. The scene remained solitary and serene, as they moved out of gunshot range across the water. Kiger's strain had caused him to guard against the white men waylaying him. Even though it didn't' make good sense!

At the bottom of his circle of vision, Adam saw that Kiger had not been relaxed by his visit with Paley. He was silent and still seemed preoccupied. More so than any paddling called for. Abruptly, Adam leaned forward. "Did ye git 'em?" he said, sharp and quick, looking into Kiger's face with snake eyes.

Kiger was bent forward, pulling his paddle through. His lean freckled cheeks stitched and he soughed automatically, on an expiring tremolo, "Ye-a-ah!. . ." As he lifted his paddle, he broke away and fixed his gaze on its movement and even a second stroke, completing it with graceful care, before he looked up at Adam again. He had got himself in hand by then. "Brother Atwell," he said with even a jocular note in his voice, "you ought to know by this time that Kiger Steele usually gits whut he goes after!"

Adam's eyes glimmering, withdrew. Seemed like Kiger meant more than he said! He nodded and lifted his face to Kiger again. "They must have been farther away than it sounded like, from the time it took ye?"

But Kiger had his pace set by now. He took a couple of strokes before he replied. "They weren't right there with the woods sawyers. Took me awhile to git aholt of 'em."

Adam continued to sit facing him, staring at the opaque water reflectively, repeating for his mind's ear the sound of Kiger's voice when he had exclaimed, *Ye-a-ah.* He was convinced that Kiger was still deeply uneasy. But why? If the letters were a bluff, it would be for Peter Bright, not Kiger to make the bluff. Adam shook his head and took hold of the gunwales of the punt and, leaning forward, put a foot behind him on the other side of his seat. He carefully faced about on the cross plank to ride forward in the boat. They were half way across the river.

When they were a couple of hundred yards nearer the other bank and still some distance above the island, a voice sang out from the shore. "Who's that you paddlin' for now, Steele?"

Adam jerked his head, his eyes walling out as he searched the vine-bush-and-tree tangle. But, after a moment, he called back good-humoredly, "I heard you, Mr. Jawn, but I kain't pick you out in the wilderness!" Then he did discover the tranquil, bronzed scaley face of John Hightower amid the green boughs of a leaning sycamore tree.

"There you be, in a sycamore tree!" Adam laughed. "Didn't know you 'uz in this country even! It's good to see you! How's the fishin'?"

Kiger seemed slow to speak but he greeted him, too. Adam began to sense complications. John Hightower would be staying with the Brights. He called out again to him. "Mr. Peter's up 'bout the house, I reckon?"

"Naw! No, he's not." Mr. John answered, on a note of levity. "Mr. Peter's with me!. . . He's right up the river there, in the bight."

Adam professed astonishment. "Naw! Hit kain't be, Mr. Pete's fishin'! How'd you toll 'im off down here to the river?"

"He'll go every once in a while," Mr. John called back.

Adam could see him fully now, sitting on the trunk of the big sycamore, which extended almost horizontally out over the river. "Le'me see your string!" he said, to continue the pleasantries.

"They're down there in the water."

"You mean they ain't ever bin took out'n the water!" They both chuckled. The boat was near enough now for Adam to employ a speaking voice. "We were coming over here to see Mr. Peter. . . .On a little business." (He paused long enough to indicate its privacy.)

Mr. John pulled up his line to look at the hook. "Well, Pete'll be back here."

Shifting tense buttocks on the plank seat, Adam came to a decision. What did he have to lose, letting John Hightower prove the letters for him, now that his own arrangement had gone awry! Mr. John didn't like the widow, but he wouldn't knowingly do her in. Of course, Peter Bright could wrap him around his finger. But he would hardly try to get him to tell a lie. Adam twisted about to look at Kiger. He said gruffly, rapidly, "You heard whut he said! Old man Peter may not be back here for a couple of hours. I'd just as soon get Mr. Jawn to prove those letters for me?"

Kiger had begun shaking his head before Adam finished talking. Then his face limbered in a mirthless, soundless laugh. "Naw!" he said, straightening up, lifting his sharp-edged nose. "Naw, that waun't the 'greement! That waun't the 'greement!. . .I got to go by the 'greement."

Adam snorted. Kiger was wall-eyed about it! They had old man Peter primed, he would guess, and they didn't have Mr. John! But Kiger's excitement, he observed, was increasing. What could it be? He called to John Hightower again. "How long you reckon it'll be 'fore Mr. Peter'll git back?"

"Oh, he's liable to be back here inside half an hour," Mr. John opined, in his slightly nasal voice. "I don't think he's goin' to find much up there to hold 'im." Now he gave his attention to his pole. He pulled in a small catfish, talking to himself and shaking his head, as he threw it back. He raised his voice again. "Why don't you all wait around? It's over a mile up there by the river and you'd have a hard time finding him."

This seemed to Adam, unbearable dawdling at a crucial moment. "Thank ye, thank ye!" He shrugged and looked back at Kiger impatiently. "Let's go!" he said.

Kiger didn't move or speak. But looked down at the paddle across his knees reflectively.

"Tain't no tellin' when he'll git back here!" Adam urged.

Mr. John spoke again. "You all might miss him—him moving along in the swamp and you on the river."

"That's right!" Kiger said and his voice rang out. He added more quietly, "Just whut I 'uz thinkin'! We'll save time and trouble by waitin'." They were now close to Mr. John's tree. He backed water with his paddle, in obvious relief, even raising a jocular note. "All it takes is a little patience, Brother Atwell, a little patience!"

Adam shrugged. "I reckon you wantin' to try out some of them worms you dug?" he said, with short humor.

Kiger raised his voice. "Mr. Jawn, ain't there a good bream hole here, near the cut?"

"Yeah," said Mr. John. "Yessiree! At the end of it. There by that big tupelo that leans so far out."

Fishing! It seemed casual, but the tightness behind Adam's jaws was growing. He didn't like any part of this, not a damned bit! Too many things happening, he couldn't account for. And he didn't have a friend in the whole lot. It was certain now that the letters were a bluff. If they were like Kiger claimed they were, there was no real reason why Mr. John couldn't read them out. As well as old man Peter! But, what was it? Adam wiped his face with a sweaty palm. What were they heading for? Unconsciously, he crouched forward on his seat as Kiger backed the boat away and let it swing into the current.

He must get another look at Kiger, he told himself and reached out and picked up the bait bucket. He could make use of it, too, he thought, as he held it up and twisted around. "Ye goin' to try your night crawlers here?" he said, continuing to hold up the bait.

Kiger dropped his gaze and had to take three strokes before he could answer him. "Yeah," he said. "Yessiree!" he repeated, somehow echoing Mr. John's tone of voice. "Tie 'er up to that tupelo when we gits there and let's fish out in the stream."

Adam set the bucket down in the space between them and turned back. The pulse in Kiger's long lean neck had been plainly visible. He's damned near panting, Adam told himself. *And I'm so thick I can't figure out why.* His face tightened in a squint. *But I'd better! And quick!* Adam had loosed the laces in his shoes, while he was under the bluff, thinking that if he had to dive in and swim for it, he would be ready. He fumbled again with them now, leaning forward on his seat, searching the bank of the river ahead, as they approached the cut between the island and the mainland.

Suddenly, he broke out into a cold sweat. This was it! The cut he had seen in his dream! It hadn't been Hannah's Island after all. This was where he had been shaken out of the green boat! Automatically he slipped forward to his knees and put out his hands to the gunwales, as he stared. But, what the hell! Would Kiger try it? Kiger sure had enough sense to know that it wouldn't drown him to shake him out of a boat!

The cut was coming on them fast. He spotted the leaning tupelo to their right, fifty yards away. But Kiger was going to try it! He could feel it in the jerk of his stroke. So! Adam wiped his loosening mouth. "Oh, little coon, little coon" he intoned under his breath. "Hell!" he grunted. The boat paddle, the heavy paddle! Kiger meant to hit him over the head, when he came back up and reached for the boat. A paralyzing lick on the head, and he would do his own drowning!

Adam's awkwardness and tension were suddenly gone. He felt balanced and limber, like a well-oiled sewing machine, ready for action—the bobbin already threaded. So Kiger had finally worked himself up to this! Adam felt shocked and a little saddened. He knew Kiger for a proudful fool, but he had not known that he, Adam, taxed him so much!

They were at the tree. Adam came to his feet. But instead of tying to it, when he took hold of the bough, he casually slid the anchor over the side, saying to Kiger, "There's a clay root down below us here, hit'll hang on. We kin swing further out in the stream this-a way." He released the tree and started to turn around. He meant to sit facing Kiger to thwart any plan for shaking him out.

But, before Adam could move his feet or turn his head, the big shake came, with great violence. At the same time, or almost so, Kiger shouted, "Hornets! Hornets!"

Still in his twist, Adam hit the water backwards. He was not there of his own choosing, but he knew what he meant to do. In the turgid, muddy stream, too turgid for thought, he yanked himself down the boat's chain to the anchor, hung behind the clay root. And, locking his legs around the root, he pulled down with the whole force of his body on the chain. Almost without pause—as if it were all one continuous motion—the bow of the punt came under the water toward him, submerging the boat.

He heard Kiger's splashing plunge into the water, on the surface above him. Then he loosed the chain. When Adam's head popped up on the surface, he saw that Kiger was below him, in the current of the cut, trying to fight his way toward the bank.

He immediately resubmerged and swam under water toward him. He came up, almost within arms length. Kiger reached out for him.

This he had expected. And again he sank, moving backward, then whirling under water. He shot bottomward beneath Kiger, pulling him under by a foot as he passed by. Kiger had on his shoes.

Adam popped up again, this time behind Kiger. Yes, little coon! He said prayerfully, as he gulped in air. One stroke put him in reach. He had seen a coon do it to a dog, swimming out after him, many times! He slapped Kiger's head under the water and circled him to do it again. He was there waiting when the head reappeared and he slapped it under again, backing out of reach of Kiger's long arms in the same motion.

They were out of the cut now and in the middle of the main stream. Already, Kiger was blown and gagging. Adam slapped his head under one more time for good measure. Then he quickly moved in on him, from behind, under water. His legs locked around Kiger's knees and his arms pinning Kiger's, Adam rode him bottomward.

The river swung and bounced and turned them end over end in the current, far below the surface. But Adam clung to this man, like a leech. Clung to him, until all struggle was gone out of him.

His own heart hammering his chest loose at each blow and his throat breaking open, Adam finally fought his way back to the surface, still holding on to his quarry. On top, Adam lay over on his back and caught his breath for awhile, only his nose above the surface. He towed a limber Kiger below him, towed him, he now realized, by the neckband of his collarless white shirt.

Adam raised his head and saw a sand bar down river from them, to the left. He was exhausted, but he managed to kick his way, dragging Kiger along behind and below him, into linc with the bar. In a little while he could stand up on the sand, though he had scarcely the strength left to do so.

He crawled into shallow water on one hand and his knees, still dragging Kiger behind him. He got his limp heavy baggage far enough up the strand to keep the current from washing it away, then he collapsed, on his back in the shallows.

But Adam rested briefly. It might well be that he had won only the first round here! Coming to his feet, he looked about him up and down the river. He discovered that their overturned boat, evidently loosed from the root by his pulling, and dragging its anchor had drifted along behind them. It was scarcely more than a hundred yards away, out in the stream.

Adam pulled Kiger's body to dry sand. He put an ear to Kiger's ribs and listened tensely for a moment, then rapidly Adam stripped off his own overalls and shirt and waded back into the stream. The water at this point was not very deep. Coming near the boat, he dived to the sandy bottom, swung the anchor onto his shoulder. And with this weight to hold him down, he walked back toward the bar. It took him three dives and walks to get the boat to dry land. He pulled it out of the water at a trot and dropped it, upside down, near the shrunken figure in tight-wet black britches and Sunday shirt.

Adam squatted by the body again and put his ear to a shoulder blade. Quickly he hauled Kiger up by the armpits and stretched him across the bottom of the punt, turning him face downward. Squatting astride the buttocks, Adam began alternately to pull up on and press down on his back. After a while Kiger's mouth opened and let out water. In time he started breathing and showed other signs of life.

Adam ceased his labors and stood over him to watch for awhile. Then he hauled him off the boat and went through his pockets. From

Kiger's hip pocket, he took a long black soggy billfold, thinking, this was enough to sink him! He unfolded and opened it sufficiently to see that letters were in it, and money, then he laid it on the bottom of the punt. He frisked Kiger about the ribs, then tore open his shirt. He thought he had felt it when he was hugging him. Kiger had an armpit holster strapped to him. Adam took it off him and pulled the short-barreled thirty-two revolver out of its sheath and broke it open. There were five rounds in it. He shook his head and looked down at his man.

Kiger was enough restored by now to be vomiting violently. Adam shrugged again, but did not speak. Nor did Kiger try to speak.

Then Adam turned the punt over and pulled it back into the river. He began a search of the bar and swamp edge for something with which to propel it. It would not take much of a paddle, since they would be going downstream. He finally decided on a light dry ash pole. Then he put his clothes back on and picked up the gear which he had taken from Kiger.

He approached him, still holding these things in his hands, and leaned over him, examining his face and throat, as he might a mule's, to see if he could travel. Finally, he said tonelessly, "Git up and see kin you walk! We goin' down the river."

Kiger lifted his head limberly and walled fear-strained eyes at him. Then he collapsed to the ground again. Adam remained motionless over him. After a preliminary trial or two, Kiger crawled to his knees mutely and staggered up to his feet.

Adam pointed toward the green punt, moored alongside the bar. He said, "You sit on the far middle board! We want the weight spread. I'm going to have to pole it. And I want you where you'll be in reach of my paddle, in case you git any crazy notions in your head!" His sarcasm seemed lost on Kiger, but he shook the gun-weighted holster in his hand. "In case you want to know: I've got your gun, too!"

Kiger moved alongside the boat to the designated seat, but he paused there. He swallowed with a heave and his slender frame swayed as if he were going to collapse, as he turned to Adam. He spoke feebly, in a sick sandy voice. "You don't' have to tell me, 'course—but, where you takin' me to?"

Adam gazed at him with calculation, thinking: *It's a good question!* "Git in!" he said, "You'll know when we git there."

Kiger got in the boat. And Adam pushed it off the sand, out into deep water, crawling aboard the back seat and scrambling into it. A good question, he repeated to himself, as he pushed the punt forward with the ash pole on the sand bottom. *He would take it up with the coon.*

22.

ADAM BROUGHT MARSE home by the middle of the following afternoon. He had found him waiting at his place when he got back there late in the day. Mrs. Hightower was taking her afternoon nap when they got to the house. Marse might have remembered that she would be, if so much hadn't happened since he had left, though it wouldn't have made any difference. Marse woke her up, tapping on the shutters of her back porch window and calling out, "Mamma, Mamma! We need to talk to you!"

He had called a second time before her alarmed half-awake voice came through the closed blinds to them on the porch where he and Adam were standing. "What is it? What is it? . . .Marse?" she cried. "What on earth is the matter?"

Marse batted his eyes soberly at Adam in front of him, and took a deep breath. "Lean over to the window, please 'um," he said, bringing his mouth close to a crack in the slats and pausing.

"What is it, Marse?" Her voice was nearer and alert now. "Why are you so late?"

Marse gave Adam the same sober glance again and, ignoring his mother's question, put his mouth to the blinds. He said, with positive and equal emphasis on each word, "Something serious has happened. There's been a drowning."

"Oh, no!" Mrs. Hightower gasped, in anguish, "not Adam?"

"No'm." Marse and Adam said at the same time. Then Marse continued. "It was this Kiger Steele. The one they call High-pockets around here." He paused for the acknowledgment and resumed. "He was with Adam, in a boat, fishing. And jumped out of it. Committed suicide, it seems like. There, just above Hightower's old ferry. . . .I stayed on, because Adam didn't have time to bring me to town. We been dragging the river for his body, but haven't found it yet. It's real strange! Here's Adam. Let him tell you the rest of it!"

Mrs. Hightower cracked the blinds. "Why, this is terrible!" she said, though her voice now was more self possessed. "Adam, my Heavens! What was the matter? I—I"—she caught her breath—"I'm bewildered!"

Adam leaned nearer the shutters. "Yessum," he said, with terse stuttering. "H-hit's got me sort of in the same fix!" He shook his head, and looking up met Marse's gaze soberly, then turned back to the blinds. "I don't know. I reckon he took leave of his senses."

"My Heavens above!" Mrs. Hightower repeated.

Adam took a more matter-of-fact tone. "We wuz fishin' along—and had bin for two-three hours—not even talkin', when it happened."

"Why, that's incredible!" Mrs. Hightower's voice came nearer the blinds. "Didn't he say *something?*"

"Well 'um, yessum. I-in a way." Adam lifted his voice. "I had said a time or two: 'Brother Kiger'—we call each other that sometime because we in the same lodge—'Brother Kiger, you mighty quiet here today!' Sort of ridin' 'im, you know. And he didn't have no comeback, at all. He just turned it off with a shake of his head."

Adam put a hand on his knee, pausing to consider. "I—I reckon there wuz 'bout another hour of sun, when it happen. I waun't watching 'im. I'd just had a bite and had my eye on my cork. I heard 'im say, 'Adam, I'm in bad trouble'—he said he was in trouble with some white mens.

"Then I look up at him and I sees that he's real wall-eyed. I said quick, 'Man alive! Whut's the matter there, Kiger?'

"But he waun't payin' me no mind. He went on talkin'. 'I tried, I tried,' he said. 'Look like I kain't settle hit no other way. I'll just settle it this way—' And with that, he pick up a loose railroad angle plate there in the boat, with a piece of chain through it. And he grab hit to 'im and jump in!" Adam paused for a moment, as if to listen for her response, then added. "I jump up from the other end of the boat, but I 'uz so took by surprise, I scarcely got up good 'fore he 'uz gone!"

He straightened up. He and Marse, one on either side of the blinds, stood looking at each other in sober mutual acknowledgment, while their words sank in. Stood, a tall mulatto man whose still, liquid eyes shared a responsibility with recognition, and a small, like standing, white boy, whose freckles and unruly toplock of red hair could not hide his face's commitment to a grave conjoining purpose.

Finally, Mrs. Hightower spoke again, her voice edged with anxiety. "Why, Adam, this thing is appalling!" She sighed and resumed, in a hesitant conjectural manner, "Do you think it may have been the same white men who sent him to you before?"

Adam and Marse had continued to look at each other, while she spoke. Now Adam looked away, bending over again to the blinds. "H-he never said enough for me to know," he said.

"But who else could it be?"

Adam shook his head. "I—I just don't know, ma'am," he insisted.

"Oh, I know you, Adam!" Mrs. Hightower protested. "You would never name a white man in anything." After another pause she added uncertainly, "Something ought to be done, but I hardly know what.

Maybe the sheriff should be called in, or the coroner. Anyhow, you ought to tell Mr. Littleton about it."

Adam and Marse faced each other, still solemn, only their eyes brightening a little, as they listened. Adam said, "Yessum. *That* wuz whut I thought. Mr. Littleton might know whut ought to be done."

"Yes," she said more positively, "go tell him now—this is Saturday and the bank will still be open."

"All right 'um," Adam said at the window. Then, as if asking a special favor, "W-would ye mind Marse going along with me?"

"Marse!" she was clearly astonished. "Marse?" But after a considerable pause, she replied, in a modulated tone of responsibility that was not without pride, "Why yes, Adam. Sure, Marse can go with you, if you want him!"

They started for the steps, but Adam turned back. "Mrs. Hightower, please 'um, would ye mind telephoning Mr. Littleton to sort of let him know you sont us on down there to 'im?"

"Why yes," she said, "Yes, I will!"

Adam stood at the far end of the director's table, in the back room of the bank, holding his hat respectfully in his right hand. His left he rested on the back of a chair, about three inches above the top of the head of Marse Hightower, who was sitting in it.

Facing them from the other end of the table was banker Littleton with the lawyer, Colonel Duke, at his side. Ranged along the left were Peter and David Bright and John Hightower. They wore, each in his own way, the mask of deliberate casualness and detached curiosity. With the exception of the elder Hightower, they could scarcely have felt more uncomfortable if they had been facing a ghost.

Putting the flat of his hand on the table and gazing toward Adam and Marse puzzledly, Littleton said, with the sound of a grunt about it, "Mrs. Hightower probably got it mixed up?"

Adam shook his head. "I—I doubt it!" he said, "hit's the curious-est thing ever happen to me!" His voice held a certain meek dignity. If his phrase *curious-est thing* had a double-edged meaning it was only dimly suggested, but his manner did not urge them to believe what he was saying.

Duke said, in a tone of cross-examination. "Did you say this Highpockets" (he glanced toward the Brights) "What's his name? You say he *jumped* out of the boat?"

Adam lowered his gaze toward the table, not pausing but a little increasing his deliberation and gave way to a dim wry smile. "I-I didn't say hit," he said positively—and now he did pause—"but I will."

Adam's ambiguity registered. Peter Bright frowned over Duke's head and Littleton shifted his hand on the table abruptly. Duke subsided.

"Just where 'bouts did it happen, Adam?" David Bright asked meekly.

Adam spoke in a factual manner. "Just off those willow piles on the Injun side, there above the old ferry landing."

John Hightower, who had already smiled a couple of times at Adam and Marse and who seemed more openly excited than the others, spoke up. "I thought Steele didn't seem up to his usual gab when you all came by me, there above Burnt Island!"

Peter Bright interrupted. "I-I was sorry I missed you all." He nodded at Adam and, without being more explicit, absorbed himself in fumbling through his pockets. He eventually brought out his pipe.

Adam seemed to be in no hurry. "Yessuh," he said with ease and great clarity and without stuttering. "Nothin' like it ever happen to me befo'!. . .We 'uz setting' there in that green snub-nose boat of Mr. Slappy's"—he sounded as if he were deliberately spinning a yarn. "I had just got a good bite and was watchin' my cork." He changed his tone to interpolate. "I had done said a time or two: 'Brother Kiger'—we 'uz in the same Corinthian lodge—'Brother Kiger, you might quiet today!' Sort of ridin' 'im, you know?" Adam paused to look around the table. John Hightower nodded his agreement blandly, but all of the rest evaded his gaze and looked uncomfortable. "And he didn't have no come-back a-tall. He just turned it off with a shake of his head."

Adam glanced down at Marse, who seemed to be absorbed in watching the men at the table. "I reckon there wuz 'bout another hour's sun, when it happen. Hit waun't dark yit when you and Bo come down to the Landing, wuz it, Mr. Marse?"

"That's right!" Marse said, looking up at him, surprised, his mouth loosening, as if for a grin.

"I waun't watchin' 'im," Adam went on, cutting off Marse's impulse to levity. (For he knew why: he had never called the boy Mister Marse before.) "As I told ye, I'd just had a bite. And I heard 'im say, 'Adam.'" (He paused again to interpolate, again glancing around the table with his look of innocent, submissive, pretending-otherwise knowingness.) "As I told you, I had my eye on my cork, not lookin' at Kiger when he said this. 'Adam,' he said, 'I'm in *bad trouble!'* "

Peter Bright clamped his pipe stem in his jaws, David shuffled his feet under the table. And Duke blurted out a question. All of them at once. "What trouble?" Duke had said. . .

Peter began smoking with absorption; David glanced over his shoulder through the doorway beyond him and Littleton frowned dourly at the table. The question lay between them, like a spewing fire cracker, in the lengthening pause.

Adam blinked in astonishment, then looked slowly, questioningly at the faces around the circle once more, as if he had not heard distinctly or could not comprehend. He shook his head gently and an ineffable twinkle came in his eyes. "Adam Atwell's not the man to tell you," he said.

Littleton shrugged, his big belly making the table quiver, and Duke's face worked nervously, but Adam did not give them time to speak. "Kiger said he was in trouble with some white mens!"

"What white men?" Duke said, with open annoyance and in a dim tone of defiance.

Adam dropped his hat. "Excuse me, please," he said, as if Duke had made an unmentionable slip of the tongue, "I-I dropped my hat." He shook his head apologetically and stooped deliberately and picked it up. But, as he straightened again, he heard the scrape of feet on the back steps and glanced at the doorway to see the glum figure of Oswald Paley entering.

Paley was wearing a white linen suit, white shirt, and collar and tie, but carried his coat under his arm. Dark hair, roached back on his narrow head, and bisters about his eyes emphasized the pallor of his sallow face. These disguised his youth and with his hump-backed nose and receding chin, gave him a ghoulish look.

But Adam gazed at him with relish. "Here, Mr. Paley!" he said, lifting his voice. He nodded toward the door. "How you, suh? How you?. . .I 'spect he want to hear this 'bout Kiger Steele drownin' hisself" Adam caught Paley's grape-like eye. "He had worked some for you, hadn't he, Mr. Paley?"

Paley, looking a little confused, darted an alarmed glance about the group. "No," he said vindictively, moving toward the table, "he didn't work for me! It was Slappy he worked for."

Littleton grunted, Duke's lips gave a dry twist and John Hightower chuckled aloud.

Adam's voice wouldn't cut butter when he went on. "Where is Mr. S-slappy, Mr. Paley? I had s-sort-a hoped he would be here." There was the first touch of insistence in the softness of his voice.

Paley looked at Duke, who apparently had been about to ask the same question. "I tried to get him to come back with me," he said, still nervously eyeing Duke. "He said he didn't have time. He had to get home."

Adam could see in the tail of his eye that Marse was gripping the arms of his chair rigidly to hold back his amusement. "Yed-yed-yessuh!" Adam said meekly, with an implicit irony that was lost on no one.

Littleton, turning his head, said, "Come around and have a chair!"

He nodded toward two empty chairs across the table from the Brights.

Adam raised his voice. "I 'uz just tellin' 'em, Mr. Paley, just 'fore he left us." Adam looked about the room apologetically, asking for an indulgence which both knew no one dared deny him. "He said, 'I tried, I tried! But look like I kain't settle it no other way.' He said, 'I'll just settle it this way!' And he grab a railroad angle plate in the bottom of the boat and jumped out in the river!"

An impulsive look of relief coming into Paley's eyes; he repeated automatically, "Well, he didn't work for me!"

Duke shifted in his seat impatiently and banker Littleton, putting his hands on his chair arms, as if to get up, said, "Well?" in his usual manner of dismissal, though not too gruffly.

Adam, turning to him, raised his voice again and the insistence was plainer. "There wuz just *one* more thing!"

Peter Bright leaned back in his chair wearily and the uncomfortableness came back to all of their faces, as Adam paused. He shifted his hat to the other hand. "Kiger never at no time say who the white mens wuz," he reiterated, reaching into the pocket in the bib of his overalls. "He never say. . .And he never say who give 'im *this*"—Adam dug in the hole with his fingers—"he just left it on the seat under the edge of the bait bucket." He drew forth a short piece of paper money and tossed it onto the middle of the table. The men at the other end blinked at it. And Duke leaned over and spread it out. It was half of a hundred-dollar bill.

Littleton remained fixed, with his hands on the arms of his chair, sweat popping out on his nose and upper lip. Red splotches crept into Peter Bright's cheeks, Duke squirmed self-consciously back into his seat. But Paley, under whose nose it lay, turned livid and his heavy breathing filled the room as he stared.

"The thing is," Adam said finally and now his voice had thickened and his own face had darkened with blood. "The thing is, I-I don't know *whose* hit mought be!" He paused and got control of the shaking in his voice. "Hit ain't mine, to be sho'!" He swallowed hard. "M-mr. Littleton, whut you think I ought to do with hit?"

Littleton grunted, belched and heaved himself up rapidly from his seat. Others pushed back their chairs, too. "Keep it!" he said brusquely, "the coroner might want to see it."

Adam nodded and moved deliberately to pick up the piece of money which he did with obvious relish. He noticed that Paley had not been able to rise from his chair with the others, but he checked an impulse to speak to him again. Taking his hand from the chair back, he turned toward Marse and winked at him solemnly.

It was after midnight when Adam got home on Tuesday. He had been to a lodge meeting, where his appetite for telling his Kiger story had taken him. The yard about his house was filled with low-lying smoke from smudge fires against the August mosquitos. And smoke, with all the doors and windows open, had got inside the dwelling, too. He had sat down before his fireplace to lay on a splinter for a little light to go to bed by, before he discovered his mother there, nodding in her chair.

She had waited up for him. And he was grateful. He hadn't been home much since his now fabulous fishing trip with Kiger Steele. And when he was there he had not had a chance to talk to her, without Babe and the boys around. He wasn't sleepy, anyhow. He didn't want to go to bed. He felt wound up for the night. But telling his whip-'emwhopper to his lodge brethren was a tepid sort of thing. He had to talk a parable. He could tell it all to ma! The lightwood blazed up and he shook her chair. "Ma?" he said, looking at her fondly, "Ma, wake up! H-hit's time for us to talk."

He had not, he supposed, ever before gone so far with a thing like this, nor done so much about it, without first consulting her. But he had not had a chance this time. He had had to take it like it came, when it got there. *That* afternoon when he arrived at the Landing with Kiger, he had found Marse with Bo and Jake there, baiting a trot line, paddling that old plank boat of his. He had to decide right then what he was going to tell them. He had already made up his mind what he was going to do with Kiger, while he poled the three miles back. He had pried into him some as they came along. Adam had tried to make Kiger tell him who the white men were who had hired him to drown him. Kiger wouldn't talk. Adam at first thought he would beat it out of Kiger, then he changed his mind. By that time Kiger was scareder of his white friends than he was of him, Adam. It was liable to get Kiger killed. It might even get both of them killed. And he didn't really need Kiger to tell him, for him to find out, anyhow.

His mother had sat up and shaken her head, without saying anything. Now she rose and went off into the next room.

Adam, looking after her, decided that she was going to wash her face. When he got to the Landing he had already made up his mind to hide Kiger and make like he had drowned himself. To keep any of the white men, whoever they were, from killing him, before he, Adam, could get to use him in court—if it came to that.

He had figured out where to hide him too: at the swamp shack of his old rafting crony, Guv Troupe, in Black Ankle, down on the Altamaha. Guv had hidden them before. But it was a long way down there. And a whole lot longer way back, paddling a boat. And he needed to get back before Hinshaw Slappy could work up enough nerve to come on the Hightower holding again.

He, of course, had needed Jake's help, for that long pull back. And he wouldn't have Bo around for any purpose! But it would surely never have occurred to him to take Marse along, if he hadn't spoken up about it. It was an outlandish thing for him to have done! But Marse was so much in for the trip, and he had always believed that the boy could keep his mouth shut. So far Marse had done fine. He couldn't really say, however, what had made him take Marse. A fragment came back to him. "Look, Adam, I'm in this, too!"—the lines of Marse's freckled face, pure and sure. . . .And he had taken instruction like a soldier. He was glad now that he had let him come along.

"Whut'd you take that white boy along down the river for? That waun't no thing to do!"

Adam raised his head to find his mother sitting at his elbow. He frowned. She could always read his thoughts!. . .He was in no mood now for the superstitious carping. "Aw, hold your tongue, ma, and listen!"

She stiffened, staring at him. "You ought not've done it and you know it!"

Adam scarcely heard her comment, as he sat gazing into the small bright fire before him with rapt gleaming eyes. He said in a guttural tone that was almost a laugh in itself, "I finally caught old Hinshaw Slappy at home tonight! On my way to the lodge."

She continued to eye him for a moment unresponsively, then sniffing spoke in still disaffected tones, "Whut about ole Coon-face?"

Adam turned to her, pausing quizzically before he spoke, his cheek slick in the firelight. "Coon-face?"

She snorted and rocked a little on her stool. "That's whut I call Milt Murdock," she said, in an even humor again.

He tossed his head. "I-I talk to him *last* night." He looked musingly into the blaze for a while, then sniffed. "He see that half-a-hundred-dollar bill. That the one time his inside music box stop runnin'!"

She stared at Adam impassively for a time, then throwing up her head she loosed a high thin peal of laughter. Her gaze settled upon the fire again and she bent toward it with absorption. . . .When she spoke her usually dried face looked swollen and there was the force of suppressed excitement in her voice. "Whut about the big un at the bank?"

Adam snorted and turned to her smiling. He looked back at the blaze to ruminate, and seemed to have dismissed her question. Then he slid his chair about so that he was facing her. He held his hands to his thighs, as if he had them on chair arms, pitching forward to get up and stared at the end of his nose. "Take it to the cor'ner!" he said, with assumed bass gruffness.

There was the lone high, but not loud peal of her laughter again.

"Yes suh," Adam was moved to add, "he stared at that half-a-hundred-dollar bill 'til sweat run off'n the end of he long nose, but he wouldn't tech hit!"

"You ought to told 'im to tear up that mortgage!" she said chuckling.

"Yeah," he agreed, adding parenthetically, "only he ain't got it no more. . . ." He sat on in the flickering light, smiling in the fullness of his sense of righteous power, both his temple and his throat pulsing with its thrust in his blood. "Yeah," he said thickly, as if to himself. "They all sit around the table there at the bank, nodding their heads to Adam. I say, 'Kiger jumped in.' And they say, 'He did!' just like they believed hit!" Adam laughed brusquely. "They know no nigger goin' to commit suicide! They think I mought've drowned 'im. Leastwise, they hope I did! But they don't dare 'spute my word!" He laughed again contemptuously. "Those low, common, thievin' white mens! Do anythin' for a dollar!" He hawked and spat on the blaze. "They ain't anything too low down for them to do, and they kin git a nigger to do hit for 'em!"

"Here, I got somethin' for us!" She turned around on her chair into the shadow and after a moment turned back with a large white coffee mug.

He took it and tasted it. It seemed, at first, to have a flat salty flavor, but he got more in the aftertaste. He swallowed it at a gulp. It was scuppernong wine.

She held up a cup, too, and cackled, her high-cheekboned face taking on a painful look. "Ole tub-o-guts say, 'Take it to the cor'ner!'"

Adam snorted. "That wuz one piece of money he wouldn't tech!" He drained his cup and looked into it. "There at the start, I'm tellin' 'em whut Kiger suppose to say. That fast-talkin' lawyer, Duke, he bin tryin' to put me on the witness stand. He kin talk faster'n he kin think. . . .I'm takin' my time. I say, Kiger he say, 'Adam, I'm in'—I kin see the muscle in old man Pete's jaws a-shakin', where he tryin' to hold onto he pipe—'Adam, I'm in *bad trouble.'* Ole slick-tongue attorney, he blurt out, 'Whut trouble?'

"I thought Ole Pete had done bit his pipe in two!" Adam gestured with his cup, grinning. "And that club-footed boy of his'n kick around under the table like a mule tryin' to git out'n a stall! And ole Bigger-ton, he heave way down inside he belly and grunt, like he sayin', 'You blame fool, he might haul off'n tell us!'"

They both rocked in their chairs with laughter.

When they had simmered down into silence she took a swallow from her mug. "Whut about that pissant Paley boy?"

Adam laughed. "Paley!" he cried out, straightening up, and wiped his eyes with the back of his hand. "That slippery, lyin' little puke got pinned in his tracks *one time!* He couldn't even squirm!" Adam laughed again.

She echoed his laughter and refilled the mugs, pulling the straw-covered demijohn around into the firelight now.

"Whut did he say?"

"He say"—Adam slumped over in token of Paley's posture and imitated his voice—"'He didn't work for me, he work for *Slappy!*'—talkin' 'bout Kiger. Dawg to the last," he added, "an egg-suckin' dawg!"

"Yeah," she said, quaffing her drink, "Yeah, Dawg." Resting the cup on her knee, she stared at the blaze, a harsh look coming over her swollen face and her eyeballs gleaming white. She said, in a bitter, tone of revelation, "He done growed up to look like Sinclair Cauldwell!"

Adam was dashed. "Aw now, ma, you needn't bring *him* up!"

She waved the mug around. "Whut difference do he make to you? You never seed 'im, nor knowd 'im. He 'uz just a couldn't-help-it, so far as you concerned."

Adam's grimace ended in a dim vindictive smile. "I reckon I couldn't holp hit, for sho'!" he said and emptied his cup.

"Yeah," she pursued, "look like Paley, but bigger and more of a man—more devil, too!"

Adam sought to divert her. "Talkin' about egg-suckin' dawgs! You ought to have seen Hinshaw Slappy back off, like a rattlesnake had buzzed 'im, when I tried to hand 'im this half-a-hundred dollar bill. He damned nigh run back in the house!"

Again she cackled grimly. "Ole Henstraw Sneaky!" she crooned in a cracked voice. . . ."And ole Coon-face! Whut did ole Coon-face say?"

Smiling, Adam reflected. "He didn't say so much," he began, after a pause. "But he looked awful hacked. And worried." Staring reminiscently into the fireplace, he added, "I don't think Mr. Milt knew whut they were goin' to do with his money when he contributed."

"Hah!" Electra said sharply, lifting her Indian-like features. "He white man just like the rest of 'em!"

Adam shook his head. "I wouldn't 've thought of 'im ag'in for nothin'—not even for the other half of that big money!" she said and poured herself another mug of wine. She turned stiffly and a little unsteadily, her dark face held high. "But, son, you done put a plaster on your ma's ole sore, you done poultice her carbuncle!" She drank to it.

Adam shook his head. "I don't know, ma. I kept 'em from drownin' me—the low, white-trash sons-of-bitches! That's all I know." He took a gulp from his cup. "If'n that helps you, I'm glad."

"You kain't know how hit do help! You ain't lived long enough. And you didn't start livin' soon enough." She looked into her cup and raised the pitch of her voice. "You ain't never had no white man to say to you, and you a green careful-brought-up girl. 'Lay down, wench, and spread your legs!' and when he git through, kick you off'n the lounge, there in he office!"

Adam jerked up out of his chair. "Here, ma, cut that out!"

"Well hit happen, happen to me—your ma. In slavery." She went on, looking into the blaze, rocking with her cup. "He looked at you one time. Took you in his hand. 'Got me a yellow baby, didn't I?' he say. Then he never would look at you no mo'. Made me send you off, when he took to comin' to my shack in the night. 'Keep that little yellow bastard out'n my sight,' he say, 'if'n you don't I'm goin' to feed 'im to the hawgs!'"

Adam spoke gruffly, from the open doorway, where he stood, peering into the gray pall on the night's blackness. "N-now, ma! You adding somethin' to hit!"

"Hit true! Hit true! I just wouldn't never tell you before."

Adam jerked around, as if to retort, but only took a drink from his mug and turned back to the darkness.

"I got back at him though, I got back at him," Electra went on in her singsong tone. "Tellin' 'im that I give Miss Minnie a brew and conjure her so she couldn't have no babies. He make like he don't believe hit, 'ceptin' sometime when he drunk. But I use to tell 'im,

'Well, if'n you don't believe it, why don't you git you one?' Then he beat me!" She threw up her head and uttered her high thin laughter.

Adam shuddered and walked out on the porch. Bending over in the half-light and putting out his hand, he said, "Here Bo's pet coon . . ." He turned back to the door. "Come on in, little coon!" he said, inviting it in.

His mother was still rocking before the hearth. "Yeah, Miss Minnie triflin' and weak in the head, like Malinda!" she said, as if to herself.

"You leave Malinda out of this!" Adam said sharply. . . .He came back to the fireplace and leaned against the mantel. "She dead now, and you kin leave 'er alone!"

This seemed to give Electra pause for a time. She filled both cups again. Then she muttered, taking up the conversation where it was broken off. "I don't know whether she so dead; you ain't doin' nothin' 'bout Babe!" Adam did not respond and, after a moment, she added, "Goin' to find you another woman, I reckon, now you done bigged this one!. . .Course she don't deserve no better!" She laughed and lifted her cup. "Whut that puke, Paley say? 'Naw, not me! He work for Henstraw!'"

Adam eyed her in surprise—she was showing her liquor, but he joined in her laughter. "Paley see that Judas money, hit like to pull 'e eyes outn' 'e head!" he crowed thickly. "And Sneaky run like a rattlesnake after 'im!" They went on laughing.

After a silence, she looked up at Adam unsteadily, and had again grown querulous. "Still you oughtn't to took that white boy along down the river!"

Adam shrugged and frowned. "Listen, ma, why you call Marse 'that white boy'? He bin out here 'nuff for you to know 'im good!"

She lifted high her face and glared at him. "He white, ain't 'e?" She reeled a little on her stool, losing her composure.

This softened Adam's face. He grinned. "You done got drunk, ma!"

"'E white, ain't 'e?" she repeated angrily. "And so is that 'oman on the back porch!" Electra wobbled. "'E white, too!" She grabbed Adam by the leg to pull herself up. "And you better leave 'er alone!" She held on precariously and Adam was about to give her support, when she broke away and wobbled into the middle of the room. Adam was shocked. He had never seen her drunk before. He moved toward her to grab her before she fell. But she was raising her mug and she threw it, as he reached for her arm, and this made him miss her. She sat flat on the floor, amid a crash of broken glass.

Adam stood over her. Then he looked through the wavering light and haze across the room. She had broken the wedding picture of Malinda and him!

For a moment he was stirred with revulsion for the small, shriveled, bundle of bones on the floor. He shook his head. Then he picked her up carefully and carried her to the head of the big double bed, pulled down the cover, and laid her between the sheets.

She muttered once more, "'E white, ain't 'e?" and fell asleep.

Adam came back to the hearth, in a fit of coughing and almost stepped on the coon. He suddenly realized that he was getting drunk himself. He felt nausea coming on him and he sat down again in his chair. He turned to the coon, sitting on his haunches, with his paws clasped before him, gazing at Adam warily. Adam extended him a finger. "Yessuh, Brother Coon," he said, "H-hit's 'bout time you took over—ag'in!"

The coon hesitantly took hold of his finger and looked up at him.

Adam's eyes wavered as he tried to fix his gaze on the right coon. "Lead me to that place, little coon!" he said before he stretched out to sleep.

23.

MARTIN SLATER, the land buyer's lawyer, placed the long envelope on the table before him, in the back room of the bank at Riverton. Lifting his lean crisp face, his thin nostrils curving faintly, he relaxed the dry line of his mouth in what for him was a smile. "Mrs. Hightower!" He looked across the table at the widow, gentlewomanly, in her white pleated-muslin shirtwaist, with its high net collar. Then he turned to Adam, seated beside his landlord, the widow, at a distance of three feet, and dressed in fresh-washed denim shirt and overalls. "I believe they address you as Adam?" he said, nodding. He glanced up at the banker, at the table-end, last. "You are, as we know, Mr. Littleton, Mrs. Hightower's unofficial adviser in the negotiations we have had."

He took hold of the letter with his long fingers, lifting it above a white cuff that extended stiffly from the gray sleeve of his alpaca coat, in defiance of the August weather. "Before I discuss this with you, I would like to transmit Mr. Lincoln's greetings and good wishes and make an introductory remark." He glanced about in inquiry and they nodded in response.

Mr. Slater's cheeks visibly convolved and his eyelids, behind his pince-nez, flickered in what was almost a second smile. "When Mr. Lincoln and I came south early last spring to buy timberland," he began, "we were prepared to encounter some new experiences—even though I had been representing him in buying land for fifteen years. But we had not expected such a—" he lowered his gaze to the envelope carefully—"such a mystery, I suppose you could call it?" He looked up at them. "Not one that would involve us, to be sure!"

He shook his head, glancing wryly at Littleton, then at Adam. "I probably have not heard all of it *yet*. . . . Perhaps, no one knows all of it!" He turned the letter lengthwise. "But a recent extraordinary occurrence on the Oconee River has brought things to a climax, and to resolution, so to speak. It has, also, put into perspective this letter, about which I'm going to speak in a minute, and which has had us greatly disturbed. Indeed, it is responsible for my return here at this time!"

He wagged his head and looked at Adam, with a hint of sly humor on his face. "A peculiarity of our mystery seems to be that it is really a comedy of errors—need not have happened—has revolved about palpable circumstances that could easily have been cleared up. . . .But so are most mysteries in retrospect, I suppose."

He now picked up the envelope and drew the letter from it. "Our first business here this morning is this communication." Lowering it to look at them, he continued, "But first let me say that this is the only one of several that we received from the sender. This one is the climax of the series and may possibly be incriminating for him. The writer began by giving us vague warnings of unspecified things in connection with the Land Deal through which we were, he said, being taken in. We didn't know quite what to make of it. Whether this man was a crank, or what. It is still possible that he is a crank. But we doubt it."

He looked at Mrs. Hightower. "That is why I asked you to bring Adam. I want, first, to question him on certain claims about him, made in the letter, to establish the substantiality of them. Otherwise, we would not bother you about them at all." He glanced at Littleton. "Do you agree to this?"

The widow's adviser bobbed his head demonstratively, heaving himself from his chins to his bulging shirt-front, with specks of ambeer stain on it.

Slater took in Mrs. Hightower and Adam in one glance, saying, "Adam, will you answer some questions?"

Adam, graver than the rest, sitting upright and apart in his chair, said simply, "I'll t-try."

After a few qualifying questions, in correct legal order, Slater said, a certain sharpening curiosity in his face, "Adam, do you know where the deposits of clay are located on the Hightower property?"

Adam blinked at the table top, then lifted his gaze firmly. "Yessuh," he said.

Slater cleared his throat. "How long have you had this knowledge?"

"I wuz with the Colonel and his engineer when they made the borings—ever one of 'em," Adam said, without stuttering, without a quiver in his face or relaxation of his gaze.

"Adam, which lots are they located on?"

"Lots a hundred and forty-five, a hundred and forty-fo' and a hundred and forty-three, on the river." Adam said.

There was a stir about the table. Littleton broke his subdued quiet with a grunt. The widow caught her breath and let it out in a soft sigh. And Slater took off his pince-nez.

He spoke again, raising his eyebrows. "Do you know that the uncertainty about the location of that clay has been a delaying complication in this deal? And that you contributed to it?"

"Yessuh," Adam said simply.

"Why?" Slater said, with a clarity of tone that amounted to almost sharpness, "Why didn't you say where the clay was long ago?"

In a visage otherwise grim, a dim smile showed in Adam's eyes. "F-for one thing, nobody axed me to."

This created further stir, though almost soundless, as the others looked at each other in surprise.

He went on. "Not directly, they didn't. And, not any way at all, and them wantin' me to tell the truth."

"Why, Adam!" the widow exclaimed.

"Course, I don't mean you, Mrs. Hightower. . . .That 'uz just h-hit!"

Suddenly Slater had the letter in his hand, restoring his glasses. "Yes," he said, glancing over the page before him. "Adam, does Mr. Paley or anyone connected with him now *exercise*, or in the past have they exercised any"—he fixed his gaze on the paper—"*persuasion and control* over you?"

Relaxing his sharpened attention, Adam nodded that he got it. He then shook his head in bafflement. Finally he slipped down in his seat, smiling wryly. "That's a big 'un!" he said shrugging. "I don't knows whether I knows whut you means, per-ekzackly. . .I-I couldn't say for certain." He lifted a struggling face toward the banker, gazing just off his shoulder. "I could-a-say, I ain't bin under his c-control"—he halted uncertainly—"ceptin', you might say, just long enough for me to h-hit the water and come up." His glance swept the group self-consciously. The widow was frowning at him in puzzlement, Littleton was glowering, Slater seemed drily amused. He shook himself and straightened in his chair. "But there wuz a time when Mr. Paley persuaded me pretty powerful." Adam scratched his head. "Couldn't say whether he *exercised* it, or no. But he sho' used other people to put the persuader to me!"

Slater's jaw dropped, his mouth opened and he uttered a token laughter. "Heh-heh-heh!" he said. "What did happen to you, Adam?"

Adam lowered his head and sat in silence for a time, then said, "I-I-I'druther not say!"

Mrs. Hightower interrupted. "Tell him about Kiger Steele, coming to you with Paley's letters from Mr. Lincoln!"

Slater bridled a little, his face growing cold. "Any letters Paley showed anyone involving us in his scheme," he said in a tone of official disclaimer, "were a forgery, let me say!" He added, sotto voce, "We did acknowledge a few of his early warnings trying to find out what he was talking about." He began folding the sheet of paper. "But we needn't go into it any further. There are obviously substantial circumstances to make this letter legal evidence." He looked at the widow. "We will turn it and three others over to you. . . .I think they constitute a basis for prosecuting Oswald Paley for attempted larceny by trick." He put the folded missive in its jacket, drew others from his breast pocket and extended them toward her. "I am not your attorney and, of course, won't advise you what to do, but I think you have a good case."

The widow took them uncertainly and a little reluctantly. "This explains many things. But it is almost as upsetting," she said directing her words at Slater, "as the long silence of you people."

Littleton looked at the letters in her hands and shook his massive head, a hesitation coming into his eyes that bordered on confusion. He said, "I owe you an apology, Mrs. Hightower!" His forehead reddened and sweat broke out on the bridge of his nose. He continued, in a downright tone of admission, "Though I don't know whether a man can apologize for being a fool!" He laughed gustily. "I was sure taken in!. . .I suppose I was too eager for the deal to go through!" He shrugged and his voice gathered assurance. "I never dreamed that Paley—well, what he was up to! Not in the least. He had seemed to me just an enterprising young man and I wanted to help him along." His voice gathered an edge of vindictiveness. "I am outraged at the way he has abused my confidence! If he's guilty of violating the law, he ought to be brought to account. I wash my hands of him! Go ahead and prosecute him!"

Mrs. Hightower said, "Thank you, Mr. Littleton!" in a noncommittal voice and laid the letters down on the table.

And Slater, without giving the interruption more pause, resumed. "About our long silence, Mrs. Hightower, let me say that you must share the responsibility with us! This proposal of yours about your Okefenokee Swamp timber has kept us busy every minute of the time. And let me tell you, we have cruised the timber in a general way. There is a very valuable stand of cypress on your holding. But clearing the titles presents a major difficulty. All of those Okefenokee Swamp titles are clouded. We would have to go into court. It will take a minimum of eighteen months, probably two years."

"Two years!" the widow, the banker, and Adam exclaimed, in one breath.

"So," said Slater, "we want to urge you to go ahead with the Oconee deal and let's wind it up. Mr. Lincoln is prepared to be here by the first of next week."

Mrs. Hightower nodded. "Yes, indeed!" she said.

Slater went on. "And I'm prepared to clear up the points of contention between us, if you please?"

The widow nodded, saying, "Terms, not contention!"

"All right," Slater said, "by whatever name. . . .We had of course, already arrived at the conclusion from Paley's letters, but we are quite willing to accept your overseer's word as final on the location of the clay"—he smiled drily—"despite Paley's blueprint! And, on the swamp field, too."

Mrs. Hightower said, "That clears the air."

He went on. "And Mr. Lincoln is quite prepared to grant your exemption on the mineral rights to the land you are selling us. That's simple enough. We're in the timber business. Not interested in clay."

He put the ends of his long fingers together before him, in an orderly measure of his grasp.

"What about the Wyche field?" she urged.

His face clouded and he shook his head. "We recognize it's on one of the fee simple lots, all right. But the field would be an exemption of a very different order," he said. "Entirely different! You would be holding out thirty acres, right in the heart of our timber holding. Think about what kind of thievery that would expose us to—if the field changed hands. Then there are three other such fields—"

"Yes," the widow said, her mouth stretching drily. "I've heard all this before!"

"Mrs. Hightower, you cannot expect us to grant an exemption that would make it practically impossible for us to resell the property?"

"I can't help it, Mr. Slater. I said from the very first that I did not want to sell this valuable piece of cotton land!" Lucy Hightower's slender face was set and she braced herself by her grip on the table edge, bending forward in her determination.

"But, Mrs. Hightower, Mr. Lincoln simply can't agree to that exemption!" Slater continued to look at her firmly for several moments. He leaned back in his chair then and turned to the banker. "Now we have a counter proposal, Mr. Littleton, which I hope you will consider. . . .It would, we believe, obtain all of Mrs. Hightower's purposes for her just as well." He glanced about him, pausing dramatically. "We will lease this field—either to you, Mrs. Hightower, or to anyone you designate—for ten years, with an option to renew, for the aggregate sum of one hundred dollars!" He beamed on her a little like a magician who has pulled a rabbit out of a hat. "Now, will that satisfy you?"

Littleton nodded and looked at Mrs. Hightower, as if to speak. But she either did not see him, or ignored him. Staring at the table top dubiously, her head weaving a little from side to side, she considered the proposal with absorption. Still ignoring the banker she turned to the colored man, a little way down the table from her. "What do you think of it, Adam?" She waited, but seeing resistance on his face, she added, "You brought the Wyche field back. And Mr. Hightower told you then you could tend it as long as you liked. I want you to be satisfied?"

"Yessum," he said, in clipped, tense stammering.

"I might die. I want you to have the use of that field, regardless." She lifted her chin. "I'll have them lease it to *you*, if you want me to? . . . How's that, Adam?"

He dropped his head, and he stared at the table with equal absorption, under a different urge. He released his words with difficulty, but he managed to keep his voice from breaking. "H-hit look like the best *kin be done.* I sho' couldn't ask no mo' from you, Mrs. Hightower! I'd be real grateful to git that lease for a hundred dollars!" He lifted his face, but his jaw was jerking so convulsively that he turned away in his chair, without trying to say any more. He kept nodding his head.

Mrs. Hightower got up abruptly, and Slater rose, too. The banker moved the legs of his chair, shifting his bulk as if to rise, then leaned over the table to Adam. "Any word about that nigger, Kiger? Ain't his body come up yet? It's been nearly ten days—well, anyhow, a week of August weather!"

"Yessuh," Adam said, his face smoothing out, as he turned to him guardedly. "H-hit do seem long!. . .I-I couldn't, myself, say whut holdin' Kiger's body down!" He got up and followed Mrs. Hightower out of the bank.

Not yet raising her sunshade, Mrs. Hightower halted under the big oak by the grated drain at the bank corner. She turned back to Adam, a few yards behind her on the sidewalk, and he approached her. As he drew near, she balanced the tip of the black and white parasol on one of the iron slats of the grating. "Do, Adam!" she began, in a voice a little lowered, her face repressing scandalized amusement. "You sounded to me like you were playing"—she paused over this, as too frivolous a word—"well, not quite serious with Mr. Lincoln, in there just now about Kiger's body!"

Adam shook his head apologetically, his countenance noncommittal. "Yessum," he said.

She examined his face searchingly, an expression of light, reproachful suspicion coming over her own. "I don't know myself what to think of that story," she said finally. "Marse has dropped me two or three dark hints!"

"H-has he?" Adam said with perfunctory surprise. He looked up and, meeting her gaze, his eye glimmered briefly.

"Yessum," he said "I 'spect he has!"

She balanced the sunshade perpendicularly before her and said firmly. "Adam, what does all of this mean?"

"Whut do hit mean?" he echoed, lifting the black hat at his knee. He righted it, as he took it between his hands. He spoke in a quiet, but carrying voice. "Mrs. Hightower, hit better for me and hit better for the Land Deal, right now, that Kiger stay in the bottom of the river." He seemed to muse on the crown of his hat. "Me and Marse, we kain't git you into our trouble."

"Marse!" she exclaimed, in motherly alarm. "What is Marse into?"

"Well, he ain't into it, sho' nuff," Adam reassured, with an air of responsible guardianship. "But he knows 'bout hit. And he kin holp me."

"Hum-m!" said Mrs. Hightower dubiously, but more willingly, shifting her parasol.

Adam added, with pride, "T-that boy, young as he is, kin keep his mouth shut!"

"Yes," she answered ambiguously, "I'm finding that out!" But she nodded after a moment. "Nevertheless, it's of elemental importance in this world."

"Mrs. Hightower."

"Yes, Adam?"

His hands at either side of his hat became rigid, as he stared at it fixedly. His mouth bunched in a hard knot and allowed his words to escape precariously, under the convulsive action of his jaw. "I—just—wanted—to say ag'in—I'm grateful—the way you stood up so long and stout—for me a-gittin' the Wyche field!"

She had lowered her gaze against the pain of watching, until he got it out. Then she lifted a face touched by the strain, and a shy smile. "Thank you, Adam, thank you! But you have no more reason to be grateful to me, than I have to you!"

"Miz Hightower!" Adam cut her off. "Whut wuz it the lawyer called the shenanigans in the land deal, he say need not to've happened?"

She blinked at him then lifted a quizzical eyebrow. "You mean, *Comedy of Errors?"*

"Yessum. That's hit! That's hit!" He shook his head several times, a fumbling embarrassment coming over him. Finally, he said "B-banker Littleton admit he acted the fool. W-well 'm, Adam did too, along the way! You don't know 'bout it, but I'm c-confessin' that he did—big fool!"

"How was that, Adam? What do you mean?"

He looked away. "Old Mr. Adam Atwell, the white man who raised me, used to say—the way he put it wuz"—Adam adopted the voice of his recollection—"'Son, you *kain't* countenance the devil.'" He shook his head. "I come mighty nigh bein' taken in by that black devil, Kiger Steele. And I want to apologize to you, too!"

With a dim apprehension of the truth, Mrs. Hightower said, "Well, I have no idea what this is all about, but I accept your apology. We are all susceptible to the devil's wiles."

He eyed the hat as he turned it upside down. "But there wuz one thing I got out'n hit. . .Them letters the land buyer's lawyer give you ain't all the letters in the case. I knows where they some mo'. And they be here when we need 'em!"

Mrs. Hightower frowned. "What are you talking about now, Adam?"

He nodded reassuringly, going on. "One of these letters—I got 'em from Kiger—hit signed, 'Archibald Lincoln.' I had Marse to read hit over to me three times. He say to Paley, something like this. 'We won't talk to you 'bout yo' proposition til after we close the Land Deal. But come to us then and'—I got his words here—'We will not be unmindful of your previous negotiations.' That's whut hit said!"

"Humm-m!" said Mrs. Hightower again, frowning and making cross hatches on the ground. "I wondered at the time!"

"Miz Hightower," Adam broke in, "we got a good case ag'in this low-down Paley boy!"

She looked up, her face flushing a little and her eyes warm. "Yes, it seems so!" she said. Then, a restraining compunction came upon her. "But we won't do anything about it now. . . .We'll see after we close the deal, next week."

"Hit's a good case! And maybe that sneaking Hinshaw Slappy, too!"

She frowned, turning away. "We'll talk about it later." She looked back with an ambiguous smile on her face. "But I was almost embarrassed at the cool cucumber you gave Mr. Littleton!"

Adam swallowed and lowered his hat. "Miz Hightower, banker Littleton waun't plumb taken by that." He looked off toward the iron grating. "They's things, at times, better not be nosed about too plain—specially where a colored man's mixed in hit."

She looked from the drain to his face, frowning a little, mystified, but knowing, too, in a shadowy way. "Yes," she agreed.

Adam went on. "Now you take that city lawyer in there, awhile ago." He spoke with a touch of indulgent sympathy in his voice "H-hit all legal or un-legal to him. He see whut he see, plain. But whut all do he see? Yeah."

Beyond the tip of her parasol, Mrs. Hightower gazed at the storm drain again, becoming conscious, as she reflected on Adam's words, of the low sound of running water far below the grating. . . His voice was farther away now. "Kiger's body, h-hit'll rise, when the time come."

She looked up to see him moving off along the walk.

24.

ADAM, SITTING IN THE STERN of the bateau, lifted his head to look at Marse the second time. Then he shifted his gaze to the middle of the river, where pale light from the sky still made a glint on the dim current-roughened water, and on across to the far bank, where dark was creeping out of the high trees and sifting down from the gray trails of Spanish moss. He said, "I don't 'spect Mr. Jawn had nothin' to do with it—why?"

Marse, in front of the boat, raised the run cord of the trotline so that the baited hook on a drop line would not catch on the gunwale as it passed over. "He acted just like he was pleased to see me," Marse said, his attention on what he was doing. "He got out of the buggy and came up on the porch of the commissary there at Adair to speak to me."

"I 'spect they just used him," Adam reiterated in a tone of voice that reflected a limited interest in the subject.

Marse, sitting astride his seat, halted the passage of the run cord across the nose of the boat to bait a line. "Now, David Bright stayed in the buggy," he said, wrinkling up his nose and glancing at Adam.

"This beef heart's pretty high!" He picked up a cube of meat to put on the hook. "He just nodded at me. Course I reckon Uncle John was coming in anyhow to get him some tobacco."

Adam shifted his paddle in the water to keep the stern from swinging too far out. He frowned and spat in the river, as if in distaste for the subject of their conversation. "I reckon Hinshaw come to Mr. Peter with their plot. But Mr. Pete, he waun't about to git mixed up in no drownin'! He made out he'd go a little way with 'em. But when the time come, he worked it so it would be Mr. Jawn there by the cut. And him off at a good safe distance—case something' went wrong."

Marse straightened up to grin at Adam. He remained hesitantly staring off into space, an uneasy look clouding his brow.

"Better make haste!" Adam said, "or dark going to ketch us here." He scrutinized again the boy's face, speckled and pale, with the cave eyes. What was Marse uneasy about? And why was he talking around about it? Adam had found him on the place, waiting for him when he got back from Deadman's. He said he was up at Adair, to spend the night with Mrs. Adair's nephews. But why did he come on down by himself? It must be to tell him, Adam, something. "Whur the Haden boys?" he asked, in a voice inviting confidence.

Marse came to with a start, settling down on his perch and pulling at the trotline, but he added a postscript to their discussion. "I reckon I can't help but hope he wasn't in on it and him being my uncle." After he had baited another hook he said, responding to Adam's question: "Jeb and Ray had to help with the milking." He drew the boat on to another drop line, then added with resolution, "But I picked a time when they couldn't come with me to leave." He pressed the point of the hook through a hunk of the tough meat and dropped it into the water. "I got to talk to you about a thing, again, Adam." He lifted the run cord to be sure there were no more drop lines to bait, then he lowered it into the river and turned around on his seat to face

Adam. "Regardless of who was or wasn't in on the plot, I think you ought to tell Mother about it now!"

Adam, his face growing impassive and a little stiff, backed water with his paddle and swung the nose of the bateau downstream to return to the old ferry landing. "They ain't no need to put hit on her—like I said befo', they just ain't no need!"

Marse raised his voice. "Well, I tell you there is, now, Adam—there is, if you expect her to prosecute Oswald Paley!"

"Yo' ma got a real tender conscience. She liable to go right down to the bank and jump banker Littleton 'bout it. And git me shot at, in these piney woods!" Adam eyed Marse closely in the swamp twilight. He hoped he hadn't done wrong to take the boy into his confidence!

Marse leaned forward, a look of grave reasonableness sharpening his high-cheekboned face. "No, she won't! She'll have a better thing to do—prosecute Paley."

Adam nodded agreement. "And when she prosecutes Paley'll be time enough to tell 'er!"

Marse was shaking his head. "You don't have to tell her *where Kiger is*. That's not necessary."

Paddling on, Adam felt annoyed and was impelled to retort that he had told one person too many already, but he only said, changing his tone, "Whut time you want to come back and fish this trotline?"

Shaking off the question, Marse went on. "You've got to at least tell her about Kiger trying to drown you in the river and the real facts about the half of the hundred-dollar bill!"

Adam spat at the darkening surface on which they glided, then lifted a dry visage and paddled swiftly for the landing. He would not discuss it further.

Marse took hold of the gunwales, pressing toward him, off the seat, squatting, raising his voice. "I tell you, Adam, she's not going to prosecute Paley unless she knows about his trying to have you drowned! She won't prosecute him just for trying to steal her clay."

Marse came closer. "She's mentioned it every day this week at evening prayers, mentioned it in a way that I know she don't want to prosecute."

Adam stilled his paddle. "Nobody *want* to prosecute, son."

The urgency of Marse's tone increased. "Just let me tell her, if you don't want to do it. I tell you, you'd better!"

Adam repeated, "How kin you know?"

"Well, I do," Marse said sharply, "I know! I know more about it than I can tell you!" He checked himself and resumed his seat, straightening up. After a moment's silence he added, in temperate positiveness, "I would be against prosecuting Paley, too, except for what he did to you, Adam."

Ha! Adam thrust his blade into the water deep. That was what he had suspected. He had been noticing a difference in Marse lately. Those revival preachers had softened him up, got a sugar teat between his teeth! Adam examined the look of conviction in his owl's eyes. Was this the Colonel's coming man? Why should he want to put all of the responsibility for prosecuting Paley on him, Adam? Breaking the pause, Adam began speaking reminiscently, mellowly, only a hint of vindictiveness in his voice. "Son, you too little to know whut he done to your pa. He ruined him! Kept the railroad from coming through by his sneakin', tattlin', and lyin'. That wrecked the plans for the clay works. And all the other things your pa and Mr. Christian DeBow aimed to do!"

"Yes. I know. I know about that!" The small unblinking eyes kept staring at Adam, and through him. "I've thought about it, all right. Many times. Burning and hurting inside. Against Oswald Paley."

Adam shrugged, frowning. "But, son, you kain't know! What that Paley did to yo' pa." His nostrils hardened. "Did to the straightest man I ever had dealings with! And, him educatin' that little puke and givin' his folks help and all, for years. Whut that damned copperhead did amounted to *killin'* the Colonel!"

“I know that, too, Adam,” Marse said, still not blinking, staring, as if he had been sitting with it a long time. “I know that, too. I used to have nightmares about it—that I wasn't equal to killing him, or that he got away from me. But not always. I've killed him a thousand times—in my imagination!” As he spoke these words, Marse had grown tense, thrusting out his feet and hands to his sides of the boat, and Adam thought that, in the dimness, he looked like a frog on a fork. Marse relaxed. “But I don't do it any more, Adam. I don't. Now I realize it's up to God to settle with Paley.”

“But, son, God works through human bein's.” Adam's voice rose, in remonstrance. “And now's our chance!. . .God's chance, I mean—by our hands!”

“No, Adam.” Marse was silhouetted like a frog on a fork again. “I know I'm just a boy, but I've been praying about it some, too.”

“But Marse, that slick, eelie, son-of-a-bitch is too mean for the Lord to have to keep on being troubled with him!”

Marse drew in his arms, folding his hands on his chest—as Adam had seen his mother do—and lifted his chin and smiled. An unfeathered bird in the nest, but sure, sure with an unquestioning inner certainty. “Adam, you're in slavery to your hate for Paley—in slavery,” he said. “I'm free!”

Adam did not reply. His hands, holding the boat paddle across his knees, were suddenly cramped by some frantic cross purpose in his muscles and his throat ached. A few moments later, the boat floating on in the dimness, grounded on the black bank at the Landing. Wheeling about, Marse leaped ashore to secure it and Adam stood up in the stern.

25.

ADAM'S RAP ON THE STEPS that Saturday morning was impatient. But he had scarcely got his Barlow back in his pocket, when the widow appeared in the doorway. And he hadn't got the frown off his face. For her first question was, "Why, what's the matter, Adam?" She was smiling, in her quiet way.

It had been raining earlier, soaking the heavy boughs of the chinaberry trees—where already, scattered leaves were yellowing—and the sun now stirred up a stench. He was scarcely conscious of this, but it was one more thing added to the conspiracy against him—of everybody and everything, it seemed.

She thrust her hand in the pocket of her plaid cotton house dress and moved nearer the edge of the porch. "Has something gone wrong about the lease?"

He dropped his gaze, in an effort to come up with some sort of smile, saying, "I s-still ain't got no l-lease!" But it sounded truculent.

She shook her head. A frown impressed her cheeks, tightening the lines at her eyes and mouth with concern. "Why Mr. Slater said he was going to leave it for us to sign! Today. I had just been waiting word from you, or the woodsman, Mr. Kitchin!" She stared on at Adam for a moment, a disturbed questioning look on her face then turned aside. "He said that Mr. Kitchin and the surveyor had gone out yesterday to get a description of the field's location, and you weren't there?"

"That's right," Adam agreed, "but they didn't tell me they 'uz comin'!"

She went on. "But I understand that the surveyor got what he needed and Slater was to draw up the lease, to be read to us. And I could sign and you make your mark and he would be back in a week or ten days to sign for Mr. Lincoln."

Adam had finally got a smile to the surface, his mouth in a set twist that did not match his smouldering eyes. "T-that whut Slater tell you last night?" He shrugged. "Well, this morning, Mr. Kitchin tell me they didn't get no d-dee-scription of it and ain't no lease bin drawn!"

She turned back to him, with her questioning gaze again. "I don't like the look of this, Adam. . . .But there at the bank, when we were closing the deal, Mr. Lincoln made it all sound plausible. And Mr. Littleton agreed with him. There were other fields involved, too. He said he had to have accurate description of their location."

Gloom swallowed Adam's smile. "Mr. Kitchin say he don't know nothin' 'bout whether Mr. Slater be back a-tall!"

"Oh, come now!" She lifted her chin. "Mr. Kitchin must have been joking with you?"

He shrugged and said soberly, "I don't like that kind of jokin', if he wuz. Hit's a po' sort-a joke that two kain't laugh at!" He could have said more. He could have told her about what he overheard in the livery stable, but he held himself to a dubious toss of his head and a dour look.

"How did it happen that you weren't home yesterday, Adam?" she said mildly.

But Adam spoke vindictively in reply, striding along by the steps. "There at the bank they said *the next day*—they was goin' to be out to the place, the next day—which wuz Wednesday. . .I stayed there at home, waitin' for 'em all day Wednesday and all day Thursday! . . .They never showed up. And they never said nothin' 'bout comin' Friday!"

"I guess they expected you to be on the place, pulling fodder now," she ventured. "But your swamp crop's so late and the other's already pulled."

"Yessum," he said ambiguously and began to subside. When he stood before her again, a low fire still in his eyes, he said, "I had to take ma over to Deadman's."

Automatically, she drew her hand from the pocket, saying, "What's wrong over at Deadman's?"

" 'Twaunt nothin' wrong at Deadman's. H-hit 'uz Ma!"

"Oh! How's that?"

Adam shook his head a couple of times and his vindictiveness receded in a twisted smile, a reminiscent look of tried patience. "Seem like we kain't suit Ma no mo'! And *she* got so contrary she wuz real hard for us to live with. But she went on her own accord. She said she waun't goin' to stay there no longer."

"Well, old folks do get notionate at times!" She put her hand deep into the pocket again, turning it upward from the bottom.

Adam spoke with slightly exaggerated casualness. "L-look like she taken exception to me and Babe gittin' married—after her talkin' for h-hit so long!"

Mrs. Hightower blinked, then broke into a hearty smile. "Why, Adam! And you hadn't told us a thing about it!" she said warmly, yet with correct detachment. "Congratulations!"

Adam's smile grew very dry, his eyes squinting and the cloudiness of a blush coming over his face. "Yessum!". . .He wagged his head.

"You said I ought to go ahead and git married ag'in," he said sheepishly, in self-justification.

She shrugged, thinking, *And probably none too soon.* But aloud, she said, "Well, I'm glad you took my advice. When did this all happen?"

"Yed-yed-yessum," he said, in sudden obscure excitement. His jaw began to jerk and a pleased, but in some indefinable way, unmanned look come over him. "We 'uz married Sunday afternoon, by our regular preacher. Mr. Arthur got me the licenses."

There was a concealed air of triumph in her cheerfulness. "Well, fine, Adam! That calls for a wedding present. It certainly does!" She stood for a moment, blinking, her shining eyes fixed on him, but absently, as she turned over in her mind what it might be. Her head jerked in an unconscious half-shake a couple of times, but she hit upon it finally and, whirling about, cried, "Oh, I know!" and left the porch.

Adam turned aside, still flushed and smiling and took two quickened steps, then slowed down. He had not told her the whole story about his mother's contrariness. Look like she never quite got over that bad night they got so drunk together. And she kept talking about Marse, sulking and quarreling every time he came on the place. Adam had not sent her to Deadman's, but he had not tried to keep her from going, either. He shook his head and turned abruptly toward the garden fence a little way behind the chinaberry trees, staring at it absently. But what about Marse? And his, his outlandish boy's notions! Adam recalled his words of the previous evening, in the twilight, on the river vividly.

The thing still shocked him. He wondered now if there wasn't something to his ma's superstition!

Mrs. Hightower was returning to the porch and Adam came back to the steps.

She held in her hands a covered, deep, brown earthenware dish, in a metal frame, her eyes bright and tender, as if she had just brushed away tears. "This is a new thing I received from Atlanta, day before yesterday. I got it on sale there. Just to see what it was like. It is very much in style now. It's called a casserole and is used for deep dish baking, macaroni and things. And you can put it on the table." She came down a step or two, taking off the lid. "I put a recipe for candied sweet potatoes in there for Babe to try out, in it. It's a wonderful way to cook potatoes. Have you ever eaten them candied, Adam?"

"No'm," Adam said, wagging his head gratefully, taking the wedding gift from her hands.

"I'm sorry I didn't have time to do it up properly," she said, looking after it, as he laid it down on top of the milk-box, beside his hat. There was a pleased, yet faraway look in her eyes, as she lifted them that was a little sad. "But I wanted, too, to show you the recipe and tell you about it," she added, turning away reluctantly, resuming her place above the steps, her features straightening. "Oh, I know!" she suddenly exclaimed, impulsive recollection bringing to her face a fleeting, half-formed look of torture, "I know where there's something I can put it in!" She whirled about again and was gone before Adam's surprised and tardy "Oh, Miz Hightower, you don't need to do that!" could have reached her.

She brought back a cardboard hat box and an armful of straw. "This excelsior will protect it and fill up the box, too," she said, wearing a pleased, but-still-not-finally-quit-of-it-look about her. "That hat box came from Charleston!" she murmured, in a tone of fond melancholy.

He ducked his head a couple of times in appreciation and said, with a reserve that came in unconscious reaction to her surprising demonstration "Well, we'll be proud to have it!" He set it on the milkbox beside the dish and turned away, moving back to the middle of the entrance, in deliberate, driving steps. He looked up, "Miz Hightower, I wanted to tell you somethin' that's bin on my mind."

"Yes, Adam." Eyeing him quizzically, she edged away in unconscious caution, in the direction whence he had come.

"I reckon I ought to tell you 'bout this," he went on, looking after her, with an air of admitting what she must have already guessed. "I, course, knows where Kiger Steele is. Kiger's hidin' out to keep out of mo' trouble." He walked counterclockwise. 'With those white mens. . . .Er-ah, when you bring up your case ag'in Mr. Paley, he'll make us a good witness. I kin git 'im here any time, with a court order."

"Adam, I don't know now—about the Paley matter!" she said, with resistance, still facing away from him. When she turned, her countenance had clouded and she went on reluctantly, "I-I debated it a long time, Adam. I wanted to be sure about my public duty, of course. But you remember how it was, there at the bank, Tuesday, when we closed the deal?" Her cheeks convolved and her mouth twisted with distaste. "It was positively disgusting! They had been glad to do what he suggested all of these months. Conspiring with him, until he was exposed. Then they came to me there, pretending to be shocked—Peter Bright and even Mr. Murdock. *Prosecute,* they said. Yes, they were all for it, since they had escaped exposure."

"M-maybe we git 'em yit, in court!"he broke in.

She ignored his remark. "And I think Mr. Littleton had some of the taint on him, too, somehow!" She moved against his direction. "And *Mr. Lincoln,* for that matter. It is certainly *not* my public duty to prosecute Paley!"

Adam stopped in the middle, staring at her with uneasy eyes. His jaw worked convulsively. "W-whut you mean, Mrs. Hightower?"

She took hold of the post near the milkbox firmly and turned toward him. "Adam, I prayed about it night and morning for three days. . .Only Paley and, of course, Hinshaw Slappy, set out to steal from me. The others connived out of selfishness and weakness and because I was easy prey." She smiled wryly. "But those are common human frailties, Adam. We are all subject to them."

His teeth chattering, he broke in, with a throaty bark, "Whut about whut that Paley did to the Colonel?"

She went on, as she had not heard him. "And, then, I thought about my own shortcomings, Adam." She glanced downward, then raised an accusatory gaze on the vacant air. "Yes, didn't I give them a right to be alarmed and upset? I threw the whole deal up in the air, by my private conference with Mr. Lincoln and my Okefenokee proposal. And I did it out of personal selfish motives—without considering its effect on them. So, I'm not spotless, either, in this sorry passage in human affairs!"

"They'd kill me!" he barked hoarsely, bafflement rooting him to the ground. His stomach burned, his chest was swelling painfully. *What, in the name of God! had come over her?. . .In slavery to your hate:* Marse's words flashing through his mind, tore him with pain and anger. "They-ey t-t-tried to"—he couldn't get it out. . . .

She summoned her strength, with a lift of her shoulders and met his glance. (He saw she had not considered, had not heard his words.) "Adam, yesterday afternoon, I wrote Oswald Paley a note, telling him that I knew what he had been up to and that I had been saddened by it. I told him that most of his former co-conspirators and others had advised me to prosecute him on the basis of evidence in hand, but that I declined to prosecute him and forgave him. And I returned to him the letters that Mr. Slater gave me."

Adam's eyes bugged out and his mouth flew open.

"You-oo-oo did whut?"

"I returned the letters!" she said positively, clinging to the post.

He jerked himself loose from the ground, wringing his hands. "Oh, Mrs. Hightower, Mrs. Hightower, Mrs. Hightower! Whut you gone and done!" He was crying angrily. His face was a swollen gray-blue, and his bloodshot eyes strained at their sockets, like chained bears. “You done ruint me! Ruint me!!” he yelled hoarsely, not knowing, in his pain, what he said or even that he said it.

Under his gaze, spell-bound, the current of their dependence blazing across the steps and a responsive anger stripping her will naked, also, she cried, “You ruined me, too! Charleston’s gone!”

He flung himself away from her, his shoulders heaving, staggering as if he were drunk.

“Oh, Edward!” she sighed and turned away, shuddering convulsively.

As he stumbled forward, Adam felt that the earth had been tilted and he was falling off of it. And fragments of painful images hit him in the face, like blowing hail—as he moved on toward bodily explosion: the moment in the green punt when he realized that Kiger was going to try to drown him, the jealous anger he glimpsed in Littleton’s face as he was rising from his chair in the back room of the bank, Paley’s profile at the back window of the lawyer Duke’s office when the white men had him surrounded, his mother’s hard, dark visage, saying “He remind me of Sinclair Cauldwell,” Peter Bright peering through the slats of his barnlot gate: ‘I had to sell that paper of your’n’, the white men’s faces in the courtroom at Lancaster that denied him a human hide, and again in lawyer Duke’s office that look, Hinshaw Slappy walking across the room: ‘lines mixed up, which uns which,’ the night after the Lancaster riot, the white man in the flat straw hat, hitting him over the head: ‘Maybe that’ll wake you up, Goddamn you!’ the whirl of darkness and strands of dim light as he and Kiger were turned end over end by the current at the bottom of the river. End over end.

But he did not explode. He took off from the ground, began to float in the air. And other feelings and images boiled up around him, bearing him upward. There was the little one-eyed trusty at Lost Mountain Prison: ‘You can get out, but you can’t get nowheres else.’ And, the Colonel, on his death bed, turning away on his pillow to make Adam realize, finally, that his dream of riches was fading on the air. And, Kiger, puking up the water and beginning to breathe. And, his ma, limp on the floor before the picture broken by her mug. And, Babe's plump, child-like hand in his own, as the preacher put it there and his realizing that it had never been there before that he could remember. And, the pale face of the white boy, killed in the Lancaster riot, the purple scar at his throat. And, old Mr. Adam's soft wheezy voice: 'Son, you can't countenance the devil.' And, the curious little coon, leading him along in the night-wood, gnawing at his hand. And, Marse's owl eyes above the words that hung in the air: 'You're in slavery—'

And, suddenly he discovered that these words didn't hurt, didn't anger him any more, and that he was beginning to find out which end was up, even up in the air. And he realized that there had been behind him all of the time, through the storm, like a mooring mast, the dim shadow of a black caped-and-skirted woman—a blackness that somehow cast a light through his balloon-like transparence, now shriveling and expiring.

And suddenly Adam was standing on the ground again, in the clear August morning sun, wringing wet, and limp and weak, standing about twenty steps away from the porch, facing the storehouse. But he knew, without thinking, that he was clean of anger and hate—hate of Paley or anybody else—and he felt within him, a mild, sweet buoyancy. He turned and saw the widow, leaning against the post, where he had left her. He shrugged and, shaking his head, walked back to the foot of the steps.

He said, not stuttering, "This thing never happened to me before in my life. It's real embarrassing to have it come on me here in front of you, Ma'am." But somehow his embarrassment did not seem to him to be the most important thing that had taken place. He shrugged. "I didn't know h-hit wuz in me so hard!" And he thought how right Marse had been.

She moved away from the post and seemed spent, herself, but there was a quiet resignation in her long serious eyes and tranquil mouth. “Let’s not dwell on the devil, after we’ve subdued him,” she said.

She now stood midway and at the top of the stairs and he faced her from the bottom. They both gazed at the five gray steps, considering the geometry that separated them and joined them. She said, only a little rhetorically, “*For now we see through a glass darkly,* Adam.” And she thought how strange it had all turned out. How she had thought she hated Riverton so much she could not possibly stay another day, if she ever had the means to leave it. How, for twenty years, she had endured her Georgia exile by the light of her dream of returning to Charleston. The celestial city!. . . Her youth? Her throat constricted and she shut her eyes to the rising image of Edward. There was to be no Indian summer for her. Her title to *wild land on the banks of the Oconee* had carried an irrevocable commitment! This was Hightower country, father and son, and Marse must grow up in it. Raw, rough, dark land, but somehow it was vital. And not the least of its vitality was in the illiterate mixed negro before her, torn from the womb of sin and slavery and curiously shaped in God’s image, the only man alive she had complete confidence in, her son’s foster father!

“We wouldn’t see a-tall, if’n w-waunt for you on the top of them steps, Miz Hightower!” Adam said. And he mused, I *know* now *I’m going to lose the Wyche field.* Mr. Kitchin said Mr. Lincoln didn’t want me to have that lease. *But I see now what the Colonel saw, lying there in his bed so close to the door. There are more important things!* And you don’t have to die to find that out but it helps. One of ‘em’s God’s freedom.

They nodded at each other formally. And Mrs. Hightower stepped over and cut down the water flowing into the milkbox, while Adam picked up his hat and his wedding present and departed.

ABOUT THE AUTHOR

From the 1958 edition

Brainard Cheney was born in 1900 in Fitzgerald, Georgia. He spent his formative years in Lumber City, a small sawmill town on the Ocmulgee River, in the piney woods region of that state. His father, a lawyer and a veteran (at 16) of the Civil War, died when he was eight years old, leaving him the only male in a widow's brood of three. His friendship from boyhood with the negro overseer of the family holdings, to the memory of whom *This is Adam* is dedicated, was a vital influence in his life.

He attended college at the Citadel, in Charleston, S.C., Georgia and Vanderbilt Universities. As a young man, he worked as a bank clerk, taught school, ran a timber camp. He married Frances Neel, a grandniece of Sam Davis, the Boy Hero of the Confederacy. He went to work as a police reporter on The Nashville Banner in 1925 and, after three years, became a political writer for the newspaper. He left this position in 1942 to serve a United States Senator as Secretary. During the past six years he has been attached to the present Governor of Tennessee as a public relations man.

Four years after he quit college he began to learn how to write in reaction against newspaper jargon; he began his first novel at 35. He has published two novels, *Lightwood* and *River Rogue,* the latter written while he held a Guggenheim Fellowship. These novels, like *This is Adam* and the one he is now at work on, are set in south Georgia, where he finds the quiet of piney woods and the aching distance of the marshes on Buttermilk Sound the most moving of all nature.

[Editor's Note: Mr. Cheney passed away in 1990, after publishing a final novel, *Devil's Elbow*, in 1969.]

This edition was printed in Georgia 9.5 font. Every effort was made to follow the original 1958 design of the work in the book's layout.

Printed on acid free paper for extended use.

www.ingramcontent.com/pod-product-compliance
Lightning Source LLC
Chambersburg PA
CBHW060546310726
48982CB00009B/1388/J

* 9 7 8 0 9 8 3 9 3 6 5 4 1 *